The Journey

Jimmy Smyth

The Journey

Second Edition

This edition published in 2016

BY EXCALIBUR PRESS

Copyright © 2016 Jimmy Smyth

All rights reserved.

ISBN: 978-0-993501555

Formatting & layout by

EXCALIBUR PRESS

EXCALIBUR PRESS

Belfast, Northern Ireland

team@excaliburpress.co.uk

The Journey

07982628911 | @ExcaliburPress

www.excaliburpress.co.uk

DEDICATION

This novel is dedicated to the thousands of normal young women who were admitted to lunatic asylums, with the use of force and deception and kept there with a diagnosis of "moral insanity".

The Reason?

Because they were pregnant and carrying an illegitimate child; often as the result of being   raped.

Many of these young women lived out the remaining forty to fifty years of their lives, locked up and deprived of their freedom and under the constant threat of torment and abuse.

Their children?

They were adopted; never to know their natural mothers or the daily nightmare they were living and the mothers would never see their children again.

"The human heart dares not stay away
too long from that which hurt it most.
There is a return journey to anguish that
few of us are released from making."

Lillian Smith

The Journey

CHAPTER 1 - THE HARPERS

A pale yellow sun dipped low on the horizon, bathing the green hills in its golden glow; putting a shimmer to the drops of moisture clinging to the grass; teasing the wild flowers with a promise of warmth; coaxing them to stay open a while longer. It was odd to see such a persistent sun at this time of year. A biting chill rushed ferociously across the southern cliffs, spreading its icy claws about, as if to put an end to any hint of clemency. Winter encroached; infusing the autumnal air with gusting winds that blew around every inch of the small cottages that lay in its path, warning that this desolate season was surely about to arrive with a vengeance. The sea mist was rising and rolling in over the land and the woman hoped her men folk would be home before the fog was so thick that a body couldn't see beyond their nose. And Mary; she should have been home before now.

"It's the weekend," Annie thought. "That miserable Mrs. Keller must have pulled out last minute jobs for my girl to do; can't bear the thought of her having a break!" Angered by the thought of her daughter's employer taking unfair advantage of her child, the mother attacked the dry clothes dancing wildly on the line. The rope that supported the assortment of rebellious rags was strung across from the lone oak tree that marked the rear end corner of the Harper property, and anchored to the heavy steel hook that stuck out of the back wall of the cottage. The original purpose of the hook was a mystery, but legend had it that great-great-grandfather Harper had fashioned this hook himself and fixed it high up on the back wall for any number of sinister purposes. Today, it held onto the Harper laundry that flapped like the gulls that flew about the cliffs. Assisted by the fierce currents of air that blew in across the sea, the clothes fought back; slipping out of the woman's grasp, they whipped her mercilessly about the face and body, stunning and stinging; refusing to be restrained.

Annie Harper was not the sort of woman to be daunted by aggressive laundry. Wrestling the elements, she struggled valiantly to collect her wayward washing. Her bare feet hugged the stony ground and the gusts grew stronger and colder as she hugged the bundle of dry clothes close to her chest. Like a sturdy plough, she cut into the wind as she trudged around to the front of the cottage; that back door had been sealed shut ever since she could remember so there was no point in expecting an opening there.

"Better to leave it as it is," Paddy had said all those years ago when he brought his young bride home. "It'll just fall apart if you force it and then we'll have a bollocks of a big hole instead of a door!" They laughed at the simple logic; everything seemed comical when Paddy explained it. And they left it at that and continued to walk around to the front door of their small cottage. During those early days there was plenty of happiness around, in spite of the many worries the young couple had.

Now, many years later, the plaster had finally fallen off the walls, exposing the irregular stones, which generations of Harpers had gathered to construct this nest. One room was all they could manage and the lean-to shed was an afterthought that clung for dear life to the rear wall like a crippled hunchback. Now two useless chickens, a goat and two sows lived in this haphazard extension. Piglets squealed around their mothers, looking for a chance to feed. Things were stored here when necessary; mostly tools, or bits of wood and coal that had been salvaged for the fire, and the meat and sausages that hung from the rafters. Salted herrings too, and sometimes there was a rabbit or two when one of the lads went hunting.

The Journey

The thatch on the roof of the cottage was weighted all round with stones as a precaution against the violent storms that lashed the coast; it was bare in places and when it rained, which was often, the place leaked like a sieve. There was grand talk of repairs but it came to nothing. It was hard enough just getting through the day; to cope with the ordeal of living and it seemed that Cliffside Cottage would skip an overhaul by this generation of Harpers for sure.

Almost eighteen years, they had used the side path that was now worn into a familiar flatness; every inch, each step was known to the occupants as they walked round the stone wall of their dwelling to get to the front door. Even in the pitch darkness of night, they could find their way around the cottage into their home. There was no way Annie would let a single worn out garment be snatched from her grasp; the woman clutched her bundle tighter to her. She gave the stubborn front door an extra shove to make enough space to get through. Like everything else in the cottage, this entrance was under pressure to accommodate the family. It gave in dutifully; scraping open noisily to perform its basic function; letting the occupants in and out of this most humble of dwellings.

Annie Harper shoved her body against the unreliable portal and gave it a kick to wedge it firmly back in place. Wearily, she dropped her load onto one of the three beds that lined the walls. Good, sturdy wooden beds they were; she bought them for a song when the typhoid took off most of the Connor family. The surviving members couldn't wait to get out of the village where stones marked the remains of their dearly departed. They had even thrown in the bedding for a few pennies extra; bleach and the sun had gotten rid of any germs that may have remained, and twelve years on, the Connor curtains still hung across the room as a partition for any privacy the family may need. Luckily, Paddy had a half decent job at the time and they had the money to spare for such luxuries. He had regretted his extravagance every day since and the Connor furnishings were blamed for any number of calamities when he had a drink too many; which was often. They were always the first things he threatened to sell and many a prospective buyer changed their mind when Annie said: "Belonged to the Connors, who were almost wiped-out by the typhoid: God rest their souls!"

The youngest girl, Sheila, was setting the plank table for the evening meal. Her red curls were pulled back into a neat tight plait; this kept the nits away her Ma said. Her big blue eyes were serious as she carefully set her father's fork beside his plate. In spite of everything, Paddy Harper always got the best his family had to offer, even though that happy, handsome young man who had brought his bride home to this cottage had long since dissipated into a philandering, drunken wastrel who was known to prefer the language of his fists to express himself.

"Any sign of Da?" Sheila asked softly and her mother sighed and sat heavily on the bed and began to busy herself with folding the clothes.

"Mary and Seamus should be home any minute," Annie replied, trying to add a cheery sound to her voice that she did not feel. "That's a right pretty table you've set, my girl." Seeing the look of concern on the nine-year-old face broke her heart.

"My babies deserve so much more than this," the mother thought as she went on with her sorting and folding. The fire beneath the cooking pot was the only light in the room; the only heat that any part of the home received was from this homely fireplace. Though the stones were crude and the joints between the stones were uneven, it was a strongly constructed hearth. All the cooking was done in that grate; potatoes were boiled in a pot hanging from a bar; bread was baked in a low iron griddle with legs; set directly over the bed of glowing coals. The family could not afford to buy wood or coal or even peat for fuel and the children scavenged whatever they could lay their hands on and stored it in the shed for when it was absolutely necessary.

9

The Journey

There was no electricity or running water for that matter, where ten to fifteen families lived scattered about the barren acres, five miles to the south of the village of Kilbarra. Rain water was collected in sturdy barrels that were scattered around the outside and water was also hauled up in a tin bucket from the well at the end of the lane; that was shared by most of the nearest neighbours. It fell upon the youngest children to fetch the water and carry it to the cottage, two to three times a week. Paddy's chair was a permanent fixture before the fireplace. Annie always had a clean throw rug to drape over this seat, so the style and condition of this piece of furniture was never exposed. The children remembered times on a winter night when the fire glowed on the hearth and the family gathered around the chair to listen to Paddy's stories of fairies, banshees and witches.

"Do you think Da will...?" Sheila asked her mother, almost too afraid to complete her sentence.

"No, of course not," Annie assured her. The items that needed darning were set aside in a basket to be tended to when time allowed. Hands were never idle in this home. "Not now, anyway! You're much too young to be away from home...to go into service...too young to start working...I want you to stay in school as long as possible...." The mother's voice trailed off as if she could not find words to convince herself and her child. Annie thought to herself, "Sheila's such a clever lass; her teachers are always singing her praises. Perhaps she will be able to get an education, make something of herself."

Her mind went back to the time when she had become one of the herring girls; she was not much older than Sheila, when she joined the crew that travelled up and down the coast, stopping at the different herring ports, following work. Consumption had finally taken her mother off, when she was six, and having no family that she knew of meant Annie had to spend the next six years of her life in the orphanage; so gutting, curing and packing the herrings with

10

her group of women seemed like a grand job to her. The work was harsh but Annie loved moving around and enjoyed the craic and the closeness of the girls. That was before Paddy laid his eyes on the seventeen-year-old and swept her off her feet.

But her Sheila had a family and Annie would fight Paddy on this one.

"I work, and I'm only eleven!" boasted Michael; pouring water, from a jug almost half his size into the chipped earthenware mugs.

"And what would I do without my little man?" Annie smiled and looked at her son. Michael was this energetic boy who dashed about from one task to another, always trying to make a few pennies for his mother. He mitched school whenever possible and he would comb the village for odd jobs, scraps of wood, or anything else that would come in handy at home. Michael was never without his old pillowcase, which he folded neatly and hid under his clothing; waiting to carry home his bounty; or booty. Today he had four freshly picked apples to add to the coal, and pennies he had accumulated cleaning the coal yard for Mr. Chambers. Sometimes, the older boys would catch Michael on his way home and strip him of his day's pickings. Then he would sit at the back of the cottage too angry to cry, until his mother came out and took him inside to clean his wounds and comfort him.

"I wish you would attend your classes as you should," Annie squeezed in the remark between her praise. "Father Kennedy complains bitterly about you every time I bump into him in the village."

"Ah, that nosy Father Kennedy should mind his own bloody business!" the boy retorted.

"Michael!" His mother exclaimed in surprise. "Don't you get too big for your boots my boy, or you'll be feeling the stick across your backside sure enough! I'll not have such disrespectful talk spoken under this roof."

The Journey

"But, Ma," Michael protested. "I can read and write...why do I have to sit in school all day, wasting my time?"

"Because education will lift you out of all this," Annie shot back, spreading her arms and hands to encompass the cottage and all its contents. The look of desperation on her face expressed more than her words could say, and Michael was sorry for causing her pain.

"Ireland had given the world some very great men, Michael," Annie said thoughtfully to her headstrong boy. Feeling bad that she had exposed her dissatisfaction with her circumstances, she added "Many of them were born and brought up in a cottage such as this." They may have been born in homes like this, but they didn't have to remain in such squalor, is what she implied.

The front door of the hovel burst open and in walked Mary and Seamus followed by a blast of cold air.

"Jesus, it's fierce out there!" said Mary, in a great hurry to get in. "I'm frozen stiff!"

"Oh, shut the door quickly," said Sheila hugging herself to avoid the draft that invaded the room. The brother and sister set the weight of their slim bodies against the front door to shut out the wind that had strengthened its gale force. Michael jumped up and threw his little frame against the door and it reluctantly slipped back into place. Mary gave Michael a hug, pulled Sheila's thick braid and then went to kiss her mother's cheek.

"Everything okay, Ma?" she asked as was her habit to do. Annie returned the affection and nodded her head.

"You're late, lass," Annie said, stating the obvious. The hands of the old clock on the shelf hung broken and unmoving as they had done ever since Paddy had brought it home as payment to settle a debt. He had been assured that a minor repair would have those hands ticking away again, putting a smile on that miserable clockface; but as with everything else in need of fixing; repair was

12

never the fate of that battered old timepiece. No matter; the woman knew exactly what the hour was.

"That nasty old hag kept me going, Ma," Mary complained. "You know how she is every Saturday. Da not in yet?" The older children removed their threadbare coats and hung them on the nail in the wall that was expressly used for this purpose. It wasn't a relative of the great steel hook outside, but it served very well all the same. The children handed their wages to their mother who counted the paper and metal and looked around for a safe place to hide the precious income. Paddy always found the cache and when he did he would cheerfully disappear for another bender, leaving the family high and dry. There were times when they wouldn't have anything to eat; which is how Annie got into the vicious cycle of taking credit. No matter how much they worked, scrimped and scraped, they never managed to get ahead because Paddy wiped them out time and time again.

"Give this to Mrs. Finnegan at the shop and make sure she writes it in her book, Mary." Annie handed the girl a note which she tucked into her bodice. At least he wouldn't get all their earnings. Annie tucked the rest of the money into a jar knowing full well he would find it and then she squinted to thread a needle and thought, "It's just not right."

"Better the old cow Finnegan gets it," Mary said meaningfully, looking at her mother. "Da will just drink it!"

"Da should be in any moment now," Annie said, her head bowed in her sewing. "And show a bit of respect for your father, my girl!"

"Da won't be home as long as he has a penny in his pocket Ma," Mary persisted. "He will be paid today and you can be sure all his wages will be spent in the boozer."

"Hush Mary," Annie scolded. "Don't talk about your Da like that! He works hard for his family, he does. It's not your place to

13

criticize your parents. You children are becoming more disrespectful by the day."

"Sorry, Ma," Mary relented. She knew how her mother hated to admit any of her father's faults and was always trying to cover up for the man. She opened the cloth in her basket. "The Missus let me have a pork pie and a loaf of bread. Made this week they were; should be a treat. Some sugar, too."

"That was kind of her, Mary," Annie replied, hoping her daughter hadn't pinched these items from the mistress she hated. "Sheila, cut the apples and let's put in a couple of spoons of sugar and stew them for after dinner." Why anyone in their right mind would give away such good food was beyond Annie's comprehension; a heart of gold was something Mrs. Keller could never be accused of having. She decided not to take the matter further; her anxious wait for her husband and her daughter's questionable traits were too much to handle, all at the same time.

The potatoes, cabbage and bits of pork in the pot were overcooked into a mushy thick soup and the fire was threatening to go out. The apples were all slushy, sweet and warm; bubbling away in their syrup and still there was no sign of the errant father. This was not unusual; Paddy now spent more time out of the cottage than in it. He said it was the work that took him away from his loved ones, but they knew better. Some of the locals always knew where he was and never failed to let them know. "Yer old man passed out at the Trainor's Pub last night, Missus;" a neighbour would call out to Annie the next morning as she trudged to work.

"Your Da bring home his fancy woman last night, Mary girl?" a stranger would laugh. "You young un's think Gertie will make a good step-ma, then? Wouldn't mind a bit of that in my bed; I tell you!" The Harper's had learned to take such remarks in their stride and usually shot back remarks that created much laughter.

The Journey

"Did yer fella find his way home from the Stag's Head, Missus? A sorry state he was in, for sure!" Annie held her head up high and tried to ignore the comments even though they cut her to the quick.

"Sticks and stones," Annie would say in the early days and this had helped them endure their father's perfidy. On this night the family sat talking about this and that; waiting for the sound of their father's footsteps while their hands moved in toil.

"I heard the new shoe shop in the village has jobs available," Mary said thoughtfully. "I would love to work there."

"Oh, I don't know, Mary dear," Annie said. "Let's see what your father thinks of the idea first. You know how hard it was for him to get you the job with the Keller's. If Father Kennedy hadn't put in a good word for you..."

"I'm sick of being bullied by the old bitch!" Mary spat out suddenly.

"Mary!" her mother exclaimed as the boys laughed. "I don't know what's come over you...such language...so unbecoming for a lass." The young girl's face flushed as she tried to find polite words that would convey her displeasure to her family. She had gotten into the habit of using swear words with Big Lucy; the Keller's generously proportioned cook, who no doubt tasted much of her own tasteless, stodgy cuisine. Together they painted their drudgery in the saltiest of language and laughed hilariously at their own ingenuity and wit.

"A right comedienne you are, Luce," Mary would gasp holding her sides and Big Lucy would strike a pose and come back with, "Could have been on the stage, I could have, Mary girl; but they wouldn't let me keep my drawers on!" Needless to say, such revelry went on behind the back of their austere mistress who was the personification of propriety and boasted she kept a house fit for the Lord to dwell in; while she tormented her employees into keeping it pristine for His coming.

15

The Journey

"I'm nothing but a slave! I'll never amount to anything at the rate I'm going, Ma," the girl insisted. "There's a big world out there and I want to be part of it; not spend my life here, rotting and slogging in this backward bog!"

"Really, Mary, I don't know what's come over you girl," Annie said sternly. "This kind of talk will lead you to a sorry end; you can be sure of that."

"Is it a crime to want to be better, to have more?" Mary asked desperately for her mother's approval. Annie refused to answer and pursed her mouth in a hard line that the children knew as her 'stop right this minute' face. Of course she wanted better for her children but the stability of a job meant more than working in some new fancy shop. At least Mrs. Keller kept an eye on Mary; who knew what would happen if this headstrong, fanciful child of hers was left to her own devices.

"There are jobs at the harbour, Mary," Seamus tried to lighten the mood. "Why don't you come by and try your luck. I could put in a good word for you, if you like."

"You must be joking? I'll not be gutting any herring, that's for sure." Mary ruffled her brother's hair and laughed.

"Gutting herrings, my ass! I'd rather die than end up like Ma," she thought. Sniffing the air she could smell the fishy odour that clung to the room in spite of all her mother's scrubbing and scouring.

"We will do nothing without consulting your father first, so let's not have no more talk about all this hopping from job to job," Annie said sharply. The other children were more easygoing; Mary had always been a handful to contain and at seventeen, her good looks and high spirits could so easily get her into trouble. Though many boys wanted to come courting, Mary flirted with them all but no one in particular had caught her fancy. The young girl got up and pulled a magazine out of her coat pocket.

"Oh, 'Movietime'!" Sheila exclaimed excitedly as she moved to sit next to Mary who began to leaf through the pages. The two girls oohed and aahed over the looks and styles of the screen sirens; the lifestyles of these stars and the films they made fascinated them. Imagining what it would be like to be one of Hollywood's femme fatales pursued by the likes of Clark Gable and Cary Grant sent them into paroxysms of laughter.

"We should pack our bags and go to America, you and I, Sheila!" Mary laughed, making her sister giggle. "I can pose as a grand lady and you can be my maid!"

"And what would you like me to pack, Madam," Sheila played along in an exaggerated docile voice. "Your torn frock would be nice for dinner with Mr. Flynn; or perhaps Madam would prefer the tattered one that is now being used as a dust rag? And shoes, Madam? What is your pleasure?" The boys laughed and added their two bits worth.

"A right ragged couple you are! Who'd look at such a pair of eejits?" A wrestling match ensued and Annie ordered them to stop when they got too wild; the girls were ruthless and fought dirty and soon had the boys hollering for help.

"All these fancy ideas you've picked up from those magazines and the films will be your downfall my girl," Annie said. "You should be thinking of settling down soon, Mary. I had given birth to two children by your age and you don't even have a fella yet."

"And how many of them babies died within the year?" Mary shot back. "Is that what you want for me, Ma?" All Mary got from her mother was stony faced silence as Annie deliberately concentrated on her darning.

"Willful girl," Annie thought angrily. "Doesn't she know I only want the best for her?" The wind whistled around the cottage and penetrated a crevice here and there when an opportunity presented

17

itself. Darkness had long since fallen and still there was no sign of Paddy.

"We should eat, Ma," Seamus said. "Da may be delayed and I have to get enough sleep to get to work tomorrow." He did not want to add that his mother should know better; she should be used to her husband's habits by now. Paddy would only return home when he was blind drunk; how he managed this was a miracle. Or he may have passed out in the arms of some woman or other; the one more sober would take advantage of the other's inebriated state to remove any items of value that remained in a pocket.

"Work? Tomorrow?" Annie asked, surprised. "It's Mass we have to attend tomorrow or have you forgotten?"

"After Mass, Ma," Seamus replied. "Mr. Chambers said I could pick up some overtime tomorrow since most of the men will be laid up nursing their hangovers."

"Let's eat, Ma," Mary said. "I'm so tired; I could fall asleep right this minute!"

"Perhaps I should take a lamp to the end of the lane and look out for your father," Annie suggested.

"It's blowing so hard out, Ma; I doubt the light would keep burning," Seamus said, hoping his mother would not ignore his logic and insist he go out in search of Paddy. "Anyway it's quite a distance to the end of the lane and freezing outside. Da can see the light in the window, and the lighthouse will help."

The big bright blue eyes of her four children looked at her for an answer. What beautiful eyes they were too, fringed with those thick black lashes just like their father's. Annie sighed deeply and gave in. She too had to rise early to get to her work at the hospital laundry after Mass. She could not gut herrings on the Sabbath Day, as Sunday was the one day of the week that she wanted to remain clean and not to stink of fish. Eighteen long years of Sundays, she worked scrubbing the dirt off the linen at the small hospital, behind the church. She had started when she had married Paddy and he had stopped her travelling around with the herring girls. Just thinking about all the stacks of laundry she has washed and ironed made her raw knuckles ache.

Luckily, Annie had found regular work at the harbour, gutting herrings. On weekdays a rickety little bus, full of herring girls picked her up at the end of the lane and transported them to the harbour in Kilbarra. She got a ride back too and this was very convenient as Annie managed to be back home in time to do her household chores and tend the animals. She refused to think of all the herrings she split open the rest of the week at the quayside. She didn't have to; they were under her skin and she reeked of them. Her hands were scarred by her years of toil. At the hospital, the staff let Annie have a hot bath with real soap when she was through with her day's labour; she lived for her Sundays; it was the only day when she felt really clean inside and out.

"Yes, let's eat," she said as she put her sewing basket aside. "Add some more sticks to the fire, Michael; let's try to keep it going till your father gets home." That would be a long, long time and a waste of precious fuel but the room was warm and the hot food filled their empty bellies, lulling the family into a false sense of wellbeing.

"The clocks go back an hour tonight; heard it on the radio," Mary said. "Mr. Keller told us to reset all the clocks in the house."

"Yes, the supervisor said the same," Seamus added. "Now it will be darker one hour earlier."

"It won't get darker one hour earlier! Teacher explained it to us; we'll have to get out of bed an hour earlier in the morning, that's all, but we also get to go to bed an hour earlier," Michael said, quick to understand the concept of this new fangled daylight

19

saving time. "We'll get used to the change in a day or two and things will be back to normal."

"It makes no difference to us," Annie remarked, frowning. "It just gives an extra hour of daylight to work in." This change in the clocks was of no consequence to the Harper family or to their neighbours. And why should it be? The sun set and rose each day no matter what the politicians said and their words were not to be trusted anyway. When did they ever do something for the good of the people?

The folks who lived along the coast between Kilbarra and Annahutton knew all about government promises; generations had come and gone listening to words that didn't mean a thing; no doubt the same would hold true in the future. Northern Ireland in 1936 was as harsh as any year for the citizens of this small community near the sea. There was no reason for life to be any different from all the previous years of misery in Kilbarra; the only light the inhabitants of this little village ever got to see was the beam that blinked from the lighthouse, set in the middle of the Lough; warning the careless mariner or jaywalker to stay clear of the dangerous precipice and the deadly tides that smashed into the rocky shoreline. On a windy day a person could be whipped right off the precipice into the swirling spume below; everyone knew somebody who had gone over the edge, willingly or unwillingly. Sometimes a distraught mother would take a couple of her children with her in her dash to depart this world. That was a terrible sin to be sure and the priests would condemn her to the horrors of everlasting damnation in their sermons. Yet, the brave souls who saw the perils of a damned afterlife as more acceptable than their lot in this Irish village, continued to jump. And now; thanks to this new-fangled daylight saving time, they had a whole extra hour to think about it.

CHAPTER 2 - THE LORD'S DAY

Paddy did not return that night. Annie couldn't sleep; she tossed and turned, worrying if her husband was safe of not. It was pointless lying in bed any longer; better to keep busy, not that she had a choice. Wrapping a thick shawl around her, she walked barefoot around the outside of the cottage. No point in wearing out good shoes they didn't have. She was just in time to see the sun creeping over the horizon and boldly stare out between the spaces of the dark clouds gathered overhead. Annie took a second to marvel at the radiant beauty and promise of warmth; before walking briskly about; trying to get some heat into her body, before going to the shed to let the animals free to forage around the yard. Apart from the few peelings and scraps from the night before she had nothing to give them; she tossed the scraps to the animals that devoured them hungrily. The little piglets squealed, around their mothers and the two big sows shoved them aside with their snouts and snorted, ignoring their hungry cries.

"Poor creatures," Annie thought. "I know what it feels like to be hungry." She took a slice of stale bread and broke it into pieces for the chickens. Driven mad by the scent of the bread, they clucked and fluttered and scrambled about, pecking frantically at the ground, picking up mud, stones and grass that stuck to the crusty bits; almost choking on the bulging lumps that formed in their craws. The bread was fair game for the goat and the pigs, who devoured the last crumbs. Annie was glad to see the goat's udders were full and coaxed some milk from the creature; thinking, "Nothing from those good-for-nothing hens; pointless keeping them; more use as a Sunday roast. Paddy can sort the hem when gets home!"

The Journey

The woman's trained eye reminded it was nearly that time of the year when the pigs would have to be slaughtered. Perhaps she could set Paddy to this task she thought, and then swiftly changed her mind; he would only make a hash of things and distribute the meat, sausages and black pudding around the village, even though the family depended on this precious cured meat to see them through the year. The piglets were almost weaned now; they clung to their mother's teats out of habit and hunger, draining the sows of whatever strength they had. They would fetch a pretty penny at the market; she must tell Michael to get rid of them; that youngster was no fool when it came to striking a bargain.

After sorting the animals, Annie took her little pail of fresh goats' milk and returned to the cottage. Seeing it was a cold day, she decided to light a fire, knowing it would make it easier for the children to get out of bed. Such good chicks they were; they deserved a treat now and then. Anne put some fat on the skillet and fried a few slices of bread. Filling the large battered teapot with water from the bucket, she waited for it to boil before sprinkling in the last of the tea leaves; wondering if there was enough for a nice hot mug for each of them.

"Get us a packet of tea from Mrs. Finnegan on tick, Mary," Annie instructed her daughter who sleepily watched her mother move about the room. "We have none left and I do love a spot of the brew to get me going of a morning."

"Will do, Ma. The old bat will be thrilled to get her bill paid," Mary said, her voice husky with sleep. "She will be begging me to take more stuff so that we remain indebted to her."

"Now, now, my girl," Annie chided her daughter gently. "It's the Sabbath. Let's think nothing but good thoughts today."

"If only Da didn't take all our money and drink it away, we wouldn't have to go without," Mary thought. "We might even be well off with a bit of savings. That's my good thought for the day,

22

Ma!" Outwardly she rose and went about, readying herself for Mass and the fun day she had planned to spend with her best mates, Jeanie and Shirley, wandering around the village and perhaps treating themselves to a film at the Picture House. Mary always kept a bit from her wages aside for herself. Mrs. Keller was always cutting her for one misdemeanor or another, so it was easy to explain the shortfall.

"Make sure you come back home after Mass and make yourself useful, Mary," Annie instructed her eldest; almost reading her daughter's thoughts on spending her day in hedonistic pleasure. "I expect dinner to be ready when I get home."

"Ma! I was thinking of meeting Jen and Shirl; haven't seen them in ages," Mary lied glibly. "Seamus will be off to work and he's bound to spend time with that girl of his. They're all over each other, they are, Ma; you should have a word with him unless you want to have a grandbaby anytime soon! Michael will disappear for the day whatever you say and that just leaves Sheila."

"I'm taking Sheila with me," said Annie sharply, not at all pleased with the independence of her family's activities.

"There you go then," Mary said. "All taken care of. I'll be home in time to make tea, don't worry; no one will be back before seven anyway."

"I can't help worrying about my family, lass," Annie said softly as she felt a rush of queasiness that she recognised but refused to acknowledge.

"I don't need this!" she said to herself. But then, when did anyone ever get what they needed? As she tinkered within the confines of her little cottage, Annie couldn't help thinking about Paddy. She wondered where he was and what could have come in the way of his nocturnal return to his hearth and home.

The Journey

The younger children had to be woken a few times before they dragged themselves reluctantly from under the covers, warmed by their body heat. The fire in the grate and the scent of fried bread helped to quicken their movements and before long the family was sipping milky weak tea from the two mugs and three chipped glasses they possessed; washing down fried bread with the hot drink. It felt like the beginning of a good day. The family went about the morning's rituals; Annie dressed in her best Sunday frock, that she got from a jumble sale and wore her much mended sensible shoes that shone like a mirror under her ministrations. Nothing but the best for the Lord. Of course, she would wear her old clogs on the walk to church and slip the good shoes on when she got there.

Walking out of the cottage, Annie was proud of her handsome brood; each of them well put together; their outer selves all smarmed and slicked, ready to cleanse their hearts and minds in His house. Even in those days of paucity it was a terrible thing to be out on the streets on a Sabbath if you didn't have a decent set of clothes on your back. There were a lot of people who stayed in all day on a Sunday because they had nothing but rags to wear. Annie knew the shame of it; having grown up in the worst kind of poverty and she crossed herself and shivered at the thought; thanking Him for His blessings.

It was a two mile walk to church and a light drizzle had begun to fall. This didn't faze the walkers in the least; they were used to making this trip in winter when the weather showed no mercy to the inhabitants of this coastal village. Wrapped in their coats; their heads covered by scarves and caps and their hands encased in mittens; the family began the trek in their old walking shoes which they would change as soon as the church spire came into view. Their warm breath fogged up the air they exhaled when they spoke to each other: once they got going the long walk wasn't really unpleasant at all, though Seamus and Michael discussed the amount of time they would save if only they had a horse and cart to take them where they wanted to go.

"And were you lads thinking of moving a horse into your bed?" Annie asked, jokingly.

"Oh, is Linda moving in then, Seamus?" Mary teased her brother, who blushed and gave her scarf a sharp yank.

"Stop it, you two," Annie scolded the siblings who were all set to wrestle each other to the ground. "I don't know where you get your fancy notions from. A horse and cart, indeed!"

"Just saying, Ma," Seamus smiled, straightening his cap and giving Mary a final pinch.

"I think we should buy a bicycle!" Mary said brightly. "Everyone uses them; then we won't have to move Linda...I mean a horse, in with us."

"A car would be even better," Michael said. "They are the most wonderful inventions ever. There are so many new ones about. Dr. Mallon just bought one; even the Chamber's are thinking of buying one; Jimmy told me."

"When your father owns a coal yard we'll buy a car too," Annie said, "Until then, we'll just have to make the best of the legs the good Lord gave us!" As the village came into view, Mary said, "Carry on, Ma, I'll run to the shop and pay the old hag before the money get's spent or pinched off me!" and dashed off towards the shop.

"Don't forget the tea, Mary!" Annie reminded her daughter who was already halfway there. The creak of the shop door opening, alerted Mrs. Finnegan who raised her head to see Mary burst in, waving a note that looked distinctly like money.

"And what brings you to my shop, Mary," she sniffed, looking down her nose at the girl. A cigarette dangled out of the corner of

25

her mouth, unhindered by the words she spat out of the other end of her thin mean lips.

"The whole ash stays on the butt until it reaches the end," Mary would say, "I don't know how she manages it; when the ash drops off it never even hits the counter!" Michael and Sheila would laugh and Annie would say, "Now, now, Mary," and couldn't help but smile at her daughter's account of the chain smoking Mrs. Finnegan.

"You planning on buying something, then?" the woman asked sourly, hardly glancing in the girl's direction.

"And a good morning to you, Mrs. Finnegan!" Mary ignored the woman's attitude; she was used to her sarcasm and it was water off a duck's back. "Just here to clear our account as we always do. Ma said, "first thing you do this morning, is wipe our slate clean and please see you do that Missus." Mrs. Finnegan snatched the note out of Mary's hand and got out her ledger to note the transaction. Sliding the book across to the young girl she didn't really want to cut all ties with the Harper's. Business was business, after all.

"We have some nice hair pins in," she said in a soft, casual tone, quite different from the way she greeted the girl earlier. "They're all the rage, I hear...." Mary checked the ledger and added 'Paid in full' as she had seen Big Lucy write when she shopped for Mrs. Keller. She signed her name with a flourish and erased the burden of debt that forced the family to make ingenious detours to avoid Mrs. Finnegan's establishment.

"No money to waste on frippery, Missus," Mary said, knowing the crafty old cow was trying to tempt her into extending her credit. "Beauty needs no adornment, Ma always says."

"Then she has no doubt overlooked the rouge on your lips and cheeks, Mary," Mrs. Finnegan replied slyly. "We have quite a demand for cosmetics; would you like to see something in our latest range?"

"I am not wearing rouge, Mrs. Finnegan!" Mary burst out. "The old bitch has eyes sharper than an eagle," she thought, and she guiltily rubbed her face with the back of her hand.

"Ah, my old eyes must be playing tricks on me then, lass," Mrs. Finnegan simpered. "Must be the blush of youth that I'm mistaking for your heightened colour. Could have sworn you had used something...."

"I didn't...I don't," Mary stammered; the fear of discovery by her mother put the wind up her. She knew the hag would bide her time and make mention of this conversation when it suited her, she continues to rub her cheeks and lips and only succeeded in making them redder.

"Not to worry then. Perhaps your mother requires some things, then?" the woman asked as she took out five boiled sweets and put them into a small paper bag which she handed to Mary, "For the children."

"Yes, she does, Mrs. Finnegan," Mary said honestly, not wanting to waste anymore time; she could see her family had walked quite a distance and she would have to run to catch up with them. "A small packet of tea then, if you please." The woman knew exactly what Mary required and handed the packet to the girl who tucked it into her shoulder bag that held her almost good shoes, and quickly signed the debt book.

"I must say I'm sorry to hear about Mr. Harper's stroke of bad luck," Mrs. Finnegan said, shutting the debt book and returning it to its rightful place. "Please tell your dear mother to come to the shop for anything she needs while her husband's away." Mary looked at the woman, bewildered at what she heard.

"Bad luck...away?" Mary repeated like an echo, not making sense of what had just been said.

The Journey

"'Tis a whale of a time your old man had; you know how he loves to use those fists of his...drunken brawl last night over that strumpet Gertie...did the other fella quite a bit of damage, I hear...in for assault and disturbing the peace...thirty days in the lock up, I believe. That man is a cross to bear, to be sure...." Bolting out of the shop, Mary raced to catch up with her family.

"You look mighty flushed in the face, Mary love; you okay, lass?" Annie remarked when she saw her daughter. "I hope Mrs. Finnegan didn't give you a hard time."

"No, Ma, she was well pleased at having her bill cleared," Mary said out of breath with the shock of the news. "Here's your tea."

"Ah, we'll have a nice hot cuppa tonight," said Annie, tucking the precious package into her worn handbag.

"She gave some sweets for us," said Mary handing one each to the delighted group.

"That's a fret; she must be in a real good mood, then" Annie smiled, rolling the sweet around in her mouth, sliding it with her tongue through the gaps created by her missing teeth. "There's goodness in everyone after all!" Mary sucked silently on a sweet, terrified over how her mother would react to the news of Paddy. There was no way she could bring herself to repeat what Mrs. Finnegan had told her.

Church was in sight and the family quickened their steps to get inside the ancient edifice. This imposing structure was built nearly a hundred years ago; mainly of granite, quarried nearby and capped by the tall limestone steeple that identified it today. A portion of the structure was rebuilt and enlarged some sixty year ago when a fire had destroyed part of the building. The family looked forward to sitting on the hard wooden pews since Father Kennedy made sure the Lord's house was dry and warm; mainly from the body heat of all those who crowded into the chapel.

The Journey

The Posh People from the Big Houses had arrived and Michael rattled off their names, identifying them by their cars that were parked at the entrance. He knew who each of the owners were and Annie wondered how, since he was not acquainted with any of these well-to-do folk. There seemed to be a lot of new cars about; these days you could hardly walk down a lane without having to step aside to make way for one of these magnificent machines. Seamus and Michael ran up to the row of vehicles and began to examine them minutely only to be shooed off by a couple of owners who stood guard over their property like sphinxes protecting the tombs of the ancient pharaohs.

"Just wanna have a look, Mister," Michael looked at the men with his large blue eyes while Seamus scowled at being told off.

"Look, but keep your mitts off, you rascals," one driver relented and when he saw how much the boys knew about cars he showed them what was under the bonnet and how the engine worked. Other boys had joined in and when the crush became too much to handle, the drivers decided it was time to stop the viewing.

"Off you go, lads! Time to pray for your sinful little souls," one driver laughed.

"Aren't you coming in?" Michael asked innocently.

"Who's going to pray for your sins, Flynn?" an older boy joked.

"I'm capable of praying for my own sins, replied Flynn. I'll be in as soon as I've finished my fag."

"Are they some kind of heathens?" Michael asked Seamus, and someone answered quickly, "They're nothing but a shower of sinners and we know where they'll end up! We should give them a good thrashing for their trouble. Too bad yer old man Paddy is in the lock up for brawling; he would be the right one to teach these uppity bastards a lesson." Seamus and Michael were alert in an instant; so that's where their father was.

29

The Journey

"Come on, Mike, let's head in before a fight breaks out," Seamus clutched his brother's arm and steered him towards the church door. "Don't tell Ma yet." Michael nodded; the boys knew how upset their mother would be at the news. Drunken brawling was bad enough but being thrown into jail was a disgrace of a whole other level.

"Someone's going to tell her for sure," Michael said, and sure enough the boys saw Annie clutch her heart, as Father Kennedy drew her aside to have a chat. The locals were a God fearing lot and this was their centre of worship; the church was always filled to capacity when services were underway. Today was no exception; Sunday Mass was the highlight of the week and the front pews were already filling up. Annie had noticed the sly, knowing looks she got when she entered the church and wondered what Paddy had been up to. She figured she would be well informed by the time she exited the church and she was right. Now she knew; the good Father Kennedy had informed her and spared none of the details.

Like a zombie, she groped her way down the aisle through the crush of Christian souls, until she found the pew where Mary and Sheila were sitting; the girls knew that Annie had been informed about their missing father, the minute they saw her ashen face. Annie sat down stiffly and looked up at the extraordinary semicircular arches which spanned the wide nave and transept. Her pale grey eyes drifted to the five rich stained glass windows in the apse and she concentrated on the stories they depicted; The Good Sheppard; The Prodigal Son; her eyes misted and for the life of her she couldn't see or remember the subjects of the other three windows. Michael couldn't bear to look at his mother and sat sullenly beside his sisters.

The warmth helped Father Kennedy's sermon of Hellfire and damnation along very nicely; his voice boomed out in censure, across his congregation, filling the building from top to bottom and end to end; each parishioner felt the scathing wrath of his words as his bulging eyes seemed to   focus on the guilty. Today, he talked about the demon, Drink. How it robbed a person of his senses and dignity; how it made one do all manner of unspeakable things under its influence; how it robbed your loved ones and plunged them into a life of pain and poverty; and of course, His displeasure and a very hot abode in the Hereafter were definitely mentioned. His body moved to stress the point he was trying to make while his hands flew in all directions to emphasise his words; his face reddened and he was most convincing as the veins on his temples stood out, fit to burst with the pressure of the sins of his flock.

Half the drunks of the village also sat in the church; but it didn't matter to the Harper family who felt the Good Father spoke directly to them; they hung their heads in shame at being exposed for all to see. All the while, the organist sat, glancing at the preacher; waiting for her cue to fill the building with the sound of holy music.

The front rows were filled with the Money People and Annie was grateful to be able to hide behind them. Though the locals knew about Paddy and most of them, like the Harper's, had a family member, or two, who belonged to the group of drunken sots that were tossed out of pubs nightly; these miserable families took pleasure in seeing others share their shame.

Seamus found his girl Linda, and they sat close together in spite of the dirty looks her parents shot at the couple, who were too much in love to notice or care. Nor did they give a fig when Father Kennedy stared right at them and ranted about fornication and falling from grace. But Annie noticed and cared; she cared greatly about what people thought of her family. She felt as if the eyes of the whole congregation were beamed on her and her children, and she suffered during the entire service. Looking at the faces of her sons and daughters, the mother knew that they knew about their father. The family tried to avoid bumping into anyone they knew

31

as they left the church, which was difficult. When they did manage to leave the building, the boys were nowhere to be found.

"Your father has got himself into a bit of bother," she began, unable to say any more. The girls made it easier for her and said, "don't be worrying Ma; thirty days isn't a long time and Da will be home soon enough."

"The shame of it...," Annie said hoarsely, and stopped.

"Most of the folks hereabouts are familiar with the inside of a cell, so don't fret, Ma," Mary tried to be matter of fact as she consoled her mother. "You ain't done nothing wrong so you just hold your head up."

"I spoke to Constable Brice; he said the best thing will be to carry on as usual since there's nothing we can do about yer Da," Annie stammered. "I really can't think straight right now...I don't know what to do."

"Why don't you go home and relax, Ma," Mary suggested as her mother shook her head. Nausea overwhelmed the older woman and she clutched her belly.

"You okay, Ma?" Sheila asked worried at the state of her mother who was so pale she looked as if she was about to faint.

"The matron will be expecting me at the hospital," Annie said absentmindedly. "All that washing needs to be done. Better to stay busy; keep my mind off...."

"Let them find someone else to do their damn laundry!" Mary said aggressively, wishing her mother would put down the heavy cross she lugged around in her head. "You should go home, Ma! You need a rest."

"I'll just carry on, Mary," Annie decided. "Why don't you take Sheila along with you while I attend to my work?" Mary screamed inwardly, "Stop being such a bloody martyr!" She was filled with a rage at her father and she did not trust herself to remain calm in front of her mother; especially when the woman made excuse after excuse for her husband.

"I want to stay with you, Ma," Sheila piped in, clutching her mother's arm. "I'll help you with the laundry." Mary was relieved with the arrangement and watched their backs as the mother and daughter walked to the hospital that was only a short distance from the church.

"Going my way, Mary?" Gerald Fegan slowed his bicycle, as he came up behind Mary. He was her twenty-year-old cousin; Paddy's sister Ginger's son; she was almost glad to see his familiar face, even if they did spend all their time together fighting about something or other. As a matter of fact, Mary had scars to show for their violent physical encounters as children and Gerald claimed to bear many of the same trophies.

"Depends which way you're going," Mary snapped and stepped aside since he and his bicycle were almost upon her. "When did you get that contraption, then?"

"Since I've been working full time, helping Da with deliveries," Gerald grinned, walking his bicycle, hoping to impress his cousin. "Want a ride?"

"I don't know...is that thing safe?" Mary joked. She had already decided to accept the offer but kept up her banter so as not to let him think she was all that needy. She knew how his mother looked down on her family and never encouraged their acquaintance. In the early days Ginger and Paddy were thick as thieves but once she married Bertie Fegan she put all her energies into being 'better'. At one stage, her betterment plan did include Paddy and she convinced her Bertie to give him a job, but that didn't work out too well when Paddy went on a bender during his first week and created some damage in the supply shed. Ginger had done her utmost to keep the families apart ever since. Now the Fegans had a flourishing glass business with three grown sons working for them.

The Journey

"My bicycle is as safe as I am!" Gerald boasted. "Come on, hop on and see for yourself."

"Not a chance!" Mary pretended to move on. "If your bicycle is anything like you, it's bound to draw my blood; be off with you!"

"Come on, Mary; we were kids then!" Gerald laughed at the memory. "When did I last make you bleed?" Mary managed to recall an incident five Christmas's ago when he swiped her across the back with a play sword and made Annie shriek when she saw a long red line seep through the thin fabric of her daughter's dress.

"Hell, Mary, you know my Da gave me a good thrashing for that!" Gerald grinned sheepishly. "How much more do you want to punish me?" Dark clouds gathered thickly, shutting the sun out, and the wind stirred itself in retaliation. Cold was inching up Mary's legs and she though now was as good a time as any to forgive her cousin.

"Well, if you're really sorry...," she said flirtatiously.

"I am! I'm so sorry, Mary!" Gerald confessed, pulling a mock penitent face and they both laughed. "Where do you want to go?"

"I was planning to go to see Jenny who lives on the other side of Kilbarra," Mary said. "Can you manage that?"

"I can do better; why don't you and I go to the pictures?" Gerald suggested.

"Because I'm going to Jen's, that's why," Mary said seriously. "Shirl is coming over later too." Shirley had got a new job as a waitress in a decent restaurant and the girls were dying to hear all about it.

"If you want to spend your time with a couple of bloody sluts, it's no business of mine," Gerald frowned as he helped Mary onto the back seat of his bicycle.

The Journey

"Don't you dare talk about my friends like that, Gerald Fegan," Mary said angrily as she jumped off the bicycle. "I don't want your stupid ride if you are going to talk like that!" She walked along hastily, prepared to walk all the way to Jen's rather than hear her cousin badmouth her friends.

"Just saying, Mary," Gerald retorted. "You're too bloody innocent to know what those bitches get up to."

"Yes, like you know everything, Mr. Know-it-all!" Mary shot back. "Get lost, Gerald!"

"Okay, I'll not say another word about your precious friends; get back on the bicycle, Mary; come on now, don't sulk. I said I'm sorry," Gerald seemed contrite and Mary decided to give their fragile friendship another try; particularly when she saw the Keller's out of the corner of her eye, piling into their new car. She got back onto the seat in silence as Gerald began to pedal forward; making room for the automobile which whizzed past them without any sign of acknowledgement.

"Snooty sods!" Mary shouted and Gerald simply said, "Bugger them!" and Mary didn't feel so bad anymore.

"Hold on tight, Mary," he shouted. "I don't want you to fall off and accuse me of drawing blood." Mary held his waist and tried to keep her balance as the bicycle rolled smoothly across the church compound and out onto the road and on the way to Jen's.

The Journey

CHAPTER 3 - BRINGING HOME THE BACON

Things at Mrs. Keller's home were quite different when Mary came to work the Monday after Paddy was imprisoned. New job descriptions were in place and this left Mary solely in charge of cleaning duties. She would only be allowed into the kitchen to scrub or wash dishes, and that too only in the presence of Big Lucy who got her ears boxed soundly for being unable to account for certain edibles that appeared to have vanished into thin air. The rest of her duties ensured that Mary was busy from dawn to dusk, cleaning the house from top to bottom; sweeping, scrubbing, dusting and polishing, after which she did the washing and ironing, cleared and washed plates after meals, and polished the rows of shoes that were lined up for her daily. And if there was nothing left to do; the silver was given to her to shine up until she could see her exhausted face in the polished surface. A million and one chores were thrown in to keep her so busy she had no time to say two words to Big Lucy or share a fag with her; the big cook now kept to herself since she was under notice of being fired.

"I can't do this anymore, Ma," wailed a dog-tired Mary when she dragged herself home night after night. "Been at it since I entered Mrs. Keller's front door this morning; I'm right wrecked now. Can hardly move!" Annie could see the toll the job was taking on her girl who looked grey, drawn and thin as a rake. She remembered how it was when she started work in earnest, and shared her thoughts with her children.

"Sit down and relax, love, while I go wet the tea. Real soft you youngsters are these days," Annie laughed. "I was almost half your age Mary when I joined the herring girls; I had nowhere to go after Ma died and not a penny in my pocket; real hard it was; I was grateful for the work to be sure."

The Journey

"At least it was exciting; all that travelling and banter with the other girls," Mary said sullenly. "I can't stand it Ma, I'm telling you; I just can't work for the Keller's anymore."

"Now, now, Mary," Annie tried to soothe the girl. "You're just tired, that's all. A good night's sleep and you'll be as right as rain."

"What was it like to travel around, Ma?" Michael asked, longing to explore the world for what it was.

"Oh, it was all well and good while it lasted. I came from away down the country, so moving around was interesting enough and I had my mates with me. My crew worked twelve to fifteen hour each day; six days a week travelling round the different herring port: starting our days at five in the morning. The fish needed to be gutted real quickly; or they would rot the same day. We worked without stopping; barely time for a snack or a mug of tea where we were. Really rough on the hands it was; had to wind cotton rags around our fingers; knife cuts and the brine, bit into the flesh of our hands something wicked. Worst was packing the fish in salt; my raw hands felt like they were on fire. Then we put the fish into barrels in a spiral kind of way; all the tails to the middle; the next layer had the heads in the middle. We had to cover each layer with salt. Don't feel it anymore; gotten well used to it over the years." Annie spread her fingers and looked at the hard roughened skin on her scarred hands.

"I don't know why you don't leave that place, Ma," Seamus said, upset at seeing the state of his mother's hands. "We work now and we can manage even if Da doesn't pull his weight."

"Your Da's had a bit of bad luck, that's all. It's not his fault; he does his best," Annie began to make excuses for her husband and could see the irritated looks on her children's faces. "It was the best day of my life when I met your father. He gave me the love and security I never had; a stable home and all of my dear children. There's things in life we have to be grateful for and are worth working hard for. We stick with each other in good times and bad; Paddy just happened to be in the wrong place and got blamed for something he didn't do; that's what he told me when I wen to the jail to visit him. Breaks my heart to see him behind bars, with all those criminals; my poor Paddy!"

"There's a police report with witnesses testifying right and left; all pointing their fingers at Da!" Mary was exasperated listening to her mother's account of the melee that landed Paddy in jail and the other bloke in hospital.

"Having this family is the best thing that ever happened to me," Annie spoke over Mary, disregarding her comment. She remembered her freedom in those days, travelling with her crew from place to place, sharing lodgings for the season. They had to carry their belongings with them almost like gypsies; bedclothes, pans and dishes followed the herring girls throughout their nomadic existence. But when she met Paddy at the church dance, all this came to an end. They were married within three weeks; Annie stayed on as a herring girl with a local crew and never again moved away from Kilbarra and the cottage.

"Once the young ones come, you'll not be working!" Paddy announced to his love struck bride who thought the sun rose and set for her husband. Babies came, one after another as did Paddy's jobs. Only these four survived and now they seemed so dissatisfied with the life their parents had provided them. Sure, things were a bit rough sometimes, but then there were those in the village who were even worse off, than them. The world was still suffering from the after effects of the Great War and the Depression. Annie sighed, thinking back, "Things are so much better these days; these youngsters were just too soft." Dragging themselves into bed that night, each one was lost in their own plans.

"We have to slaughter the pigs this weekend," Annie said before she closed her eyes. "You boys, make sure you get to it."

The Journey

"Yes, Ma," they answered sleepily, knowing they would have to complete this chore if they knew what was good for them.

"I'm going to change my job," Mary promised herself, snuggling under her covers; what better time to do this than when Paddy was away? Annie could tell him when she visited him in jail and soften the blow before he returned home. The fact that her friend Shirley earned more in a day, waiting tables, than she did slaving away for a week, didn't sit well with the girl at all.

Mary shared her dissatisfaction with Gerald who mentioned he knew of many jobs going in the village centre and even said he could get her a good deal on a bicycle, to use to travel to and from work. Gerald had got into the habit of giving her a ride on his bike after Mass and now she could handle the bicycle like an expert; how she loved that machine; she would give anything to own her own bike! I can do this, she kept telling herself and Gerald encouraged her ambitions. It seemed like a dream, but this was one dream she was going to turn into a reality right away.

Nothing would induce Annie to take a day off from work; after Mass, she gave instructions to the children and walked off to the hospital. They were more than capable of slaughtering their two pigs; they had watched their Da do it for years and should know by now how the job was done.

"Not today, Gerald," Mary said when her cousin offered her a ride. "Got to get our two pigs slaughtered today or Ma will have something to say about it!"

"Okay, so I'll drop you home," Gerald laughed casually. "If you're a good lass, I'll even help you with the pigs."

"No, Gerald, you carry on," Mary smiled. "I'm sure you have better things to do with your day."

The Journey

"What could be better than helping my kinfolk in their hour of need?" Gerald said with all the drama he could muster, making the siblings giggle.

"I'll race you Gerald," Michael challenged, already off at a run. "Bet my legs are faster than that old bicycle of yours!"

Seamus and Linda were strolling hand in hand towards the cottage; with Annie out of the way they intended to add a bit of fun to the day.

"Come on, girls," Gerald said to Sheila and Mary. "Let's race Michael to the pigs. Sheila got on the back seat and Mary hopped onto the bar and soon they were flying past the courting couple and about to catch up with Michael. Mary could feel his body against her back as Gerald leaned forward, clutching the handlebars and peddling for all he was worth. He panted to keep up his speed and his breath warmed her neck. His strong arms stretched out on either side of her, almost holding her, and all of a sudden, he seemed much too close.

"Get off, Gerald!" she said, struggling to loosen the bond between them, and he answered by moving in closer and giving her a kiss on her cheek.

"You stop that, Gerald," Mary pushed his chest and turned her face. "Behave yourself, or I'm jumping off your bike right now!" Gerald roared with laughter and stopped the bike since Mary was struggling to make her threat good.

"I'm just kidding, Mary! Frig, you take everything so seriously!" Gerald couldn't stop his laughter and Mary thought she may have been making a big deal out of nothing after all. Sheila was enjoying the bicycle ride and didn't quite understand what was going on.

"Let's go all the way home on this bicycle, Mary," Sheila pleaded. "It's such fun; please Mary, get back on."

The Journey

"Come on, Mary! Don't be a spoil-sport," Gerald said innocently; and Mary decided to give him the benefit of the doubt. The girls got back on and sailed past Michael with loud cheers and waves while Gerald pedaled the rest of the way back to the cottage.

"That was grand, Gerald!" Sheila laughed, cheeks flushed and eyes bright.

"You're welcome, chick," Gerald said happily and wheeled the bike to the back of the shed where he and Mary waited for the boys. Gerald took a packet of cigarettes out of his pocket and offered one to Mary; she took one out of the packet and stuck it between her lips, as did Gerald who lit both their cigarettes.

"Da will knock your block off if he sees you smoking," Sheila gasped, shocked to see her sister indulge in such behaviour.

"Well, he's not here, is he?" Mary asked boldly, looking at her stunned sister as she blew tendrils of smoke out of her nostrils. "He smokes, doesn't he?"

"Your Da does a lot of things he shouldn't do, don't he?" Gerald said, grinning slyly.

"You shut your mouth, Gerald Fegan," Mary lashed out. "Ain't none of your business what my Da does!" Sheila held her hands over her face, trying to block out the ugliness; she wished her mother was here; she would know what to do.

"Don't be a baby, Sheila!" Mary said harshly. "I'm grown up now; I can do what I want!"

"Is that a fact, Mary?" Gerald teased. "And what is it you'll be wanting to do now?"

"I'm going to give in my notice first thing tomorrow!" Mary blurted out the words that she was dying to say. "And then, I'm finding myself a proper job; maybe waiting tables like Shirl. She said she could get me fixed up if I want."

The Journey

"There's this guy I know, Mary; owner of the Royal Hotel in Kilbarra, he is. A right posh place that is and all. I could have a word if you like; old Reg owes me one."

"Would you, Gerald?" Mary was delighted by his offer. "I'd be ever so grateful."

"And how grateful would that be?" Gerald leered at Mary.

"As grateful as a grateful cousin can be," Mary smiled, trying to keep their conversation light. She felt uneasy but she couldn't afford to alienate Gerald; she did need all the help she could get in landing a job, and he had all these great contacts.

"Grateful enough to give me a kiss?" Gerald asked, giving her scarf a tug over her face. She grabbed the scarf and flipped it at Gerald, hitting him squarely on his nose. Gerald retaliated by snatching the end of the scarf and wrapping it around her arms, tying her so she was unable to move. She tried to kick out, but was helpless in the strong grip of the young man who made a point of showing her who was in charge. Sheila laughed at the roughhousing; this rowdy play was something she was familiar with; the siblings couldn't be next to one another without delivering a pinch or a prod.

"Stop, Gerald, Stop!" Mary squealed; all out of breath and red faced. "Here come the boys. Let's get ready for the butchering."

"You come to the hotel early tomorrow morning, Mary," Gerald said confidently. "And you'll have a job before you give in your notice, I promise you, girl!"

"Really, Gerald?" Mary clasped her hands together and did a little jig around the stones that dotted the back yard. Gerald nodded, and his eyes followed his cousin.

"Just look at yourself, happy and leaping about the place like a dopey mare!" Gerald laughed. Sheila looked at her sister and worried about the trouble she was going to get herself into; leaving her job with the Kellers.

"Please don't let her do this, Gerald," Sheila begged. "Ma's going to be furious and there's no telling what Da will do when he gets out."

"Don't worry your pretty little head, Sheila girl," Gerald said, tossing the red curls that framed her lovely face. "Everything will work out fine, you'll see. Mary deserves to work in a place that's more fitting for her; once your Da sees how much she earns, he'll be okay. Sometimes a person has to make a bold move to get out of bad situations and slaving for that bitch Keller is a bad situation, to be sure." Mary ran up and hugged Sheila. "Everything's going to be fine," she said happily, convincing her little sister that it would. "Don't say a word right now; let me break the news my way when I'm good and ready. Now not a word, mind; to nobody; it's our secret." Sheila smiled and kissed Mary; she liked the idea of sharing a secret with her big sister; besides Gerald had said everything would work out.

The boys and girls changed out of their Sunday best; they were facing a messy job to be sure. Seamus gave Gerald an old pair of Paddy's trousers and a torn shirt and then he quickly changed out of his suit and joined the group outside. They couldn't resist climbing up the oak tree and the huge boulder that someone had placed at the base of the tree, before anyone could remember, served as a perfect step up into the low spreading branches. Linda was first up and she could see the whole village in the distance.

"That is a pretty sight for sure," Linda said and Seamus responded, trying to kiss her, "Not half a pretty as you, lass!"

"Get down here; there's work to be done!" Mary yelled and all hands presented themselves for duty. They fetched the two big sows out of the shed for the kill. There were normally two kills each year; one in April and one in October; it was near the month's end now and high time to refresh their meat supply. The process was a natural part of the lives of country folks; these animals were kept in even the smallest of homes. A few would be kept for the family's own use, with others reared and sold on. There was a fine litter of piglets this season; a good income could be expected when Michael sold them at the market. That would make Paddy happy. Having cash to throw around the pubs and treat the local Tarts, thrilled him to no end.

Annie had prepared the tub of brine and left out the buckets, knives, water and the sack of salt before she left the cottage. A pile of wood for the fire was also stacked neatly just waiting to be lit. The men made quick work of stunning the pigs and slitting their throats. Seamus and Michael were used to doing this job; with Gerald and Linda there to help them, the work went even quicker than usual. Mary, Sheila and Linda done whatever they could; setting the buckets to catch the blood that drained out of the lifeless carcasses to make black pudding. They lit the fire to boil the heads and salvage whatever meat possible.

Not a bit of the animals went to waste. Entrails were removed and the liver and kidneys were saved. The intestines were rinsed out to hold the black pudding, which was mixed with oatmeal, herbs, spices, salt and pepper. Once stuffed into the intestines and tied up into lengths of a foot, they were put on a tray and steamed over boiling water for several hours. The lengths of black pudding were then hung up in the shed. The boys split the pigs down the middle, and placed the sides on the flat stones the family had kept for this event. Paddy and Annie had discovered these slabs while walking near the rocky shore and it had taken them a while to bring them home. But, they were always glad they did; a number of tasks were performed on these old stones and in the summer they even served as benches to sit on outside and enjoy the sun.

The gang set upon the sides of the pigs with handfuls of salt that they rubbed in; first on the flesh side and then the skin side. Salt

45

was fundamental to the curing of pork, not only to preserve the flesh but to kill any bacteria that threatened to infect the meat. Then they placed the skin-side down and wrapped the sides in pieces of sacking after which they placed the four sides in the shed. After a few days, the salt would be further trampled in by standing on the sacking. The sides would then be hung up on hooks; still covered by the cloth. When required, portions were cut off which made a hearty meal for the family.

After the chore was completed, the work gang was covered in the remains of the slaughtered swine. It was late afternoon and though there was a chill in the air they raced to the cliff to follow their route down to the beach. The only way to get clean was to bathe in the sea and the six of them ran into the waves. It was exhilarating and they stayed in the water long after they were washed clean; all of them could swim like fish and darted through the water until their muscles ached. Dragging themselves back to the cottage, they changed into fresh clothes and sat about talking and laughing.

Annie came home that night to find the pigs had been butchered and everything neatly scrubbed and cleaned and back in its place. A rich stew of head meat and some freshly baked bread was warm in the grate but the inmates of the cottage were so stiff, they could hardly move. It was back breaking work they had done that day and they were sore and exhausted.

"My angels," Annie smiled as she kissed each one of her children. "What would I do without you?"

"Linda and Gerald helped a lot," Seamus said and Annie went over to plant a big kiss on their cheeks as well.

"Such kindness," Annie said, overwhelmed by emotion.

"You stay and have supper with us; I have an apple tart from the hospital kitchen. Matron insisted I have it, bless her."

The Journey

"Yes, please stay," Sheila didn't want the excitement of the day to end. "Mary makes a lovely stew; there's lots of food for all of us.'

"It's late. Perhaps you can spend the night?" Seamus tried to see how far he could go with his mother. She was so tired and grateful that all she said was, "Yes, spend the night!" Linda and Gerald were thrilled and didn't need a second invitation.

"I can give you a lift to work tomorrow morning, on my bike," Gerald said knowingly, giving Mary a wink. "Save you time, it will."

"That's so good of you, Gerald," Annie gushed. "It's times like these when one gets the real measure of family."

"My pleasure, Auntie," Gerald said smugly. "You need all the help you can get with Uncle Paddy being away and all." Linda sat much too close to Seamus but Annie was almost too happy to care; she did manage a halfhearted scowl or two in their direction which kept them mindful of their behaviour; they were just grateful to be able to spend all this time with each other. The girls slept together and the boys slept together. Annie lit the oil lamp and left it burning all night, "For decency's sake." She needn't have bothered; the tired household was asleep as soon as their heads touched the pillows.

Mary was awake the moment she felt her mother's hand on her shoulder. Annie had lit the fire and the mother and daughter sipped a mug of hot tea before waking the others.

"Isn't this grand, Ma," Mary said cradling the warm mug between her hands. "I wish it could always be like this." Annie did not miss the inference in her daughter's words. 'Always like this' as opposed to 'like it, when Paddy creates chaos and keeps us penniless'. Annie woke the others with a mug of tea which they sipped in bed; it was sheer luxury for the family to spend time like this. Mary dressed with care and looked almost too stunning to go and slave at the Keller house.

The Journey

"You look lovely, Mary," Annie said looking at her daughter. It had been a long time since she looked so serene and happy.

"We had better get going," Gerald said to Mary. "We can give Sheila a lift to school; would you like that Sheila?"

"I would love that!" Sheila exclaimed, throwing her arms around Gerald who was already taking over the place of her absent father. "I love your bicycle!"

"Now don't you start getting used to all this fanciness, girls," Annie warned, to make them realize that Paddy would be back soon and life as they knew it would resume again. She quickly remembered the baskets of herrings she would be filling today. The baskets used by the women represented time and money to them. Each filled basket was one more to fill each barrel that brought their wage. How relieved she was at the end of the day to see the last basket of herrings disappear into the barrel. Nausea made her dash outside and throw-up by the side of the shed. There was no mistaking her condition any longer; another baby was definitely on its way.

As he had done the day before, Gerald pressed his body against Mary as he rode the bike. The minute they dropped Sheila at school, she got off the bar and sat on the seat. Gerald merely grinned; he got a kick out of playing her moods. They rode into Kilbarra and it took all of fifteen minutes to make the trip, which would have otherwise taken a good hour or more on foot. Plus, there was no wear and tear on their shoes.

"This is a real swanky place, Gerald," Mary said nervously when they stopped at the hotel side entrance. "Are you sure I can get a job here?"

"Won't find out till you try, will you, Mary?" Gerald laughed. "You wait here a minute and put on a smile when I come to get you." He walked off and entered a side door; it was obvious he knew his way around. Mary shivered in her shoes. The enormity of

48

what she was about to do dawned on her and all her bravado began to disappear through her chattering teeth. She watched the traffic on the street and the people all going about their seemingly busy lives. Mary could not believe how many bicycles there were about and how many women rode them. She was stunned to see a woman drive past in a car; this was really the place to be and she hoped against hope that Gerald would find her a job; the thought of staying on with Mrs. Keller was just too abhorrent to consider.

By the time Gerald returned Mary was weak with anxiety. The smile on his face was deceptive; he always had a cocksure look regardless of the situation.

"What did your friend say, Gerald?" she asked, unable to read his expression.

"What did I tell you Reg would say?" he teased.

"What did he say, Gerald?" she pleaded. "Please tell me!"

"Well he says if he thinks you're pretty enough and can handle the work, he'll give you a try," Gerald said slowly and Mary forgot herself and threw her arms around his neck.

"Hey, steady on, girl," Gerald went on. "You will be under training for a month after which Reg will see if you're suitable or not. If you are, you'll become a waitress in the restaurant; how's that?"

"I'll work so hard," Mary burst out and then remembered to ask an all important question. "Will I be paid during the training, Gerald?" She couldn't take the job if she wasn't earning, that was for sure; she had to back up her action with positive results. Her family depended on their pooled incomes.

"Well, it won't be a fortune to start with, but after the training you will get a good salary and you'll be allowed to keep your tips," Gerald assured her and when he told her how much she would be earning, the girl went weak at the knees; that was more than she ever dreamed of earning in this job.

"That's if you're hired in the first place, girl," Gerald teased, holding her hand as he ran with her through the side passageway, ducking into a side door and into the plush interior of the building. "Come on, let's not keep Reg waiting."

Mary had never been in such a place before; in fact, she had never even seen the likes of it, even at the picture house. As they walked into Reg's office, she caught a glimpse of the posh folks breakfasting casually in the grand restaurant, that Gerald said she would work in, if Reg said so. Hushed voices murmured and blended with the clink of crockery and cutlery laid out on fine linen tablecloths; fresh flowers were all over the place; this seemed more like heaven or at least another world and for the life of her she couldn't make a connection to her reality.

How she got through the interview was a miracle; mostly Reg and Gerald talked while she stammered incoherently. Mary felt lost in the big leather chair and intimidated by the well-to-do man in the neat brown suit. What he had in common with Gerald was beyond her, but they seemed friendly enough.

"Well, you seem a likely lass," Reg said gruffly. "Sure pretty enough to add to our establishment's style and refinement; a bit of training will polish the rough edges. I'll give you a try; if it works out; the job is yours. You have Gerald to thank; he insisted I give you a chance; the rest is up to you." Mary rose weakly and thanked Reg with a minimum of words. She could not believe her luck and floated on air out of the hotel and back to Gerald's bike.

"I've got to scream!" she said joyfully. "Pinch me and tell me I'm not dreaming!" Gerald pinched her until she begged him to stop. He took her to a café, in the village, for a cup of coffee and a sandwich; she'd never tasted coffee or a sandwich like this before and this was the first time she'd been in a place such as this where one paid for food that was made by someone else: it was all too much for one day.

"Now how are you going to handle Mrs. Keller?" Gerald asked grinning, and Mary laughed; nothing could faze her now; she was on her way.

Mrs. Keller was almost foaming at the mouth and about to have a seizure when Mary arrived for work, one whole hour late. The bad tempered old hag began with a tongue lashing to chastise the girl for her crime. Mary waited demurely until the ranting and raving woman was out of words and breath; then she said simply, "I'm not going to be working for you anymore, Mrs. Keller. Today is my last day."

The Journey

CHAPTER 4 - NEW JOB

While Mrs. Keller ranted and raved, Mary went about her work with a dedication that made her employer even more enraged at losing her maid's services. Silently, the girl took down the lace curtains and put them to soak while she ran a damp cloth over the panes before she put up a fresh new set of frothy white ones. She dusted the drapes and drew them open to allow the sun to come streaming into the house. Starting at the top of the stairs, she made her way down, meticulously cleaning and polishing each inch of the place. To look at her work, it seemed as if being in service was her calling.

"You can't up and leave without giving notice, you wretched, ungrateful girl," the woman shrieked. "To think I only took you in because Father Kennedy asked me. I have a good mind to call the police for you; you've robbed me blind; you deserve to be behind bars with that rotten father of yours!" Mary went on with her work without a murmur which infuriated the woman even more.

"What am I going to do on such short notice," Mrs. Keller shouted, and shoved Big Lucy aside. "Get out of the way, you useless, good for nothing lump; you're going to have to do her work as well as yours; see how you like that!" The cook was a nervous wreck; where would she ever find such a job if the Missus decided to toss her out. What was Mary thinking?

"Don't go, Mary," Big Lucy managed to whisper as the women crossed paths during their chores. "Don't leave me alone with this bitch!"

"There'll be a new lass in here before you know it," Mary replied. "I've got better things to do with my life."

"Where will you go, girl?" she asked as if Mrs. Keller was the last place on earth for young girls to be enslaved and brutalized. "What are you going to do?"

"I'll manage, don't you worry, Lucy," Mary said softly, not wanting to share any of her plans. They were too precious to expose and she held them closely inside her. "You just take care of yourself; see the cow doesn't take advantage of you." Mrs. Keller came into view, accompanied by her tirade and threats and the women went on with what they were doing.

At the end of the day Mary set the table for the evening meal, adding little flourishes that she had noticed in the hotel. She put out the best linen, even though it wasn't Sunday, using the good china and silver, and added some flowers from the back garden, in a vase as the centerpiece. Even Mrs. Keller was momentarily stunned into silence by the perfection of the room, and when she finally recovered her speech, all she could say was, "My, oh my!"

"I'll be off now, Mrs. Keller," Mary announced, not waiting as she usually did to be dismissed for the day. This was the time Mary usually served the evening meal when Mr. Keller returned home from work, and then cleared up after them.

"The cheek of you, standing there all bold as brass, and telling me what you aim to do!" Mrs. Keller was beside herself all blustered and rambling; she didn't quite make sense anymore. "If you think I'm going to pay you a penny for your insolence, you've got another thing coming! As for a reference; everyone's going to hear of your criminal behaviour; chip off the old block you are; see if you get another job when I've finished with you! I must speak to Father Kennedy!" Mary was glad she had collected her wages at the weekend so there was only one day owing to her. She thought,

The Journey

"You keep today's wages as my gift to you, Missus. I just pray I never have to darken your doorstep again."

"Well then, I'll say goodnight to you, Mrs. Keller; and thank you for all your kindness," Mary said graciously to the stupefied woman who stood by with a gaping mouth. She clutched her coat around her, gave Big Lucy a wink and swept out of the front door.

Walking home that night, Mary was glad of the distance that gave her a chance to assimilate her thoughts. The fresh cool night air whipped around her but she was unaware of the chill. She took the cigarette she had swiped out of Mr. Keller's packet, lying in his bedside drawer, and lit up with the matches that she picked up as well. She was on top of the world. She had to begin her work at the hotel in two days and the excitement overrode all her other emotions. Quitting her job was a huge decision but that paled in comparison to what she had accomplished today. She would have to break the news to her mother but she could handle that; she could handle anything after today.

She saw the lighthouse standing in the distance; its revolving light shone brightly as it swept over the landscape. The tides hissed towards the shore, assaulting the rocks that impeded their onrush; crashing and splashing, until the ocean current drew them back only to return them with renewed force. In spite of her busy day, Mary was not the least bit tired; she felt as if she was walking on air. The minute she shoved open the cottage door, reality hit her and she ducked her head to avoid Annie's glance. She removed her coat and wished she just had a little more time before she faced her mother.

"You alright, Mary dear?" Annie asked. A mother knows when something's amiss and Annie had a second sense about such things. "Mrs. Keller give you a rough time, then?"

"She didn't give me anything, Ma," Mary said bluntly. "I gave her my notice!" There it was out; relief washed over the girl and she shrugged and sat before the fire. Every pair of eyes in the room was riveted upon her and every mouth hung open; she had the undivided attention of the family who were aghast at what they had just heard.

"Oh, Mary, what have you gone and done, girl?" Annie was white as a sheet.

"Well, first thing I did this morning was get myself a job at the Royal Hotel in Kilbarra; a waitress I am to be, after the training. I join on Wednesday," Mary babbled, firing the details at her shocked listeners. "I'll be earning more than double of what I earn from Mrs. Keller; I get to keep my tips too."

"And why would anyone be paying a lass like you, all that money?" Annie asked skeptically. "Up to no good is what they're up to! You're not going to work in such a place, and that's that!"

"It's all very respectable, Ma," Mary said. "Gerald got me the job; he knows the owner."

"What am I going to say to your Da, lass?" Annie could not get beyond the fact that her daughter had quit her job; a job that Paddy had twisted Father Kennedy's arm for. How were they going to explain this ingratitude to the priest?

"Well you can tell him I got me a job with better pay and better working conditions, that's what you can tell him!" Mary said belligerently and Annie was grateful that her husband wasn't here at the moment. A good pasting they would have all got; Paddy believed in equality for the innocent as well as the culpable. Aiding and abetting, he called it; guilt by association. That man could explain things as only he could; he had such a way with words. And he explained so much better when he was loosened up by a drop of the hard stuff; and using his fists to embellish his speech; the man was a genius, no doubt about that.

56

"Don't you get sassy with me, Missy;" Annie was reinforced by the thought of her husband and what he was going to make of his daughter's bold step. "You discuss things with your parents; you just can't go and do as you please!"

"I discussed this with you, Ma; I said I couldn't work with that bitch any longer!" Mary reminded her mother.

"It's that Gerald behind you; giving you fancy ideas, is he?" Annie folded her arms across her chest to hold herself together. She thought, "It's that mother of his; thinks she's too good for the likes of us; it's all too much to cope with without Paddy by my side."

"I told Gerald how I felt; he took me to see this friend of his and I got the job," Mary explained. "At least someone is listening to how I feel!"

"I'm listening, girl," Annie said angrily. "And I don't like what I'm hearing. We're a family; we decide things together. I know nothing about this hotel of yours; is a young girl like you safe working there? Your father hasn't met your employer; God only knows what sort of man he is! You have no right to make a decision without discussing it with your parents first; getting too big for your bloody boots, you are!"

"Gerald recommended the place; his friend owns the hotel. Right respectable Mr. Calhoun is too; a proper gent. What's wrong with me getting a better job, Ma?" Mary wailed. "It's more money for the family; more money for Da to drink away. I'll be happy in a better place; Da will be happy with more of my money; it's good for the whole family!"

"I don't like your tone, Mary; have a care! And I don't like the way you keep talking about your father!" Annie was not used to arguing with her children; they usually did as they were told, and now here was Mary, taking advantage of Paddy's absence, challenging her authority. The other children sat around, eyes and mouths open wide, listening and watching the mother and daughter battling for supremacy. This would never have happened if he was around. "You go back to Mrs. Keller and apologise and hope she takes you back, or else!"

"I'm sorry, Ma," Mary said stubbornly as she got into bed. "I'm starting my new job on Wednesday morning and delighted I am to be doing that. If you're so concerned, why don't you go and work for Mrs. Keller?" She covered her head with a blanket to block out her mother's voice; it had been a long, eventful day and Mary wanted to savour the pleasurable bits; the best being telling Mrs. Keller she was leaving; that was real priceless. Annie stood lost in the little room; disoriented by the blast of Mary's insolence while her children looked at her to see what she would do next.

"Let's sleep on this," she muttered helplessly. "Things will be clearer in the morning." It was already clear to all that this round had been won by Mary.

Mary was asleep when the family rose early as usual the next morning. Annie stroked her cheek gently and tried to wake her. The girl stirred and the mother asked, "You'd best be getting up for work now, Mary love?" Mary growled from under the covers, "I will yes!" and Annie knew the girl wouldn't be going to the Keller house today, or any other day for that matter.

Annie thought it better to leave Mary alone to cool down, and decided to take time out to see Mrs. Keller. Someone would fill in for her at the harbour; there was always extra hands waiting to earn a few extra pennies. It was more important that Mrs. Keller bore no grudge at Mary's resignation; she didn't know exactly how it went but Mary did hint that the parting was bitter and that was not a good thing. Father Kennedy would have something to say about this and she just couldn't face that on her own. Her stomach would not cooperate and heaved as she walked to the Keller household. On the way she passed her transport chugging along to pick up the crew and waved them away.

The Journey

"What's up Annie love? You sick or something?" Murphy shouted out. She never missed a day's work if she could help it which made her a valuable member of the group. Annie thought, "Yes, I'm sick; sick and tired of the whole bloody thing, I am!" Instead she called back cheerfully, "Be in later, Murph! Got something important to take care of first!" The dilapidated vehicle continued on its way while the crew concurred, "Must be that bugger Paddy; he'll be the death of that woman!"

Climbing up the front steps of the Keller house, Annie tried to tidy her hair and straighten the wrinkles in her skirt. She suddenly realised she was not fit to walk up to the grand front door and she quickly made a detour to the side entrance of the kitchen. Big Lucy's surprised hazel eyes popped out of her pox marked face. Her greasy, dark brown hair was pulled back and a few rogue strands defied their imprisonment and made a break for freedom, dancing about her lined red forehead.

"I'd like to see Mrs. Keller, Lucy," she told the servant who stared at her as if she had taken leave of her senses.

"Oh, I don't know, Missus," Lucy said wringing her hands. "She's in a right state, she is..." At that moment the lady of the house herself came into the kitchen and stopped her tirade at the sight of Annie.

"Could I have a word, please Mrs. Keller?" Annie said before she lost her nerve.

"Well, I never!" Mrs. Keller spat out. "The cheek of you people! You'll not get another penny out of me so don't waste my time."

"I would like to apologise for my Mary, Missus," Annie said. "If you would allow me to work for you in her place I would be happy to do so." Where did that come from? Annie had no idea, and it made no matter once the words were out of her mouth. After releasing a flood of complaints, Mrs. Keller simply said, "Stop hanging about then and get to work!" Annie put on an apron and got stuck in. After twenty-two long years, her work as a herring girl was over. What would her family make of that?

Paddy took it better than she expected; he had a lot on his mind. Paddy now decided his talent lay in throwing in his lot with the nation's builders and discussed his plans with his wife who listened meekly to her husband's political ambitions without understanding a word he said.

"I'm turning over a new leaf, Annie love," Paddy said as his wife gazed at him with hope in her eyes and a nagging doubt in her heart. The unsanitary conditions of the jail were evident, and the foul stench that filled the place made Annie's stomach do somersaults. She wondered if this was a good time to tell Paddy about the pregnancy, but thought better of it. She had unloaded a lot of news and he had taken it all so well; why risk ruining his mood by unburdening herself further? Paddy was talking about getting the support of Father Kennedy and Councillor Reagan for his campaign. Annie wondered how that would pan out since it was the Councillor's brother-in-law that Paddy had given a beating to.

"Must convince them to place me somewhere in a position of public service," Paddy who hadn't held a job for more than six months at a stretch was indicating that his expertise at drunken brawling would in some way qualify him for public service. Annie was totally confused as to how this talent of his would support his new found aspirations. She shivered when the huge steel gate clanged shut behind her and couldn't wait for the end of her husband's thirty day sentence to be over so that she would not have to come this way again.

Annie was certainly glad she had kept the peace with Mrs. Keller and Father Kennedy who both seemed much happier with the new arrangement. Annie was more passive than her daughter Mary and gave no reason for conflict in her new job. She was a born slave and did exactly as she was told. She was much more at ease working indoors in a comfortable, clean environment and didn't miss the herring gutting one little bit; it was almost like looking after one's own home and Annie wondered why it had taken her so long to make the change. Scrubbing around the Keller household had almost gotten rid of the stink of herrings from under her skin and having time to eat made the bones on her face less prominent. She couldn't remember a better time for the family and looked forward to the day her husband was released.

Seamus had proposed to Linda and though her parents said no, the girl said yes. Annie said she would prefer that the couple stayed on in the cottage. She knew that her boy didn't earn enough to set up a home and support a wife.

"God knows what would happen when the babies come along," the mother thought, looking suspiciously at Linda's waistline. It was decided to build on a much needed room for them at the side of the cottage. It would hardly cost anything, Seamus promised and the family all pitched in to collect the stones that would form the walls and looked out for bits and pieces in the scrap yard. They found sturdy bits of timber that could be used as rafters and collected slabs of slate from the cliff side which Seamus and Michael primed for the floor.

Mary never came home without a couple of stones for the room in the basket of her bicycle. She had told her family she had hired the bike but she had actually bought it on tick from a friend of Gerald's. There was even a discussion about Seamus getting a bike at some point, seeing as how useful Mary's transport was turning out to be. The whole family had learned to ride her bike; even Annie, who did agree that it made life so much easier.

The Royal Hotel had many Americans passing through; the ones that had left Ireland penniless and in rags years ago, now came back to show off their new found prosperity. Some returned just to get a whiff of Irish air, to dampen their feeling of being homesick. Others had come to marry a sweetheart, or take back family members with them to enjoy a better life across the pond; or else they were tourists just coming to enjoy the historical sites and the majestic coastline. Whatever the reason for their presence, the Yanks were really generous with their tips.

Mary couldn't believe how much money she had to spend on herself; of course she kept her purchases in her locker at work and never disclosed how much she actually earned. Putting something aside for a rainy day was something Reg advised her to do. It was always Shirl gave me this, or Jen gave me that, and no one ever doubted her. Since she earned so much more than her previous job, her family never thought to question her finances and they did enjoy the day old food she managed to bring home from the hotel. The girl blossomed and bloomed in her new job; she was conscientious in her duties and Reg was well pleased with her work. She had a way with clients that made them ask for her and became a popular member of the Royal team.

"This one's a gem," Reg told Gerald when the young man came by to check on his protégé. "A right little treasure she is, that's for sure."

There was no time for socializing but Gerald managed to stay in touch with Mary at Sunday Mass after which they sometimes rode their bikes into town to see a movie. Mary was so grateful to her cousin for literally changing her life; she could hardly deny him anything. If his lusty advances towards her made her uncomfortable, he always laughed them off and apologised and while she overlooked his actions, she made it known how she felt about his familiarity. Neither wanted to offend the other and so they made a great effort to maintain their tenuous relationship.

Since Gerald was no longer considered the instigator of Mary losing her head with Mrs. Keller; he was welcomed at the cottage by the family and spent many happy hours there. He was always ready with advice or a helping hand and Annie had begun to rely on him as did the others.

The Journey

"You'll be having a bite with us, won't you Gerald?" Annie would ask many an evening when the young man showed no sign of leaving.

"No thanks. Don't be troubling yourself; Auntie Annie," he would reply and shift himself as if to leave.

"Ah go way outta that, of course ye will!" Annie would insist while the others said, "Please stay, Gerald!" and he settled back into the chair.

"Does your Ma know how much time you spend with us, Gerald?" Annie once asked him. "Bet Ginger wouldn't approve of you mixing with the likes of us. Always thought she was the Queen of Sheba, your Ma did!"

"Ah, Ma's got a good heart and high hopes; that's all," Gerald laughed. "Wants us all to do well, she does. You mustn't mind her; we don't."

"And doing well you are, my boy, working with your Da. You're a good sort, Gerald," Annie said. "No airs and graces about you; always ready to give a helping hand."

"Family is family, Auntie," Gerald said innocently and it was hard to doubt him. Even Mary felt guilty at losing her temper with him at times and tried her best to steer away from situations that would force them to be within touching distance. Such peace and tranquility reigned in the lives of the Harpers that they almost forgot how it was when they went to sleep hungry and afraid; when Paddy was so ossified he lost control of his senses and his bodily functions, and would drag himself home after spending the night in a ditch; all wet and filthy like a stray dog and still have the energy to strike and abuse his family even as they tried to clean him up and put him to bed.

Then Paddy returned; one evening he surprised the family with his presence and they were not fooled by his bright smile and boisterous promises. Annie was the only one who was delighted, but after a while she too remembered; Paddy reminded her that things were back to normal.

"I think I'll have a round in the pub; see what's happening while I've been away; see about getting a job!" Paddy said, tucking some of the family's hard earned savings into his pocket and putting on his coat that had hardly time to dry off. "It's a new man I am now; learned quite a lesson inside, I did. Going to make something of myself; make my family proud!"

"There's a good pot of stew about ready, Paddy," Annie said hopefully. "Why don't you stop in tonight and get some nourishment?"

"I'll be back in a while, Annie love," he said pinching her cheek affectionately and making her blush in front of the children. "You can feed me yer stew then; right looking forward to it I am." He did not return that night for Annie's meal, preferring instead to be nourished in the loving arms of Gertie who opened a few bottles of whiskey to celebrate his homecoming. Then he got himself into trouble when he went to settle his tab at Trainer's, so he could rack it up again. He got into an altercation with the four Mulligan brothers who were enjoying a peaceful drink and discussing the future of the country. The argument escalated into a wild scrap that left the pub looking like a bomb site.

Paddy couldn't leave it at that; when the police arrived, he abused them sorely, hurling curses at their families including their saintly mothers. When they tried to restrain him, he let the cops feel the force of his knuckles and injured several of them in the process. That was three months in the clink and he was whisked away without even having had a taste of his wife's stew. Annie wept bitterly while the children were ecstatic to see the back of their good-for-nothing father: though they rejoiced in silence, not wanting to upset their dear mother.

The Journey

CHAPTER 5 - PRISON LIFE

The high security prison was quite a journey from Kilbarra, but she walked, hitched a ride on a cart, or caught a bus, and then walked some more. Annie managed to make this trip every weekend; come rain or come shine. The sight of the enormous penal complex constructed of black basalt rock, spreading its tentacles over ten acres, chilled her to the bone; the rigors of travelling and the usually inclement climate only added to the gloomy unforgiving atmosphere. Head down and coat pulled tightly across her chest, she braced himself against the cold wind that blew her backwards, as if to keep her away from entering the hostile gate.

Built within a five-sided wall, the four wings of the prison reached up to four imposing storeys in height and fanned off from the central area which was known as The Circle. Annie knew that beneath her feet ran a tunnel linking the Courthouse on the other side of the Prison to the Holding Cells, the Hospital, the Hanging Cell, and Graveyard. A man could be sentenced and dispatched to meet his Maker without ever seeing the light of day. The woman crossed herself and said a silent prayer for the long life of her husband. At the bleak Gate House, a series of bolts released the barred gate which slid open and then closed noisily after her. The whooshing sound of the airlock echoed through the pathways like a hissing snake slithering after its prey. When the main door slammed shut behind Annie; cold fear ran up and down her spine and her knees felt weak and wobbly as she whispered, "Holy Mary, Mother of God, pray for us sinners..."

A prison guard carried out a body search on Annie, to check for any contraband secreted among her person; as he stroked her body once, she knew his hands lingered longer than they should and when he began to repeat the process, she knew he was up to no good.

"Ah, get on with you!" Annie protested. "One would think I'm the criminal."

"Can't be too careful, Mam," the guard said flatly and continued to pat Annie down. "The things we find on a body...shocking I tell you, shocking it is...do anything for your men, you girls will. Tis human nature, that's what it is!" He gave her bottom a final squeeze and motioned her on to the next counter. Annie thought, "And you should know, you cheeky blackguard!"

Uniformed guards came and went, performing their duties like robots. The frostiness of people and the place matched the iciness of the weather outside. Annie was always dismayed by the acrid harshness and bleakness of the visitor's room. She hoped she would see some signs of motivational efforts to make prisoners opt for a better way of life but so far there were none.

"The prisoner will have cuffs on his wrists and ankles during the meeting for security, Missus," the guard warned her; he could probably smell the apprehension oozing out of Annie's pores. It was not her husband that made her fearful, but the starkness of the place; she knew how captivity would affect her husband and her pulse raced as she waited. Paddy was led into the room; the chains impeded his normal gait but the set look on his face belied the fact that he was in any discomfort. He sat down heavily and Annie knew how violently disturbed his spirit was; Paddy's eyes swept madly about the hostile space looking for an opening to make a run for it; but the truth was that he was going nowhere, and then he focussed of Annie; she would do very well as his escape for the moment and he took refuge in her presence.

When his dutiful wife made her trips to the High Security Prison, her husband was never in the best of humour. He was furious at

67

being back in the clink after savouring a mere two days of freedom and this time it was a hundred times worse than the local jail, in the police station in Kilbarra; this place was something else. News of home and offerings of a few homemade treats made no impression on Paddy. He was wrongfully incarcerated for no fault of his own, is how he saw himself, and his anger at his situation could not be contained.

"Fecking eejits!" Paddy raged. "I'm in and those useless Mulligan bastards are out to spread their shite! Bloody hell!"

You hush now, Paddy love," Annie tried to get him to calm down. "It's enough trouble you've got yourself into; don't make it worse, now."

"Can't get any worse! 'Tis no advantage to anybody to try to be good in here, lass," Paddy responded by kicking the table legs, banging his fists, and glaring at the guards; this was the most physical damage Paddy could do at the moment, but he struck out with his speech. His attitude and words were duly noted; he was a troublemaker. This time Paddy was sentenced to hard labour and since any kind of labour was against the man's nature, he raved bitterly against his unjust ninety day sentence. The hard labour class of inmates had to do the washing in the laundry, whitewashing and pumping water. They had to dig trenches, and break rocks for brick making; all this physical work was done in chains for twelve hours a day and in some cases even more.

Industry was seen as an important aspect of prison life as it promoted regularity and prevented idleness; Paddy was never idle for a moment if the warden could help it. Keeping prisoners busy also helped with managing the internal discipline which may have had a lot to do with the designated working hours that were from daylight to dark. These were dangerous times for a country shaken by social and political upheaval. In this restless society within the walls of this High Security jail, many unholy alliances were formed and groups were created, each with divergent views and treacherous aspirations.

"Working prison? My arse! Slave labour is what it is, I tell you; keep us going from morning to night they do, the bastards!" He showed his roughened palms to his wife, who knew all there was to know about backbreaking labour and savaged hands. "Food a dog wouldn't eat, they give us! They aim to kill me, one way or another, Scumbags; the lot of them!" Annie rubbed Paddy's calloused palms gently with her own scarred hands and made comforting sounds, trying to get her husband to calm down. Seeing the dirt ingrained in the lines of his hands and under his fingernails reminded her how Paddy loved to be clean and dress up all smart when he was sober. Their home may not have been all that, but compared to this cesspool it was grand. She prayed to the good Lord and all the saints in Heaven, begging them to give her Paddy the strength to survive the harsh environment, the most basic of prison food, the dangerous inmates, unsanitary conditions, and the cruel separation from his loving family.

"A right shower of savages I'm locked in with, Annie love; have to watch myself, lass: sly and vicious they are!" Paddy said when Annie counselled him. "These buggers are out to get me!" Just who were these people who targeted Paddy was never clear; yet the miasmic group of faceless, nameless individuals continued to pursue him relentlessly in his imaginings.

"I know it's hard for you love," Annie murmured, trying to comfort her man and Paddy retorted, "And what the fuck do you know?" Annie found herself wondering what on earth she should or could have done differently; as if somehow she was guilty too.

"I know what it's like to be left to pick up the pieces, deal with the children and the reactions of people; forever making excuses for you, afraid and embarrassed to bump into anyone, I am; scuttling around like I've done something wrong myself," Annie thought. "And I know all about that bitch, Gertie." She immediately felt bad to have such feelings of resentment and said a silent prayer for forgiveness.

When Paddy said, "Met a whole bunch of men in here; real outspoken they are; some right interesting notions they have," the hair on the back of Annie's neck stood up, alerting her to trouble. Then he said, "Tis the government that's to blame for the troubles of the people," and Annie went faint with fear.

"Don't be talking about such things, love," she responded, hoping no one heard. "Just concentrate on getting outta here and coming home."

"If it's a jailbreak you're suggesting, lass, perish the thought," Paddy said half seriously. "The government built this place to keep us in, and keeping us in it is. Built real solid this shite hole is, and everyone's a nark; can't trust any of these villains." The distraught woman stammered, "That's not what I meant, Paddy," and he just said, "Damn bloody government." Mary crossed herself quickly and begged, "Please don't be saying things like that love; puts a real fear into my heart, it does!" The law of sedition was frequently used in prosecutions when a person or member of an organisation stored or distributed anti-state literature or spoke out against the state. Any such actions were considered as the subversion of the state laws or incitement against the state, and an imposition of fascism upon the working class and poor peasants of Ireland.

"Don't you be telling me what to do, lass, I get enough of that shit in here, I do," Paddy growled, raising his voice and staring at the guards. "If I want to say fuck the government, I'll say fuck the government and bollocks to anyone who hears me!" Annie was almost glad when a buzzer signalled the end of the visit and as guilty as she felt, she couldn't wait to get out of there. She felt like she had lead in her veins; she could hardly move. Woodenly, she went through the process of leaving, in reverse; each stage seemed more tedious and added to her stress. When she finally got through her cottage door late at night, her children were waiting for her with a fire going strong and a mug of hot tea laced with whiskey to bring her back to life.

Apart from the man of the house being incarcerated and the shame of it all; things went well for the Harper family; the children agreed among themselves that Paddy's absence was the reason for their wellbeing and hoped he would stay where he was forever. By the look of things, it seemed as if they would get their wish; Paddy committed one misdemeanour after another and kept adding time to his sentence, much to Annie's dismay. There wasn't time to dwell on good fortune or bad fortune; there was much to be done and so little time to do it in; and who could argue with the good Lord when he sent down tests for the Harper family.

Mary was delighted with her work at the Hotel and her job was confirmed as soon as her period of training was over. She had made new friends; Mairead and Maureen, the twins, who worked in housekeeping; the three girls stepped outside for a fag and a chat any chance they got. There was Kelly Ryan who was so sophisticated Mary tried to copy everything she did; the two of them discussed fashions and their ambitions to meet a man who would give them a better life than the ones they had. Mairead said of Kelly, "Right snooty bitch she is, that one!" and Maureen agreed, "Thinks no end of herself, she does!" but Mary said, "Oh, she's alright; give her a chance will you!" to which they replied, "It's her that doesn't give us a chance, uppity cow!" Mary tried to remedy the fact by inviting them all for a meal of scrambled egg on toast after work at the cafe down the road; none of the three girls spoke to each other and Mary decided it was okay to keep her friends apart.

Grace O'Brien was a few years older than Mary and was married to Billy, a good hardworking man who adored her. His mum looked after their two daughters at home while the couple worked and saved whatever they could so that they could immigrate to

71

America. As Grace explained, "Tis a better life and good weather we're after," backing up her statement with fascinating success stories of acquaintances who had crossed over the water. The free spending Irish yanks that frequented the establishment were evidence of the life Grace and Billy dreamed of; sometimes Kelly and Mary wondered if such a move was a possibility in their mutual plan of self-improvement.

If Mary saw less and less of Jen and Shirl, it was because her work took up most of her days and she had so much to do with the precious time she had left over. She loved strolling down the Main Street after work, looking at the clothes in the shop windows and the fancy shoes in different styles and colours lined up in the shoe shop window, almost begging to be bought. She had never owned a new dress or new shoes in her life and hardly knew where to start. Luckily she had Kelly to advise her and she did make a few sensible purchases. However it was the twins who knew how to find the best bargains in the thrift stores they frequented. When Mary saw the framed mirror with a glass shelf, she had to have it to hang on the wall of the new room. And when she spotted a white lace dress hanging on a rack of second-hand clothes, she couldn't believe her luck. She thought, "Sweet Jesus! Which fool would get rid of such a beautiful frock; must be right out of their minds, for sure. Maybe the woman needed the money or died," and she shivered at the thought but that didn't deter her from holding on to the garment. She knew this was perfect for a bride and bought it for Linda. When Kelly said, "I wouldn't mind wearing that myself," and offered to buy it off Mary, she knew she had gotten a real steal and refused to part with it.

"Become quite the fashion queen, you have Mary," Kelly said eying her friend's newfound fashion sense, acknowledging she had stiff competition. The fact was that Mary was blooming in her improved circumstances that were an appropriate setting for her grace and beauty. She had her hair cut at the salon that Kelly frequented and the result was stunning; her gold streaked chestnut bob framed her pretty face and accentuated her features; her big blue eyes seemed bigger and bluer if that was possible! The girls experimented with cosmetics, and subtle make-up was now a part of Mary's grooming. Her naive simplicity added to her charm and kept her grounded; Reg saw the lady in her and was always protective and respectful towards the girl.

"You alright, Mary?" he would ask when he saw her, and she would smile and say nervously, "I'm grand, Reg, thank you." She never got over the fear of this imposing man who was responsible for hiring her and could just as easily fire her.

"You come to me if you have a problem," and she would nod her head, blush and say, "Thank you, Reg, I will that."

When Linda saw the white lace dress, she burst into tears. Seamus said, "Thank you, Mary, I'll pay for it," she just said, "Aw, get away with you; just fix the mirror on the wall when you build it," and he promised, "I will, sis, that I will," and hugged her tight and Mary saw he was a whole head taller than her now, and she hugged him back.

Explaining her purchases to Annie, it was always,

"Kelly gave me this." Or "Shirl gave me that." Annie could not understand fanciness, as she called it, and could not get used to having more money than they needed, not that Mary ever gave her mother an accurate picture of her finances. Her tips placed her in a whole other world and she did not know where to hide her money until Reg explained to her about banks and even marched her to his branch up the street and had her open an account. It was such a huge move for Mary until she found out that most of her friends at work had bank accounts too and she felt foolish when Kelly laughed, "You been hiding your cash in your mattress, then; dear oh dear?" and explained how her money was growing safely for when the time came to execute The Plan.

The Journey

The men at work flirted with Mary as did many of the residents of the Hotel. She was asked out constantly but she was standoffish with her admirers, which pleased Reg to no end; familiarity on the job always created problems; staff had to be sacked and new employees would have to be trained, only to have the process repeated when relationships soured and acrimony spilled over into the workplace. Standards had to be maintained; the Royal was the finest hotel in the county and Reg meant to keep it that way.

The one man who would not tolerate her aloofness was Gerald and he made demands on her time that she found hard to refuse since he never let her forget who was responsible for her good fortune. Gerald would turn up at work and sometimes would hang around Reg's office, or he would have a snack in the hotel restaurant and watch her work, insisting on her serving him. He engaged the girl in conversation and touched her every chance he got. His mood darkened when he saw Mary exchange words with the male staff and he glared at them furiously, complaining to Reg about their bad service.

Mary was always nervous when Gerald was around since he often insinuated that her continuance in the job was up to him.

"Reg was asking me if I was happy with you working here, Mary," he said and the girl paled with fright. She loved her job and her cousin knew it.

"And what did you tell him?" she asked and he replied nonchalantly, "Oh I don't know; I'm not sure if it's the right place for you; all these fella's trying to get you into bed." The girl gasped in shock and retorted, "You know that's not true, Gerald; I do my work and don't fool around!"

"Seems to me you have lots of time to fool around with your fancy new friends; make a load of excuses when I ask you out," Gerald complained like a petulant child and when Mary said, "That's just not true, Gerald!" He said they could see a picture after her shift ended and she quickly said, "Yes." In spite of all his kindness, Mary recognised there was a demon lurking under the man's skin and wondered when he would choose his moment to strike. He had made his intentions very clear; often times Mary wished she could have romantic feelings for Gerald but he repulsed her in that way. It was increasingly hard for her to accept his friendship but she was caught up in the situation having accepted his favours.

Meeting at Sunday mass was a regular feature and they usually did something after that whether it was going back to the cottage or riding into town on their bicycles to see a picture. If the weather was fair they would ride over to the orchard across the road from Cliffside Cottage or go down to the shore and have a swim. Gerald had ingratiated himself so much with the family that Annie would say, "Keep an eye on my babies, Gerald," before she dashed off to the hospital laundry or the prison to see Paddy. Once he had even accompanied Annie on one of her visits to the prison; something her own children had refused to do, and Gerald had been beatified ever since in her eyes; the lad could do no wrong; even Paddy changed his impression of his nephew from a turd to a toady which was a big step up and Mary tried to deal with the uneasy situation the best way she could.

When Seamus decided it was time to start the construction of the new room at the cottage, it was only natural that Gerald rolled up his sleeves and pitched in too, and an even closer bond formed between the lads. Mary would come home from work to find Gerald sprawled out in her father's chair before the fire, being waited on hand and foot by her family and giving advice and opinions on the construction or any other business he decided to poke his nose into. The family worshiped Gerald and Mary found herself alone in her growing aversion towards her cousin.

Seamus seemed to have money on him these days and explained it by saying, "Doing a lot of overtime," or "Ran an errand for

75

Trainor." Mary realised he bought things for the extension including a couple of cans of white paint to cover the old windows, a wide bed with a good spring mattress and a sturdy door to replace the old front door; no one in their right mind would give these things away and Mary realized that like her, he was not telling the truth about his earnings.

"Good for him," Mary thought. "Pointless to slog just so Da could drink up our earnings." The family were all so delighted with the prospect of extra space that no one thought to question how it came about. When Mary said, "Wish we had a real toilet, instead of using the dirty old bucket or going in the ditch!" Seamus said, "Why not?" and decided to repair and extend the old shed and add an outhouse on to it. A dry toilet was fashioned with a wooden seat that had a hole in it and an enamel bucket underneath it to catch the waste. It had to be emptied every few days and that task fell to the youngsters who did not see the point to all this added work since they still used the old chamber pot at night.

"Have a bit of class," Seamus said in answer to Michael's complaints. "Now you can sing in peace and have a good read while you're at it! And we don't have to suffer the sight of your fat bum."

"At least we don't have to stink up the house!" Mary said with disdain. Annie smiled at the fancy ideas her children had picked up and put it down to the changing times. She said, "Never even thought to change our lives; now you children have actually changed everything," and Mary said, "It's called modernization; we have to move on or we perish," and the children all mocked her and said, "Oh, Miss. Lah-de-dah!" and the room was filled with the family's happy laughter.

Gerald got a good deal on the thatched roof which included the fixing of the old roof, and Mary and Seamus chipped in for the cost. The new room had a back door and an entrance to the old room was created by knocking out an archway of stones in the wall. It had a window at the front, Seamus said, "To see who's coming and going." The new front door was put in and the old front door replaced the old back door, which was repaired and installed on the jacks; now all these wooden portals swung open and shut without a battle.

The girls were to share the new room with Seamus and his bride; he had partitioned it cleverly to give enough privacy; after the whole family living in one small room, this was like the last word in gracious living. The old room was now a communal area with Paddy and Annie's bed off to the side; the chairs around the fireplace and the table against one wall. There was also a food cupboard Michael had dragged home one day and restored. Annie was delighted to have this separate storage space for her cooking utensils and food items. Better than leaving things in the open, for the rats to get at! The room looked quite empty once the girl's bed was moved to the new room but it filled up once everyone sat together around the hearth. A space here for a pallet for Michael would be sorted later; for the present he would share a bed with Seamus. It was strange having all this space, and from time to time one of them would get up and walk around, marvelling at the changes in their home which was transformed from a hovel to a very respectable dwelling. Seamus put up Mary's mirror as promised and the glass shelf now held a brush and comb. Everyone clustered around it to check themselves before they went out or sometimes they simply stood before the mirror to admire their images.

"Pride goeth before a fall," Annie would quote when she caught her children gazing at their reflections while the siblings wondered how they ever existed before the precious mirror came into their lives.

Annie made sure she told Paddy about each new development as things progressed so that no shocks were waiting for him when he got out. When he said, "And who's paying for all this extravagance, then?" she was quick to tell him the children scavenged the material and said, "Mary gets a fair bit in tips; she and Seamus paid for the roof," and added, "Gerald managed to get the thatch for a bargain; our home doesn't leak anymore!" When he shot her a dirty look, Annie said, "You'd have fixed it love, if you'd had the time, I'm sure." Paddy just grunted and said, "See they don't waste any bloody money; it don't grow on trees!" and Annie said, "Yes, love, I'll tell them you said so."

"And tell that boy to forget any ideas of getting hitched," Paddy added. "He's much too young to have a bloody wife and kids hanging round his neck." Annie nodded and repeated Seamus and Linda's intentions on her next visit and Paddy burst out, "Tell him I'll be dealing with him if he doesn't give up his crazy bloody notions! Explain it with a strap across his backside, I will, if the friging eejit doesn't understand!" Then one day Annie said softly, "They have to get married, Paddy love," and her husband laughed incredulously and said, "Oh, shit!" and that was that. The family waited for Paddy's release from jail and set the wedding date with Father Kennedy accordingly.

Gerald borrowed his father's van to pick up Paddy from the prison when his time was done. Annie had taken time off from the Keller's and was so delighted she could hardly contain herself; the thought of having her man home again filled her with happiness that was unfortunately not shared by her children. Paddy tried to conceal his joy by fussing about this or that and all his wife said was, "Don't you fret, love."

"Bet you won't recognise your old home, Uncle Paddy," Gerald said on the drive home and Annie's heart almost stopped.

"A lot of nonsense been going on then, lad?" Paddy asked and Gerald said, "That's for sure, Uncle; but it's a home that befits the likes of you! Real solid character it has; just like you!" Paddy laughed and said, "You'll get nothing out of me by flattery, lad." Annie's blood began to flow again until Paddy said, "It's a long

78

drive back to Kilbarra; worked up a mighty thirst I have these last months; let's stop for a nip, what do you say, Gerald."

"I'll stop for a bottle; gotta get this van back to Da by nine sharp so drink it on the way," Gerald said and pulled up at the next public house.

"Please, Paddy, the children are so excited to see you again," Annie said pleadingly. "Please don't spoil it; I can't see you back in jail again." She put her arms around his neck and he patted her back and reassuringly promised, "I'll not be going back, Annie love. Just a wee drink, that's all; it's been so long." Then Gerald returned with a half pint bottle and handed it to Paddy who couldn't wait to get the cap off.

"Aah!" he said as the sweet liquid wet his parched throat and flowed into his dehydrated body. "Aah!" He cheered up so much Annie couldn't remember when she last saw him in such good humour. He talked and laughed and told them of his plans.

"Been offered some real work, I have," he said. "Bloke who was in with me gave me a contact; chance to make some good money, it is."

"And what kind of work would this be, love?" Annie asked suspiciously, and Paddy answered, "No need to be worrying your head none, lass. I'm home now," and she began to worry in earnest. Gerald laughed and said, "Women! What do they know?" and Paddy had a swig and replied, "What the feck do they know, eh, lad?" and they broke into raucous laughter while Annie bit her tongue to avoid an argument on her husband's first day home that would drive him straight into the arms of that wicked trollop Gertie.

"So it's a working man you're going to be, Uncle?" Gerald asked slyly and Paddy checked him, "It's a rich working man, I'll be, lad. Maybe you'd like to come in with me, huh?"

"Tis working with my Da and brothers, I am," Gerald answered. "The family business needs me; doing pretty well we are." He thought, "I'll not be messing in your monkey business, Uncle Paddy; I sure don't have any ambition to be your cellmate!"

"Let me know if you change your mind, lad," Paddy offered. "You've been right by my family while I've been away and I sure appreciate that; owe you one, I do."

"Family is family," Gerald said, and Paddy said, "And that's the truth of it; family is family," and Annie nodded in agreement while her husband took another swig from his bottle.

"And what's to be your line of business, Uncle?" Gerald prodded casually and Paddy said vaguely, "Export and import, lad; that's where the money is."

"That's for sure," Gerald agreed. "We have so many orders we can't keep up with the demand. Have to expand, we have to, I keep telling Da."

"Not feeling the pinch of the economic war, then?" Paddy asked slyly and Gerald lied, "Not a bit, Uncle; just keep finding new markets for our products."

"You've a smart head on those broad shoulders of yours; when did you grow up and become so clever?" Paddy slapped him on his shoulder. "Must have got your brains from that mother of yours!" Annie thought, "And when did that snotty mare have a brain in her head? Must be the booze talking!"

"So this import and export business of yours; what commodities will you be dealing with, Uncle Paddy?" Gerald asked and Paddy just said, "I have to meet with this man tomorrow and I'll have the exact details then. Promise of good money there is, for sure. Time for my Annie to take it easy; I see you have a bun in the oven lass, when were you going to tell me?"

The Journey

"Paddy!" Annie exclaimed and put her face in her hands, and Paddy reached out to pat her stomach, and laughed, "Don't you be going all shy on me lass; did you think you could hide anything from me?" Paddy was in a mellow mood by the time the bottle emptied just as they got home. It was light enough to see the cottage and Paddy stared at it with his mouth open.

"What the...? You brought me to the wrong cottage, now take me to the right cottage, Gerald!" he joked. The fact that Paddy was smiling put everyone at ease and the children, momentarily forgetting their animosity towards their father, threw their arms around him to welcome him home. As he walked through the cottage, Annie kept reminding him softly, "It's what you would have done, Paddy love, if only you'd had the time," and Gerald pulled out a large bottle of whiskey and handed it to Paddy saying, "To celebrate your homecoming!"

"You're a good sort, Gerald," Paddy said, grasping the bottle with both hands, kissing and cuddling it lovingly. "Now that's a present and a half; thank you, lad!"

"My pleasure," said Gerald. "Gotta go now, I'll leave you folks to enjoy the remains of this happy day." Annie insisted, "You stay and sup with us," and Paddy said, "You gotta stay; have a drink, lad," but Gerald said, "My Da will be waiting for me," and Annie and Paddy said, "Well, sometime soon then?" and Gerald promised, "For sure, for sure!" and made his way out of the new front door. Annie and Mary followed him outside and the girl asked, "Why the hell did you give him the booze?" and Gerald replied, "Let him drink at home and he'll not be going out; at least not tonight!" Paddy had his family around him and was the centre of their attention. He regaled them with stories from the past and they wished it could always be like this although they knew this was not possible.

It was as Gerald predicted; filled with whiskey and good home cooking, the exhausted man passed out in his bed before the new clock on the food cupboard struck the midnight hour. Annie lay beside her man, gazing at his handsome face. Lovingly, she smoothed back the hair that fell across Paddy's forehead and beheld the miracle of her husband lying beside her so peacefully. It was the first time in over seventeen years since they shared a room together without any of their children sleeping beside them. Annie looked at him until the embers in the grate stopped shedding their light; the room became dark and she snuggled up against Paddy's warm body and drifted off to sleep thanking the Lord for his infinite kindness and mercy.

The Journey

CHAPTER 6 - A SMUGGLER'S LIFE

Sheila returned from school in the late afternoon to find her father getting ready to leave the house. It was hard to tell if it was colder inside or out; rain lashed down, blown about by gusting winds that swept over the sea and came rushing in over the coastline, flattening the grass and slamming the cottages that stood here and there like the remaining teeth in an old crone's mouth. The sky was dark grey, packed with thick towering Nimbus clouds, almost black in places; it looked as if there was going to be no let up in the ominous deluge that heralded one of the mighty storms that hit the coast each winter.

The storm warnings were announced on the radio; the schools informed children, who informed their parents, who could tell by just sniffing the air, that they were in for a big one. The girl was soaked to the bone and quickly removed her sodden coat and scarf.

You going out, Da?" she asked. "It's coming down something fierce out there." Shaking like a wet dog and dripping water around her she rushed to get a fire going; that's what Annie had told her to do the minute she got home.

"See your father's comfortable; keep the fire going and see he gets some hot tea inside of him," Annie told the children; the first one in would have to comply. Keep him warm; keep him fed; keep him home, is what she ordered; Sheila's mind raced frantically, looking for ways by which such a feat could be accomplished.

Within minutes, the fire was lit and the kettle was on the boil. "I'll make you a hot cup of tea, Da," said Sheila. "Wouldn't say no, girl; got anything strong to put in it?" replied Paddy as he tied the laces on his shiny shoes. She wasn't quite sure if it was okay to get out the bottle of brandy that was kept hidden for medicinal purposes; Annie always swore her mother would have perished much earlier if it wasn't for the brandy that warmed her chest and kept her going as long as she did.

"Give him whatever he wants," her mother had commanded, and the girl darted out to the shed and pulled out a bottle from the straw under the chickens who clucked angrily at being disturbed on such a miserable, damp, blustery day. There was barely an inch of the deep amber liquid in the bottle and Sheila returned to the room more wet than ever.

"This is all there is, Da," she said guiltily, as if she would rather have given him a big bottle full, but his face lit up and he said, "That will do very nicely, lass," and downed the contents on the spot in one gulp and Sheila thought, "I don't think he knows my name," and wondered if she should tell him she was Sheila. Paddy clasped the steaming mug with both hands and sipped the hot brew. Sheila watched him relish his tea and asked, "Would you like something to eat, Da?" and Paddy said, "No, lass, gotta go see this bloke about a job; is that umbrella any good?" The girl took the big, black umbrella off the nail on the wall and Paddy unfurled it to check its condition; apart from a couple of small holes, it was in good nick.

"Oh, 'tis bad luck to open an umbrella inside the house, Da!" the child looked at her father with alarm in her eyes, and he laughed, "Yer make your own luck, girl, remember that." Donning a thick scarf that his wife had knitted for him, and his overcoat that had seen much better days, Paddy set out like a knight on a quest. Shielded by the big black umbrella that threatened to blow inside out, he dove into the murky, wet gloom, slamming the cottage door behind him, leaving his daughter bewildered and panicked. Stunned by her failure, Sheila squatted before the grate and hugged her knees as she buried her face in her arms. How would she explain to Annie that she let her father get away?

Annie got the picture the minute she came in. Her daughter helped her out of her wet things; she sighed and sat down heavily before the fire, sticking her palms out as if to grab some warmth. Sheila put a mug of tea in her hands and Annie accepted it gratefully.

"I gave Da the brandy," the daughter confessed, her big blue eyes dark with worry. "Wanted something strong for his tea, he said."

"You did the right thing, Sheila love," Annie answered, deep in her thoughts.

"Da said he had to see somebody," she explained, trying to shift any blame that may come her way for not keeping him home.

"Yes, lass, he'll be back soon, for sure," Annie said, and the women busied themselves in preparing the evening meal while the absence of Paddy loomed like an enormous emptiness in the room. Mary and Michael came in and made no mention of their missing father. Seamus would be in late; these days he dragged himself home at all hours of the night; too exhausted to do anything other than close his eyes.

"Working for my wedding," he would say and Annie would tell him to slow down. "Trying for a good start for Linda and me, I am. Gotta keep going while I can."

"Good start, indeed. What foolishness is that? Never thought of such things in my time; we made the best of what we had or didn't have," she mused, shaking her head at the strangeness of it all. "Didn't have a penny to our names when we wed; Paddy and me; love and hard work got us through the bad times just like the rest of our neighbours. We were all without, all in the same boat we were, so we never even realised we were poor. We shared what we had and comforted each other in rough times; it's all changing now; everyone for themselves they are."

"Going to bed cold and hungry isn't a childhood memory I cherish, Ma," Mary said. "It's all very well to have love and work yer fingers to the bone, but a bit of planning goes a long way. I think Seamus is a smart lad."

"Not so smart to keep his trousers buttoned up, was he?" Annie thought; then she remembered Paddy and her when they first met, and softened. Couldn't keep their hands off each other; magnets for each other they were, and she sighed inwardly, "Love is a powerful thing, for sure."

"Want my wife and children to have more than I did, no offence, Ma," Seamus tried to be gentle. He had already stated that he did not want Linda working outside the home once they were married and often said that Annie should quit work and relax but she didn't know how.

"That's a good thing to want to care for your own," Annie would say. "But it seems to me a mighty greed has sickened my children and I'm afraid for you all. Trying to be something you're not, trying to change this and that; getting above yourselves you are. No good can come of being dissatisfied with what the Lord intended for you." The younger children listened to the discussion intently, wondering which side they should take. They liked all the improvements and treats but they also loved their mother dearly; she was the centre of their little world and if it came to a choice, Annie would be the winner; no question about it.

"He helps them that help themselves, Ma," Seamus laughed. "Just giving Him a helping hand, that's all."

"Don't you blaspheme, Seamus Harper!" Annie was furious; few things made her angry and taking the Lord's name in vain was top of the list. "You'll feel my shoe on your backside, big and all, as you are, boy!" He put his arms around his mother trying to tease the annoyance out of her.

"Now stop with your foolishness and let's eat," Annie grumbled, not really as upset as she pretended to be. There was no mention of

The Journey

Paddy and the family slept soundly, energising their exhausted minds and bodies for the coming day of more toil.

The village of Kilbarra is by the sea and about five miles south of the village; the sea flows into a Lough. A Lough that separates the north of the country from the south of the country. This Lough was being crossed in the dead of night by two men in a small rowing boat, smuggling alcohol and tobacco from Southern Ireland; knowing the huge profit that was to be made selling their contraband in the north of the country. They crossed the treacherous waters without lights, not wanting to be spotted by the customs men who kept a close eye on the Lough. In the pelting rain, the small boat was rocked back and forth by the turbulent current; they were prepared to risk life and limb for the huge rewards that the success of their illicit mission would bring. They had already sold their consignment to a contact boat and now headed back to the shore to split the profits and return home.

The former fellow inmates of High Security Prison struggled against the elements to remain afloat; the raging squall was upon them and whipped up the sea. Above and below, the men faced mortal danger by being where they were. They shouted out to each other but their words were ripped out of their mouths by the wind and scattered haphazardly in all directions. Without the contraband to act as ballast, they tossed about in the wooden tub; much of the time they were lost and Carrick tried to get their bearings by checking the compass he kept in his pocket. This was an exercise in futility since it was too dark to see; they couldn't have a lamp or a flashlight and risk being spotted by the coastguard that patrolled the waters looking for the likes of them. It was a relief when they finally spotted the lighthouse of Kilbarra off in the distance beckoning the boat to shore.

Numbed by the rigors of their strenuous exertion, the men looked forward to the end of the trip. As they entered the sheltered inlet, they began to discuss the division of the spoils. It was to be a seventy-thirty split; it was Carrick's boat and he had the seed money so seventy percent was his share; according to him. Paddy tried to up his share while Carrick tried to beat him down further. Much of what the men said was lost anyway as the deafening sounds of the storm drowned out their voices. The alcohol the men had consumed and their tiredness made them foolhardy in their accounting. Tempers flared and where wisdom is lacking, a physical exchange usually ensues as was the case this night.

The men began to shout abuse and jab each other with their oars; the unstableness of the situation would have given an air of comedy to the circumstances but the men fought in earnest: each intent on pocketing all the money for himself. Paddy lunged for Carrick and the two men were at each other's throats. Paddy was the bigger and stronger man and Carrick lost his footing and hit his head against the tiller which snapped, making a deep gash in his neck. A jagged spike pierced the man's skull. Blood gushed from the wounds as Carrick lay motionless at the bottom of the boat. Paddy checked for vital signs but he knew a dead body when he saw one and Carrick was a goner for sure. Paddy pulled out the wad of notes from the man's pocket, stripped him of his watch and shoved his evil gain into his own jacket pocket. He rowed to shore and pushed the boat out to sea. Half drowned himself and gasping for breath, he clambered up the craggy rocks of a cliff to find the familiar path he knew since he was a child; he stumbled along, until he found his way almost instinctively to his cottage.

Annie shot out of bed the moment her husband appeared and was appalled by his state.

"What happened, love?" was all she could manage and he stuttered; "Terrible storm!" as she stripped him of his wet things and got him into bed where he shivered and shook until sleep finally overcame him. Annie threw some wood in the fire that had not quite gone out and hung Paddy's wet things on the line inside

89

the room; then she lay awake beside her husband wondering what crime was committed tonight.

If the children were surprised to see their father asleep in bed when they readied themselves for work the next morning, they did not show it. The family went their separate ways and Annie knew her husband would not wake until she returned from work. No one would have guessed at the devastation that had just visited Kilbarra; the day was bright with not a cloud in the sky, nor was there a wind to upset its perfect stillness. The Keller's were away visiting family for the week, so Annie left a couple of hours earlier than she normally did. She stopped at Trainor's pub to pick up a large bottle of whiskey for Paddy and a small bottle of brandy to hide away for medicinal purposes.

Deserted us, has old Paddy, eh Missus?" Jerry, the barman joked. Annie answered, "Not at all, Jerry; he'll be on his feet again and you'll be seeing him then, for sure!" She stopped in at Mrs. Finnegan's shop and the woman was quick to spot the bottle of alcohol peeping out of her bag.

"Celebrating the return of your husband, Mrs. Harper?" the woman asked slyly from behind her veil of smoke, hoping to elicit some information she could spread about.

"Seems to have a chill, my Paddy does," Annie tried to be polite while keeping her answers to a minimum. "Was a fierce storm that blew in last night, wasn't it?"

"Indeed it was," said Mrs. Finnegan. "Blew the roofs off the Cleary and Adair cottages; did some mighty damage to many a home in the village, I hear. Sheila tells me there's quite a bit of work you've done to your place, Missus? Lucky, that; or else you could have lost your roof like some of the unfortunate ones who can't afford the fixing."

"Mary and Seamus; work really hard they do; want all sorts of improvements," Annie explained cautiously. "I say better to save your pennies for a rainy day. That rainy day could have been last night though; would be a sad state to have no roof. Must go round the village to see where I can help; I'm sure you'll be doing the same, Mrs. Finnegan. Could you throw in a couple of packs of Woodbine, please?"

"I'll be doing my bit for sure; always do," the woman said while her cigarette danced about between her thin lips. "And a couple of packs of fags it is. Anything else?" Annie said, "No thank you," and Mrs. Finnegan asked, "Will that be cash or credit then, Missus?"

"Credit, if you please, Mrs. Finnegan," Annie didn't want the woman to know she could have paid cash for a dozen packets and had money to spare. "I'll see it's paid for by the end of the month, I will."

"Not to worry," Mrs. Finnegan said. "You keep your accounts up to date; not like some I could mention."

"Tis hard when a family is not working," Annie replied and both the women recalled the time not so long ago when the Harper's could barely make ends meet.

"Is Paddy looking for work then?" asked the woman boldly. "'Twill be difficult for sure; so few jobs these days and it's few around these parts that would employ a convict."

"My husband has served his time, Mrs. Finnegan," Annie said curtly. "Having a temper hardly makes a man a criminal. He will be up and about as soon as he shakes his chill, for sure." Annie thought, "A good punch in the kisser would do you the world of good, you miserable, spiteful cow!"

"Well, I suppose there are worse things a man can do, Mrs. Harper, but a bad temper does lead to all kinds of mischief," the woman answered. "I heard they found a dead body of a man washed ashore on the beach, pretty close to your end; did you know that? No doubt a bad temper was involved in the man's demise."

"No, can't say I heard; hard to keep up with all the gossip; too busy working, I am. Good day to you, Missus!" and Mrs. Finnegan said brightly, "Get that big fella of yours to give you a hand, then." Annie tried to keep her dignity as she sailed out of the shop with her head held up high, but once outside her heart began to pound and she felt faint with fear.

"Sweet Jesus," she prayed. "Don't let Paddy have had anything to do with the body on the beach. Please protect this family and keep us all out of harm's way." She walked briskly, breaking into a run as she neared the cottage; hoping against hope that she would find her husband safe at home.

Paddy stirred when he heard the cottage door slam shut. Through his half open eyes he could see his wife looking at him and he reached out his arms for her. Without a moment's hesitation, Annie was beside her man, lost in the magic of his touch as his hands roamed freely about her body. She closed her eyes, taking pleasure in the sweet whispering of his kisses as his lips caressed her skin, taking her to another place where everything was perfect.

"I better get up, Paddy love," Annie said, not really wanting to break the spell as they lay luxuriating in each other's arms. "The children will be home soon."

"You stay where you are, lass," Paddy held her close in his strong arms and began to caress her again. "Won't be the first time they've seen you in bed with their father. I missed you, Annie love." It was impossible for Annie to deny her husband his rights; her body was on fire at his touch and there was no way she could turn away.

Paddy smoked a cigarette and sipped his whiskey as he leaned against the pillows propped up against the wall, and watched his wife move about the room as she tidied herself and began organising dinner for the family. "What a strong woman she is," he thought and was glad she was on his side. He felt loved and protected and wondered why he did the things he did which could very easily cost him his family. The months in prison were unbearable and he was determined that he was never going back; then he thought of last night's fiasco and cursed himself.

"Where did you put my jacket, love?" he asked, Paddy suddenly panicked, remembering the roll of money he had stashed in his pocket. Annie said, "Here you are, Paddy," and handed him a pile of the dry, folded clothes he had worn last night. His hand went straight to his pocket and he felt the wad of notes exactly where he had put it and he began to breathe easy. As he climbed into his pants, he heard Annie say casually, "A dead body was washed up on the beach last night; wonder who the poor man was." His heart sank and he had a hard time slipping into his shirt and buttoning his trousers. He didn't trust himself to look at Annie and said, "'Twas a fierce storm last night, it was; could've been a sailor, swept off the deck of his ship."

Michael and Sheila came in at that moment bursting with the news of the dead body practically on their door step.

"A terrible night to be out," Paddy said, and Sheila said, "But you went out in the storm, Da," and he quickly said, "To be sure I went out but I saw all hell let loose outside and I came back real quick; ask your mother." Annie said, "That you did, love; you were in just as the children went to bed," and repeated for good measure, "Your father was in all last night, and a good thing that was too."

"Policemen all over the place, asking questions," Seamus said when he came in, "Wonder what happened." Mary said, "It's all over the papers it is," and took a newspaper out of her coat pocket and the children made a grab for it to check the gory details.

The Journey

"Let me have a look at that," Paddy said and they sat around him in bed as he read the news aloud between puffs on his cigarette and sips of his whiskey.

"The body of Mr. William D. Carrick.....," Paddy read the account and said, "This bloke was in prison with me; got out a month before me, he did; eleven kids he had; talked about them all the time, God rest his soul." He read, "Suspected involvement in smuggling...." and Mary said, "Met Officer Brice on the way home and he asked me if I noticed any unusual activity on Monday and I said, "No, couldn't see further than my nose, so fierce the storm was," and he asked if you were in all night, Da, and I said, "Yea for sure; all night." Annie said, "That's right, yer Da was in all night; now enough of all this talk about dead bodies and let's eat."

Paddy stayed home for the rest of the week, fearful of the constabulary that were combing the area. He was ready for Brice when he knocked at the cottage door.

"Sorry to disturb you, Paddy," the police officer said. "Just need to ask you a few questions, if you don't mind."

"Ask away, Arthur; don't mind at all; glad to be of any assistance, I am." The two men had grown up together and the cop still held a grudge for all the times he got a pasting from Paddy when they were kids.

"Heard the story, have you? Body washed up on the shore," the policeman pointed to the beach.

"That I have, Arthur; in fact I met the bloke while we were both in; a real tragedy it is," Paddy replied.

"Did yer old cell mate come to say hello then Paddy?" the cop asked, and Paddy said, "You're the first person to come over to visit me, Arthur; just got out on Sunday; been nursing a cold since then, I have."

94

"Have to ask, Paddy," Arthur probed. "Seeing as you and Carrick were such good mates in the slammer."

"You think I had something to do with....aw, get away with you, Arthur. I may have a bit of a temper when I've had a few, but I ain't no killer, man!"

"Not saying you are, Paddy. Just seems to me your quick fists have led you into a lot of trouble...could've killed me a couple of times, for sure," Brice looked Paddy in the eye and the men laughed, remembering the scraps they had got into as children. "You saying you were in on Monday night then, Paddy?"

"That's right, Arthur, ask the family, ain't got out since I came home," and Brice said, "I asked them and they all stick to the same story. I kinda believe you though; you haven't been to your usual haunts and you ain't visited Gertie; she's asking all over for you."

"That's all over and done with; put my family through too much I have; I'm a new man and this man ain't going to see the insides of prison ever again," Paddy confessed and Brice raised an eyebrow and replied sceptically, "That I don't believe so much, boyo!"

"Well then, it is what it is," Paddy said shrugging his shoulders, and Brice said, "For sure we always get our man; you can count on it. If it's a man that did Carrick in, he's going to swing for it, no doubt about that! Going to put a stop to this smuggling lark once and for all! Aim to put all these criminals behind bars as soon as possible."

"And good luck to you I say, Arthur," Paddy said, "you're a man of principal, you are." The cop said, "I do my best for the community, I do. Isn't easy with all these violent savages about, I tell you."

"Thirsty work, it must be, chasing after villains all day and all night long; have a drink before you go?" Paddy offered and Brice replied, "I'm on duty man," and Paddy said, "Oh, go on; have a wee one to warm you up, 'tis a nippy day." "Okay then, a wee one for the road," said Brice and they sat outside on the old stone wall reminiscing about the old days until they finished the bottle of whiskey. "Well goodbye, Paddy, don't get into any trouble, mind," "Bye Arthur, no trouble from me you'll be having."

There was no way Paddy would stir from the cottage. He followed the case of Carrick like a detective, questioning the children about any new developments and what people were saying. He went over and over the newspaper Mary brought home for him daily, keeping each edition next to his bed so that he could reread the newspaper and refer to his material in case he made a connection to some piece of information he had missed before. He was furious when Sheila removed the entertainment page that had something about the case on the back of it. He shouted at the girl as if she had committed a serious crime and would have given her a taste of the back of his hand if Annie hadn't intervened.

"No one is to touch Da's newspapers," she ordered, trying to hold her husband off.

"What sort of Morons am I living with?" His booming voice raged as he stood menacingly, all red faced with his veins standing out on his temples and his threatening fists flailing about, ready to make contact. "Break every bone in your body if you put one finger on my papers again!" and the family knew he was responsible for the body on the beach and at that moment they feared for their lives. Never again did anyone interfere with his precious newspapers and not a scrap of sacred newsprint could be sanctioned for the jacks without his express permission.

Then one day, Paddy read that accidental death was ruled as the cause of Carrick's death; the man was out, up to no good, on a bad night; he slipped, hit his head on the tiller and drowned as a result, and the case was closed. However, the local constabulary and the coastguard had stepped up their efforts to apprehend the smugglers that infested the area and Paddy looked over his shoulder constantly. The two hundred pounds hidden under the chickens was a lot of money to have lying around and he broke into a sweat just thinking about it. It wasn't that Paddy was a coward by nature, but the thought of being incarcerated again was too much to deal with at the present. As long as his family plied him with booze, he saw no reason to invite trouble by stepping out of the safety of his cottage.

Annie loved having her husband home and sometimes came home from work early to be with him. Mrs. Keller was threatening to sack her but she managed to placate the woman with her good nature and hard work. When she told Paddy about this he said, "Nothing but a bitch! You quit right away, love." "Have to bring in money to keep us going." Replied Annie. "That's it!" said Paddy "I'm going to get me a job and you're going to stay home!" Annie didn't want the situation to change and would have worked even harder to have her man safe at home, but he was adamant.

"What'll you do, love?" she asked worriedly. "Jobs are real scarce to come by these days; I don't want you to have to slave away among savages; you know you can't do that!"

"Going to ask about, I am," he said. "Time for me to stand on my own two feet. I'll talk to Father Kennedy on Sunday and Arthur, too; they may know of something that would suit me." Showing off a sober Paddy beside her at Mass made Annie giddy with joy. "When He gives, He gives with both hands," she thought; her whole family lined up beside her in their Sunday best for all to see; was a dream come true.

"What's the job situation at the harbour?" Paddy asked Seamus one evening as they sat outside on the stone wall, waiting for the rest of the family to come home.

"Not good at all, business is slow; lots of good men being laid off," he replied. Paddy said thoughtfully, "Is that so, then? I hear a man

97

can make a penny or two shifting crates, if you know what I mean."

"Place is crawling with coppers and narks because of the clampdown on smuggling; not the best place for you at the moment, Da," Seamus advised, adding, "You had a lucky man to have escaped the last time, so leave it at that." Paddy turned to look his son in the face and it was clear to both the men what was being discussed here.

"You cheeky beggar!" Paddy laughed, tossing the boy's hair with his big hand. "Since when do you have a monopoly on the business, then?" Seamus remained silent and kept his eyes down. Paddy said, "Here, have a fag, lad." "Got my own, Da," replied Seamus and pulled out his pack offering his surprised father a cigarette. He stuck one between his own lips and lit up for the first time in front of Paddy who doubled up with laughter.

"Seems to me there's a lot you know, lad," Paddy said once he got the better of his amusement. There was something in the boy's eyes that carried a message he didn't quite understand. "Care to share your knowledge with your Da, then?"

"I know that booze muddles up a man's thinking," Seamus said meaningfully and Paddy was alert in an instant. "Messes with his logic when he's on the job; puts him at risk of being caught. I saw you that night, Da."

"Stop talking bloody rubbish, lad," Paddy said seriously. "You saw nothing of the sort!"

"I drove the truck that supplied you and your cellmate with the booze, Da. I was the man in the mask and hood," Seamus replied bluntly. "If you were sober, you would have noticed who you were dealing with; if it was another driver, he would have identified you, and Carrick's mates would have put a knife in your back by now."

The Journey

"You've got balls of steel, talking to me like this, lad!" Paddy said slowly. "I have half a mind to squeeze the cheek out of that scrawny little neck of yours!" he looked at his son and realised the boy's neck wasn't scrawny anymore; in fact the lad was stockier and taller than his father; in a fight Seamus could probably take him quite easily.

"You asked me," the boy replied flatly. "Just giving you an honest answer, Da. I saw you were too tight to handle the job and I was right. You are a lucky man, you are. Could have been swinging at the end of a rope, if the police had discovered you."

"Well, they didn't, so shut yer gub; not in a mood for none of your lip," Paddy mumbled, genuinely disturbed by Seamus's revelation; that the boy was right was even more annoying.

"Carrick! I mean are you serious Da?" Seamus couldn't stop. "Partnering with your jailhouse buddy who had no idea what he was doing on his first run? What were you thinking?"

"Just shut the fuck up, you little shit!" Paddy retorted. "Trying my patience sorely, you are!" The men puffed on their cigarettes in silence and Paddy corked his bottle and put it aside.

"What would I have to do to make a success of the business, because I aim to have another go when things cool down?" Paddy asked, as normally and naturally as if he wanted to know the time of day.

"For a start, you need to choose yer partner carefully," Seamus answered casually. "I suppose that person would be yourself, then." Answered Paddy.

"All depends," Seamus said vaguely, irritating his father no end. Paddy asked, "Depends on what?" Thinking his son was toying with him.

"Depends on your self control, Da. Need to be able to trust you at all times," the son replied and Paddy said, "Hmm...Anything else, then?"

"No drinking on the job and I need to know you won't be shouting yer mouth off in the boozer and throwing yer cash about; making a show of yourself every chance you get."

"Right fine opinion you have of your father, I must say!" Paddy shook his head to be sure he was hearing right. "Sound like Father Kennedy in his pulpit, you do."

"We're talking about business, Da," Seamus put his hand on his father's shoulder. "I'm talking about our lives, here; I must know I can depend on you completely."

"You can; I give you my word," Paddy promised and for once he meant what he said. "And what else?"

"Expenses and profits split right down the middle, no argument," Seamus stated. "In fact, no arguments at all if we can help it. Must keep a level head at all times." The men could see Annie and the two younger children approaching and they stood up and shook hands.

"You got a deal, lad." "I hope it turns out that way," said Seamus. "Oh shut the fuck up!" Replied Paddy and hugged his son tight.

"It's for my future, I need the money, Da," Seamus whispered. "I'll go straight once I've enough, I swear!"

"Your future looks real bright, lad, not to worry," Paddy laughed and thought, "Can you ever have enough? I doubt it.

CHAPTER 7 - HOLY PADDY

Paddy's first appearance at Sunday mass created a stir; gossip flitted across busy lips and bets were made on how long he would stay out of prison this time. Sooner, rather than later was the favourite to win. The Harper's didn't care; Annie was so pleased at having her family together she felt she would burst with pride. The date for the nuptials of Seamus and Linda was set in two weeks' time, and Father Kennedy made a mention of this after the service. This gave an occasion for people to shake hands and congratulate the family. Annie and Paddy saw the malicious intent in the sly eyes and probing questions but they put on a brave front and got through the scrutiny and ill will.

"Pack of wolves, they are," Paddy said, squeezing his wife's hand. "Ignore them and they'll be off to their next victim." Annie was experienced at ignoring the cutting remarks of her fellow men, and women. All water off a duck's back she claimed it was to her, but inside it hurt which is why she was so happy to show off her handsome family today. Informing relatives, friends and neighbours were given importance as no one must be left out of the celebrations. The family passed the message around and made a point of going from house to house to ensure everyone who was invited knew of this.

It was cold and wet on the day of the wedding that united the Harper and Brogan families. The Fegans were in attendance to offer their support: there may not have been a lot of love lost between them but when it came to such important milestones, family was family. It was wonderful how families and close friends pulled together for important occasions. Seamus wore a dark suit lent to him by Gerald and though he was broader than his cousin who was taller, it looked like it was made for him. Seamus waited excitedly with his best man Gerald, waiting for Linda to appear.

The bride came from a very poor family who lived over in the next village and she was overwhelmed by what she considered the affluence of the Harper family. Her mother, Joan Brogan was permanently pregnant; her sickly father Tom could not exert himself to labour beyond his husbandly activity. At sixteen, Linda was the eldest of eleven children who didn't have a decent pair of shoes between them. The seasons made no difference to their attire; they went barefoot in summer and winter; mostly they wore rags and went hungry for days on end. The Harpers went bare foot in the house, but they would rather die than venture out unshod.

"A sorry state those Brogans are in, to be sure," Annie would say. "Feel sorry for them, I do. I remember a time when I went barefoot and hungry. A tragedy it is to be brought so low."

"You got off your arse and did something about it, lass, didn't you?" Paddy replied. "A right lazy, spineless bunch they are. I hope Seamus knows what he's stuck with!" The Brogan children resorted to stealing to keep them alive and it was a mystery how they survived under such appalling conditions. Linda tried to work, but given the family's dysfunction, it was not in her hands to be any different. Seamus met his love at a local ceilidh and they had been together for two years. It was inevitable that they would wed one day, though that day arrived much sooner than expected.

Linda dressed with care on her special day; she looked lovely in her white lace dress that Mary had bought her and white shoes that her mother had borrowed from a relative; her hat and gloves were lent for the occasion by Dr. Mallon's wife. Her little bouquet consisted of a few cloth flowers tied together with a white satin ribbon; it was made by a neighbour, Mrs. Burns who said it was much too cold to find any fresh blooms growing in the fields of

The Journey

Kilbarra that day. "It's beautiful, Mrs. Burns," Linda said gratefully, kissing the woman's cheek. Annie hugged her friend and said, "Thank you, Muriel; it's a fine job you've done; a real good sort, you are!"

Mrs. Murphy hit the keys, and the strains of 'Here comes the Bride' resonated throughout the church. Every bride looks beautiful on her wedding day and Linda was no exception. She walked with grace down the aisle on the arm of her limping father who had one too many on the way to bolster his nerves and only succeeded in messing up his coordination. The slender young girl was glowing when she took her place at the altar beside her groom. If her waist was a couple of inches wider than it should have been, no one noticed or suspected anything other than that young love prompted this marriage.

Father Kennedy officiated over the ceremony that bound the couple together in holy matrimony; he took his time over the readings and in his homily, elaborating on the theme of marriage.

"This is a sacred opportunity to join with family and friends in dedicating the marriage of Seamus and Linda to God, the author of all love," the priest's loud voice was easily heard above the hushed congregation. "Be attentive to our prayers, 0 Lord, and in Your kindness, pour out Your grace on Your servants Seamus and Linda who come together before Your altar, that they may be confirmed in love for one another. What therefore God hath joined together, let no man put asunder." The women were teary eyed when the couple exchanged their vows and rings; the lovers were the first children in their families to marry and their youth made them all the more endearing.

The service ended with a Blessing, and the bride and groom walked back down the aisle, followed by their families and friends. They were slowed down by well wishers who delayed their progress to offer congratulations. Seamus had borrowed a neighbour's horse and trap to get his bride and him over to

Jenkin's barn, which had also been borrowed for the wedding celebration, since their house was too small to host so many people. The wedding procession grew larger as relatives, friends and neighbours made their way to the ceilidh. There was a good attendance of people, from the community of Kilbarra and the celebration gave them a chance to meet, eat, drink and have a good time. Father Kennedy would be there and he encouraged these ceilidh's, as they were one of the few ways that local people from the poorer end of the community could socialise without extra cost to anyone. It was also one of the few places where young people could see and be seen and many marriages came out of these get-togethers.

There were over forty people assembled in the barn and everyone brought something with them; as was the custom. The bread, the meat and the vegetables for the Irish stew were all given by the people attending, so that the expenditure did not put a strain on one particular family. The whiskey and the poteen that flowed were also donated by neighbours. The musicians who played were amateurs who didn't get paid for their services; they were just happy to get a free meal, a couple of drinks, and a chance to meet the lasses. It was no wonder that this custom was so popular at a time when poverty was a guest in most of the houses in Ireland.

It was the talk of the evening that Paddy hadn't left home during the three weeks since he had returned from prison. No one knew of a couple of forays across the Lough, in the dead of night with his son; and though everyone had a joke at his expense; they did begin to wonder with grudging respect; if the man had turned over a new leaf after all.

"A shock can cure a man of his bad habits for sure," Father Kennedy opined. "The prison experience is in truth a great shock for any man to endure."

"If that ain't the truth, Father," Paddy said. "Just looking for an opportunity to spend my time in gainful employment." And the men believed him and were impressed.

"Why don't you come and see me at the hospital," suggested Dr. Mallon. "I think I may have something for you there."

"That's good of you, sir," Paddy thanked the man. "Real Christian of you, for sure. I'll be seeing you first thing tomorrow morning and you'll not be sorry you gave me a helping hand."

"You make sure you stick to your promise, Paddy," Father Kennedy looked him in the eye. "It's not easy for a man to get a job these days; specially one who has fallen foul of the law," and to the Doctor he said, "I hope you don't regret your kindness, Dr. Mallon; trusting our Paddy here is a consideration bordering on foolhardiness." Paddy thought, "You can always count on the compassion of the clergy, the miserable buggers!"

"The Hospitals Trust Board is administering additional funds that have been allocated to small hospitals," Dr. Mallon said. "This is allowing for huge changes to the health system and with the expansion, new jobs are being created. I think Paddy would benefit by working in this supervised environment; a man must be useful or else he will find undesirable ways to dissipate his energies. I'm willing to give Paddy a chance."

"You fall short and you'll be out on your ear, Paddy," Father Kennedy said. "So you'd better think twice before you blow this chance." "I will, Father; right grateful I am for this chance," and thought, "Damn clerical fool; rumbling like thunder; always rumbling!" The priest went on to rumble and rant against the immorality of the day. He blamed the bad influence of the cinema for affecting everyday Irish life and the demoralising effect of films on the young, undermining their Christian standards of morality and decency. Annie and Sheila came up and heard what was being said.

105

"I'm going to be a nun, Father," said Sheila. "I'm going to give my life to the Lord." Annie gasped, "Oh my," and Father Kennedy exclaimed, "'Tis a night of miracles, it is!" Paddy looked at his daughter, wondering how much poteen she had sipped and said, patting his wife's stomach, "Let the church have the lass; we've another child arriving shortly; so we can afford to be generous!"

"Ah, 'tis no finer calling than to spend a life dedicated to His work," the priest said. "But there are other considerations in becoming a nun...perhaps you would like to join as a lay sister, my child?" A lay sister was in effect, a servant to the nuns. Like servants in the Big Houses, lay sisters lived in special quarters and ate either before or after, and apart from the nuns. Their habit included an apron and it looked like a drab maid's uniform.

"A Bride of Christ my lass wants to be; not a bloody skivvy!" Paddy lashed out. "If it's the nun's dowry you're thinking about, Father Kennedy, you shall have it!" Paddy said, his temper rising out of control. Seamus was beside him whispering sharply, "Hush! Have a care, Da!"

"You have the best intentions, Paddy, but it may not be in your hands to make such promises to the girl." Father Kennedy tried to mollify the irate man and only succeeded in adding fuel to the fire."

"My daughter will have the damn dowry, Father," Paddy retorted, his face red with anger at the priest's arrogance. "I will pay you the dowry required!"

"Paddy wants the best for his children, Father, 'tis the whiskey talking, that's all it is!" Annie smiled her sweetest smile while Seamus was trying to physically drag Paddy away from the conflict that was getting the attention of other guests.

Once outside the barn, Seamus said, "You promised, Da! What do you think you're doing?" and Paddy just swore. "Who the hell does he think he is? If its dowry money he wants, I'll shove the bloody dowry money up his big arse right now!"

"Da, get a hold of yourself! You'll have us all arrested this night if you don't control yourself," Seamus was sick with fear. "Stop talking about having money: do you want them to dump us both in prison and throw away the key? Stop, please stop!" Seamus tried to shake some sense into the drunken man who struggled to return inside to make good his words.

"Don't tell me what to do, you little shit," Paddy shouted. "I'll do what I please!"

"Does it please you to go back to prison then, Da?" Seamus asked his father, who replied spitefully, "If I go back, I'll take you with me, you bloody pompous bastard!"

"What have I done?" Seamus thought, and he knew for sure that one day his father would be his undoing.

Annie came outside and handed a drink to her inebriated husband whose incoherent words were now flying out of his mouth with the saliva he could no longer contain.

"What are you doing, Ma?" Seamus shouted angrily. "Hasn't he had enough?" as Annie helped pour the brew down her man's throat and said, "He needs to shut his gub, lad; this'll do it for sure. Help me pour another one down his gizzard; then off you go; this is your wedding day and you'll only get one chance to enjoy it. I'll handle your father, don't worry." Paddy passed out within fifteen minutes and Seamus and Gerald lifted his limp body and put him in the back of the van. Annie covered him with a few empty potato sacks, to keep him warm.

The dance floor was crowded and the musicians were spurred on by the appreciation and alcohol to perform their most popular music. The children ran in and out and all over the place, up to all kinds of mischief. Old men hallucinated and reached out to squeeze a breast or pinch a buttock whenever possible, while the old women complained to each other about everything under the sun. The able bodied tried to make the most of their opportunities and couples followed up their mating rituals in dark corners. Writhing bodies pressed together in passionate desperation until these frenzied pleasure seekers managed to unite in horizontal ecstasy in the field behind the barn. Husbands cheated on their wives and wives cheated on their husbands and the singletons just struck where ever they got lucky. Discovery would mean a belt or a boot struck by an irate party; sometimes a wrestling match or a catfight ensued and added greatly to the entertainment of guests.

Many a baby would be born as a result of this ceilidh without ever knowing the true identity of his or her father; unless there was a striking resemblance to the culprit, in which case there would be hell to pay. But for now, everyone seemed to be having a grand time; even Seamus had relaxed enough to enjoy the festivities with his bride and laugh at the ribald jokes that were usual fare at such gatherings. Mary was charming and danced with every man and woman who was up for it; Ginger Fegan let down her guard and clapped and tapped her feet as she watched her lovely niece take the Fegan men through their paces.

"That lass of yours is something special, Annie," she conceded. "Got all the class from her father's side, she has." Annie smiled graciously and said, "Thank you, Ginger," and thought, "That's why there's none of it left over for you, you common cow!"

"So your young one wants be a nun?" Ginger asked slyly. "Ambitious girls you have, don't you?" "Its child's talk; is all it is;" Annie said laughing, "one day she wants to be this and the next day it's something else. She has no idea how much it costs to enter the convent." Ginger replied smugly, "That's a fact; which is why the nuns are from wealthy backgrounds; daughters of comfortable, large farmers or shop owners, they are. A hundred pounds or so for a dowry is no small amount to pay unless you're made of money. We would help; it's an honourable vocation to be sure, but things are difficult for everyone these days."

"I know; the likes of us can only dream," Annie said casually, trying to downplay the incident. "Good in school she is, my Sheila. I'm trying to keep her there as long as possible. Anyway, it will be years before it's time to make a decision. So many new jobs opening up for young women these days; who knows what her chances are when she's ready?" Ginger seemed to lose interest in Annie as she watched her husband talking intently to the Meg Davis who looked stunning in black; she got up abruptly and decided to join the conversation before the widow got any fancy ideas of coming out of mourning.

It was past midnight when the older folks began to drag themselves away from the revelry to embark on their long trek home. The band counted the pennies that were tossed into the hat in a spurt of drunken extravagance; there was even a sixpence and three shillings, and they wondered what motivated such generous donations; they had no illusion it was their talent. They divided the cash between them and finished up, tired and happy. Carts and cars were filled to capacity with the bodies of the legless and the wedding ceilidh came to a successful end, even though it would be kept going by the gossips for weeks to come.

Mary had arranged for the bride and groom to spend the weekend at the Royal Hotel; it was half empty due to winter and Reg was more than happy to grant one of his best employees this favour. She was happy to do this for Seamus; the brother and sister had always been very close and their relationship had endured and strengthened with the hardships of their childhood. They confided in each other and supported one another and it saddened Mary that their lives and priorities would now take different paths. She hoped this transition would create a new chapter in their lives, and make their bond even stronger; yet she couldn't help the feeling of sadness and the lump in her throat that kept her on the verge of tears.

The Harper family was driven home by Gerald and the plan was to drive the newlyweds into Kilbarra to their weekend retreat.

"Why don't you join us, Mary?" Gerald suggested; hoping for a chance to be alone with the girl. "Be company for me on the way back." Annie saw Mary's expression and said, "Take Sheila and Michael along too; I'm sure they would love the ride into the village." "Yes, we want to go too!" Shouted Michael. They all piled into the car and Gerald tried to slip his hand up Mary's skirt as he helped her into her seat. The love birds were in each other's arms in the back while Sheila and Michael hung out of the windows excitedly taking in the sights and commenting on what they saw; Gerald took full advantage of the situation to harass Mary.

"Stop it, Gerald!" Mary snapped as she tried to stop her cousin's hands from roving. He retaliated by nastily whispering, "Cold bitch!" and continued his advances whenever an opportunity presented itself.

Though she had talked much about the Hotel, her siblings weren't prepared for the grandeur of the place. Their mouths hung open at the sight of all the luxury as Mary took them on a tour of her workplace. The intimate and charming atmosphere, high quality comfort and hospitality were unimagined by the siblings and yet Mary fitted in so naturally with this elegant setting.

"Oh, Mary!" Sheila exclaimed at everything she saw. "How beautiful!" Michael constantly asked what was this or that and was stunned when he found out. "What does a person need so many spoons for?" and "Hot and cold water taps! Sweet Jesus, what will they think of next?" and "Room service? What the hell is that?" Gerald said, "Stop being such an ignoramus, Mike." Mary replied, "Shut up, Gerald. The lad's just curious." Gerald replied in her ear, "I'm curious too; you going to show me around and explain what's what?" Mary sighed in exasperation and gave him a shove, but he only came back for more. Reg intervened, "It's late; why don't you and the little ones spend the night? The staff rooms are mostly empty." Mary hesitated, "I dunno; they have school tomorrow." Reg coaxed, "Aw, let them miss a day. It's a special occasion; they'll learn more here in a few hours than a year at school; it's a lesson they won't forget for sure!" "That's God's truth," said Seamus. And Mary relented, "Oh, alright then, I'll put them on the early bus in the morning." Gerald looked like he was going to have a stroke.

"That was a cheap trick, Mary; now I have to drive alone all the way home!" Gerald said when he got her alone, twisting her arm viciously to make his point. "Stop it Gerald, you're hurting me!" Mary said as she pushed him away roughly. "We're cousins, what will people think if they see you carrying on?"

"I don't care; give me a kiss, Mary," he begged and tried his best to plant one on her lips without success. "Oh, come on Mary, just one kiss!" Mary threatened, "I'm going to tell Da!" Gerald scoffed, "As if he'll believe you; thinks I'm a saint and I'll tell him you led me on."

"Auntie Ginger will believe me; I'm going to tell her if you don't stop! It's disgusting, you are!" The mention of his mother's name made him recoil instantly.

"Disgusting is it? Not so disgusting when you take from me without giving, is it?" Gerald's face was crimson with anger. "You're nothing but a bloody whore!"

"We're cousins for Christ's sake, it's a sin," Mary protested, walking quickly to join the others. "Besides, I see you more like a brother."

"And a fucking chauffeur, and your bloody slave," he raged. Reg arrived and said, "Well good night Gerald," and Gerald stormed off into the cold night. Before she went to sleep, Sheila confided, "I want to work here when I grow up, Mary!" and Mary replied, "And what happened to being a nun?" Sheila mumbled sleepily, "This is as close to heaven as I'll ever be," and Mary thought, "You could be right, our Sheila. You could be right."

Michael tried out the shower and didn't want to get out of the wonderful warm water; he had never been so clean in his life.

"Stop flushing the toilet, Michael, and get to bed right now," Mary called out to her brother who still could not get over the wonders of the hotel. He pulled the chain one more time before he climbed into bed and buried his face into a soft white pillow.

Paddy was up early the next day and went to the hospital to see if last night's offer of a job held good or if it was just a drunken promise.

"Well this is a surprise Paddy; I didn't expect you up and about after last night's celebrations!" the doctor exclaimed.

"It's a job I'm after, Dr. Mallon," Paddy showed no sign of wear and tear after the excess of the previous night and the doctor was impressed by his commitment. "You asked me to come and see you and here I am. If it's inconvenient at this time, I'll thank you and be on my way,"

"Not at all, Paddy, I'm about to make my rounds; walk with me and let's chat."

"Just give me a job, man," Paddy thought; father and son decided that he would need a day job as a cover for his nocturnal activities. His head throbbed and he wanted to go home and sleep off his hangover. Dr Mallon talked about the hospital as he walked down the long corridors and large wards, and every sound jangled in Paddy's throbbing head. The starch in the doctors white jacket crackled like chalk on a blackboard every time he moved; the clank of steel hospital implements and each footstep on the tiled

112

floor was a sharp nail hammered into Paddy's brain and he cringed in agony.

There was a lot of activity in the hospital and there were patients with all manners of ailments. The hospital had staff accommodation, a busy kitchen, a small restaurant, a laundry, and even a little church. There were plenty of people about and Paddy had difficulty deciding, who were the patients and who the visitors were; they all looked sickly, miserable specimens, waiting their turn to depart this world. There wasn't a bed to spare and nurses and orderlies in crisp uniforms moved about administering to the stricken as best they could.

A priest sat at the bedside of a man who gasped laboriously in an effort to move on; the holy man whispered to him, promising eternal damnation if the creature didn't repent before he crossed over. Old Fred was a sinner in life and unremorseful to the end. The priest realised the futility of his mission and began to administer the last rights as a loud, rasping death rattle beat frantically in the dying man's chest, urging him to give up. Paddy thought, "Poor sod; no peace in life and no peace in death; and not a chance of it where he's going either!"

Dr. Mallon stepped into a ward that treated patients from the army; men that had suffered injuries in some far flung corner of the Empire, fighting for King and country. Their wounds were mostly of a severe nature; limbs and organs blown away by blasting shells, gaping wounds seeping pus through their bandages, the trauma, exposure and disease had eaten them away. They endured the agonising journey home only to have the gangrenous parts of themselves removed; the surgeons whittled away their bodies until there was nothing left to sustain a life.

Dr. Mallon examined a delirious patient who suddenly lunged up at him. Paddy pulled the man off the doctor and tried to calm him down. Dr. Mallon held up his hand to stop the two orderlies who dashed to his rescue and watched Paddy restrain the combative

113

patient. The feverish man relaxed in Paddy's strong arms and seemed to believe him when he said gently, "It's alright, boy; everything's alright, don't you fret." As the doomed man slipped back into the merciful arms of delirium, Dr. Mallon said, "This is what you should be doing, man. You've got yourself a job as an orderly if you want. Controlling aggressive patients, assisting physicians, escorting patients and any other tasks Matron may think up for you in this department. Eight hours a day; six days a week; fifteen shillings a week; what do you say?" "That will do very nicely, Doctor, and I'll take it, thank you very much!" Answered Paddy.

"You have to stick to the rules, Paddy; we run a tight ship here," the doctor insisted. "Regular attendance; no nonsense; no arguments; no fights; no drinking; you got that, man?" Paddy answered, "For sure, Doctor." The doctor added, "Don't let me down, now; I'm going to take a lot of grief for sponsoring a jailbird such as you. Out on your ear you'll be at the first hint of trouble, I mean it!" Paddy thought, "What the shit have I got myself into?" and swore to his benefactor, "I won't let you down, sir."

"Let me take you to meet matron; she'll fill you in on the details," Dr. Mallon said to Paddy. Just at that moment a uniformed woman turned the corner. "What a stunner!" Paddy thought: "Sweet Jesus; I've died and gone to Heaven!" "Ah, here comes Matron Cairney now," said Dr Mallon and introduced the two. Then he said, "See you tomorrow, man; bright and early, mind."

Paddy assumed his gentleman posture and a personality he used with particular success, when dealing with the ladies. He listened intently, nodding seriously as if every word the woman spoke was gospel. He gazed at her just long enough to make her uneasy and then lowered his eyes respectfully, making her feel guilty for her suspicions. He stared at her full breasts and she pulled her cardigan together; he eyed her shapely rump, making her squirm; Paddy's work related conversation was so serious that Matron Cairney blamed herself for her imaginings. Wishing her goodbye, Paddy promised to report for work the next morning and they both looked forward to the new day.

The good news was welcomed at home; an employed Paddy was a rare thing indeed and the family treated the man with the consideration he deserved. Annie believed in her heart that this was not a possibility, but then neither was having her husband home, and both these wonders had taken place.

"It's time you quit working, Annie," Paddy insisted and she found it hard to make such an extreme decision. She gave in her notice at the laundry much to the surprise of the nursing staff who promised, "Your job will be waiting for you anytime you want to return, Annie." Parting with Mrs. Keller however, proved more difficult than expected.

"Having a baby, I am, Mrs. Keller," Annie replied in answer to the woman's protests. Her employer got on well with her and was pleased with her work. "My husband says I am to stay home now; how can I refuse to do as he says? He's not a man to be trifling with."

"So I hear, Annie," Mrs. Keller was not ready to grant her slave complete freedom yet. "Surely, we could come to some arrangement; perhaps Mr. Keller could have a word; speak to your husband and tell him how reluctant we are to let you go."

After much discussion it was agreed that Annie would work every other day and train a new girl who would fill in for the time when Annie was promised a whole month's leave for the birth of her child. This worked out well and Annie was secure in the fact that she still had a job. However things could change overnight and in her heart she knew Paddy was up to no good and it had something to do with the body on the beach. He slipped out at least once a week without explanation and Annie almost wished it was to see

Gertie, but she knew that wasn't the case; he had a new fancy woman; that she knew; a wife always knows when her man's attention is elsewhere, but this was not the reason for his absences. What was worse is that Seamus was somehow involved and she prayed to all the saints in Heaven to keep her son out of harm's way.

"Sometimes Seamus doesn't return from work and comes home in the wee hours of the morning," Annie prodded his young wife for an explanation.

"Says he is working overtime, Ma," Linda said innocently. "Such plans for the future he has." Annie thought, "This poor lass has a lot to learn about men."

The wad of money Paddy thought was hidden from his wife grew steadily and this terrified Annie. She had no idea of what was going on, but something was happening and she was sure the results would be explosive and rip her family apart.

"Make sure whatever you do is for the good of the family," she would say as they all sat together. "Never do anything that will damage us."

"Too much time on your hands, Ma?" the children would joke. "Now you spend your time worrying about us. Relax; this family has seen the worst; nothing and no one can come between us."

Annie enjoyed the extra time she had at home and Linda proved to be another daughter. She showed the new bride her ways and the girl learned fast; soaking up her new environment. Together they got a vegetable garden going again; they added to the henhouse and now had chickens laying eggs on a regular basis and a nice roast on the table every Sunday. They sat together while Annie told stories of the old days and they lovingly sewed little garments for the babies that were soon to make their appearance into the Harper family. Life couldn't have been better.

The Journey

CHAPTER 8 - THE HOSPITAL

It was a hard life but then, when was life in Ireland ever easy? In the cities, houses were damp, overcrowded and lacking in basic amenities. Jobs were scarce and people took up the most menial of jobs to sustain themselves. In the villages, at least there was fresh air, but the people suffered the same poverty that afflicted their city cousins. Some managed to put something in their bellies, by growing vegetables and keeping chickens and goats or pigs; if they could, but mostly the ordinary person couldn't even afford to do that and hunger was a normal part of life.

"'It's sad to see young ones about with no shoes on their feet and little in their stomachs;" Mary would think when she passed through the poverty on her way to and from work.

"Shoes and stockings were seldom seen on children and often not on grownups and people went barefoot in all kinds of weather. I don't remember it any other way." Annie would say when Mary related what she saw every day.

"'Tis no different now, Ma. The rags men and women wear are so tattered and complicated, that it is hardly possible to imagine what article of dress they originally belonged to." The conditions never failed to appall the girl.

The environment in which people existed was a breeding ground for disease and crime. Hospitals were for those who could afford medical care and there must have been enough of them because those places were full to overflowing. There was help from the government and from religious and charitable organizations, but this was negligible and frequently the destitute dropped dead where they were.

"You'll be escorting Greg and Pete to the Big House today, Paddy. Make sure they have their jackets on tight and buckled up; a feisty pair they are for sure," Dr. Morgan handed Paddy a release order. "Take Dan to help you and don't leave those two alone for a minute." The Big House was the doctor's name for the asylum in Downgullion, where all aggressive patients and those with mental illness were sent. Morgan attended to patients with psychiatric problems and if ever a man loved his job, it was he. Judgmental, with a fixed and inflexible attitude based on Victorian values; he is not among the most popular people at the hospital. The staff were afraid of this tough and ruthless doctor, but strangely he and Paddy got along well together and formed a special bond.

Paddy worked closely with Morgan since most of the doctor's patients were violent and needed to be restrained. Paddy also accompanied Morgan on his monthly trips to the asylum, where Morgan administered shock therapy by applying an electric current through the brain of a patient for a brief period by means of electrodes that were placed on the head; sometimes this was used as a treatment for severe mental depression. Unfortunately, the side effects inevitably included memory loss.

Paddy monitored patients after Morgan had performed a lobotomy on them. He enjoyed watching the operation; the way the doctor deftly drilled holes in the patient's skull on either side of the prefrontal cortex and injected the connecting fibers with alcohol to destroy them. Then a wire hoop was inserted to sever the white matter between different areas of grey matter.

"You see, Paddy," Barden explained. "By severing the connections that the frontal lobes have to the rest of the brain, the patient's emotions are calmed and their personalities are stabilized without doing away with their intelligence and motor functions." This was not always the case.

119

The Journey

Since most mental hospitals didn't have operating rooms or surgeons on staff; some patients were sent to Morgan at the hospital in Kilbarra. He became so adept that he often performed lobotomies as outpatient procedures in his office with Paddy assisting. Many of these operations had adverse effects on patients. Some were left with the mental capacity of an infant. Others couldn't speak intelligibly or control their bodily functions. Some lost their higher intellect or had no long-term memory, or just spent their day staring into space. Most spent the rest of their life in an institution.

There was also insulin coma therapy, where patients were pumped full of insulin to put them into a hypoglycemic coma. Many patients died as a result of this treatment. There was a very high death rate and a very high rate of brain damage. There were no trials for these procedures and no evidence base; the doctors just had huge populations on which to experiment and they made good use of the opportunity. Mental healthcare in Ireland was ignorant and cruel and conditions in hospitals were barbaric.

Paddy asked questions and Morgan would always take the time to explain and often said, "You could have been a medical man yourself, Paddy, if you'd had put your mind to it." Paddy agreed with him, but the good Lord tests His creatures sorely and the Devil litters a man's path with so much temptation that it's hard to find the right way.

"'Tis too much to dwell on," Paddy would say honestly. "A regular beggar I was; never wore shoes until I was twenty and that pair was from the charity box. Lucky to be where I am today and that's the truth." He held down patients who displayed an uncooperative nature while Morgan injected intramuscular medication into the unmanageable, so that they would comply with hospital rules. On the doctor's recommendation, most of these patients were sent to the Big House.

120

The Journey

While Morgan was disliked, Paddy became a great favourite around the place. He was popular with the patients and staff, particularly Matron Cairney, who found every excuse to consult with him.

"Since my husband went I feel so alone in the world; all I have is my work; thank God for that," she confided to Paddy; she always referred to her departed spouse as 'my husband' and Paddy never found out the man's real name; not that he had any interest in knowing the identity of his predecessor to Mrs. Cairney's affections. He was more concerned with the welfare of the buxom widow who was well respected for her capabilities and no nonsense manner. Paddy believed that under her stern and proper exterior was a woman that was worth getting to know, in a biblical sense, of course. He gave her little gifts; a box of chocolates; fancy gloves, and even a pair of tiny pearl earrings.

"Oh, I can't accept your gifts, Mr. Harper; it wouldn't be right," she protested but Paddy talked her into changing her mind and she sometimes wore the pearls to work and smiled when he noticed. "There's a necklace that matches those two, lass," Paddy whispered seductively, leering at her ample breasts.

"Stop being coarse, Mr. Harper. Too many liberties you take! You wouldn't want me to lose my job would you? "The man replied, "Not at all, Matron; call me Paddy; I love it when you say my name."

"Get away with you, you ridiculous man," she would admonish harshly and then add with a smile in her eyes, "Paddy, take these notes to Morgan and make him sign them." The games they played only heightened their desire for one another. The sight of her moving about in her dark uniform and starched hat made Paddy think unholy thoughts that should never harbour in the mind of a righteous man. But then, Paddy was not the most righteous of men, and he shook his head and said sympathetically, "'Tis a sad thing to leave a widow behind and sure a woman needs a man to take care of her."

"Oh, I don't know, Mr. Harper; my husband left me well taken care of and I've managed very nicely," Mrs. Cairney assured him, but he insisted, "'Tis a man you need, Mrs. Cairney; if there's anything I can do for you just say the word." He undressed the woman with his eyes but his words were spoken with such sincerity that Liz didn't trust her judgement, and would have preferred to have a second opinion. Alone in bed at night, she begged her husband to give her a sign to help her on her way through life; of course she never mentioned how hot and bothered Paddy made her. Whether her husband advised her from beyond the grave or not, was academic; Mrs. Cairney and Mr. Harper were in bed together within the month.

During the day they were all business as usual; respectability mattered a lot to Matron Cairney and Paddy was now beginning to see the upside to maintaining a decorous front. Father Kennedy congratulated him at church and Dr. Mallon beamed with pride at how well things had turned out, and those that did not know him called him Mr. Harper. Paddy was a world away from the wretched drunk and jailbird; yet sometimes he felt a thirst so strong that he longed to visit his old haunts just one last time and go on a mighty bender. He resisted the urge and diverted his energies towards his new hobbies; smuggling and his paramour.

Furtive glances and a quick touch at work only fueled their need for each other but they had to be careful; gossip spread like wildfire around the hospital. Night time at her neat little house was a different story; she was perfume lace and wild abandon; Paddy knew exactly how to comfort a lady in the absence of her husband. They fed their hungry appetites with such a greedy passion; when Liz wrapped her voluptuous thighs around Paddy and nearly squeezed the living daylights out of him he gasped and thought,

"Jesus Christ, what a woman! No wonder her poor wee husband had a bloody heart attack!"

Annie didn't have much time to worry about her husband's affairs; they always ended with him coming home to her. Gertie looked about for Paddy when he dumped her and even had the gall to show up at the cottage door one afternoon in search of him. Annie flew for her with her broom and sent the woman running down the road.

"Got in a few good blows, I did; enough to make the strumpet think twice about ever showing her face here again," she told Paddy later in bed that night. He laughed, "Ah, my Annie, what would I do without you?" He gave her a box of chocolates that had been rejected by Matron Cairney and lied; "For you, my love; just for you." It was his forays into the night that disturbed his wife most of all, and the amounts of money he brought home each time scared the life out of her. He now took it for granted that Annie would put his ill gotten gains away in a safe place and didn't even bother to hide the cash as he once did.

"Where do you get to at night?" she would ask. "What is Seamus doing with you?" Paddy would say, "Picking up extra work at the harbour, we are." Annie wouldn't let the matter go and said, "But you have a job, Paddy love; and a good one it is too. Why do you need the extra work?"

"Seamus isn't the only one with big plans for the future, lass. I've got plans too!"

"It's a lot of money you bring back from the harbour Paddy," Annie persisted and Paddy growled; he had humoured his wife enough and was tired of the woman's questions. "How about you open that box of chocolates, enjoy them and then we get some shut eye. All this working is tiring business, it is." He put his arm around her swollen middle and drew her to him, licking the chocolate inside of her mouth.

123

The Journey

Life has a habit of never running smoothly; indeed it can be utterly miserable; in which case one has to be resigned to one's fate. On the other hand, it might not be so terrible, and that's a mercy. But for some reason that only He knows; it can never be all good, because that's when the real trouble begins. Mary had her cross to bear and that was Gerald, who kept hounding her. Her life was perfect, but for the odious attention of her wretched cousin.

"How about a kiss Mary? Just one little kiss, please Mary; how can you be so cruel?" Gerald continued to accost her and his behaviour alternated between being aggressive and being remorseful. He became ridiculous in his demands; he would say, "Marry me, Mary," and she would answer for the hundredth time, "Don't be silly, Gerald, we're first cousins!"

"Do you love me, Mary?" Gerald would ask and when Mary said, "No, Gerald, not in that way," he would abuse her; going through his entire range of foul words; then calmly ask, "Why don't you care for me? What can I do to make you love me?" Mary would say, "Stop it Gerald, you're behaving crazy!" and he would laugh and reply, "Yes, I'm crazy about you, I am." Gerald never missed a chance to touch her, and whenever they happened to be alone, he grabbed her and a wrestling match ensued. One day Kelly walked in on them and they quickly jumped apart.

"What's with you and your cousin, Mary?" Kelly questioned her bluntly and Mary said, "He's just a disgusting pig! Keeps on at me." Kelly said, "Tell your brother Seamus to sort him out."

"He's harmless," Mary said. "It's no big deal. He did do me a favour, getting me this job; I can manage him." Mary tried to deal with Gerald's erratic behaviour when forced to, but mainly she avoided him like the plague.

Mary forgot Gerald in the business of her life. She loved her job that kept her on the go and for the first time in her life she was able to concentrate on herself. Love must have been in the air because

124

The Journey

Maureen met Phil who introduced his best friend Eric to Mairead. The couples became inseparable and went everywhere together, and the twin's conversations never strayed to anything other than their fellas. It was Phil did this, and Eric said that - from morning to night; it's strange what love can do to the hearts and minds of simple young girls. Then Kelly met Ralph Maher, who was fifteen years her senior, but he loved her to bits and spoiled her rotten, which suited her just fine. When Mary asked, "What about The Plan?" Kelly just shrugged. "Ralph is okay, I guess; could be he's part of The Plan," and Mary said, "Does he know this?" and Kelly laughed, "He already thinks he is!" "Be kind to Ralph; he seems like such a nice person," Retorted Mary. "I will, he is a great person," Replied Kelly.

They met quite by accident; Mary was about to turn into the Royal for work one morning when the handsome young man stopped her to ask directions to the army camp. The minute their eyes met, that was it; in that instant, they found in each other the people they wanted to spend the rest of their lives with. It seemed so natural, standing on the pavement outside the hotel; to introduce themselves and to make plans to meet later. It wasn't the uniform that attracted Mary; a lot of uniformed men frequented the Hotel. But it may have added to his mystique; here was a man ready to fight for his country, and now here he was ready to battle for her affection.

Kelly was the first person she told as she dashed into work that day.

"Slow down, girl," Kelly said. "You just met the guy; what do you know about him?"

"I know, Kelly! I just know he's the one for me," Mary said excitedly and Kelly laughed, "And you got all that after five minutes?"

The Journey

"Wait till you meet him, Kelly; he's special, so different to all the other guys I've met. You'll see...," Mary went on to describe the minute details that only a person struck by Cupid's arrow could see or appreciate.

"There's one born every minute! What happened to The Plan?" Kelly interrupted her litany of praise and Mary said, "Plan? What plan?" and the girls giggled and hugged each other.

Jeremy Fields came to the Hotel to pick Mary up and she introduced him around. When Reg smiled and said, "The lad's okay," Mary couldn't have been happier; Reg's approval meant a lot to her. Jeremy Fields was in Kilbarra for ten days but he assured Mary they would never be parted; within a week he had proposed to her and she saw no earthly reason to refuse his offer. She told her brothers a bit about her Jeremy as they were walking home one day, when she was so full of happiness: she just had to share her news. "Don't say anything yet," she said. She was sure the family would be as thrilled as she was with Jeremy when they finally met him, but for the moment she guarded her precious friendship.

On his last day in Kilbarra, they walked about, held hands and kissed; it was a bitter sweet parting and Mary tried to concentrate on his return in a month's time. The days would fly by and they consoled each other as they clung together, savouring every magic moment before Jeremy had to leave. What the couple wasn't aware of was that they had been spotted by Mary's cousin. Gerald couldn't believe his eyes when he saw them by chance, strolling arm in arm, stopping intermittently to steal a kiss. He viewed the scene in horror; to him it was the worst kind of betrayal; his girl was cheating on him with another man. The pain of rejection was so acute, he couldn't bear it.

The enraged man stalked the lovers, following them as they talked and hugged and with each passing minute, his anger grew until he was crazed with fury. This was Mary; his Mary; how could she do this to him? If he couldn't have her, he swore no one else would. He watched in the dark as they said their goodbyes and Jeremy boarded the bus that would take him back to his home town in the South. A tearful Mary then rode her bike home, lost in thought of her beloved Jeremy. She was halfway there when she heard the sound of a motor behind her. The beam of the headlights outlined Mary on her bike; the glare was so bright she couldn't see the vehicle, but from the sound of the horn she knew it was Gerald following her. She signaled him to pass and moved off to the side of the narrow lane, hoping he would overtake and drive on.

"Come on, get in the car," Gerald shouted, following Mary so closely that his bumper nearly touched her back wheel. She tried to steady the handlebar but the wheels continued to wobble along the potholed, uneven path. The man honked his horn, keeping his hand on it as it shattered the calm night with its shrill maniacal blast. Mary stopped and said, "I'm going home, get on with you!" and Gerald shouted, "Get in the car; I want to talk to you!"

"I have nothing to say to you, Gerald," Mary shouted back, annoyed by the man's persistence. "Get out of my way; it's late, I'm going home!" Gerald stopped the car and got out. He loomed over her menacingly; Mary clearly saw that she could not move forward or backward and knew she had a fight on her hands.

"Well, I have something to say to you, bitch! Get in the van before I drag you in," Gerald looked insane and Mary sighed, "Say what you have to say then and be done. I'm not getting into your bloody car!" Gerald snatched the bike out of her hands and tossed it like a toy into the back of the van. He grabbed Mary by her collar and shoved her into the front seat. She was more angry than afraid; Gerald had gone beyond the limits even for him, and she decided that she was going to have a word with Seamus or even Reg.

"I've had enough of you, Gerald," she said struggling to sit up straight. "I'm going to tell Seamus about you; you've gone too far!"

"Is that a fact, then," Gerald asked viciously, bringing his face close to hers. "I'll show you how far I'm going to take you! You'll be begging for mercy by the time I've finished with you, you fucking whore!"

"What's gotten into you?" Mary shouted as they struggled with each other, and Gerald shrieked, "What's gotten into me? What's gotten into you?"

 What are you talking about? Let me go, Gerald, stop it!" Mary yelled and Gerald said, "I saw you kissing that bastard! Saw him sticking his tongue down your throat, you lying whore! What else has he been sticking into you?" It suddenly dawned on Mary what the issue was; her cousin was maddened at the thought of her with someone else. He had always considered Mary as his private property and even though they were cousins, in his mind he would overcome any obstacles that stood in the way of their being together.

"I was with Jeremy; he's my fella; we love each other," Mary said, trying to explain her situation, but her words were a sharp knife in Gerald's heart and like a wounded animal, he struck back, grabbing her by the shoulders and shaking her till her teeth rattled.

"Jeremy, is it? You rotten, shameless bitch! Your fella? You fucking whore!" Gerald was beyond recognition; his voice belonged to a creature from another world; he could have been speaking in a foreign language because his words were undecipherable. He was in pain and he wanted to inflict the same pain on Mary; he struck her sharply across the face with the back of his hand and she felt as if her head flew off, parting from the rest of her body. Dazed and stunned she could not make sense of what was happening and struggled against her attacker, who screamed, "I'm going to show you! You can't mess with me Mary! I'll fix you and that mother fucker, I will, you filthy bitch!"

The Journey

Gerald started the van and raced down the road. Mary sat crouched in her seat shocked by what had happened, with tears running down her cheeks. The speed and the erratic movement of the vehicle swerving from one side of the uneven road to the other frightened her, and she held on to the dashboard to avoid falling about while Gerald cursed and heaped abuse on her. He switched off his lights as he entered Kilbarra and Mary could see they were near the Church. Gerald drove up to the land behind the cemetery and turned the engine off.

"Why have you stopped here? Take me home, Gerald," Mary said and the insane man snarled, "Don't tell me what to do, bitch! How can you do this to me?" Then he changed his tone to a whine, "We can make this right, Mary; I love you," he began to plead; "Just one kiss, Mary love, please, please," and she struggled all the more against his touch; grabbing his hair with both hands, she pushed him away.

"You're disgusting, stop, stop!" and in that moment she found the strength to open the door and bolt out of the van. Gerald was out in a flash and caught up with her; even then Mary felt anger rather than fear. How dare he do this to her? If her family would have been there, they would have thrashed him soundly. Her thoughts were scrambled and her heart pounded wildly; as she saw the steeple of the church she thought, "It's going to be alright; he just wants to rough me up a bit and then I'll go home."

It was when he caught her and threw her to the ground that she knew she was lost. Gerald unbuckled his belt and swung it at her. It lashed her thighs and made her scream, "Stop, Gerald, stop," and he hit her again across her outstretched hands. Searing pain made Mary roll up on the damp soil beneath her and she wanted her mother. She could hear Gerald raging like a lunatic. She raised her head to look at him and saw him unbuttoning his trousers and then she was afraid; so afraid that she thought she would die from the sheer fright of the moment.

The Journey

Gerald was upon her and they wrestled; writhing together on the ground as if locked in some strange kind of dance; his hands were everywhere and she could not help herself as she lay, flailing about helplessly as his strong body pinned her down. He pulled up her skirt and ripped off her knickers. Mary was so shocked that for a second she forgot what he was about to do and was ashamed of her nakedness.

"You dirty rotten bitch!" Gerald slapped her again and again and Mary fought back with all her little might, thinking, "If I'm going to die, I'm going to make it as difficult as I can for you to kill me."She thought this was his intention; Gerald was going to kill her because of Jeremy; she had no idea what men actually did to women. No one really spoke to her about such things. By the look in his eyes, Gerald seemed totally possessed and mercifully, Mary drifted in and out of consciousness as he violated her. She felt a searing pain inside of her and in her disoriented state; she couldn't fully comprehend what had happened. Then Mary realised that the screams she heard were her own.

The man was yelling and crying wildly as he smashed her bicycle to pieces and she wanted to say, "Oh, don't do that; I've got to get to work tomorrow," but the words wouldn't come out of her swollen, bloody mouth. He saw her looking at him and picked up two fistfuls of dirt and threw them at her. He roared abuse between the gulping sobs that wracked his body and then got into his van and drove off into the night, leaving Mary lying on her back on the rough stones and grass in the light drizzle that had begun to fall.

Mary got up off the flattened shrubs and grass where she had being lying. The revulsion she felt at what Gerald had done to her made her sick to the core. All the whispered innuendos and the hinted allusions about what men and women did fell into place like pieces of a puzzle.

"I've been raped; it's entirely my fault. My parents will be disappointed and disgusted with me and everyone else will see me as a low life." Irrational thoughts raced round the girl's confused, aching head. "I've caused grief to my family and disgraced us all. What will people think of us now?"In the space of seconds she made a conscious decision that no one need know about this; it would remain her secret. Her body throbbed with pain and the shame she felt was agonizing. She sat hidden by the long grass that surrounded and shielded her. What they concealed her from, she did not know, but she was glad of their cover. Mary held her head in her hands and sobbed endlessly, and the torment that was racing round her head was unbearable.

Mary pulled her clothes together and tried to gather her thoughts along with her scattered possessions. She saw her handbag and a shoe, but had to look around before she found the other one. She took her handkerchief out of her bag and tried to wipe away the mud and bits of grass that stuck to her skin, and the wetness that seeped between her thighs. Feeling weak, Mary made her way to the road, hoping to get home quickly in case Gerald decided to come back again. The rain came down harder and the wind was whistling; in her weakened state it was difficult to walk against the gust. Mary sensed a darkness in the air, not from the night, but from an ominous energy, and stepped up her pace, occasionally stopping to see if anyone was following her. She knew the Devil was not far behind.

Annie was waiting up for Paddy when Mary staggered into the cottage.

"Holy Mary mother of God, what happened to you lass?" the mother cried out, holding the shivering girl. "Mary love, who did this to you?" Mary shook her head and said hoarsely, "I don't know, Ma." The kettle was on the fire and Annie quickly put some warm water in the small tin basin and sponged her child, gasping at the sight of her cuts and bruises that had begun to swell up hideously. Only a monster could have committed such brutality.

The mother wrapped her child in a blanket and tried to find out what happened just as Paddy and Seamus came in.

"Jesus Christ! What happened, Mary?" Paddy shouted so loudly he woke up the rest of the sleeping family who crowded around the stricken girl.

"Tell me who did this to you, Mary," Seamus cried. "He'll not live to see the morning, I swear!"

"It was some lads; jumped me on my way home. Stole my money and my bike; beat me up," Mary lied, and Michael said, "Did you see their faces, Mary?" and she said, "No, it was dark; it happened so fast."

"Where did this happen, Mary," Seamus asked and when she said, "In the churchyard behind the cemetery," hedashed out into the night with Michael.

When they arrived at the churchyard they soon found the damaged bicycle. "Who would steal a bike to break it to bits?" Seamus wondered, holding up the mangled bicycle while Michael remarked, "It's madness, for sure! They could've sold it; why destroy a thing of value?" Something caught Seamus' eye and her picked up a white piece of cloth and realised it was a pair of women's knickers; he quickly put them into his pocket.

"A person only destroys a thing of value out of spite; when he can't have that thing himself," Seamus replied and their minds went to Mary's new fella and they were sorry when they heard he had left town. They looked at the deep tyre tracks in the soft earth and Seamus said, "Someone left here in a hurry." Michael sat on his haunches and examined the treads in the beam of his flashlight.

"These marks were made by Gerald's van," the young boy said.

"Are you sure lad?" he asked and Michael nodded. Stunned by what his brother said, Seamus repeated, "How do you know this for sure?" and Michael explained that he had noticed unusual tyres

132

on Gerald's van. The brothers walked home in silence and went straight to bed; they would find out what happened and the culprit would wish he had never been born.

The next morning, before he went to work, Seamus sat beside his sister and kissed her cheek softly, making her grimace in pain. He slipped the knickers under her covers and said, "Who did this to you Mary? Was it Gerald?"

"Please, Seamus," she whimpered. "If you love me, don't ask any more questions," and Seamus ran out of the cottage to hide his sorrow and rage.

When Reg found out Mary had an accident on the way home, he drove over to the cottage to visit her. He was shocked to see her condition; the cuts and bruises had not yet fully subsided and mentally, the girl was a wreck.

"Just tell me who did this to you lass," he begged. "I'll sort the bastards out in no time; I know people who can deal with this sort of thing." Mary just repeated what she told the others, "I don't know, Reg. Some lads knocked me out; it happened so fast." Reg had to ask, "Was it Jeremy, love?" Mary protested, "Never! Jeremy would never do such a thing!"

"You just get well soon, Mary," Reg said. "Come back whenever you're ready; your job will always be waiting for you. If there is anything that I can do for you just let me know" "You've been so good to me Reg, and I appreciate what you have done for me so much," said Mary. "Not at all, Mary; just wish I could get my hands on the bastards that done this to you," and he shook his head to try and get the image of the broken girl out of his mind. She thanked him woodenly for his gift of pies, pastries and fruit, beautifully arranged by the Royal's chef himself in a basket tied with a fancy ribbon; she was relieved when he left the cottage.

Life resumed its usual pace and Mary went through the motions of functioning in her little world, weighed down by a constant feeling that something was terribly wrong. Her old confidence had deserted her and she had problems with her ability to cope with ordinary, day to day stuff. Everything seemed to overwhelm her. She withdrew into a private cocoon, feeling detached and estranged from others. At such a young age, she was not that self aware and carried on in a silent state of confusion. Her life had changed overnight; there was no way she was the same Mary anymore; her personality had altered and her soul was asleep.

When Jeremy returned, he called at the Hotel with a bright smile on his face and his eyes full of love for his girl. Mary greeted him coldly and dismissed him callously, as if he was some wretched stranger. He begged her to tell him what the matter was and without emotion, she broke his heart by telling him there was someone else. When he walked away, Mary didn't even glance in his direction and went on with her chores as if nothing had happened.

Reg did his best to help Mary but she hardly responded and went about her chores like a robot.

"See if you can make sense of all this," Reg said to Kelly in passing. "You're her friend; she talks to you."

"Not anymore, she does," Kelly replied. "She has hardly said two words to me since she got back." Reg said sadly, "I wonder who could have done such a terrible thing to the Mary?" Kelly replied, "I'm thinking you might ask Gerald that question." Reg looked surprised and Kelly explained, "After her like a dog, he was. Used to pester her all the time; I told her to tell her men folk to sort out the crazy bugger."

"They're cousins," Reg said quickly. "Best not to put such gossip about; the Mary has enough on her plate. Just be her friend; she needs you now." Reg drove out to the Fegan house to see Gerald but was told the boy was making his rounds. He asked Bertie Fegan to tell his son to call with him regarding some supplies and

134

as he left, he said casually, "Sorry about Mary. Your niece is a lovely lass; any idea what really happened?" Bertie said, "Don't have a clue, Reg, not a clue. Things are changing; a person ain't safe in their own home these days. Three weeks ago thieves broke in while we were all out; got the wife's jewellery and the money we had in the cupboard; it turned out that the maid was in with the criminals; no trace of any of them at all."

"Well, I'll be off then; Gerald hasn't been round at the Hotel in a bit. Do give him my message."

Gerald saw Reg's car and wondered why he had called. He hid during the visit and waited for his friend to leave before he came out.

"What did old Reg want?" he asked his father who replied, "He wants you to see him about some supplies. Go and see the man; we could use his business, things being as they are. Why are you avoiding him? I thought the both of you were great friends." "Wasn't avoiding him; just didn't want to do some jobs for him; busy that's all." Replied Gerald.

"Well, you should be man enough to tell him to his face instead of hiding like a little girl!" Bertie scolded. "Just make sure you go see him, he came all this way to see you; have some manners, for Christ's sake!" Gerald nodded and said, "I'll go in tomorrow, if I can." As his son was about to leave the room, Bertie said, "Asked about our Mary, he did. Any new developments in her case? Your mother went to see her; shocked she was at the girl's condition." Gerald's blood froze and he shook his head, "No, nothing new, Da."

"Good for nothing police! Haven't found our thieves yet either and it's been nearly a month. I tell you, it's a new world we're living in; no respect for the law and every man for himself! String up the lot of them I say; make some examples!" Bertie enjoyed his little rant and didn't even notice his ashen faced son leave the room.

The Journey

In Church, Paddy asked, "What's the matter with Gerald? Real attitude he's sporting!" Ginger Fegan replied, "Aw, the lad's in one of his sulks. Can't get a civil word out of him; you know how kids are these days; no respect for their elders!" Paddy said, "That's for sure; got my own villains to contend with." When he caught up with Gerald, Paddy said aggressively, "What's up Gerald? Too high and mighty to meet and greet your elders?" Gerald hung his head and said, "No, Uncle Paddy; not feeling so good. Just in a real rotten mood I am, that's all."

"Mood? What the fuck is that, you rude, miserable bastard! You need your arse kicked, if you ask me!" Paddy shot back and Bertie complained. "Brought up too soft your sons are, Ginger! You better get the lad off his backside and pulling his weight, or I'm going to boot him out, I swear I will; let him have his fucking moods on his own time!"

"Now, now, Bertie. We're in the House of the Lord. You're too harsh with the boy," Ginger said, all ladylike as she inwardly cursed her husband for his authoritarian attitude towards his son. Changing the subject, she said, "So sorry about Mary, Paddy," and Paddy replied, "Not as sorry as the bastards who did it are going to be when I find them!"

"Well, don't be putting all the blame on the lads, Uncle Paddy," Gerald said when he was alone with his uncle. A shocked Paddy asked, "What do you mean by that, boy?"

"Seems to me that Mary has been pretty free and easy with the chaps at work. That boyfriend of hers was all over her before he dumped her and disappeared in a hurry. Behaves like a tramp she does; seen it with my own eyes, I have."

"There's nothing worse than having your own children shame you!" Paddy said furiously. "Damn you for getting her that bloody job; thought she was very grand earning all that money; now see where it's gotten her! A bloody disgrace is what she is!" Gerald

136

said slyly, "What you need is a good drink, Uncle. Let's stop in at the Trainor's; they've missed you sorely there, the lads have." Paddy didn't need a second invitation and he drunk himself into a sorry state and Gerald had a hard time taking him home on the back of his bike.

Mary was unaware that Gerald's torment of her was not complete; he continued to poison her father's ears and turn him against her. She sat in church and listened to Father Kennedy's sermons assuring the flock that the darkest hour comes before the light, but there was no light and Mary believed that for the rest of her life she would have nothing but darkness. She continued to fumble around in the dark, slowly closing down, more and more inside. As far as Mary was concerned, all her dreams had gone forever and her life had ended.

The Journey

CHAPTER 9 - DESPAIR

Paddy and Seamus left the cottage for work in the morning and Seamus' bike was not leaning against the wall where he usually left it. The morning mist filled the air and dawn was breaking over the cliffs. It was a breathtaking sight to behold and the men would have commented on the splendor of the countryside, had it not been for the missing bicycle.

"Someone's stolen my bike, Da!" Seamus said and then it dawned on Paddy where it was.

"Calm down lad, calm down, it's not stolen, I borrowed it last night to go down to the Lough; I had a few drinks and forgot and left it in the cove, I did."

"What? What were you doing with my bike, Da? You're going off alone now, are you? Have you lost your mind?"

"Don't give me any of your bloody lip, lad!" Paddy said and they both broke into a run to retrieve the misplaced bicycle. They reached the cliffs and heard voices below. They furtively looked over the edge; through the misty haze they could see a lot of activity down on the beach. One policeman had the missing bike with him while some others dragged a small boat along the sand. Paddy said, "Oh shite, they've got the boat!" Seamus looked at his father incredulously and retorted "They've got my bike! What have you done?"

"Let's get the hell out of here," Paddy shouted to his son, and they raced back to the cottage.

"That's my bike! They'll know it's my bike!" Seamus shouted at his father. The butterflies in Seamus' stomach were nothing as he felt the hangman's noose tightened about his neck and he felt as if his soul had already departed his dangling, lifeless body.

"Shut the fuck up, boy," Paddy said "Don't panic, for Christ's sake; the thing is not to panic!"

"Not panic? They've got my bike; they'll be coming for me in a bit and you tell me not to panic!" Seamus was a nervous wreck. "Two minutes with the police and I'll be singing like a canary!"

"Calm down, lad!" Paddy waved his hands about. "We have to think of something. "Annie popped her head out of the window and said, "You'd best go down at once and report your bike stolen," she said, and Paddy said, "Bloody genius you are!" and the two men dashed to the police station to report a missing bike. They were taken aback to see the bicycle propped up against a constable's desk and the boat already in the yard.

"Buggers move fast when they want to," Paddy remarked.

"Come to report a missing bike we have, Officer Magee," Paddy said. This was a familiar place for the man; almost like a second home. "By the looks of it, you've found it already, thank you very much."

"Not so fast, Paddy," the officer said. Paddy was well known to the policeman; they had often come in contact with each other when Magee was called to sort the man out, during his drunken brawls. "A few questions I have to ask you; Take a seat."

"That's my bike," Seamus told Magee. "See it has my name on it." He pointed to his name etched into the black paint on the bar.

"And what was your bike doing hidden in the cove, then, laddie?" Magee asked pointedly and Seamus felt his knees turning to jelly.

"In the cove?" Paddy exclaimed, feigning surprise. Seamus said, "My bike was missing this morning when I was about to ride to work. I'm late already; let me take my bike and go; dock my wages they will if I show up late."

The Journey

"Work with Jack McColgan you do?" Magee asked and when Seamus nodded, he laughed. "Nothing to worry about, boy, you don't have a job to go to. Arrested the man, we did; locked up the whole crew, we have. A nice little smuggling operation old Jacko had going. Lucky you weren't there or you would be in the clink too. Night off was it?"

"What? Bloody Hell!" Seamus was genuinely surprised; "I don't believe what I'm hearing; there must be some mistake!" McColgan was always so careful; he seemed invincible. There had been many police raids at the Harbour, and McColgan was always as clean as a whistle. The young man had followed his boss's example and prided himself on being cautious.

"No mistake, lad," the Magee said looking at Seamus suspiciously. "You saying you had nothing to do with last night's goings on? How about you Paddy, old son? Walking the straight and narrow these days, I hear?"

"Don't know what the hell you're talking about, man! Accusing an innocent person of a crime he didn't commit; that's low, even for you lot!"

"Just give me my bike and I'll go," said Seamus weakly, and Magee replied, "Sorry, lad; keeping it as evidence, we are."

"Well, if you please, I have to be at work," Paddy said brashly. "You're free to go now boys; we know where to find you once the McColgan gang starts squealing." Chuckled Magee. "No bike, no job," muted Seamus and he held his hands over his face. The police officer joked, "Don't cry son; would you like to have the boat, then?"

"Stop tormenting the lad; he's had a mighty shock, he has," Paddy said, putting his arm around the boy's shoulder as if to comfort him but actually pushing the distraught boy out of the door under the guise of fatherly concern. As the father and son left the station, Paddy could feel the flesh tremble under Seamus' shirt.

The Journey

"Keep calm, lad. They have nothing or they'd have hauled us in," he said confidently. "Wait till I get home tonight and we'll put together a plan." He seemed so calm and Seamus cursed the day he involved his father in his business.

"I'm in big trouble, Ma," Seamus blurted out the minute he entered the cottage door. "Mr. McColgan has been arrested for smuggling and my bike was found on the beach; they suspect I'm involved."

"But you were in last night; your Da...," it dawned on Annie that Paddy had let the side down. "Hush, lad; be strong. You take your wife and leave this place at once; go as far away as you can and don't ever come back!"

"How can I leave you, Ma?" Seamus asked hoping she would tell him to stay and that it was all just a bad dream.

"I'll not have my son behind bars. You have responsibilities lad, you have to do your duty to your wife and child. Go!"

Within minutes, Seamus and Linda were on their way into the village but he couldn't leave without saying goodbye to his dear sister. Mary got out the travel brochures and time tables from the front desk at the Royal. Guests always needed information and bookings; so this would be the best way to plan her brother's way out of danger.

"You taking a trip, Mary?" Reg asked and Mary said openly, "My brother and his wife have to get away from here and I am checking the bus and boat times." Mary knew she could count on Reg; he always knew what to do.

"They could be on the boat to America; it sails in three hours," Reg said pointing to the schedule.

"That's really far away," Linda said worriedly and Mary decided, "That's where you're going, then."

"Do you need some money, Seamus?" Mary asked and her brother replied, "No thanks sis; I'd like to leave some with you."

"I have enough, thanks," Mary refused but he insisted, "Keep it for the family or bad times then. Only God knows what's going to happen now."

"I'll hold it for her, Seamus," Reg said, and Seamus handed him a thick envelope.

"After a while, when things have settled down, write to your sister here at the Hotel in my name; I'll see she gets your letters." Reg gave Seamus the name and address of a friend of his who would meet them at their destination. Then Reg called a mate who agreed to drive the couple to Belfast and put them on a ship bound for New York.

When Paddy got home that night, the first thing he said was, "Where's Seamus?"

"Lost his job, he has; he and Linda thought they'd visit with her folks awhile and then go on to London to see if there's work to be had there," Annie said casually. Mary sat motionless, unable to believe her beloved brother was parted from her. Never had the mother and children been separated and the pain they felt was unbearable. She could not believe that Seamus was involved in any criminal activity, but the amount of money he had with him implicated him and she did not know how to process this shocking information.

"Better he's out of the way when the police come nosing around," Paddy frowned. "The lad was falling apart at the station this morning, he was, and they hadn't even charged him with anything yet!" Hate filled Mary's heart, "That's because he's not a hardened criminal like you," she thought. "All you care about is yourself, Da!"

"Will the police be visiting then, Paddy?" Annie asked as if it was an everyday expectation. Perhaps it was.

"You never know, lass," Paddy stretched out and yawned as if he hadn't a care in the world. "Seems they're really clamping down on the smuggling trade. Suspect everyone they do; Seamus' bike was found in the cove; they must think he had some involvement; especially since he works for McColgan."

Mary couldn't take any more of her father; how could her parents be carrying on this normal conversation when their Seamus was gone. She wanted to scream and cry and bring him back to safety. She couldn't bear that she was so powerless and the helplessness of her life overwhelmed her; all she could do was jump up from the chair and through the front door into the darkness of the night.

"What's up with the lass?" Paddy asked and Annie answered, "Upset she is about Seamus leaving; very attached to each other, those two are."

"Hasn't been right in the head since...," Paddy couldn't say the words. Annie said, "I know; needs time she does, that's all."

A week later the police decided to call at the cottage. It was late afternoon and Sheila was weeding the vegetable patch when she spotted them coming and alerted Annie who was preparing supper inside. Mary said calmly,

"There's no need to worry, lass; we've done nothing wrong. Let them come and do what they will. Probably want to ask a few questions, that's all." When Constable Brice knocked on the door, Annie was relieved to see his face.

"Need to conduct a search of the premises, Missus," he said, feeling bad for the heavily pregnant women. The others were not so polite and barged into the room and began to push and pull things apart. Annie said, "If you tell me what you're looking for, I could give it to you and stop my things from being broken." One officer made a vulgar remark about what he was looking for and another said, "Shut your mouth, Griffin! There's ladies about!" while the others joined in the laughter.

The Journey

"Steady on, lads; it's not Annie's fault," Brice said. "Not blaming you at all, Missus; we have a job to do, that's all," and they went on wrecking the place. To distract the bare footed, angry woman, Brice asked, "Where's Paddy?" and Annie replied; "at the hospital working, he is. Should be home anytime now."

"I hear Seamus has skipped," Brice said, and Annie said, "Fed up, he was. Gone to London to see if he can get a job there. Nothing left for the young ones here. Sad it is when honest sorts can't stay in their own country. A good, hardworking lad is my Seamus."

"Irish folk have been leaving the country for years," Brice replied. "To be sure 'tis a tragedy when a man can't live at home in dignity. "Annie heard Sheila shriek and ran out to see a police officer stabbing at the freshly tilled soil; scattering their vegetables all over the place.

"Holy Mackeral! Is it a body you're looking for then?" Annie shouted and tried to stand between the man and her cabbages. "Stop! That's our food you're destroying!" Another officer with a stick pushed her aside and started poking at the soft earth. Sheila ran about trying to salvage the battered vegetables that were lying scattered about; injured like hapless victims of some terrible battle, while tears streamed down her miserable, frightened little face. Michael arrived and said, "What the hell is going on here?" Griffin smirked and said, "OH, the man of the house, is it?" and the others laughed except for Brice who just repeated, "Take it easy, boys!"

After the police officers had ransacked the cottage, they began to prod the roof with their sticks, destroying the work that had so recently been done. They disturbed the homes of resident mice that squealed and darted about the thatch.

"No need for that, lads," Brice said sternly as pieces of reed and dust rained down to form a layer of debris on the floor. "Let's finish and move on." The animals in the yard fled in all directions, frightened by the noise and strangers, and Sheila and Michael ran

145

after them to bring them back. The whole time Mary just sat on a chair with her hands over her face.

When they were satisfied with their investigation of the vegetable patch, the men moved on to the shed and left it in a mess.

"And what do you hope to find in there?" Annie asked, too stressed to care that she was weeping bitterly at the destruction of her precious home.

"Ah, you never know, Missus," a cheeky one said. "God! It don't half hum in here. What the hell are you saving your shite for?" The bucket hadn't been emptied in days and was half full of faeces. The constable held his nose and grabbed the wooden seat out of the small enclosed space. He tossed it out and it broke with a loud crash as it hit the ground; Seamus' workmanship couldn't withstand the onslaught of the law and pieces of wood from the shattered commode flew in all directions. It was more than Annie could bear, and she howled at him to stop. He began to prod the bucket with his stick. Annie stepped inside and grabbed the bucket. Picking it up, she tossed its contents at the uniformed man.

"Take that, you bastard!" she screamed at the top of her lungs at the stunned constable who stood rooted to the spot, dripping with the foul excrement.

Just then Paddy arrived just in time to take in the scene, and shouted," Aw, Annie, love. What have you gone and done?" Annie just howled and wailed like a demented animal "Really Arthur! Was this really necessary?" and Brice said "Sorry man, we had to search the place."

"Arrest the bitch! Assaulting an officer of the law; get the cuffs on her!" The waste soaked victim shouted, but no one was particularly keen on apprehending the hysterical woman who had shit on her hands, legs and clothes. Brice turned to his men and said, "We're done here lads, let's go," and away they went. The police officers couldn't contain their laughter and they all kept clear of their colleague who was still covered in urine and faeces.

"Did they get the cash, lass?" Paddy asked casually as if he wanted to know what was for supper. Annie moved the loose tile in the floor of the jacks and took out a tin packed full of money. She aimed it straight at her husband's head and it hit him right between the eyes.

"Take your bloody money then and damn you to Hell!" she screamed like a raving lunatic. The tin fell to the ground and the notes scattered everywhere. Paddy had never seen his wife like this before.

"Calm down, Annie love," he tried to get through to her but she was clearly beyond control. How the mother and children got through that day and the days that followed, only they knew. With spirits crushed and broken, they tried to repair the damage to their home. The children lugged buckets of water to wash away the grime and wreckage, and boiled kettles of water for baths to scrub away the filthy scum of their lives.

Mary listened as Grace said, "Haven't had my friend visit this month and got the morning sickness."

"You pregnant again then, Grace?" asked Kelly and Grace placed her hand on her stomach and replied with a shaky laugh, "Sure looks like it." In spite of the closeness of their living quarters and the many pregnancies of her mother, Mary was unaware of the functioning of her body, mainly because no one ever spoke about such things. The printing, publishing, distribution or sale of publications advocating contraception or abortion, as a means of birth control, was banned. The argument was that the sexually explicit nature of such information made it unacceptable; there was a fear that spreading such knowledge could lead to indecent conduct and public immorality. The law prohibited the importation and sale of contraceptives; among Catholics, the very subject of contraception was a taboo.

"I'm pregnant," Mary thought. "Oh, God, I'm going to have a baby!" With that realisation, the enormity of her situation hit her like a ton of bricks. Having known a man outside the sanctity of marriage was a scandal on its own, but to have sex with your cousin; that was unthinkable. Having a baby out of wedlock was the biggest transgression of all. Unmarried mothers were shunned by society; all had a great fear of how family members, neighbours, employers and the whole community would judge them.

While many women concealed their pregnancies from their employers because they would be fired, others hid it from their families for fear of being thrown out of their home, or in some cases, a more violent reaction. Illegitimate children were considered lesser beings than other children and viewed that way in the eyes of the law. Infanticide was tried as a capital crime in the Irish courts, yet in some cases, the sisters, aunts, mothers and fathers of the unmarried mother and the infant's father were involved in killing the baby. Infanticide and the taboo surrounding unmarried mothers pointed to attitudes towards illegitimacy, sex, poverty, birth control, women's rights and protection of infant life, revealing much about the complex nature of Irish conservatism during that period.

"I'm going to kill myself," Mary thought but then she remembered that taking one's own life was a grievous sin and if she committed suicide, she would never know Heaven. So much sin heaped upon her fragile body was too much to bear and she blocked it out of her mind and left her fate in the hands of Jesus. Annie was watching her girl and her suspicions grew. One day when they were alone she confronted her daughter.

"You're pregnant, Mary love?" she asked and Mary said without hesitation or emotion, "Yes, Ma. I think I am."

The Journey

"You're not going to tell me who the fella is then?" Mary shook her head ,"I don't know, Ma."

"Your father's going to have to be told about this, love. Don't know how he'll take it but he has to know." Mary shrugged her shoulders and thought, "Sod him, I don't care what that hypocrite thinks!" Strangely, a flood of relief washed over her; her secret was out and her parents would decide what was to be done; she was free from the burden of making decisions, and it was like a great weight had been lifted off her.

When Paddy got home that night and the children were asleep, Annie said softly, "Our Mary is going to have a baby." Paddy sat up, stunned for the moment as Annie added for good measure, "She won't tell me who the lad is."

"'Tis a terrible sin; a great shame for this family," he burst out; his face red and the veins on his forehead sticking out. "I'll speak to Father Kennedy first thing and see what he has to say. Maybe I'll have a word with Dr. Morgan and Matron Cairney; they know a lot about medical things. This is too much for a father to bear; I don't know what to do, but I won't be letting this family's name be dragged through the mud, for sure!" Annie thought, "This family's name has been well dragged through the dirt thanks to you! When did you become so grand?" But it was a great shame to be sure, and the matter had to be dealt with; Paddy would find a solution to their dilemma.

Father Kennedy shook his head and repeated,"Dear, oh dear!" Paddy waited until the priest had composed himself and then asked,"What's to be done, Father?"

"Ah, these young people; no self control at all, they have. What about the father of the child then? Will he not accept his responsibility?"

"The lass was raped, Father," Paddy said."Raped and beaten in this very churchyard, she was. She doesn't know who did this. 'Tis a shame for the family, it is."

"Ah, it's a scandal to be sure," Father Kennedy agreed."The girl will have to be sent away to have her child; that's the first thing that comes to my mind, Paddy. She can't stay here and flaunt her shame for the entire village to see. There are places where we send girls and I can make the arrangements as soon as possible. These things have a way of getting out, so let me know what you want me to do and the sooner the better."

The Irish solution to the disgrace of pregnancy outside marriage was to conceal it. Pregnant girls and women were sent to mother and baby homes run by religious orders. The neighbours were told they had gone away to work. The babies were adopted, went to orphanages, or if they were very unfortunate they were sent overseas to places like Australia; often to suffer physical, mental and sexual abuse. This all happened to children without their mother's consent or knowledge. After the birth of their baby the woman returned home with her reputation and that of her family, intact. The system of secrecy employed by the religious orders gave the mothers of these children the opportunity to work, marry and raise families in the normal way by ensuring that nobody knew their secret. But much of what was done was done harshly or even cruelly and little attention was paid to the immense suffering of the women concerned, who were given little or no say in what was happening to them.

It is fair to say that when a girl became pregnant outside marriage, she lost control of her life. Some made the choice themselves to go to institutions and have their babies secretly; but if they had not made that choice, then the choice would be made for them and the outcome was exactly the same. While an unwed pregnant girl was in the institution, her contact with the outside world was censored.

The Journey

"You look a bit down in the mouth, Paddy," Dr. Morgan said as he monitored the machine that sent charges of electricity into his patient. Paddy sighed and shrugged.

"What's troubling you, man? Tell me; I may be able to help you." Paddy said,"My daughter's pregnant; I feel ashamed to say this to you, I do. Such a shame for my family if it gets out; don't know which way to turn."

"I take it there's no prospective husband to remedy the situation," the doctor asked, raising the voltage on the machine. Paddy watched the patient convulse and replied, "No, there isn't; the girl was raped." Dr. Morgan thought, "That's what they all say," and responded, "Well, there's always a solution to every problem. Girls in her condition are usually unstable; you may have noticed symptoms of dementia already."

"Now that you mention it, I have. Hasn't been herself since...I was telling her mother this...."

"There you are. The best thing would be to have her admitted to the Big House where she will be out of sight and well looked after. They help out many girls there. Once the child is born it can be adopted and your daughter can return home if you so wish." Paddy relaxed for the first time since he heard the disturbing news.

"It seems like the perfect solution, Dr. Morgan, but how's a poor man like me going to afford all this? Father Kennedy says there are homes for girls to go to...."

"The Big House is the best place for her; she will have proper medical treatment for her mind and body there. You don't want her to come out and repeat the offence. They'll sort her out, they will. I can do this for you, man. I will have the girl admitted and the adoption charge will go towards her upkeep while she's at the Asylum."

The Journey

"Adoption charge?" Paddy asked, and the doctor said, "You don't think babies are given out for free, do you, man? Couples pay a good amount for a child; it's common practice for unwed mothers to give up their babies for adoption; works out well for everyone in the end. Have the girl come in; tell her it's for a checkup; we don't want any fuss and bother when we transport her to the Big House." The patient convulsed violently and suddenly stopped moving and Dr. Morgan said casually, "Check the vitals, nurse; I think we've lost another one."

Matron Cairney saw his face and soon got the story out of Paddy. She was shocked and horrified at the decision he had made, "How can you do that to your own daughter, Paddy? You know the baby can be aborted and the girl will be right as rain within the week."

"Are you bloody insane, woman? You're talking about the worst kind of sin, you are!" Paddy forgot himself and Mrs. Cairney arched her eyebrows and said sternly, "Get a grip, Mr. Harper; I can think of worse sins and I'm sure you can too. Never took you for a hypocrite and I don't like what I see."

"Come on, Lizzy love. 'Tis a right predicament I'm in and I expect you to support me!"

"Well, I do not agree with you, Mr. Harper and I certainly will not support your heinous plan. Now if you'll excuse me, I've work to do!" It took a week of apologies and a gold bracelet to make up with Mrs. Cairney who never forgave his inhumanity to his own daughter and made him pay for his treachery in a hundred different ways.

Paddy tried to broach the subject with Annie, but she was disturbed at the thought of Mary going away to a home for girls as suggested by Father Kennedy.

"Mary can stay home and have the baby here!" she insisted and her husband decided not to openly disagree with her. He had not mentioned the things Gerald had told him about his daughter and the sight of Mary enraged him. Annie was in the last stages of pregnancy and extremely cranky. She had lost her son and would never see her grandchild. After the raid, Paddy treaded carefully around his wife; he still had a scar on his forehead to show for that encounter and he didn't want any upset of his plan which seemed like the only way out. A pregnant, unwed daughter was the last thing he wanted, and Paddy had made up his mind that his daughter would be nothing but trouble; so he was determined to be rid of Mary for good.

"Dr. Morgan wants the lass to come in for a checkup," he said and Annie said, "Well, I suppose a checkup won't do any harm. Many girls are going to the hospital to have their babies these days."

Mary felt nervous with her father as she entered the hospital. It was clinical, shiny and busy and she was impressed by Paddy's ease around the place and how he seemed to know everyone. She had no idea what a checkup entailed. Mary became apprehensive when she met Dr. Morgan but he soon put her at ease by making small talk and showing an interest in what she said. When he said it was time to go to the special maternity wing of other hospital, she had no idea what he was talking about but got up and went with her father. She was a bit surprised to see Father Kennedy waiting for them downstairs, but everything was strange to her in this place so she took it in her stride; no doubt it would all become clear later.

Dr. Morgan drove his fancy new car with Paddy beside him. Mary sat in the back seat with Father Kennedy, patiently waiting for the other hospital to appear and have her checkup. No one spoke and the road seemed unending. The long drive relaxed Mary. She sat back; from the car window and watched the world go by with no particular interest. The world went by without showing any particular interest in her either. People went about their business and Mary did notice how many mothers went to and fro with their little ones holding onto their skirts as they held their babies in their arms or pushed them in prams.

Suddenly the large red brick building came into view and as they drove through the grounds, Mary's first impression was that it looked really old. There were bars on all the windows and the girl thought, "This is more like a prison. Do the bars keep people from getting in or getting out?" She realised how foolish her notion was; it seemed that nothing but inane thoughts flitted through her mind these days, when she would be better off trying to get a serious handle on her life.

An elderly doctor greeted them introducing himself as Dr. Lowry, the Medical Superintendant of the County Lunatic Asylum.

"Why am I in a lunatic asylum? "Mary asked and Dr. Morgan, quickly replied, "There is a special maternity wing here for girls like you." They followed Dr. Lowry to a room where he said he wished to check the patient and a cheerful nurse asked Mary to lie down on the examining table behind a curtain. The girl was tapped, prodded and asked for dates and symptoms; all of which were noted on a chart by the nurse. The doctor asked her about her alleged rape; he pressed her for the name of the father and asked her what she intended to do about the baby. Uncomfortable with the bluntness of strangers, Mary was vague and irrational. As she lay alone in the examining room, she heard Dr. Lowry talking about her to the others.

"A textbook case of Moral Insanity," he said and Mary wondered what that was about.

"I agree with your diagnosis, Dr Lowry," said Morgan. "I was telling Mr. Harper I suspected this. The girl is vacuous and shows no signs of remorse for her situation; I would go so far as to say there was no rape; she brought the pregnancy upon herself due to her low morals; it's quite obvious she's touched in the head."

The Journey

Paddy was furious with Mary; what these learned men were saying was the truth; his daughter had disgraced the family; that's what Gerald had said.Dr. Lowry commented, "You made the right decision to have the girl admitted here. We know how to deal with such patients and I assure you Mary will have the care she needs right here with us." Mary was off the examining table in an instant and pulled the curtain open. The nurse tried to restrain her, "Come girl, calm down. The doctors know what's best for you." She panicked and struggled all the more and the four hostile men looked at each other knowingly as if to say, "How right we were!"

"I've come for a checkup! I'm not stopping here;" said Mary and the men smiled indulgently as Dr. Lowry replied, "Of course, Mary. Don't fret. "To the men he said, "You can leave her with us now," and when they stood up to leave, Mary grabbed her father's arm.

"Don't leave me here, Da!" she pleaded and he just looked at his child with loathing and said, "You got yourself into this mess; now deal with it! Disgraced your family; so ashamed I am. I never want to see your face again!" Father Kennedy said, "It's the best thing for you, lass. You can come home when this is all over. "The men turned their backs on Mary and walked out of the room. Mary ran after Paddy and two white uniformed orderlies stepped in to restrain her. She screamed and thrashed about like a wild animal caught in a trap and her behaviour only confirmed Dr. Lowry's diagnosis. She was strapped into a straight jacket and ankle cuffs and transported in a wheelchair to a ward where there were other young women like her.

"Ma! I want my Ma," Mary cried pitifully, but no one bothered to listen to her pleas.

When Mary didn't return home with Paddy, he explained to an anxious Annie that the doctor had kept her in for a few days as some of her tests showed irregularities.

155

The Journey

"What kind of thing is that?" Annie asked and Paddy replied, "What do I know; I'm not a doctor." When the girl didn't return for a week Annie said, "I'm going in with you to the hospital to get my girl. I don't like her being there on her own; I want to know what's going on!" It was then that Paddy told her Mary was in a home for unwed mothers and she would return once her baby was born. He also mentioned the child would be adopted and the whole problem would be resolved and that this whole ugly incident would be no more than a bad memory.

Annie began to scream and lash out at Paddy. He couldn't calm her down and the two younger children stood by in horror at seeing their mother fall apart. She didn't stop cursing and screaming even when Paddy slapped her across her face. That tactic usually worked with hysterical patients at the hospital but it made no difference here. Annie howled and cried and damned Paddy to Hell. Clutching her stomach, she double up and Paddy shouted to Michael, "Go get the midwife, for Christ's sake, fetch the midwife!"

When Muriel Burns arrived two hours later, Annie was still screaming and thrashing about on the bed in which each of her six living and dead children were born. Sheila was by her side, stroking her, whispering loving words to make her see reason; desperately trying to calm her down.

"Mary!" was the only word Annie called out constantly between her tirade, and Paddy said angrily, "Alright then, I'll bring Mary home if it means that much to you!"

"You must relax Annie, or you'll harm yourself and the baby," Muriel said to Annie who only screamed louder and tried to kick the woman away. Hours passed and the baby didn't seem to be eager to make an appearance, and why should he? Annie moved about violently and moaned as she tossed about, while Paddy and Michael tried to restrain her. The midwife began to worry about the amount of blood Annie had lost and talked about calling the

156

doctor. Annie's son was born in the wee hours of the morning. The mother and child showed no signs of life and the midwife pulled a sheet over them, and left the stunned family to deal with their emotions as best as they could.

CHAPTER 10 - THE FUNERAL

That day, and indeed the days ahead, a cold and bitter wind crept in from the Lough and blew across the countryside. The wind was so sharp and harsh that a person could be forgiven for accusing it of tearing the heart right out of their chest. The hearts of the remaining Harper family had been ripped out by the death of Annie. It made no difference to them whether they were inside or out; their grief rendered them insensitive to the assault of nature whipping around them as if to punish them for letting the precious life slip away. It was as if the Banshee herself had taken up residence at the Cliffside cottage and spilled over into the surrounding area, screaming and lashing out violently, chastising the guilty along with the innocent for the senseless loss of Annie.

Screeching over Kilbarra, the messenger from the underworld rode the wind; the grey cloak of the raddled old hag spread out and overshadowed the village as she swept over it, filling the land with a deep depression, making sure everyone felt her presence. Her long grey hair streaked behind her in her wake, striking chimneys and causing the tiles to fly off the roofs in terror. Her piercing wail shattered the glass on many a window pane and penetrated homes, chilling them with her gloom as she lamented the tragic loss.

Annie would have been surprised to know how much her passing affected her neighbours. In fact, the whole community expressed grief at her death and wished it could have been that no good Paddy Harper who had departed, instead of his wife. Mrs. Keller shed a tear when she heard the sad news.

"A fine woman," she remarked to Big Lucy, touching the corner of her eye with her delicate lace handkerchief. "Such a good worker; I don't know what I'll do without her." Mrs. Keller was never known to shed a tear ever, even when her own mother shuffled off this mortal soil. Lucy had to mention it and before long everyone was trying to outdo Mrs. Keller's astounding reaction with fantastic Annie tales of their own.

In death, Annie had become the saint of the village; examples of her goodness and humbleness became greatly exaggerated and exalted; she would have had a laugh herself if she could have heard some of the anecdotes going around in her name. Mrs. Finnegan said, "Never a harsh word did she speak about anyone," and refrained from gossiping about Annie and the rest of the Harper family for a day or two, though she couldn't help adding, "I wonder where that Mary Harper has gone to at a time like this!"

"A grand lass was Annie, for sure," Constable Brice remarked whenever her name came up. He shuddered when he remembered their last encounter and wished things had turned out differently. Grudgingly, Ginger Fegan admitted, "Not a bad sort was our Annie," and even the drunks in the local pubs raised their glasses in a toast, "To a good wife and mother!"

"Salt of the earth she was!" Muriel Burns sighed, and the herring girls repeated, "The best friend one could ever have; would do anything for you!" Matron Carney shook her head at the tragic loss of life and vowed to redouble her efforts to help women in distress. She spoke of Annie to a group of women, that she had round for dinner and there wasn't a dry eye in the room when she finished. Of course, she didn't mention her part in the family dynamic; it wasn't really relevant to how she saw her affair with Paddy who was becoming more redundant to her by the day. Dr. Mallon simply said, "May her soul rest in peace."

The funeral was a small affair arranged by Reg, Michael and Sheila, helped by Bertie Harper whose brother Paddy went on a week-long binge and was too drunk to be of any assistance during the burial of his wife and infant son. The young siblings evoked the pity of the congregation; who would take care of these young ones now that their mother had passed and their older brother and sister had disappeared without a trace? Surely not that no-good father of theirs who was barely alive, so pickled he was with alcohol. Sitting on a pew propped up by his brother on one side and Gerald on the other, Paddy was almost comatose in his response to the proceedings. Had he been somewhat conscious of his surroundings, he would have felt the sharp censure of the villagers who were livid with anger that he was still here instead of his wife.

 If truth be told, Annie was a huge part of Paddy's life; without her he was reduced to this half person, and a shallow, useless, fragmented creature he was at that. It wasn't so much that love for Annie had laid him low; it was more the reaction of a man who suddenly learned he could no longer see or walk, and he used the contents of his bottle to disconnect him from his reality; he didn't care who else suffered as long as he was protected. It suited him perfectly to remain in this intoxicated condition; it absolved him of participating in the final send off of his wife and therefore, accepting the truth that Annie was gone. Michael knew that nothing would bring his mother back and it was better to escort her to her grave in peace and dignity than have Paddy make a boisterous spectacle of himself. He also knew that this inert Paddy was better than the riotous father, and he kept his Da's whiskey supply topped up.

Annie was buried in a far corner of the churchyard with her son and she was in good company as many members of the Harper family were laid to rest under that stony ground; including her four babies that did not survive beyond their first month. Her husband had to be helped to her graveside; alcohol impaired the functions of his mind and body and he bobbed about like a marionette on tangled strings, manipulated by an unskilled puppet master.

The Journey

"Get a grip, you savage," Father Kennedy snarled sideways at him when the man stumbled and almost slipped into his wife's yawning grave. "Tis a disgrace is what you are! Stand up, man!"

"He's beside himself with grief, Father," Gerald quickly said loudly enough for the others to hear." Wants to join his wife, he does, poor Uncle Paddy!"

"'Tis the drink that's driving him, Gerald Fegan," Father Kennedy retorted angrily. "The man's an affront to the Lord! Just look at the state he's in!"

"Deadened his feelings he has, Father," Gerald persisted. "The man is grieving the only way he knows how. Loved his wife he did. Right shattered he is; you can see that. Pray for him, Father."

"Shut your mouth, Gerald; hold up your damn end," Bertie panted, struggling with the dead weight of his brother. The irate priest hurriedly said the prayers as the cheap wooden casket was lowered into the ground; the sooner this funeral was over the better; no telling what that drunken clown would do next. It wasn't soon enough to escape the man's parting gift to his wife; Paddy outdid himself by spewing a stream of vomit just as the last shovel of earth was tossed over Annie's grave. The strong, swirling wind blew it in all directions and Bertie and Gerald who were shoring him up, bore the brunt of the odious emission.

"For fuck's sake, man; sorry father!" Bertie cried out in horror and revulsion. Gerald exclaimed," Ah, sweet Jesus!" Their best suits took the majority of the gooey, stinky assault; they jumped aside momentarily, releasing Paddy to examine themselves and the unsupported man slumped face forward into the freshly turned mud. Michael and Sheila were horrified at this insult to their mother as were the other mourners who had taken the time out to be there; despite the inclement weather. The swollen faced, red eyed siblings stared in dismay at the final degradation of their

161

precious mother and pure hatred for their father welled up inside them.

"Get him out of here," shouted Father Kennedy. "This man is bound straight for Hell, for sure! Lower than the lowest animal is he that has no respect for His teachings! No respect for his late wife; no respect for the cloth; get him out of my sight!" He looked down to notice flecks of vomit splattered along the hem of his vestments and went crazy, spluttering and repeating wildly, "Get that wretch out of here! Take him away! Get him out of my sight!"

After Annie's funeral a small group arrived back at the cottage with the Fegan's and a few neighbours stopping by to raise a glass to her memory and speak of her with kind words. Mrs. Burns had helped Sheila arrange tea and sandwiches and biscuits and the guests relished the food, washed down by alcohol and a helping of genuine sorrow. No one could say a harsh word about Annie even if they tried. Her life had been one of loving and giving; of restraint and self sacrifice. In their hearts, the guests marveled at the irony of fate that had taken away such a precious parent and left behind one so worthless instead. It made the locals quite livid with anger to witness this travesty of justice and they heaped curses on Paddy, whenever he appeared or when his name came up in conversation. They even cursed him when he blighted their thoughts and they made the sign of the cross on their foreheads as protection against the scourge of such a wicked individual.

Though her time on earth had not made a dent in the scheme of things; Annie's absence would greatly alter the lives of the two young children she had left behind. Their mother was their mainstay; their rock; and now they were bereft of her support, deprived of all hope and happiness, left in the incapable care of their father who had passed out, snoring loudly and intermittently breaking wind to remind the others of his demonic presence.

Michael and Sheila looked around and wondered how they would survive. The brother took time out from his grief to console his sister, but her miserable little face showed there could be no relief for her suffering. Seamus had gone; who knows where, and Mary had disappeared; there was no one to lean on during this troubling experience and their little hearts trembled with fear for the coming days, weeks and months ahead.

"We'll manage, Sheila," Michael said trying to be the man and failing utterly as tears rolled down his cheeks. Sheila sat unmoving as she tried to manage her broken heart. She tried to remember her mother's dear face and inwardly cringed when the image of Annie on her death bed flashed before her. She longed for Seamus and Mary to help her through this unbearable moment in time, and Michael wished they would suddenly appear and lift the burden that was crushing his small shoulders and squeezing his chest so tightly he could hardly breathe.

When the last of the guests left the cottage, the children sat in silence as darkness descended. A sound, that sounded like the Banshee continued to howl outside; it seemed as if she had brought her sisters along to provide a chorus for her frenzied song. The wind shrieked in wild applause and the dense sea mist rolled in to add further chaos to the night. Kilbarra closed its doors tightly against the assault. The beam from the lighthouse could not penetrate the gloom as it blinked sporadically from its post in the middle of the Lough. The children must have fallen asleep out of sheer exhaustion sometime during the early hours of the morning, slumped where they sat, uncaring of the discomfort of their positions; just grateful for the merciful embrace of sleep.

The days that ensued followed a familiar pattern. Paddy had been fired from his job at the hospital and he lay about the house in a drunken stupor, or dragged himself off to the pub, when his legs would allow. Michael didn't care to replenish his father's stock of alcohol; he didn't care what the man did and tried to stay out of his way. Sheila did her best to bring some semblance of order to the home but soon gave up a losing battle and the cottage deteriorated into a shambles. The rooms that Annie had so lovingly and efficiently tended became untidy and even though Sheila knew how much her mother would have disapproved at her bad housekeeping skills; there was nothing she could do about it.

There was no point of focus to the young girl's existence now; it seemed futile to make a bed only to get back into it again; to light a fire when she could never get warm; to cook a meal when no one ate. She wore the same clothes day after day and didn't comb her hair, allowing her long curly red locks to sit in tangled snarls about her pretty face like a serpentine Medusa. She stopped going to school, even though Michael begged her to continue; he reminded her how much Annie had wanted her to complete her education. The girl remained unmoved and refused to venture out of the cocoon she had encased herself in. It was all too much for the child to cope with and without a guide to show her the way, she was totally lost.

Michael was the only one who somehow had his wits about him and kept a keen eye on his sister's welfare. With the help of their neighbour, Mrs. Burns, he managed to get Sheila to eat and make her move from the chair; she made no effort to get out of unless she was forced to do so by her brother.

"Come on Sheila," he begged."We have to try to manage; Ma will be sad to see how you're neglecting yourself." She shrugged her shoulders in a helpless gesture of resignation.

"Ma's gone," she whispered; her voice broke with the strain of expressing herself and speaking of her mother."She's not here to see anything. Makes no difference; nothing will bring her back."

"Ma will be alive as long as we remember her, Sheila," Michael said, fighting back his own sorrow to help his sister with her grief."We must live on as she wanted; we have to be strong and we need to help each other." Sheila shrugged her shoulders again and hung her head as tears began to flow. Michael hugged her and tried to soothe her with the promise of a better tomorrow, if they stuck together and soldiered on as their mother would have done. One morning he got her to dress and took her to school on the back of Seamus' bike; which had been returned by the police for lack of evidence against him.

Sheila's delighted teachers welcomed their bright student back and the girl found her day passed quickly and painlessly in the company of her books. Michael was there to pick her up and she smiled for the first time in the six months since her beloved mother had passed. It was a weak smile, but it was a smile nevertheless. Michael was relieved that she had turned a corner in her struggle to emerge from the darkness that had enveloped her. Sheila was no longer a prisoner of her grief and each day thereafter, she made small but meaning steps to move forward.

"I'm so proud of you Sheila," Michael would praise his sister."Ma would be real pleased if she could see you now." The girl no longer cried at the mention of her mother; if she wept into her pillow many a night it was still early days and Michael let her have this release.

"Do you think Seamus and Mary will ever come back?" Sheila would ask and Michael always answered, "For sure! They'll be back before we know it."

"Where do you think they've gone?" Sheila asked, unable to understand why her older siblings were absent at such a time. "Do you think they know about Ma?"

"I certainly don't believe they have any idea about Ma, or they would have been here to bury her," Michael replied."I think Seamus is hiding somewhere because he thinks the law is after him; he probably doesn't know there was nothing on him. As for Mary; it's all too strange. That night I heard Ma scream at Da to get her back from an asylum. Mary's not mad. Don't know what that meant but I'm going to do everything I can to find out."

The Journey

"Wouldn't it be wonderful if we were all together again," Sheila said wishfully. "Imagine, Linda must have had her baby; we have a niece of nephew somewhere; I'm an aunt!"

"And I'm an uncle!" he laughed, and added, "I know we'll all be together again, I know it for sure. We need to stay strong for each other, that's all; we'll get through this Sheila, you'll see." They had this conversation many a time; it was their comfort in pain and something to look forward to in overcoming the sadness of their endless days. Some days Gerald came by with a bottle or two; him and Paddy drank themselves into oblivion. Other times they would haul themselves off to Trainor's pub and end up passed out on the side of the road; a familiar sight for the residents of Kilbarra.

"Lord God you were fairly ossified last night," Constable Brice remarked to a hung over Paddy when he visited the cottage one day. "Think of the young ones, man. Annie would have expected you to look after them." He groaned some incoherent response and held his throbbing head, as Michael said, "We manage okay."

"I'm sure you do lad; but this is no life for kids," Brice replied. The children were doing their best but from the look of things they were struggling. The place was a pig sty and Brice wondered if they could afford food, since Paddy was out of a job. He seemed to have a constant supply of booze but when did the children last eat?

"Half of Kilbarra has drunks for fathers and they manage; so will we!" Michael retorted. "Sheila is ten now and I'm twelve, we're old enough to take care of ourselves!"

"True enough, but a family can be found to look after the both of you; temporary like, you know. There's time enough to grow up." Brice spoke out of concern and the children were alerted to the possibility of being taken out of their home and even being separated by the authorities. Horrified at the prospect, Michael quickly said, "We have a home and a loving father; he's just upset by Ma's passing; he'll be okay soon enough and we'll manage just

166

fine until then, thank you very much." Sheila added, "It's what Ma would have wanted; she always said we must stay together. This is our home; we're staying right here!" Out of respect for Annie, Brice didn't pursue the matter; the children had already undergone the loss of their elder siblings and their mother; any further change in their lives could prove harmful rather than helpful. He decided to keep an eye on the brother and sister, for the sake of their mother.

Sometimes in the dead of night, Michael would lie in bed and listen to the slurred conversations of Gerald and Paddy as they spoke loudly in the other room. Mary's name was often mentioned by Gerald and she was reviled by both the men. He heard enough to know that Mary was pregnant and had gone away to have her baby. Michael was young but streetwise: he heard the other boys talk and the men joke, and knew what went on in the world of men and women. Putting things together and remembering him and Seamus seeing the tyre imprints of Gerald's van at the churchyard, he was now sure it was his cousin that raped Mary that night; Gerald had all but said this. Once, in their drunken states, Michael clearly heard Paddy accuse Gerald of raping his cousin and Gerald didn't deny it; he abused Mary and said it was not his fault; she had asked for it.

Michael knew his sister and remembered her state that night; she had fought her attacker with all her might; she would never have encouraged Gerald. She had a fella and she was in love; why would she do such a thing? The more he thought about it the more enraged he became. It was Gerald's fault that his sister's life was ruined. If his mother was not so devastated at Mary being sent away, she may have survived and he could have had another brother. He knew that if Seamus was still here, that he would deal with Gerald, but as this was not the case then it was down to him, and he became fixated on taking revenge and spent all his waking hours trying to devise a plan to teach Gerald a lesson he would never forget. When he watched Gerald look greedily at the wad of notes Paddy took out of his pocket, he knew exactly what he was going to do.

Greed will turn the head of most men. In the case of weak men like Gerald it does not take much to tempt them into immorality. Michael had hidden the bulk of his father's money safely in a deep hole under the now dry vegetable patch, but he kept enough on hand to allow his father to buy all the alcohol he wanted. The boy often wished Paddy would be run over by a vehicle while he was lying passed out in a dark street or simply wander off the cliffs one night, when the fog was heavy. Fortunately for Paddy, alcoholics have a rare sense of self preservation; the drink gives them an uncanny ability to bounce right back and live on to torment others before they themselves ever succumb to any accident.

"It worries me how Da throws his money about," Michael confided to Gerald, one day, as they walked to the pub to buy some booze.

"Is that so, Michael?" Gerald said, at once interested in the subject of Paddy's money.

"He has a lot of money," Michael baited his hook. "But it will finish sooner or later if he keeps on spending the way he does, and him out of work and all. Gave Gertie ten quid for nothing the other day when we passed her on the way to the off-license. I don't know what to do; you know he doesn't listen to anyone."

"Now there's a problem, Mike," Gerald agreed. "Frittering away cash is not on. He'll be skint, before he knows it. Where does he keep all his money anyway?"

"If I knew where Mary was I could ask her," the boy said. "She kept it in a bank for him."

"Well, she's not here so that's the end of that," Gerald seemed disappointed but Michael quickly asked, "Where is she? If I asked her she would tell me for sure. It's a lot of money he's got stashed away."

"She's in some asylum," Gerald volunteered this information casually. "I don't know which one and anyway no visitors are allowed. We'll just have to wait until she's back after having the kid; shouldn't be long now." Michael was delighted to learn that his dear sister Mary would be returning soon, but this was not really part of his plan for Gerald.

"Da also has a lot of money here," he said and his cousin was once again caught in his net. "Going through it like water he is; it's enough for me and Sheila to move away from here and live off the interest for the rest of our days."

"Is that a fact, then?" Gerald's eyes glistened with interest. He slapped the boy across his back and laughed. "What do you know about money and interest and the like? How much is there? Where does he keep all this money, kiddo?"

"Oh, there's a lot of money," Michael replied stoking Gerald's hunger. "Last time I counted it there was over a thousand pounds."

"A thousand pounds!" Gerald shouted in shock. A thousand pounds! Jesus! That's a fortune; do you know what you're talking about?"

"I counted every single note and I know a thing or two about counting money. I do it at the coal yard when Chambers prepares the salaries every week. Says I'm a real mathematical genius, he does. Ma took care of Da's cash when she was alive and I helped her," Michael said truthfully. "The police couldn't find it when they tore this place apart looking for it. I sure know exactly where the money is because I hide it from Da and I only give him enough to keep him happy!"

"Smart little bugger you are and all!" Gerald said, fully taken in by what Michael said."Where do you keep all the dosh?"

"Oh, in different places," the boy said casually. "I wouldn't want him to find it all at once; no telling what he would do; he wouldn't

169

give a damn if Sheila and I were left without a penny to our names."

"True enough," Gerald agreed. "Your father is a feckless frigger at the best of times. Would you like me to keep it in a safe place for you?"

"I'm thinking, maybe you could help us, Gerald," the boy said. "I would have to keep his whiskey supply going or he would kill me for sure. Bet he doesn't even realize how much he's got. Made a killing smuggling alcohol and tobacco and he would still be at it if he wasn't so sozzled all the time."

"We could make sure he never finds out. You and I together could save this family from ruin. It's what my dear Auntie would have expected of me; to look out for you and Sheila; but you know Mike, that will take money. Let's keep the money safe." Gerald was already planning his future in his mind. His family never treated him with the respect he deserved. His father always favoured his older brothers and treated him like an idiot. Get the kid's confidence and get him to reveal where the loot was hidden and Gerald imagined he would be home free and a very rich man to boot. Here was his chance to make a fortune without even exerting himself; all he had to do was reach out and take the money. What could be easier?

"You're right; it's what Ma would have wanted," Michael replied. "She really trusted you. Give me a few days to get it together. Today's Tuesday; how about you come by on Friday? That will give me enough time to get the cash together without making Da suspicious. Let me know what the plan is, then."

"Good lad, Mike!" Gerald couldn't hide his joy; he was positively salivating at the prospect of getting his hands on his uncle's wealth. He thought, "I have a good plan, Mike old son! I'll take the cash and vanish; trust me, you won't even see my dust when I head out of this dump." Michael read the thoughts that were clearly written all over his cousin's evil face and thought, "This one's for you Mary!"

Michael waited for his father to stir from his stupor the next afternoon. He was beside him with a hot cup of tea and some oatmeal biscuits from Mrs. Finnegan's shop.

"Here Da, try to get this down you," he coaxed.

"Get...away...from me...you...damn...eejit!" Paddy snarled, mouthing unintelligible words. He clutched his pounding head that felt as if it was about to explode. Trying to unite himself with his aching, shaking body, he crawled about the bed making strange moaning sounds. Even in that weakened state, he managed to aim his leg and kick out at Michael who managed to step aside and save the tea, but the biscuits went flying.

"Come on, Da. You'll feel better; have a sip of tea and a biscuit;" the boy needed his father to attain some small level of sobriety to tell him what he had to know.

"I need...a drink...get me...a drink," he slurred. "Where's my...bottle?"

"I'll put a wee drop in your tea, Da," Michael promised. "Just like Ma used to do. Please, Da, I have something to tell you; it's important, you've got to listen to me!" He quickly added a shot of whiskey to the brew and Paddy grabbed the mug and gulped it down. The blood began to flow through his veins and he started to come alive.

"Don't bother me...got enough problems...stop tormenting me," his garbled words were hardly audible."Gimme that bottle...right now...before I give you...the kicking of your life...little shite!" Michael knew it was now or never; this was as lucid as his father was ever going to get, and the words poured out of him.

"It's Gerald, Da," the boy burst out. "He wants me to show him where your money is hidden. Wants me to give it all to him, he does." The man was alert within seconds even though delirium tremens made his body shake uncontrollably.

"What?" he shouted and then winced and held his sore head, whispering "What the fuck did you say, boy?" Michael took his time to pour his father a small drink; it would sharpen the man's senses just enough for him to grasp the situation. He could see that his words had registered and had the desired impact. Michael continued, "Tell me what to do Da! Gerald is after your money; bullies and threatens me all the time to make me tell him where it is. He took me to the edge of the cliff yesterday and said he would chuck me over. I'm really scared, Da. What should I do? He said he'll be over Friday afternoon and kill me for sure if I don't show him where the money is. Please help me."

"So that's what the spineless cur is up to," Paddy said coldly and calmly. "I'll show the bugger he's barking up the wrong tree. You leave him to me lad!" Michael could see the cogs turn in the morass of Paddy's soggy mind as he struggled to form a strategy.

"He's big and strong, he is, Da," Michael said. "I don't know how much longer I can hold him off. Do you understand what I'm saying, Da?"

"I get the picture, lad. That Gerald Fegan has always been a sneaky rat!" he answered. "Don't worry I'll be more than ready for him and I will rip that bastard apart, I will! Thinks he can mess with me; I'll show him who's the boss! Tell your mother to mix me some of her special remedy...gets me on my feet...where the hell is Annie?" Michael thought, "You should know where my mother is, you crazy dog; six feet under, and you put her there!" Instead he said sweetly, "Mrs. Burns sent over some really good stew, Da. Do you the world of good to have some. Real nourishing it is, she said."

"Well, I have to revive myself if I'm to battle that bloody Gerald," he said resigned to his fate and determined to beat his enemy.

172

"Give me a wee bit, then." No sooner than he had got the bowl of hot stew down him, when it came right up again onto the slate tiled floor beside his bed.

"Not to worry, Da," Michael soothed his father. "'Tis a shock to your system is Mrs. Burns nourishing stew. You can have some more later. Whatever stays down will get you on your feet in no time at all." Paddy moaned as his stomach heaved and he longed for a glass of alcohol to steady himself. His instincts ordered him to resist; there would be plenty of time for a drink when he had dealt with Gerald. He felt much better when he got up from his nap and downed the tea that his son had spiked with a little brandy. He went for runs on the beach and a dip in the ocean, and Michael was beside him all the way, goading his father to make short work of Gerald. By the time Friday rolled around Paddy was longing for Gerald to come by.

"Gerald should be around in about an hour or two, Da," Michael said, watching his father pace the floor. "What do you want me to do? I may be able to hold him off for a few days but not much longer."

"I'm going to deal with that bastard today, once and for all," Paddy had gone over Gerald's impudence in his mind and resolved to put a stop to it right away. "Thieving skunk! Who does the little shite think he is? Doesn't he know who he is messing with? Is he crazy?" These thoughts rattled around his head and Paddy walked up and down the room, working himself into a frenzy of rage.

"That's a good idea, Da. Set him right today," the boy said simply." 'Twill be good if Gerald's not around when Mary comes home."

"What's that? Mary coming home?" Paddy spluttered. "That bitch is not going to darken my doorstep again; she's never going to get out of the loony bin, that's for sure! She's going to stay there where she belongs!"

The Journey

"The tide is out, Da; why don't you have a walk on the beach; the fresh air and exercise will really clear your mind," the son suggested, holding his anger, and the father started out of the cottage door and sprinted unsteadily towards the beach. As soon as Paddy was out of sight, Michael dug the money box out of the vegetable patch and stuffed the paper notes into the inside pockets of his coat. The faded plaid jacket had belonged to Seamus; the young boy had not yet grown into it and the garment hung loosely about his slender frame concealing the padding that lined and weighed it down. Michael climbed to near the top of the oak tree and kept an eye out for his cousin. Paddy returned from his walk just as Michael spotted Gerald far off in the distance, making for the cottage.

"He's coming, Da!" Michael shouted to his father as he clambered down from the tree."What do you want me to do?"

"You can get the fuck out of here and let me handle my business!" Paddy shouted back. Paddy placed a couple of large knives under his pillow and slid the axe under the bed. As Michael turned to go, he noticed the gun winking at him from under a newspaper and a wave of panic washed over him. He recognized the Police revolver that Jerry Rafferty had taken off the body of a New York copper in a gang fight. He had fled back to the home country and the weapon was a memento of his time spent in America; that and the ugly scar that ran from one side of his face to the other.

"Where did you get that gun, Da?" he stammered; perhaps he had gone too far; perhaps he should warn Gerald? Then he remembered what Gerald had done to Mary and any sympathy he had for Gerald quickly disappeared and he left the cottage. He ran outside and jumped onto Seamus' bike to go and get Sheila from school. When he came up to Gerald, his cousin caught his handle bars and stopped him.

174

The Journey

"Where do you think you're going in such an almighty hurry, boy?" he asked. "'Tis all pale and trembling, you are; what's going on, then?"

"It's Da. He's in a right old state, he is," Michael answered. "Taken all the cash and shoved it into his mattress. Thinks thieves are going to break in. I'm going to pick up Sheila now. You just be careful of Da."

"Yeah, right; I'll be real careful!" Gerald laughed and gave Michael a shove."You go and pick up your sister. Oh, I'll handle your Da with kid gloves, I will!" Michael watched as Gerald walked down the lane to the cottage, impatient to get his hands on the money in the mattress. The boy walked his bike down the road, giving Gerald enough time to reach his destination and then adding another fifteen minutes extra for the altercation between the men to take place. Michael looked at the cottage and wondered when he would come this way again. He then rode the bike to the police station and said to the constable who was standing at the front gate,"Please, sir, my father Paddy Harper and my cousin Gerald Fegan are having a terrible fight; Da says he's going to kill him; please send some policemen out to the Harper cottage!" Michael then rode off to pick up Sheila.

CHAPTER 11 - END OF THE ROAD

Paddy lay on his bed, propped up against the pillows. He hadn't been so sober in a long time and the pain of being in contact with reality made him twitch with anxiety. The DTs made his flesh itch and he imagined there were bugs crawling underneath his skin, trying to eat him alive. His unease had reached fever pitch by the time Gerald opened the door and let himself in. In Paddy's fragile mind, the bugs morphed into his nephew who took on a menacing look; grinning viciously and coming towards him to swallow him up.

"Not drinking, Uncle Paddy?" Gerald pulled out a bottle of whiskey from a paper bag and asked, "Can I pour you one, then?"

"Who invited you?" Paddy spoke angrily and surprised his nephew. "Get out of my home Gerald, before I put a bullet inside you!" Paddy pulled the gun from the folded newspaper on his lap and Gerald jumped back when he saw the steely glint of the barrel staring right at him.

"What's the matter with you, Uncle Paddy? What are you aiming Rafferty's gun at me for?" he asked, startled by this unexpected turn of events. Michael never mentioned his father had a gun. "Calm down; I've just come to see you, that's all."

"Indeed? Is it a friendly visit you're after?" He asked suspiciously, eying the danger that threatened him. "Or have you come to rob me blind?" Gerald looked shocked that his uncle was on to him. "Michael must have told Paddy or how else would the man have come to such a conclusion?" he thought, trying to size up the situation.

The Journey

"Don't be ridiculous, Uncle Paddy," Gerald tried to make light of the matter. "Why would you even think of such a thing?"

"Calling me ridiculous, now? Is that how bold you've become, telling me I'm ridiculous, you heartless savage!" The uncle shouted and waved the gun around and Gerald kept his eye on the weapon, hoping to make a grab for it whenever possible. "Bullying and threatening my son, are you? Attacking and raping my daughter, wanting to steal my money? Who the fuck do you think you are? I'm going to teach you a lesson you won't forget in a hurry, you dirty, lowdown skunk!"

"Come now, Uncle," Gerald said patiently. "We're mates, you and I, remember? Steal your money? What's Michael being saying to upset you? He's just a kid, what does he know? It's the drink that's messing with your brain."

"Really? I'll show you how I'm going to mess with your brain!" With that Paddy squeezed the trigger and fired a shot at his nephew. The bullet only missed him by inches and a stunned Gerald now realized just how precarious the balance of his uncle's mind was. He lunged at his uncle, trying to grab the gun and the demented man fired another round straight at his nephew. This time his bullet went through Gerald's shoulder and the young man looked incredulous as blood stained the whiteness of his shirt.

"You dumb fucker!" he screamed, his eyes popping out of his head. "You've shot me! Are you mad?" he grabbed the mattress with one hand and tipped it over with Paddy on it. With the armed man lodged tightly between the mattress and the wall, Gerald began to rummage around for the money, reaching deep into the mattress filling to locate the hidden cash. The fragile fabric of the Connor mattress gave way at a touch. Frantically, he pulled out handfuls of the filling and tossed it about until his shoulder began to throb painfully. His left arm refused to function anymore and hung limply by his side; yet his greed was so intense that it powered his treasure hunt and gave him the strength to keep going.

Regardless of the pain and danger, and the right and wrong of his situation, he soldiered on.

Managing to right himself, Paddy began firing blindly at Gerald from behind the padded partition. Two bullets struck him and he screamed out in pain and horror. He knew his thigh bone had been shattered and had to get away from this lunatic. Paddy pulled the trigger again but the revolver misfired; it may have been the very old ammunition he was using or a weak mainspring that caused the problem, but when Gerald heard the dull click, he jumped at Paddy who threw the gun aside and grabbed one of the knives that he had hidden under his pillow. He plunged it into the young man just as he came at him; it was as if the victim willingly met the weapon in a mutual embrace.

Gerald clutched his stomach, dripping a trail of blood as he staggered towards the door, trying desperately to make his escape. He heard the loud sounds of the police shouting and banging about outside, and cried, "Help! Help me!" as he tried to unhook the heavy steel latch of the wooden front door. Paddy saw the axe and took hold of it; aiming and hurling it at the back of his nephew. The axe struck; with a sickening crunching sound, it sank into vital flesh and bone; finally severing the cord of life in the severely wounded body.

He reloaded the gun as the police threatened to break down the door. Opening a window, he fired at them. The three policemen were not prepared for such an outcome and one of the men dashed off for reinforcements while the others remained at a safe distance under cover to watch the cottage. Soon a truck-full of constables arrived and the men quickly surrounded the place. One of the constables shouted an order at Paddy to come out with his hands in the air: Paddy responded by firing off another round of bullets and calmly reloaded Rafferty's revolver. The well worn wooden grips pounded the web of his hand as he fired indiscriminately through the window of the cottage. Two constables received bullet wounds, and now the situation escalated from a simple arrest to a shoot to kill directive.

People had heard the news of the ongoing standoff and gathered around, making it difficult for the police to operate and maintain safety. The old oak tree was studded with eager spectators perched among its branches. To the entertainment starved locals, this was better than a night at the pictures and it was free. A wide cordon was set up safely away from the cottage to keep the public at bay and the head of police was called in to coordinate the effort. The audience cheered or booed every move. They oohed and aahed and shouted advice, reminiscent of ancient Romans watching Christians being thrown to the lions.

It wasn't long before Ginger and Bertie heard that their son might be with Paddy and the stricken parents rushed to the scene. Ginger Fegan made a tearful appeal to her brother to let her son out but she received no answer to her plea and had to be supported by her two other sons who swore to have Paddy's guts for garters if he harmed a hair on their brother's head. Father Kennedy arrived to see if the power of religion could bring an end to the impasse.

"For the love of God, come out and stop all this nonsense Patrick Harper!" he roared at the top of his voice. "Repent and you will be forgiven; stop before it's too late!" His words were met with silence and it was obvious that Paddy and the good Lord were estranged this night. Darkness was falling and the policemen were anxious to end the conflict and apprehend Paddy. Under the sharp criticism of the crowd, they didn't fare well, so it was time to make a bold move. The head of the police ordered one of his constables to set fire to the thatched roof of the cottage and this was quickly done. The plan was to smoke the villain out but he stayed inside, refusing to budge or even negotiate his freedom. Thick black smoke billowed out of the Harper home, blackening the whitewashed walls. The blaze had gotten out of control and threatened to engulf neighbouring cottages; a fire truck arrived and

179

tried to douse the flaming thatch that lit up the night sky, while a light breeze tossed the burning cinders about in a spectacular and dangerous firework display.

As the flames of hell were dying down, a shot was heard from within the cottage and the police rushed up and broke down the back door. Inside, the constables found two bodies. Ginger Fegan shrieked when she saw her bloodied son being taken out on a stretcher and when a sheet was pulled over his face, she dropped into a dead faint. The Fegan men made no show of manliness and howled openly. They did not care who saw or heard them; they were not prepared to handle their sudden loss, and broke down under the pressure of grief. No one said a word for Paddy. He didn't look much worse for wear; one clean bullet to his temple had been administered by his own hand and it had ended his miserable life and the only emotion expressed by those who knew him was one of relief. Onlookers gawked at the dead man in ghoulish fascination as his open blue eyes stared off into the darkness.

The question remained; where were the children? What had Paddy done with Michael and Sheila? Speculation raged throughout the night and neighbours were questioned; no one seemed to have any idea where they were and the police planned a manhunt for the little ones as soon as it was daylight. Brice regretted that he hadn't followed his instincts and removed the children out of harm's way. Local volunteers came out in full force to assist the constabulary who had also brought in the services of sniffer dogs.

When Reginald Calhoun's call came through at the police station, a wave of relief swept over the village.

"The children are safe, they spent the night at the Royal and they are with me." Reg had heard from hotel customers; accounts of what had transpired the night before and he didn't quite know how to break the news to the children. He asked for Constable Brice to come to the Royal, as the children had requested. Michael was ready to take up the constable's offer to place Sheila and him with a family, as long as they were not separated. He had explained this to Reg when he arrived with his sister at the hotel to ask if Reg knew the whereabouts of Seamus or Mary. Reg had previously told them to come to him if ever they needed help. Well, here they were and they were desperate. Reg heard them out and comforted them, fed them and got them to sleep; promising to sort things out in the morning.

Brice arrived at the Royal Hotel with his superior officer and a lady from the child protection services. They had the matter of the children to sort out and of course, there was a body to bury. Reg asked his wife Jill to sit in on the meeting and without bothering with the preliminaries, Reg said straight away, "My wife and I would like to foster Michael and Sheila Harper until their elder brother and sister can be located and are able to take care of them." The automatic protestations of officialdom were aired and Reg allowed the visitors to wrap themselves in red tape until they had exhausted all their assertions.

He listened quietly and plied them with the finest tea, poured into delicate bone china cups by Jill herself who passed around a three tiered tray of cakes and sandwiches that the company couldn't resist.

"You men are a credit to your profession," Reg said. "The way you have handled this case speaks of your expertise. Every year I make a large donation to the police force comforts fund and this year my cheque is going straight to the Kilbarra police station. As for the children's protective services; 'tis a splendid job you folks do! What would our little ones do without your able ministration? If there is any way in which I can be of assistance in helping your service, please don't hesitate to give me a call."

He handed each of his visitors an embossed calling card and as they ran their thumb over the raised gilt letters, they knew that here was a man that meant business. Over a cup of tea, Reg talked about the services provided by the Royal and when he said, "We arrange the best weddings and the bridal suite is thrown in free if the reception is held at the Royal: the wedding guests, who stay overnight, always have the rooms at special reduced rates. You all have my admiration and as a token for the work you have done, you will all be welcomed anytime at the Royal, as my guests, and at my expense." He spoke so sincerely that no one could have accused him of trying to influence the authorities. When he said it might be in the best interest of the children to let them remain with him and his wife, the visitors merely nodded.

"Well, they can stay until we decide what'll happen long term and we will certainly consider your offer to let them remain with you and your wife," the pale faced child protection worker said primly. Her daughter was about to be married and she had a lot on her mind.

"That is very good of you Mrs. Collins. It is the sensible thing to do right now; the children have been through enough already without being shunted about more than they have to be. I will take care of the funeral, of course," Reg went on. "I will call at the undertakers in the afternoon and make the arrangements. With your permission, I would like to stay in touch with you all until this ugly mess is sorted out."

"Yes, of course," the visitors replied almost in unison. They had a million other things that required more immediate attention, so if this is what Mr. Calhoun wanted, why not let him go with it, as long as all the necessary formalities were complied with. As they left the hotel, Jill invited them to stop in for tea anytime they happened to be passing by. The visitors were all smiles and good cheer; spending an hour in the splendour of the Royal Hotel was a far cry from the grimy environments they frequented in the line of duty; the experience and gracious company had lifted their spirits. Mrs. Collins thought, "Wait till I tell our Bridget about the wedding offer!" Brice said to his boss on the drive back to the station, ""It's right for the children. The Calhouns are decent people and they'll take very good care of Michael and Sheila."

When the children had arrived at the hotel, Michael had introduced himself as Mary Harper's brother and asked to see Mr. Calhoun, the nice gentleman who had invited them to spend the night at the Royal when Seamus and Linda got married. Michael hastily told Reg about the situation back at the cottage and asked him if he had any idea where Seamus and Mary were and the kindly man took the children under his wing. He told them Seamus was in Boston and promised to get in touch with him for them. He said he had asked around but he had no idea where Mary was. Michael told him what he knew about his sister and Reg promised they would search for her.

Following the meeting with Mrs Collins and the two police officers, Reg took Michael and Sheila into his office.

"There's been an incident," he said cautiously. "I'm sorry to tell you that your father is dead, and so is your cousin Gerald Fegan." Reg and Jill watched the children as they received the terrible news. Their faces were expressionless and they sat still, until Michael reached out and held Sheila's hand.

"First, we need to bury your father," Reg began, "We have money, we can do this;" replied Michael and he began to pull out the bundles of pound notes from inside his jacket pockets; the Calhouns were surprised to see all this money on the boy.

"Where did you get all this cash?" Reg asked, and Michael replied, "It's my Da's money; it's what the fight was over; please take it and use it. We don't want it; it's brought us nothing but misery and bad luck."

"Money doesn't bring problems; it's what we do with it that makes the difference," Reg said softly as the boy pushed the notes away from him. "Seamus left some money with me for Mary to use for the family. I will add this to that amount and it will come in handy

183

one day, you'll see. You both stay here, at the Royal, until after the funeral and then you can move into our home with us. Let's hope the authorities will allow this to be a permanent arrangement; at least until Seamus and Mary decide what they want to do. Jill and I are delighted to have you with us and you are welcome to stay with us as long as you like. Please call us Uncle Reg and Auntie Jill; if you like, that is."

Michael went with Reg to the police station in Kilbarra. Riding there in Reg's new car, just like the shiny ones that were parked outside the church every Sunday; he couldn't help feeling good until he remembered where they were going and why. As they neared Kilbarra's police station, Reg could see the boy was apprehensive.

"You're not to worry, lad," he said kindly. "I'm with you and there's nothing to be afraid of. Just a few formalities to be completed, that's all."

"Thank you, Uncle Reg," he said, genuinely grateful to the man for making his troubles almost disappear. He thought it was no wonder Mary went on and on about Reg; he was wonderful. Yet the young boy couldn't shake his anxiety and he grew pale as they got nearer to the station. He needn't have worried; the adults took over while he sat silently with his head down.

"The cottage and the acre of land it occupies is the property of the family;" Police Chief Griffin said. "It has been sealed for the investigation and after that the heirs can decide what they want to do with it."

"That's fine for now. I intend to get in touch with Seamus Harper. Is there any case against him?" Reg inquired.

"No, not at all," Brice answered. "I remember his bike was found in the cove and Seamus reported it stolen. There was no evidence that he was involved with the smugglers. We had an eye on Paddy; quite sure he was involved in the smuggling racket." Michael breathed a sigh of relief and so did Reg. Seamus was free to return if he pleased. Now his main job was to find Mary.

Before they left, Brice gave Michael a large heavy brown envelope and said, "I found this photograph while going through your home this morning and had old Phil frame it; thought you would like to have it." Michael removed the frame and saw his whole family looking back at him. The photograph was taken at the wedding of Seamus and Linda and the happy smiles on each face were genuine. Who would have guessed that within less than a year, things would change so drastically? Michael clutched the picture to him and began to cry. Large gulping sobs tore out of his body and the men watching him crumble in anguish as they stood by helplessly.

Brice put his arm around the boy's shaking shoulders and said, "Sorry Michael, I only wanted to cheer you up, lad." Reg took the framed photograph from him and held the child close, whispering words of comfort to him as he wept tears that could not be stopped. He guided Michael back to the car and sat him in the back seat, placing the photograph on the front passenger seat.

Reg got into his vehicle quickly and drove back to the Royal.

At the Royal, Michael and Sheila huddled together and drew strength from each other. Children are resilient and with each passing day their grief became more able to bear. Reg and Jill comforted them and talked to them. They had never had real conversations with adults, as they were always told what to do and simply obeyed orders. Being consulted and advised about their lives was a new experience and it was exciting to have options laid out before them and make choices for themselves. Children can't be taught to behave better by making them feel worse. When children feel better they behave better.

Their living conditions helped ease their misery; who could remain unhappy amid such beautiful surroundings? They ate the best and had never seen most of the stuff on their plates before. Michael couldn't get over the showers and he used every excuse to have a bath. Jill took them out and bought them new clothes and shoes. These were children who were lucky to have one decent pair of shoes; now they were spoilt for choice and by the end of the week, no one would have recognised them as the scallywags from Kilbarra.

A problem arose over the burial of Paddy Harper. He had shot himself and his death was considered a suicide by the church. Father Kennedy remained adamant on the matter and his personal dislike for Paddy heavily influences his stance; funeral rites would not be provided at the funeral and Paddy would not be laid to rest beside his wife in consecrated ground. Reg went to see the priest in the hope of getting some leniency in the matter.

"The man committed suicide; no chance for redemption in this life or the hereafter when one causes his own death, either by positively destroying his own life, as by inflicting on himself a mortal wound or injury, or by omitting to do what is necessary to escape death, as by refusing to leave a burning building."

"That's a bit harsh," Reg shot back. "The liturgy on occasions like these stresses divine mercy. The dimensions of God's mercy are as far as the east is from the west; as high as the skies above the earth. Isn't that what we are told?"

"Don't come here in your fancy car; in your fancy suit and quote to me!" Father Kennedy said in disgust. "The Catechism of the Church clearly states that suicide contradicts the natural inclination of the human being to preserve and perpetuate his life. It is gravely contrary to the just love of self. It likewise offends love of neighbours because it unjustly breaks the ties of solidarity with family, nation, and other human societies to which we continue to have obligations. Suicide is contrary to love for the living God."

"Except in cases of insanity; do you honestly think Mr. Harper was in his right mind when he took his own life?" Reg returned angrily, and Father Kennedy said, "Ask young Gerald what he thought of his uncle's state of mind, when he was shot, stabbed and hit in the back with an axe. But of course you can't ask him; he was brutally murdered by Mr. Harper! The Book of Common Prayer is quite clear that the Burial Service is not to be used for any that die unbaptised, or excommunicated, or have laid violent hands upon themselves. This means that such persons cannot be buried in consecrated ground."

Reg mentioned the problem when the four of them sat having dinner that night.

"Why not bury my father where ever they allow him to be buried?" Michael asked. "Makes no difference as far I can see, to Da or anyone else. He has to be buried so why not get on with it?"

"What happens in this kind of funeral, Uncle Reg?" Sheila asked timidly, and he answered, "Well, first of all there can be no funeral rites; it seems that Father Kennedy will not even attend or say a prayer over your father's grave. He has to be buried in a separate area in the churchyard. We can select the spot and have the grave dug. The casket will come from the funeral home and be interred with just us there to say a prayer."

"We should bury my father," the girl said quietly. "What do you think, Michael?"

"We should," he answered and thought, "Seems to be more than he deserved," and then guilt washed over him and he said, "It's all my fault!"

"Nonsense, Michael," Reg insisted thinking it was grief that visited the boy once again. "You're just a child."

"I told Da that Gerald was after his money and I told Gerald there was money lying around the house," Michael said woodenly. "I set them against each other; it was revenge I wanted for Ma and Mary! So you see, it is all my fault."

"You've been through so much, losing your mother, brother and sister. Things have been distorted in your child's mind," Reg explained patiently.

"You don't know what Gerald did to Mary!" the boy said bitterly and Reg said softly, "I do, Michael, I do know." Michael put his head in his folded arms; he was too ashamed to face the others. Jill stroked his thick brown hair and whispered gently, "It's alright, love, don't fret. You're only a little boy." Michael felt like a little child; for the first time in his life he didn't feel like he had to be strong and grown up.

"Some disaster would have struck sooner or later; it was inevitable the way things were," Reg said calmly. "It's certainly not your fault, lad; don't blame yourself!"

"Let's bury Da peacefully," Sheila's little voice was firm. What she really wanted to say was, "I've had enough; let's get this over with and put it behind us; let's move on, out of this mess!" Michael understood her message and said, "Sheila's right. We should bury Da and be done."

Patrick Harper's funeral took place two days later just as Reg had described. As the children viewed his face for the last time,they were surprised to see how well their father looked lying there in a smart suit and tie, all peaceful and rested against the satin cushions that lined the casket. This serene picture was to stay in their minds whenever they thought of their father and it was a blessing.

The wooden casket was transported in a hearse to the grave site which was ready and waiting to receive Paddy. It was a quiet, solemn affair with Reg, Jill, Michael and Sheila in attendance. Arthur Brice turned up to support the children and the two grave diggers added to the company. Each of them had a little prayer to recite, and as they said the words the children could see the grave of their mother on the far side of the cemetery. On their way out they stopped to say prayer for her and it is then that their tears flowed freely. They stopped on the way home at Mrs. Finnegan's shop for some sweets; a treat from Reg and Jill. Her cigarette was put down the minute they entered; the woman did not recognise the children and served them with deference. They did not care to enlighten her as she fawned shamelessly over them.

"Would little miss care for these cherry flavoured drops or the mixed berry ones?" and "Would young sir prefer the lemon drops?" she simpered, and even opened the door for them as they left her shop, staring after them as Reg opened the car door for them and drove them away. Nellie and Ruth walked into the shop and Mrs. Finnegan looked down her nose on them.

"Don't the children look grand, missus?" she said trying to make conversation and have a bit of a gossip. Ruth said, "Gawd, I wouldn't have recognised them if Father Kennedy hadn't mentioned it!" They saw Mrs. Finnegan staring blankly at them and the older twin said, "You do know who those two that just left your shop are, don't you?"

"I certainly recognise gentry, if that's what you're getting at," Mrs. Finnegan sniffed as if a bad smell had wafted through her shop. Nellie broke into uproarious laughter and slapped her thigh. Her sister laughed fiendishly in chorus and said, "Gentry my arse; them two are our own Michael and Sheila Harper! Who else has eyes like that?" Mrs. Finnegan's eyes expanded into big circles and she said, "Never!" and the twins went on to enlighten her.

So concerned were the new foster parents over the welfare of their charges that they spared no effort to see that the children lacked for nothing. They had locked away all this special love when they realised they would not have children of their own; now they lavished this pent up affection on Michael and Sheila. The children moved among genteel people where swearing and loud voices were never heard. They didn't have to be constantly on their guard, anticipating some form of attack. Their needs were amply satisfied and they mellowed and bloomed in their new surroundings. The only thing Reg and Jill asked of them was that they study hard and never miss school. The children were well mannered, industrious and were well liked where ever they went.

The Calhoun home was a spacious detached house on a beautiful tree-lined street. It was elegantly decorated and had all the modern conveniences to make work easier. There were so many surprises for the children who had no idea that people lived like this outside of the movies. Jill had a maid who did all the housework and dinner would be sent over from the hotel. She even had her own car and they would drive to the pictures, go shopping or to other places the children never even knew existed. They went to an art exhibition and a flower show; Michael and Sheila had no idea that people spent their time admiring such things and Jill showed them there were books on the like, and their minds soaked up the knowledge their new world brought. At least once a week, they would turn up at Reg's office and while he was enjoying a cup of tea, Michael and Sheila would manage to drink two whole glasses of homemade lemonade. Reg's eyes always lit up at the sight of them and he indulged them hopelessly.

"I've written to Seamus and I've begun to make enquiries about Mary;" he told Jill and she replied. "Oh Reg, I don't think I could bear to part with the children." "I know, love," and he wondered how he would cope when the time came for them to leave.

"I wonder what Ma would have made of this?" Sheila would say and Michael would imitate Annie's voice and say, "Ah, get away with your fancy nonsense!" and they would both laugh. They each had their own rooms and were encouraged to have their friends over. Their days were full of happiness that was a buffer against the haunting memories of the past. Life was like a dream; the only things missing in their near perfect world were Seamus and Mary,

The Journey

and   Reg   was   going   to   find   them.

CHAPTER 12 - THE ASYLUM NIGHTMARE

If people wondered where Mary had gone; she thought the same thing; every day since she had been abandoned in the Lunatic Asylum, along with the hundreds of other men, women and children, she lived within the confines of this Victorian torture chamber. The inmates were closely guarded and regularly tormented by their captors and other inmates: this place was a Hellhole that sucked every ounce of energy from a body and a mind. Few were allowed visitors and most relatives and friends quickly forgot that their nearest and dearest were slowly rotting away in this dungeon from the past; leaving expectant patients, every second of every day, gazing into space praying for a familiar face from the past to show itself. Nothing was ever explained to them and privacy was non-existent. Wards were able to house up to fifty patients, in very close proximity with little personal space. The daily regime was strictly regimented, with little scope for variation and always under the watchful eye of staff. If you weren't mad when you arrived at this place, then you soon would be. The asylum didn't cure insanity, it created it.

"What is this dreadful place and why am I here?" Mary asked herself, and anyone who would listen; but no answers were forthcoming. Where was Da? Surely Ma would ask for her and they would come here to take her home, if not today hopefully tomorrow.

"Moral insanity is what you're in for and you can't leave unless you're cured;" she was told by the staff whenever they cared to answer. "Better accept this and try to make your stay here as tolerable as possible or else you can struggle against the system and go to hell burning yourself out!"

"There's nothing wrong with me," she protested. "Please let me go home."

"You ain't going nowhere, that's for sure," she was told umpteen times. "Your father admitted you and only he can get you out. You don't think he's in a hurry to do that, do you? Settle down; at least till your baby is born." Mary glanced out of the window and saw the high wall and a large set of gates that enclosed the asylum and its grounds. The orderly on duty recognized that trapped look on the girl's face and said quickly, "All the doors are locked and there are bars on the windows." What she really meant was that patients at the facility were lifelong prisoners; at the mercy of the doctors and caregivers and there was no point in harbouring notions of escape. Mary understood her message but she wanted desperately to run; to fly; to flee this terrible place and go home to Annie, Michael, Sheila and Kilbarra, and she missed Reg and all the girls at the Royal so very much.

Mary protested during those early days at the asylum, and most of her time was spent in the constraints of a straight jacket or in a padded cell. She fought against her captors until the energy for such remonstration slowly seeped from her mind and body. She was then considered fit to be among others like her; when the drugs took hold, she became placid and was herded into her place in a ward. The long room held fifty patients and Mary hit a solid wall of noise the second she entered the bedlam. She barely heard the heavy metal door clanking shut behind her; everyone, it seemed, was yelling, laughing, crying, and trying to slam things about. Fifty frantic inmates was a lot of people and it was destabilizing to have to share intimate space with so many human bodies.

The décor was based on metal covered in chipped paint, and every sound echoed through the long, dirty, untidy ward. It was filthy and the stench of all those bodies packed together in unhygienic conditions was enough to make a newcomer wretch. The cleaning staff tried to keep the wards tidy, but the disorderly patients soon undid their efforts. In this cacophony of human discord, Mary felt as though she had entered some kind of hell. Inmates, jostling each other; some of the women were in various stages of undress; a couple of them had their dresses pulled over their heads and one woman kept saying, "They've taken away my clothes; they're forcing me to wear other people's clothes!" She preferred to remain naked rather than wear the smock that was given to her.

Mary passed a little old lady who seemed quite sane and conscious, sitting in bed and shaking with terror. She put her arms around her and said, "It's alright, love," even though she knew it wasn't. The old lady cringed at this alien gesture of compassion and looked askance at Mary. The nurse on duty said sourly, "Don't interfere with the others and upset them. I've spent all morning getting them to calm down!" If this was calm; Mary wondered what the room was like when the patients were really upset.

Observing the callousness of the staff; it appalled Mary that people could be so indifferent to human suffering. It would have sufficed if they simply performed the job they were paid to do, but it seemed as if that was asking too much. These caregivers were given the opportunity of looking after people who are hurting every day; people who trusted that they would listen to them, try to understand them, not laugh at them, and not think that they are stupid, crazy, or horrible. Instead, many nurses merely followed the attitudes of their unconcerned supervisors and doctors and allowed their patients to flounder in a sea of confusion and pain.

Cruel tortures were devised to calm patients. Mary hated the bath torture which seemed to be a favourite among the caregivers. Patients were put into an almost freezing bath, then quickly into a very hot bath, back and forth between baths. This was meant to calm the agitated, but it was the exhaustion of it that wore them out; a body couldn't move a muscle when they were through with those dreadful baths.

Some of the other patients made her life miserable; they beat her whenever they could and no one came to her rescue. Once her nose was broken by this woman who said Mary was the devil; she punched Mary so hard that the girl blacked out while the woman continued to stomp on her face. A right bunch they were and when the patients weren't having a go, some of the nurses and doctors had a go. If some of the nursing staff didn't like you, then you were in big trouble. The amount of time Mary spent in a straight jacket or a padded cell beggared belief.

The asylum was a largely self-sufficient institution. Its large farm provided the hospital with milk from fifty pedigree cows and meat from its own abattoir. Acres of vegetables were grown in the hospital grounds. The able bodied were put to work in and around the hospital; men ran the farms and traditional male activities like the upkeep of the grounds and gardens; they were also employed in various mechanical, carpentry and electrical workshops, and would fix any breakdowns that occurred. The females managed the laundry, kitchens, and general housekeeping duties around the wards. The sick and infirm patients were housed in their own wards and spent the majority of their time there.

Angry, violent or suicidal patients were housed and restrained within the wards, and on occasions, locked within a padded cell. Seclusion rooms were also employed, but these were mainly used for patients who would disturb others during the night. There was also a cemetery on the grounds and most of the patients who passed away were buried right there; if they had families, these were usually uninterested or unable to claim the bodies of loved ones who had departed long before they died.

Dr. Lowry was Mary's nemesis; she hated the times when she had to go to his office for her evaluation. He seemed to take pleasure in letting her know how evil she was and how he was there to make sure her vileness would never spill over beyond the confines of the asylum. It made no difference how she presented herself; in his

195

eyes, Mary was the Devil incarnate. Mary was attacked by Jane every time she passed her bed, which she had to do in order to get to her own. The woman pulled out clumps of Mary's hair during their scuffles; so Dr Lowry ordered the head nurse to chop off Mary's long locks leaving an inch of growth on her head.

"Completes the picture," Dr. Lowry laughed sardonically when he saw her; it was the only time he ever commented on her appearance and she wondered what he meant.

It did not mean everyone at the asylum was unfeeling and merciless; there were angels of mercy among the staff and though they were few, they brightened the lives of those they touched. Mary was fortunate to meet Eileen Doyle, a head nurse on the women's block. Though any form of friendship between staff and patients was not allowed, the two women formed an instant bond. They spoke a word here or there; or in short sentences when they passed each other; otherwise their smiles said what they could not articulate. Some times they were thrown together when they had to sort the cupboard, or distribute linen; then they would take full advantage of their situation and would chat till their jaws ached.

"Do you think I'm crazy, Eileen?" Mary asked and the nurse answered, "You're as sane as I am love. There is nothing the matter with you at all and that's my expert medical opinion!" The women laughed softly, and Mary asked, "Then why am I here? I know I'm pregnant, in which case I should be in one of those homes that nuns run for girls in my condition. I don't understand why I'm in an asylum."

"A family member doesn't need much of a reason to lock a person up. I've come across alcoholism, time of life, puerperal mania, laziness, egotism, fever, jealousy, moral insanity, and even novel reading and these are just a few of the weird reasons for that lead to a person being locked up in a lunatic asylum! One could be committed for having a short fuse or being outlandish in behaviour or dress. Heck, a landlord can have a tenant committed for not paying rent and a boss can do the same thing to an employee, if the employee was an inept worker."

"Does a person in here not have the right to protest and to put their case forward?" Mary asked horrified.

"Once you're in here, there's no question of reason. Husbands are always committing their wives; they may be fed up with them or fancy someone else. Anyone who deviates from the things society thinks is right; is in danger of ending up in an asylum," Eileen told the distressed girl. "Asylums are places to hide away those that don't fit in; anyone who falls through the cracks in society most likely ends up in the madhouse. All a person has to do is tell a court that a relative of theirs is insane, and he or she will be committed. You can go to court and claim that your relative is a dangerous lunatic and the judge will say;" "Fine. Lock him up!" Mary shook her head in dismay at the highhandedness of those in a position to make such decisions.

"What have I done to make my father hate me so much?" Mary whispered. "How can one's own flesh and blood be so cruel?"

"It's devilish easy, Mary," Eileen answered. "Anyone who can persuade two doctors to sign certificates of insanity can put away inconvenient or embarrassing relatives in an asylum."

"Am I to be locked up in here forever?" she asked in desperation. "My father will never sign me out and the authorities will never let me leave this hellhole! I'm going to rot in this lunatic asylum; it would be better to kill myself than live like this!"

"Hush, now Mary, love," Eileen cautioned her friend. "Trust in God and he will bring you comfort and deliverance." The women parted and went on with their work; neither of them wished to jeopardise their relationship. The next week Eileen got Mary assigned to the laundry. The young woman welcomed the chance to leave the main building and meet other girls who were capable of working. The few pennies they earned afforded the cigarettes or sweets from the hospital shop. It made them feel more a part of the world, to be able to function as productive human beings.

Some of the other girls, working in the laundry, were pregnant and they openly discussed their condition, even though the supervisor tried to maintain silence at work. During the tea and cigarette breaks, they talked about the time when their babies would arrive. Mary enjoyed their conversations and wondered how she was so naïve about pregnancy and what it entailed. There was so much she didn't know. It was when Karen said, "I'm not going to give my baby up!" that Mary first realized what was going to happen when her baby was born and she recoiled in horror.

"Give your baby up?" she asked surprised. "What do you mean, Karen?" She needed the girl to explain her statement; she wanted to be clear about what was in store for her so that she could prepare herself for that eventually.

"Don't be so stupid, Harper!" Jackie snarled, brushing aside the hair that played about her forehead. "What do you think happens to babies that are born in here?" At that moment, Mary hadn't the faintest idea; she hadn't even thought so far into the future, and she stared at the girls with a confused look on her face.

"Our babies are taken from us the moment they're born," Karen said, close to tears. "They are taken to the nuns in Dublin; one of the staff told me. Our babies are then sold to the highest bidders; they're given up for adoption and we never get to see them again." Karen began to sob and the other girls cautioned her that the supervisor was making her rounds. Mary stood still; for the first time her baby was a reality; a living being inside of her; a part of her. She heard Beth say, "A right old racket is this adoption business! The minute the little mite pops out, the nuns are waiting. Fairly lining up for babies, folks are. I even heard that some yanks paid top dollar; fly in from the States to pick them up and fly straight back they do, with our little ones in their arms; there's plenty of local customers too."

The Journey

"You mean to tell me babies are taken from their mothers? They're sold to adoptive parents?" Mary was shocked at this revelation. "Do we have to give permission for this?"

"You're a laugh a minute, Harper!" Beth guffawed and snorted. "Permission, my arse! Step out of that fantasy world you live in; like you gave permission to be here. Did you sign a permission letter, Harper, to have yourself committed to the loony bin? You're crazier than you look, girl! And yes; our babies are sold to the highest bidder. They say the money covers our expenses; like we aren't already slaving for them every waking minute."

Mary felt as if her mind was disintegrating like the cinders off a burning log. She felt herself descending into an abyss of darkness; floating deeper and deeper into the spiraling vortex of nothingness. She was alone in this immense space and though she felt no pain, her agony was excruciating. How she got back to the ward, she didn't quite know; when she got to her bed she got in and curled up into a ball and slept the sleep of the dead. She had to be shaken awake the next day and stumbled around trying to complete her chores.

"What's the matter with you, Harper?" Matron Wells asked. Infection control was unheard of, so when an illness ran through the building many people got sick and some died without medical treatment. The common flu bug took many lives each season in lunatic asylums around the country, and it was that time of year again. The nurse tried to check Mary's pulse and the girl slapped her hand away.

"Come now, Harper," the woman looked surprised. "What the hell has gotten into you?" The docile Mary turned into a wild thing.

"Get away from me!" she shrieked, attacking the nurse with her outstretched hands. "You have no right to keep me here! I'm leaving this place; you will not take my baby from me; you have no right!" Mary may have been poor and she may have been bossed around by the men in her life, but she had never been a prisoner. The woman tried to hold her and she sank her bared teeth into her arm, drawing blood. Reinforcements arrived within minutes and Mary was strapped and taken off to a padded cell. She lay there unattended for hours and flitted in and out of sleep. Finally, a couple of orderlies stepped in and removed her restraints. They noticed the welts and mumbled words of regret. They asked her if she intended to behave herself or not, and Mary nodded, yes. They seemed pleased with her response and walked her to a seclusion room with nothing but a mattress on the floor. Mary dropped down on the mattress; all the fight had gone out of her; she had no intention of getting up again; ever.

A couple of days later she was marched into Dr. Lowry's presence.

"You're getting manic," he pronounced, and prescribed heavy doses of drugs for her.

"I don't believe I am manic," she said lucidly and realized that in her delirium she didn't even know what that meant. Dr. Lowry raised his eyebrows in indignation, and Mary continued. "I feel perfectly fine; you just need any excuse to perform drug experiments on me!" The orderlies smiled and Dr. Lowry shouted, "Wipe those silly grins off your faces or I'll do it for you! Get this lunatic back to her room and keep her there! Make sure her medication is given on time."

Mary thought that people were reading her mind and laughing at what they heard her think. She was frustrated and angry and confronted the nurses on this but they pleaded innocence. This didn't satisfy her. She wasn't convinced she was sick either; she thought that, realistically, this peculiar phenomenon taking place didn't have anything to do with mental illness, or mania in particular. She was right; it was the drugs that were playing hell with her body. Her mind was being stretched and bent and she was filled with feelings that were beyond her understanding and control. She was promised that the drugs would be stopped once she returned to her normal state; but how could this take place when it was the drugs that kept her in this heightened state?

Eileen was shocked to find Mary in such a terrible condition when she returned from her weeklong break.

"What have they done to you, love?" she asked, knowing the answer. Patients were given new medications with terrible side effects. They were used as human guinea pigs to test new drugs and some patients died as a result of the side effects of that medication. This was all covered up. Eileen wrote a strong note in Mary's file, mentioning the disastrous results these drugs could have on the girl's unborn child. Eileen's uncle was on the hospital management board so the senior nurses and doctors were always mindful to be respectful towards Eileen. The drugs were stopped and Mary returned to her old self, though she became extremely introverted and suspicious.

The days passed by in meaningless pursuit; some days were manageable while other days were sheer torment. For Mary, time was one long continuous nightmare from which there was no chance of waking. She was scrubbing clothes on the washboard when she felt a rush of wetness down her legs. For a minute Mary thought water had splashed over from the basin, but when she felt a warm gush down her thighs, she stepped back, wondering if she had an accident; she felt a constant pressure on her bladder and had to make a dash to the toilet. Katie saw her looking at her wet shoes and said, "Oh my God! Your water's broken, Mary," and she yelled out to the supervisor, "Harper's water's broken!" The woman came over and asked, "Any pain yet?" and a puzzled Mary said, "No."

"Finish your shift then," she instructed. "Go see Matron Wells when you're through."

"Your baby's coming, dummy," Iris laughed at the puzzled look on Mary's face. "Probably be out before dinner!"

The Journey

Mary was in labour for twenty hours and it was a long and painful experience; she was certainly not prepared for the agony of delivering her first child. She screamed the place down and in her panic and ignorance, she could not respond to the instructions of the midwife which made the delivery even harder for her.

"Ma! Ma!" she called out over and over again, begging for her mother. "I want my ma!"

"Behave yourself!" the nurse scolded her roughly. "Women have babies all the time; it's natural; stop making a bloody spectacle of yourself!" The midwife called the doctor and he was contemplating sending her to the general hospital when Mary finally gave birth to her son. She heard him cry and saw the nurse wrap him up in a little blanket. The young nurse saw her looking at her baby and put the infant in his mother's arms, telling her, "It's a boy!" Mary looked at his precious face and watched him adjust to the alien conditions of the harsh new world he had entered. He looked at his mother and she saw he had the blue Harper eyes. She remembered Annie saying all new born babies had blue eyes, and that one had to wait awhile to see what the real colour was. Mary knew her son's eyes would remain bright blue. She breathed in his newborn's fragrance as she kissed his rosy cheeks.

"Take the child away!" the midwife shouted at the nurse who quickly lifted the child out of his mother's arms and took him out of the room.

"Where are you taking my baby?" Mary asked; her anxiety at being separated from her child made her panic.

"You've had a hard time; you need your rest and the baby needs to be attended to in the nursery," the midwife said firmly and Mary was too exhausted to argue and dropped off into a deep sleep. When she awoke, the first thing she asked for was her baby. She longed to hold him and look at him. She remembered his dear face and thought, "So like our Sheila he is; red hair and all. His name is James; my little James; suits him, it does."

Mary became agitated when no one responded to her calls. She tried to get out of bed and her stitches made her cry out in pain. A nurse tried to stop Mary but she struggled against her. Matron Wells was called in to sort out the problem that was escalating by the minute.

"I want to see my baby," Mary insisted aggressively and would not be calmed. "Bring my baby to me or take me to him!"

"You're not giving the orders here, Harper; I am! And I'm telling you right now to stop all this nonsense and settle down!" Wells stood over the girl, menacing her with her militant presence.

"Please, Matron, I just want to see my baby," she pleaded, looking to the woman for some sign of mercy. "I think I need to feed him," she added, touching her tender, engorged breasts.

"Let me make myself very clear, Harper!" Wells raised her voice and spoke slowly and deliberately as if Mary was hard of hearing. With her hands on her hips to make her message more impactful, she said angrily, "The baby does not belong to you, Miss! You forfeited all right to him when you decided to have a child out of wedlock. He doesn't need a slut for a mother. He will be going to new parents; decent people and at least now he has a chance for a better life; forget about him because you will never see him again!" Mary could not believe her ears.

Somewhere nearby, a wild animal howled and thrashed about in maniacal frenzy and vaguely the girl realized it might have been her. Wells barked, "Restraints, nurse!" and before long, Mary was strapped and contained, though she continued to shout until she lost her voice in the straining vocal cords. She realized how futile her protests were but she was powerless to stop. It was only when a sedative was injected into the muscle in her hip that she stopped her fight against the atrocity that was being perpetrated against her.

203

Throughout the day more drugs were administered; they calmed her enough to sit still without lashing out; this suited the staff since she no longer posed a problem and she done as she was told; moving robotically as if her legs were filled with lead. During her visit to see Dr. Lowry she perked up enough to say, "I want Ma!"

"Your mother and father are dead," he said coldly, looking at her squarely in the face. "Dead, I say, do you understand me? You have no one left on the outside; you are here to stay, so the sooner you get used to this fact, the better!" Mary looked at the man quizzically, as if there was something wrong with what he was saying but she couldn't quite grasp what it was. Her parents were both dead? How was that possible? Why did they continue to lie to her? Why didn't her mother come for her?

During the weeks ahead Mary protested again and again and each time she was seen by a doctor who prescribed stronger medication. She was then seen by Dr Lowry who decided that Mary needed electric shock treatment to calm her down and to help her forget her baby. She was taken to a room, where this Electric Convulsive Therapy was carried out. There were no drugs given before the treatment, to relax the muscles, which meant that the muscles could contract so severely that fractures in the patient's bones could occur. She underwent this horrific ordeal as did many of the other inmates at the asylum. Eileen managed to get her out of the vicious cycle of drugs and shock treatment once again. She pleaded with Mary not to fight against the system.

"I was able to get the drugs stopped when you were pregnant, but I have no excuse now and Lowry would love you to act up so that he can use you as a guinea pig for new drugs. Please try not to lose your temper, Mary," her friend tried to make her see reason; she couldn't bear to see Mary beaten down and in despair.

"Seems it makes no difference one way or another, Eileen," Mary said. "They have taken my baby, heaven knows where. They say

204

my parents are dead. What I do or don't do is not going to make any difference to my life now."

"Nonsense, Mary. Where there's life there's hope," Eileen said. "Please don't stop hoping."

"Hope for what? I have no one outside of this place and I am not allowed to contact anyone or receive visitors. I am not even allowed to write letters or get any mail," Mary said. "I cannot leave this place and if I protest, I am restrained and drugged. I have no rights and I am being treated like the scum of the earth; always at the mercy of the staff and that's the truth of it. What's there to hope for?"

"There's always a chance that things may change," Eileen said. "This system cannot be allowed to continue and it is possible that you may be sent home one day."

"I have no home," Mary said bleakly, "I have no one."

"That's not true, Mary," Eileen said. "You have brothers and a sister on the outside; you have good friends, you've mentioned them many times to me. Besides, I'm here for you."

"You have been so kind but I feel I have nothing to live for," Mary said. "I am thinking of killing myself; may God forgive me but the thought is becoming more appealing to me each day. Going to hell could be no worse than this place."

"Mary; that is not the answer. Please don't have those thoughts, please Mary!" Eileen was shocked by this revelation. "Mary; promise me that you will reject those thoughts of suicide and I'll promise you that I will do everything in my power to help you."

"You've been wonderful, Eileen," Mary replied. "Without you, my life would have been much worse; thank you for caring for me." Mary saw how visibly upset Eileen was and felt guilty for unburdening herself at her friend's expense.

The Journey

"I'm here for you, Mary Harper!" a male voice broke into the conversation and Mary turned around in surprise. Eileen said, "This is John Magowan, a new nurse here. John's one of the nice ones. See, already you have a new friend. So don't give up hope, Mary."

"I'm not going to let you give up, Mary," John's smiling eyes looked into hers and Mary was at once aware of how shabby she looked and tried to smooth down her short hair. "I'm an old admirer of yours, even though I obviously didn't make an impression on you. Saw you first at the Royal Hotel." It was such a surprise to hear that place mentioned; to be connected with her other life came as a shock to Mary; it was as if she had always been here and had no existence beyond the walls of the asylum. It was grand to know she had, and here was someone who acknowledged it.

"You worked at the Royal Hotel; I used to go there for evening tea, with my parents and the truth is; I only went to get a glimpse of you Mary." John smiled. "I was working up the courage to introduce myself when you suddenly disappeared. I was quite heartbroken: asked around but no one could tell me where you went. Fancied you a lot back then; you were so beautiful...sorry, you still are beautiful. It is so wonderful to see you again." John blushed and Mary started to laugh; her first laugh in a very long time...three years ago in fact, when she told her young brother and sister about Jeremy and her plans. For a brief moment, her heart felt a small glimmer of hope. Eileen was right; she must never lose hope.

CHAPTER 13 - ESCAPE OF BE DAMNED

They had to be careful but John and Mary met whenever they got a chance and over the next few months they got to know each other well. Mary would slip out for cigarette breaks and they would meet behind the old wooden shed. When she hung out laundry John would slip in between the lines of sheets and they would exchange a few words, and sometimes even a quick kiss. Their feelings for each other became so strong that it became painful for them to be apart. When they couldn't meet, they sent messages and notes through Eileen who was delighted to encourage the friendship, but also cautioned them to make sure no one saw them together.

"There'll be hell to pay if someone spots you both." Eileen said more than once. "Please be careful, Mary. There's no telling what they'll do to you if they find the notes you are sending John, or find out that John and you are overly friendly. He'll lose his job for sure and you; I shudder to think of what punishment they'll devise for you." Eileen spoke at length to John and asked him straight what his intentions were towards Mary.

"I love her, Eileen, I've loved Mary since the first time I set eyes on her in the Royal hotel" John said and she believed him; his feelings were clearly the focus of his life and Eileen was afraid for the couple. "I don't know how I'm going to manage it, but I intend to marry Mary one day. I love her so much, I think I always have."

"Mary has had so much bad luck," Eileen said. "Don't add to her torment; please don't take any risks. Please stop passing each other notes and tell Mary to stop writing them; she'll listen to you. If anyone finds out about you two it will be the end of her world in more ways than one. These savages will show her no mercy!"

The Journey

Eileen's fears were confirmed when a note was found. It was a mere scrap of paper with the words, "I love you," on one side and "I love you more," on the other side. Just some nonsensical words that lovers say to each other, but when the note was turned in, it created quite a hue and cry. Who was conducting a romance under our noses; this was totally against the rules? Dr Lowry wanted to know, and the ward nurses were questioned and asked to be more vigilant.

"There is nothing going on with my patients," Nurse Doyle said, when she was asked. "Perhaps it's love among the staff? Have you thought of that?" If they hadn't, they did now and new restrictions were put in place making relationships between the staff in the asylum a reason for instant dismissal. Eileen breathed a sigh of relief when the enquiry died down but she still begged John and Mary to be careful; but still they continued to be together at every opportunity, and lived for those special moments.

Mary told John everything about herself and he was shocked at all she had been through. John also shared the details of his life with Mary.

"I come from Kilbarra; the northern end of the village is where my family live," he told her. "There's my Mum and Dad living there now; I'm the youngest; I have two brothers and a sister who are all married and live close by. I worked at the hospital in Kilbarra before I came here."

"That's where my Da worked for Dr. Morgan," Mary said. "Did you ever bump into them?"

"I never met your father but everyone knew Dr. Morgan. He wasn't very popular."

"He brought me here; him, my father and Father Kennedy, an unholy trinity if ever there was one!" Mary shivered.

The Journey

"Do you remember when you first came to the asylum?" He asked softly. "What was it like, Mary?"

"I remember that day; it was all so unexpected. I went for a checkup at the general hospital and ended up here," Mary said, still somewhat surprised by the events of that terrible day. "By their action, I lost my family and became a prisoner; tortured and tormented at every turn until I was so dehumanized I hardly recognized myself."

"I don't know how you've endured all this suffering, Mary," John's heart broke for her.

"It was terrible, John, from the minute I stepped into this dreadful place," Mary continued, lost in her memories. "I was so frightened when I came here and found out it was a lunatic asylum, I couldn't understand why I was imprisoned here. They said I was insane but that was untrue; I wasn't; not in the beginning anyway."

"There's nothing wrong with you, Mary," John insisted. "There are many like you here; mentally healthy men, women and children who are here for ridiculous reasons. It's criminal, the number of normal juveniles who are mixed in with mentally ill and violent adults. They are kept here indefinitely without any hope for future release."

"There are some women who have been here for up to fifty years," Mary agreed. "They have been left to rot here, just like me."

"You are not going to rot here, Mary," John protested. "I'll see to that; I need you to trust me and stay strong. They can't keep you here forever."

"They said I would be free to go home once my baby was born, but that was just a lie as well. They took my son away as soon as he was born. I never saw him again, but I can still see his little face; so beautiful he was!" Mary smiled, she hadn't given up hope of finding her little boy.

The Journey

"After the birth, things went from bad to worse. They made me work from morning till night, seven days a week. Sheer torment it was, wondering where my baby is; no one will tell me anything; it's so frustrating to be locked up like a common criminal. In a way I am a criminal; I had a baby without being married. Even though I was raped, that was an unforgivable crime, for sure. No one ever came to visit; Ma would have moved heaven and earth to come to me; she would never have let me remain here. Now they tell me they are both dead. Sometimes I believe this. I'm sure they would have come for me if they were alive." Mary went on painting a vivid picture of her stay in the asylum, and John wondered what he could do to get her out of there.

"I think I should go to Kilbarra and ask around; see if there's anyone who can help," John told Mary. "I have to get you out; they have no right to keep you here."

"Go and see Reg Calhoun at the Royal Hotel," Mary suggested. "He's a very powerful, resourceful man; who was always so good to me. Got my brother Seamus and his wife Linda out of the country, when they were in trouble. He's bound to have some ideas." John had some accumulated leave due and decided to go that weekend after he cautioned Mary to be on her best behaviour while he was away.

Mary missed John but the memory of him kept her going and she had his return to look forward to. Eileen teased her about moping around because of John and Mary always brightened up at the mention of his name. She told Eileen about John's mission and they both hoped he would come back with some good news. It was that weekend, that some of the inmates decided to make a break for freedom. The siren went off and its shrill, eerie whine alerted the whole complex.

A group of five male patients had broken out; they managed to get hold of the keys to the main exits and were able to get as far as the front gate before they were discovered and surrounded. Having tasted a few minutes of freedom, the men were in no mood to surrender quietly and put up a valiant fight. They were beaten, restrained and then pumped full of sedatives. They never attempted to escape again; but for one of the group who managed to escape the asylum, by hanging himself. His mortal remains were interred in the asylum graveyard; his soul had left, but he was never really free of the place.

The asylum was in an uproar at this breach of its systems. Security was tightened and the weak links were severed; three attendants lost their jobs, for being negligent while on duty. The rest of the staff was under orders to attend to their duties or face the consequences.

"Poor souls," Eileen said. "They must have been so desperate to try and escape from this place. Didn't they know it's next to impossible to break out of here?"

"They must be insane, then," Mary remarked sarcastically. "This is why they are here in the first place, isn't it?"

"That's not true, Mary," Eileen replied. "I know those men and they are as sane as you or I. Admitted here for a number of reasons, that hadn't anything to do with their mental health. One of the men was admitted at the request of his brother; who bribed a few of the right people and then he inherited the enormous family farm. I feel so sorry for them all. Do you know that they released a woman from the main block last week? Sure gladdens me when such things happen." Mary was suddenly all ears; this was a rare occurrence and she asked, "How did she manage that? Why did they let her out of here?"

"Well her husband passed away and an elderly relative came to see her; he was able to have her released into his care. Helen was a quiet, slender, dark beauty. She defended herself against extraordinary physical and mental abuse by her husband who had her admitted here fifteen years ago. Then she had to contend with the torment and abuse that this place hands out. She was not a criminal or insane, yet she was subjected to electro convulsive therapy, drugged, ridiculed, raped, and mentally abused by others there. She is no longer beautiful and weighs twice as much as she did when she was admitted. However she managed to keep her sanity and now she is free." Mary was thoughtful; she didn't know how to evaluate Helen's freedom; she asked Eileen, "After all the torment the woman had been through will she ever really be free?"

"I can't say, Mary," Eileen replied. "She never broke, in spite of whatever they threw at her. I do believe Helen will make a go of things on the outside; at least I pray she does. The main thing is that she's out of here, and that's all that matters. I wish her all the luck in the world."

John was bursting with news for Mary when he returned from his trip and it was agonising not to be able to share it with her immediately. Security was tight and patients were constantly watched. Dangerous as it was, he wrote everything down in a letter and asked Eileen to hand it to Mary. Tucked inside the letter was a photograph of Michael and Sheila with Reg and Jill and another one of Seamus and Linda, with their two girls, Annie and Mary. Mary wept with joy when she saw their dear faces smiling back at her. They all looked so well and Mary couldn't pull herself away from looking at the pictures to read the letter; she simply couldn't take her eyes off her family.

It was only when Eileen asked, "What's in the letter?" that Mary remembered to read it. Going over the words during the brief moments when she was alone, Mary would read a paragraph and return to gaze at the pictures. John wrote that he had been to Kilbarra and had been given a full account of the death of her parents. He didn't go into detail because he wanted to spare her the pain of knowing exactly how they died. He had met Sheila and Michael who were under the Calhoun's care and they were well and happy.

212

"I was asked a hundred questions about you; they were all so excited to have news of you. Mr. Calhoun had recently discovered where you are; he came here but was not allowed to see you. He wants you to know that he has never stopped looking for you and will not rest until you are home." Tears welled up in Mary's eyes and she went on to read that Seamus had just recently written to Reg, informing him of his whereabouts. "Reg has written to Seamus and begged him to come over and release Mary, since he was her only remaining adult relative; Bertie Fegan had refused to have any contact with the Harper family and blamed his son's death on them. Reg is waiting for Seamus to respond; war has broken out and mail is slow in coming. In the meantime, Reg is working with his own connections to try and get you out." Mary savoured each precious word of John's letter and as for the photographs; they revived and renewed her spirit, and she kissed the images whenever she was alone.

"Please destroy the letter, or at least give it with the pictures to Eileen for safekeeping," John requested. "We can't take any chances in case it's discovered; we will both be in a lot of trouble if it is found."Mary just couldn't do this; she kept the envelope on her and read the letter and looked at the pictures over and over. It was nourishment for her soul, and parting with the letter would be like being separated from her loved ones all over again. She cheered up immensely and began to take care of herself. Others began to notice and the girls at the laundry teased, "What's up Mary? Got a fella?" and she would say, "Aw, get away with your nonsense!" and smiled even more broadly.

John was in a state of panic over Mary's lack of concern for her safety. He discussed his concerns with Eileen and asked her to talk to Mary. "I haven't signed my name as a precaution but if she's caught it won't take long for them to get my name out of her; they will pump her full of drugs and she'll tell them everything." When John heard what the girls at the laundry were saying, he knew that he would have to take matters into his own hands; and soon.

The Journey

"I will have to quickly get Mary away from here and across the border. The authorities here have no jurisdiction in the South and Mary will be safe there," said John. "But how can I get her out of here?"

"Please don't even try to get her out of here that way," Eileen pleaded with fear in her eyes. "No one has ever escaped from this place. You'll be caught and that will be the end of Mary and you know very well what they'll do to her." While he promised to reconsider his plans, John was determined that he was going to get Mary out of the asylum. He must help her to escape; if they could only get across the border into Southern Ireland, his girl would be free. When they got there, they could marry and start to search for Mary's son. Love had made both of them delusional and they did not see beyond their noses to notice the forces gathering against them.

Dr. Lowry was quick to notice the change in Mary and was under no illusion that anything at the asylum could brighten her spirits to this extent. She was like a new person and he had to get to the bottom of her transformation. Of course he had heard the gossip from the laundry room; nothing escaped the man and he would soon find out the reason for Mary's good cheer. Was that note that was found from her, to some man here? A male inmate or even a member of staff?

"You're looking positively radiant, Mary," He said pinning her down with a suspicious look. "Have we finally managed to make you happy?" Mary blushed and mumbled some flustered reply that answered the doctor's question fully; the girl was up to no good. John was hanging around in the corridor outside the doctor's office; he knew Mary was scheduled to visit Dr. Lowry and he waited hoping to catch sight of her; it was all they had now since he refused to meet her behind the shed, seeing each other in passing would have to do for the present. As John turned to go after Mary as she passed and they had exchanged loving looks; Dr. Lowry came out and handed Mary's file to the duty nurse.

"Get Dr. Craig to schedule a Prefrontal Leucotomy for Mary Harper as soon as possible; sometime next week would be ideal," Lowry instructed. "Do it right away." The nurse quickly checked with the concerned department and was given an appointment for the following week. When she relayed this to Dr. Lowry he said, "Perfect!" He thought, "If that girl thinks she can outsmart me; she's got another thing coming;" and casually went back to whatever it was he was doing. John overheard the whole conversation and was horrified; he remained rooted to the spot until the man with the tea trolley shouted, "Hey you! Get outta my way! You in love or what?" and then laughed at his own joke.

This was no laughing matter. John immediately sought out Eileen who was as alarmed as he was.

"I have to get her out of here, Eileen; you see that, don't you?" Eileen nodded and said, "Yes, John. There seems no other solution. If she stays here, Lowry's going to turn Mary into a vegetable. My uncle, who is on the management board, is fed up with my complaints about the asylum so there's no point in appealing to him to try and have the operation stopped."

"I'm going to have a word with Mr. Calhoun," John decided quickly. "Perhaps he may have some ideas about the situation."

"Yes, do that. You're going to need all the help you can get," Eileen agreed. "I have a plan; I'm the only nurse on night duty in Mary's ward on Friday night; she can escape then. I will take a sleeping tablet with my late cup of tea. Mary can take my keys and open the ward door; where you will be waiting for her. I can say that Mary put a sleeping tablet in my tea."

"That's a great plan, Eileen," John said. "I haven't even thought the process through; I'll give all this information to Mr. Calhoun and see what he makes of it."

215

"I'll give Mary the details just before the plan goes into action, so she doesn't have time to worry. I won't mention the Prefrontal Leucotomy," Eileen said. "Don't want to put more pressure on Mary than is necessary."

"When they discover Mary is missing, there will be an extensive search to find her and they won't stop until they apprehend her. This lot won't give up easily and Lowry will leave no stone unturned. I'll have to hide her while the police and the asylum authorities look for her. I could take her to my quarters in the attendant's accommodation; it's not a place they're likely to search. After that, I can wait for an opportunity and slip her out of the gate. What do you think, Eileen?"

"I think you have a chat with that Mr. Calhoun first before you decide what to do," Eileen replied. "I wish you the best of luck, John. You're braver than I!" The woman tried to hide the fear she felt for the young couple and she didn't see how they could pull off this daring escape; but there really was no other option. Mary was doomed if she stayed and damned if she was caught. The operation would be the end of Mary; if she survived, she would be too damaged to return to her old self and she would spend the rest of her days as a docile creature, if things went well; if not, she could end up rotting in a vegetative like state until infections and bed sores ended her life. There was even a chance she may not survive the operation; this was perhaps the most merciful outcome of the procedure. If there was half a chance in hell that she could escape this nightmare; then she must take it; Eileen knew Mary had nothing to lose.

"Thanks Eileen; I can never repay you," John said gratefully.

The next morning, John took a day's leave on the pretext that his mother was ill and he had to go see her. He looked so distressed that his supervisor granted his request, even though they were short staffed on John's ward. He lost no time in travelling to Kilbarra and was met by Reg as soon as he arrived at the Royal Hotel. Reg could see something was wrong the minute he saw John but he never guessed that the situation would be so dire. As John blurted out the details, Reg knew they had to rescue Mary; he just wished he had more time; Seamus had given him hope that he would return to have Mary released. But now there was not a moment to lose. It was only a few days until the operation was to be performed so it was now or never.

"Get Mary out of the ward as planned and keep her hidden in your room," Reg advised. "I will phone you and I'll tell the operator I'm your father and I am calling about your mother's health. All I need to know is whether the job is done. I'll arrange for her transfer from the hospital and her onward journey across the Lough to Southern Ireland and freedom. I will let you know the details soon when I have the arrangements in place." John was relieved; getting Mary out of the hospital grounds was the hardest part and now that was taken care of. Mary was going to make it.

Reg's wife, Jill, always the practical one said, "I'll give you something for Mary to wear; she'll need to get out of her hospital clothes." She also tucked a bag of biscuits and cake into the bag, "These things won't spoil; at least Mary will have something to eat while she's in hiding." When they parted, anxiety was etched plainly on their faces; they all realised what was at stake here; a young girl's life hung in the balance and it was up to them to save her from a fate worse than death. There could be no slip ups; the plan had to succeed.

On the way back to the asylum, John's mind raced wildly as he went through the details of his part in Mary's escape. He was so worn out by the time he returned, and as he passed the reception area the nurse on duty asked, "Has your mother taken a turn for the worse then?"

"She's well enough," John replied. "Brightened up when she saw me. But you can never tell..."

The Journey

"Bless her; sometimes parents can be a worry," the nurse said. It was night and she felt like a chat and John was in no mood to indulge her; he didn't want to hang around longer than necessary. The place was empty but for the odd member of staff walking to and from the wards. The staff mostly slept at night, as the difficult patients were well sedated so problems were not expected. The duty nurse asked, "What's in the bag, then?" and John felt the blood in his veins freeze.

"Just a couple of shirts and a pair of shoes that I can wear on my days off; no point in keeping them at home. Mum never lets me leave without making sure I take a good supply of her baking with me," he tried to laugh. "Here, have a biscuit with your tea, my mum is a really good baker." He held open the brown paper bag and the duty nurse helped herself. "Thanks John! These biscuits look delicious." John said, "Go on have a few more; try the ginger ones; there's plenty here and between you and me I don't even have a sweet tooth." He piled biscuits on the side of her saucer and the nurse grinned, "Do tell your mother; these are the best ginger biscuits I've ever tasted."

"I will, for sure," John replied. "Mum loves to be complimented on her baking. 'Night then, Madge!" He left the duty nurse with crumbs on her chin and hurried to his room. He tossed and turned all night and dropped off in the wee small hours of the morning. He was woken by the sirens that marked the day's routines and jumped up to get ready for work. As he passed Eileen in the canteen she mimed, "What happened?" and he whispered, "It's on for Friday night as planned!"

"I managed to get the letter from Mary," she said softly and John replied, "Good; one thing less to worry about!" He paid for his tea at the counter and walked out. He could not help the thoughts that streamed through his mind, even though he told himself not to over think things and complicate the issue; he mentally walked through each step of the plan and then repeated the process.

218

The Journey

By the time Friday arrived, John was a nervous wreck. As if that wasn't bad enough; it rained cats and dogs throughout the day and the inmates were on their worst behaviour. As he walked past a group of men to the therapy room, one man ran off and dashed out into the rain. Everyone laughed at the sight of old Henry dancing in the rain. John called him back but he refused to return and kept on going through his repertoire of dance steps for the amusement of the staff and inmates who gawked at this unexpected entertainment.

There was old Henry, in his element; being pelted by the elements. Undeterred, he flailed his bony limbs about, in time to some mysterious music in his head; now a waltz and then a foxtrot, followed by a spirited tango; he danced with his fantasy partner. Passing orderlies stopped to watch and cheered Henry on as the man kept his audience in stitches.

"Get back here, Henry!" John shouted. "You'll catch your death of cold, man." Two inmates went to bring old Henry in and out of the rain, but it wasn't long before the whole group joined Henry to dance in the downpour. John had to return all the men back to the ward so that they could get into dry clothes and he was given a telling-off by the therapist for being late. He tried to see Eileen to have a word with her about Reg's plan, but they were both so busy that day he didn't get a chance.

It was almost nine at night when the heavy deluge knocked out the power in parts of the asylum. John thought; "There goes the plan! That's the end of that!" Electricians would be all over the place trying to restore the electricity and that would put everything in jeopardy. He was so relieved when he heard that it was decided to repair the lines at first light the following morning; the men didn't want to risk their lives working on live wires in the dark wet night. Candles were issued to the wards and John helped to distribute them, making sure Eileen's ward was one he had to visit. They were relieved to see each other; Mary was already in bed and asleep as were the other inmates.

"It's on," John said and Eileen nodded and crossed herself. "Three o'clock in the morning, I'll be outside at the back, waiting for Mary." He could see Eileen's lips move in silent prayer. As he left the ward he glanced at Mary, looking so small and fragile in her narrow bed and a new strength filled his being. All his anxiety left him as he readied himself to rescue the woman he loved so dearly.

At a few minutes to three, Eileen shook Mary gently. She was awake in an instant and her blue eyes were full of fear as she tried to comprehend what was going on. Eileen put her finger to her lips to caution her to be quiet. "Come, Mary," she whispered. "You're leaving this place. John is waiting for you at the back; go to him." The woman in the next bed stirred and turned over; the two froze and waited until they heard soft snoring coming from the sleeping woman. Mary slipped her feet into her run down shoes and Eileen helped her put on her raincoat which was miles too big for her. It didn't matter; the object was to get to John. She tucked Mary's letter into a pocket and Mary smiled.

The women embraced, almost reluctant to let each other go. Eileen said, "Stay safe, love and good luck." Eileen ushered Mary into the darkened hall that led to the walkway where John would be waiting. The noise of the rain deadened the sound of her footsteps and Mary had no problem leaving the building. Eileen returned to complete her part of the plan. She took a strong sedative with her tea; one that the patients were given to knock them out, and was relieved as the effects of the drug eased the tension that gripped her entire body. She had never been so frightened in all her life. She put her head down on her desk and passed out.

The Journey

CHAPTER 14 - OLD FRIENDS

At three, on the dot, John was ready and waiting for Mary. It was pitch-black outside and John had to find his way almost by instinct. The sky was overcast and it continued to pour. Without the lights that usually illuminated the open walkways of the building, it was nearly impossible to see where one was going; not that there was anyone out at this hour on such a miserable night. Mary was standing there waiting for him and he saw her as clearly as ever. He held out his arms to her and she walked straight into them.

"Come, love, we have to get out of here quickly," John said as he led Mary by the hand along the wall of the building. "I'm taking you to my room, you'll be safe there."   They could have been lovers out for a walk in a park; it was as easy as that. They moved stealthily from one building to the other and no one crossed their path. They were drenched when they walked into John's tiny room on the first floor, but they didn't care; they were together and they were safe; for the moment. Mary got her precious letter out of her pocket and was glad to find that it was dry. She undressed in the darkness and slipped on one of John's shirts, and John changed out of his wet clothes and they curled up against each other and fell asleep.

A nurse found the inmates on Eileen's ward roaming freely about the place and ran to investigate. She found Eileen with her head on her desk, snoring soundly.

"I don't know what came over me," Eileen said groggily. "I drank my tea to stay awake and suddenly, I couldn't keep my eyes open." When a head count was taken, there were forty nine patients

222

instead of fifty; one was missing. Eileen's keys were also gone and they were soon found, tossed outside in a flower bed. To say the asylum was in an uproar when Mary's absence was discovered was an understatement.

"You have been drugged, Nurse Doyle," the supervisor said. "Mary Harper has made a fool of you!"

"There must be some mistake," Eileen acted out. "Mary would never do a thing like that. Where's my coat? It was hanging on the hook on the cupboard."

"Well, Mary Harper has taken you in, hasn't she, Doyle?" Dr. Lowry shouted. "Ask her where your bloody coat is!" He was livid when he heard the news and had come to the ward to investigate the matter himself. The staff were raked over the coals and no one was spared his tongue lashing. He ordered a complete lock down; all the inmates were to remain in their wards and attendants had to escort staff to their posts and back. It was another rainy day but the electricians were ordered to restore the electricity; the cover of darkness was blamed for easing Mary's getaway.

John feigned ignorance and surprise when his mates told him what had happened. Staff and inmates were rigorously questioned and the place was searched thoroughly, but there was no sign of Mary. Reg phoned John and asked, "How is everything?" John replied, "All's well Dad; working hard as usual. How's Mum?" Reg answered, "Your mother is doing very well and has to leave the hospital on Monday night at nine."

"I'll be ready," John replied. "An inmate has disappeared and they are turning the place upside down, looking for her. Very strict with people coming and going, they are right now, but I'll try to be there. Take care of Mum." They knew the operator could be listening in and didn't want to take any chances. The message was clear; Mary would be moved at nine on Monday night. John was relieved; the authorities were going over the place with a fine tooth comb, and sooner or later they would search the staff quarters.

No patient had ever escaped from the asylum and everyone was incredulous. Dr. Lowry's anger had no limits and he continued to rant and rave and abuse everyone who crossed his path. Exaggerated reports had Mary scaling the walls and running off into the night. There were many sightings and John was happy about this as it threw the searchers off her track. The police were called in and they even brought in their sniffer dogs but they couldn't find a scent because of the rain. Dr. Lowry ordered an inquiry; many questions needed to be asked and Nurse Doyle would be made responsible for the escaped inmate; someone had to take the rap.

John and Mary could not help rejoicing in each other's company, in spite of their precarious situation. It was sheer heaven to be able to talk freely. Their commitment allowed them to plan for a future together; they knew they would marry one day soon, when this was over. John told her the news of what was taking place outside and they were reminded of the fragility of their togetherness. Mary was not free yet and in a second, their happiness could be snatched away from them. Knowing this, they valued their time together all the more, if that was possible.

There was a moment when it looked like it was all over. Mary was in the toilet by the stairs when one of the male nurses walked by. John jumped forward to hide her, but not before the man had already glimpsed a woman inside.

"Take it easy, John old boy," the nurse laughed, seeing his consternation. "I didn't see anything, that's for sure!" He winked at the frightened young man and went on his way. The male nurses smuggled girls into their rooms regularly and it was an unwritten rule among them that no one snitched. John quickly returned Mary to his room, but they were both terrified and waited anxiously for Monday night, wondering when Reg would give them the details of the plan.

Early on Monday morning, the postal van pulled up into the hospital as usual. Among the mail was a package for John and the postman said it was a special delivery; he would have to sign for in person. The duty nurse at reception saw it was from his mother and laughed, "I'll give it to John. It's more of his ma's biscuits, I'll bet."

"Sorry, Miss, I'm to hand the parcel to Mr. John Magowan and that's what I intend to do." John was called and the girls looked on smiling as he signed the slip. The nurses were so busy giggling they didn't see the man motion to John to see him outside. He tore open the wrapping and sure enough, it contained a tin of biscuits from Reg. Quickly, John handed most of the biscuits to the delighted girls and their colleagues who had gathered round, and left them squealing with delight as he followed the postal worker outside.

"A delivery van will be here at nine tonight with electrical supplies and Reg says to have the girl ready," the man told John and got into his vehicle and drove away. John couldn't wait for his shift to end so that he could tell Mary the good news. As sorry as they were to part; they were both glad to end this dangerous impasse. Mary put on the dress and shoes that Jill had sent. They piled her belongings into an old pillowcase; nothing of her must remain for the authorities to find when they searched the room; word was out that the nurses' quarters were to be searched shortly. Tensely waiting for the appointed hour; they both promised each other that they would be reunited very soon. This didn't ease the distress of their parting. They couldn't help trembling at the prospect of what they were about to do.

The delivery van pulled up outside the main gate and the driver honked and shouted, "Open up! Electrical supplies!"

225

The Journey

"A bit late for bloody deliveries," the gateman growled. "I have no instructions about a late delivery of electrical supplies." The driver shoved his work sheet under the surly man's nose and said, "Sorry, mate, got delayed a couple of hours by the weather. Dr. Lowry ordered these supplies; lost power in most of the building, I hear. I can always come back another time, if you make a note of your refusal to accept the goods and sign your name to it. No skin off my nose, pal."

"Oh, get on with it, then," the gateman said grumpily. He had just eaten his dinner and needed to stretch out for the night, but hearing the mention of Lowry's name he decided to comply, and asked, "How long will you be?"

"Just as long as it takes the lazy buggers at the stores to unload the stuff," the driver replied. "Shouldn't be more than, fifteen minutes. If you don't know about the consignment, it's likely the louts at the stores haven't a clue either. Be a good chap and buzz them so we don't waste anymore time. I'm not going to unload the van; not my job." The gateman picked up his interconnecting phone and spoke to the stores' supervisor who was equally put out by this additional work.

"What the hell, man!" the man in charge bellowed. "Been awake since the damn power breakdown and we're trying to fix this bloody mess; all my men are busy right now!"

"Well explain that to Dr. Lowry," the gateman said. "He ordered this stuff, himself. I'm sending the van over to you, so deal with it." When the gateman waved him inside, the driver said, "Aren't you going to check the delivery?" and the irate gateman replied, "Get on with it, will you, I don't need to check everything that comes into this bloody place!" The driver joked, "You better check me on my way out! I hear the inmates are escaping regularly."

"Aw, get the fuck out of here and deliver your bloody shit," the man said angrily, "I've got better things to do on this miserable night than wait on you."

"Sure yeah; like you need to rest your fat arse!" the driver laughed and drove in through the gate. The electrical supplies were off-loaded by three unwilling, moaning workers; they were male inmates who had been quickly rounded up to do the job; they certainly didn't want to be out on this dark cold night, but the threat of Dr. Lowry made them go to the stores and get on with the job. They were in a hurry to be done, and signed the work sheet without bothering to read it. No one waited to see the van back up in the darkness towards the male nurses' accommodation and they certainly didn't see Mary quickly jump into the back.

John gave the driver the thumbs up and the man drove his vehicle back to the main gate. He honked at the gateman who opened the gate and waved him out with a rude sign. The driver laughed his head off and shouted through the grill between him and the back of the van, "We're out, Miss! You can relax now; we'll be in Kilbarra in less than an hour!" It had all been so easy and Mary couldn't believe that with each passing minute, she was getting further and further away from that hellhole. Mary was out of the asylum after four long years and she never wanted to set eyes on the place again. It was a matter of luck, bad luck, that had brought her here and it was sheer luck, good luck, that set her free. It was cold and she took Eileen's big coat and put it on. She stretched out on the long seat, and using her packed pillowcase to rest her head, Mary let the rhythm of the vehicle lull her to sleep.

They arrived at the Royal Hotel through the delivery entrance and were met by Reg who picked her up in his arms and carried her up the back stairs. Kelly knew that Mary was due and quickly opened a room that was kept in waiting for her. Reg was in tears when he set Mary on the bed.

"What have they done to you, love?" he cried as he held her close.

227

The Journey

"Dear God!" Kelly gasped and burst into tears at the sight of Mary. It was no wonder they were shocked at seeing her condition; Mary looked like a little old woman; she was skin and bones and her short uneven hair made her look like a waif. She trembled constantly. Gone was the beautiful, sophisticated, confident Mary; if they hadn't known this was her; they would never have recognised her as the girl they used to know. All Reg and Kelly could do was hug her, stroke her and promise that everything was now going to be okay.

While Reg and Kelly were overwhelmed with sadness for Mary; she, on the other hand, thought she was the luckiest person in the world to be where she was and couldn't stop smiling. It was as if everything she had suffered was excused by this single miracle of being out of the asylum and among loved ones, once again. Kelly fed and bathed her and Mary smelled the familiar fragrance of soft scented soap and relished in the warm water that moistened her dry skin. Kelly rubbed moisturising lotion into her cracked hands and feet and Mary got into a fresh cotton nightie, before slipping between the clean linen sheets. "It's the most wonderful thing in the world to be here!" She exclaimed, and no one but Mary knew exactly what that meant.

That night, Kelly and Mary slept together, just like in the old days. Kelly told Mary about Ralph; they were married now and she said he was a lovely man. He had enlisted in the army and was posted overseas at the moment and Mary could see that Kelly missed him and worried for his safety. Mary couldn't bring herself to go into detail about John. Nor could she tell her friend about her baby; her throat constricted and her chest hurt when she thought of them. She couldn't speak of her siblings or her parents just yet. Instead, it was better to talk about the people they knew and things they used to do. It was her first step on the road to normality and she had to tread lightly and not dwell on her past in the asylum, or she could stray off course and into the realm of the insane. She told herself to remain in the present and stay focused.

228

"When can I see Sheila and Michael?" Mary asked excitedly. She longed to see the young ones, and the photographs she had showed how much they had grown and how well they looked; she couldn't wait for Reg to bring them to her.

"Jill and I have been thinking about this," Reg said thoughtfully. "You are in hiding. Should we burden them with this secret? They are so young and happy and we were wondering if seeing you and managing this situation would stress them unduly. What do you think, Mary?"

"I never thought about it like that, Reg," Mary answered. She could see how much though and planning the Calhouns had put into the care of her siblings and she appreciated that. Their world was a far cry from the haphazard ups and downs of her existence. "You are right; I shouldn't disrupt their lives; but I do miss them so."

"I'll arrange for you to see them without their knowing," Reg said kindly. The children meant the world to him and he would never let anything upset them. "Would you like that, Mary?"

"Oh, yes, please, Reg," Mary replied happily. "That would be wonderful!" In the meantime Reg gave her two photograph albums, showing the children's progress since they had come to the hotel, up to the present. Jill had a camera and kept clicking away; recording the lives of Michael and Sheila and lovingly filing the photos in the album, dating each of them, so that there was no doubt of the memory. Mary went through the albums and marvelled at how fortunate Michael and Sheila were to be under the care of the Calhouns. She shuddered to think of what would have happened if things had been different. She thought, "Reg is right, let them have this perfect time and stay safe. I can't be selfish and only think of myself now."

A couple of days later, Reg invited Mary to his home to see Michael and Sheila from behind the heavy wooden screen that divided the kitchen and the dining room. They tried to have dinner together here at least three times a week and this would provide the ideal opportunity for Mary to see her dear brother and sister. Mary was so excited, as she sat in the dark behind the screen: even though she had seen them in dozens of photographs, the reality was something else. Her breath nearly stopped when they walked in to the room with Reg and Jill.

Thirteen-year-old Sheila was so tall; quite the young lady and a real beauty, and fifteen year old Michael was so like Seamus; for a split second, Mary's heart skipped a beat; she thought it was Seamus. They looked so well and how their foster parents doted on them; that was obvious in every move and word. They lavished affection on the youngsters who took it as a matter of course and returned it in full. Mary couldn't believe these smart, confident teenagers were her own brother and sister, and thought, "this is how it should be." Watching the family through her tears, she blessed Reg and Jill for being the lovely people they were.

Mary stayed locked in her room, at the Royal. It was luxurious, but not being able to get about, kept her feeling as if she was still a captive; even though she understood she had to remain hidden until she had crossed over to the south. The search for her was still on and she had to be careful. It was agreed that Mary should remain at the hotel for two to three weeks; Reg insisted he couldn't send her off in her present weakened condition.

"You've got to be stronger before you make the journey," he told her, and Jill coaxed her with special food, to make sure she was well nourished. Kelly bought her chocolates and had to beg her to try them; Mary's stomach had shrunk and it was hard for her to eat anything but miniscule portions and even then, her insides constantly heaved with nausea. It would take a while to become accustomed to good food. Still, she tried to please her hosts and did her best to listen to their advice, and her improved diet was working; she blossomed by the day, and her carers marvelled at the results of their attention.

When Kelly brought in her breakfast on a silver tray, Mary chuckled, "Now I'm sure I'm not in prison." Kelly watched her eat and commented, "You're free love. Don't think about that horrible place." Mary couldn't help thinking about the asylum; John was still there and without him she could not rest in peace. What had happened when they found out she was missing? How was John? She missed him so badly and wondered when they would meet again: and what about dear Eileen? Had she gotten into any trouble over Mary's escape?

"Have you had any word from John?" she asked Reg and he answered, "I phoned him when you arrived to tell him all was well. He's a grand young man; I have no doubt he'll catch up with you soon enough, don't fret."

Mary would have been very upset if she knew what her good friend had to undergo because of the incident. Finding no one else to blame, Eileen became Dr. Lowry's scapegoat. He couldn't put his finger on it, but all his senses told him Eileen had something to do with Mary's departure. The nurse was removed from her ward duties and was assigned work that did not bring her into direct contact with the unfortunate people she cared for. Lowry believed she was the main person of interest in the case of Mary Harper's disappearance and she was told not to leave the premises; pending an inquiry where her fate would be decided.

Eileen's uncle visited the asylum and called her into the office to have a word. He told her to stop involving herself in things that did not concern her; how the asylum was run should be no concern of hers.

"The welfare of the people I care for is my concern, Uncle," she told him straight. "The doctors here rely too much on medication with dangerous side effects and other brutal outdated so-called treatments. There is a significant lack of psychological and social therapies, and I find this very disturbing. We need a deeper understanding to provide humane and caring services to some of the most vulnerable people in our society."

"The doctors know what they're doing! Do your job and stay out of their business," the uncle advised. "In a harsh environment, harsh measures are sometimes required; stop your interfering! It's embarrassing for me to have my niece constantly undermine an institution that I represent as a member of the governing body."

"The treatment at the institution that you represent is enough to make a sane person crazy; enough to push troubled souls further over the edge. Do you know that patients of this asylum are subjected to beatings, starvation, and used as cheap labour? They are chained, shackled and drugged to ensure complacency," Eileen could not stop. "Do you know what goes on here? Human beings are given new medications with dreadful side effects; used as human guinea pigs to test new drugs. Have you any idea of how many die as a result of this testing? Do you know how many perfectly sane people are locked up in here for ridiculous reasons? It's hard to comprehend, that such things happen in this day and age."

"Get a hold of yourself, or get out, Eileen!" the old man said angrily. "Don't waste my time with your misguided sympathy; there's no place for weak stomachs at the asylum; you being a nurse should understand all too well! May I remind you, this is a lunatic asylum, not your bloody house? We're done here, lass and I don't want to hear any more nonsense from you and please don't let me get any more negative reports about you, or I'll be forced to sack you myself!"

Eileen knew that this was the end of the line, as far as their discussion about the asylum was concerned. She got up and commended, "Thank you for explaining your position to me, Uncle, but I will continue to treat the people within these walls with the care and dignity they deserve. Please don't feel that you're obliged to defend me, or involve yourself in any way on my behalf; I'll not be asking any favours of you."

"You're a stubborn girl, Eileen; just like your mother," the Uncle said in a lighter tone. "You're twenty-six now; isn't it high time you found yourself a husband and settled down?"

"I will give your suggestion due consideration. Goodbye, Uncle," Eileen smiled; men didn't take a woman seriously. As long as a female didn't rock the boat, she was allowed to muddle along. Eileen could never consider marrying anyone other than an equal and until such a man materialized, she would continue to be a spinster quite happily.

The inquiry took place with all the senior staff and board members in attendance. Dr. Lowry led the proceedings and began to question Eileen. He went on and on describing the events of the night and Eileen knew he was leading up to her connection with Mary.

"Would you say you had a special friendship with Mary Harper?" he asked her.

"Yes, I believe I had a special friendship with Mary; just as I do with all the people under my care," she answered boldly, quite unafraid of the monster's penetrating gaze which was aimed at her.

"Is that so?" he asked slyly. "Would you say your friendship encouraged her to escape from the asylum, Nurse Doyle?"

"We talk about treating people with a mental illness with compassion and gentleness and see them as being more than a diagnosis," Eileen said. "It's time we start doing, instead of talking. It's time we start treating all the people who come to the asylum for help with dignity and justice."

"Just answer the question, Nurse Doyle," Lowry insisted. "Did you have any part in the escape ofMary Harper?"

233

"If I did, I'm glad!" Eileen burst out. "Mary is sane and yet she was in here with no chance of leaving. She was tormented, mistreated, brutally restrained, drugged and she was abused by patients, staff."

"Calm down, Nurse Doyle," Lowry broke into her tirade. He wasn't comfortable having the asylum's dirty linen aired in front of the governing body and he wasn't sure whether to stop the irate woman or let her continue and hang herself. "Are you accusing the doctors here of malpractice? This is a very serious charge, wouldn't you agree?"

"I do agree. I am a professional person and I deal with serious matters," Eileen said. "The welfare of the people in my care is a serious matter and when doctors cross the line and put them in danger; it is a very serious matter to me!" Dr. Lowry opened his mouth to speak, when one of the board members interrupted and asked, "Could you be more specific, Nurse Doyle? In what way do the doctors endanger the lives of the inmates; that is your accusation, is it?"

"Yes it is!" Eileen said. "I accuse Dr. Lowry of malpractice and attempting to endanger the life of Mary Harper." There was an audible gasp around the room and Dr. Lowry spluttered with indignation.

"How dare you?" he raged, and before he could go on, Eileen said, "I dare, because what I say is true!" He began to form his reply when the board member said, "Can you explain yourself, Nurse Doyle?" Dr. Lowry retorted, "I'm not under investigation here! How dare this woman speak to me like this?"

"Nurse Doyle has made a very serious statement and she must explain herself, or face a charge of slander," the board member replied. "We are here to look into the facts of this case and that is what we must do. Please explain yourself, Nurse Doyle."

Dr. Lowry has always had it in for Mary Harper," she began and the board member said, "Stick to the facts, madam; your personal opinions have no bearing on the case."

"The fact is that Dr. Lowry is responsible for prescribing excessive doses of drugs for Mary; no other doctor ever thought she was in need of such extreme treatment; no other doctor ever prescribed the high doses of medication that Dr Lowry did; certainly not when she was carrying her child. I myself made a note on Miss Harper's chart about this and the drugs were stopped at that time. A week ago Dr. Lowry ordered Dr. Craig to perform a Prefrontal Leucotomy on Mary Harper, even though Dr. Craig examined her and made a note stating that she was not an ideal patient for this operation; she was a healthy female who exhibited no signs that warranted such a harsh procedure. Do you know what this experimental procedure does to a human being? Holes are drilled into the patient's skull and the prefrontal cortex is injected with alcohol to destroy all the connecting fibres; then the frontal lobes are severed by a sharp wire that is inserted into the skull. By doing this, the patient is left with the mental capacity of an infant; they can't speak intelligibly or control their bodily functions: that is, if they survive the operation. Why did Dr. Lowry insist that Mary Harper, a sane individual who was able to perform her duties in the laundry, undergo such a procedure, even when Dr. Craig questioned this? She displayed no aggressive behaviour; in fact she was so well and happy that her colleagues remarked on this. She was scheduled to have the operation on Saturday and if she somehow managed to avoid this horrendous operation; I say good for her!"

"Dr. Craig, is this true?" the board member queried the doctor who answered simply, "Yes, it is." The room was in an uproar. Even the staff who didn't give a fig, for the people in their care, distanced themselves from Dr. Lowry. Disparaging remarks against him filled the room and the senior board member had to bang his fist on the table and call for calm.

235

The Journey

"There is no evidence against Nurse Doyle, so this enquiry is terminated. I would just advise the staff that if they have a complaint, don't take the matter into your own hands; please send in a report to the members of the board so that we may address the issue appropriately."

"I wish to tender my resignation," Eileen said loudly and clearly.

"Your ten years of service here has been exemplary, Nurse Doyle," Dr. Craig spoke up. "My colleagues and I hope you seriously reconsider your decision."

"Thank you, Dr, Craig," Eileen replied. "I've made up my mind. I am going to enlist, as a nurse, in the army and try to ease the suffering of our soldiers who are wounded in fighting for freedom and justice for all our people. As for a report; I intend to write a comprehensive account of the goings on at this asylum; you can be sure of that!"

"We can settle the other matters in a private session with all the senior staff present," the board member suggested. "I think we can move on now."

True to her word, Eileen Doyle wrote a comprehensive sixty page report on her findings at the lunatic asylum; backed up by evidence. She mailed a copy to each of the board members, and one to a national newspaper. The newspaper serialised the report which attracted so many readers that its print run doubled. The expose brought to light the harsh conditions in lunatic asylums in the country and supported the ongoing debate for a radical change of their function and a stop to the practice of admitting people, other than those who have a mental illness.

John met with Eileen, on her last day at the asylum; they embraced, generating the kind of energy that only comes about when the souls of two good people touch. They exchanged addresses and promised to stay in touch: a letter or a phone call to the Royal Hotel would always find John or Mary. As Eileen departed with her suitcase in hand, she promised John that she would be present on the day that he and Mary get married. Two days later, John resigned 'for personal reasons', and caught the bus to Kilbarra and Mary.

CHAPTER 15 - FREEDOM

Mary heard a knock on her door and went to open it. She couldn't believe her eyes when she saw John standing there with a huge grin on his face. She flew into his arms and he embraced her; they had waited for this special moment and now it was here. It was minutes before they found their voices.

"You look amazing, Mary!" John said surprised to see the remarkable recovery she had made. She had definitely improved in the few weeks she had been at the Royal. Flesh had begun to cover her bones and her cheeks had a rosy glow. Her hair had been styled by Kelly and even though it was still very short, it looked quite glamorous. Dressed in beautiful clothes, and perfectly groomed, Mary was no longer the patient at the asylum.

"It's all thanks to Reg, Jill and Kelly and their tender loving care," Mary admitted, and the questions poured out of them. What had happened since they had been apart? John told Mary about what had taken place when she left the asylum.

"Lowry was furious; he couldn't get over the fact that you had slipped away under his nose," John laughed. "Do you know that you made history? You are the first person to escape!"

"I don't know how we managed it, John," Mary said. "It was so easy; it still seems like a dream."

"We had the help of people who care, and luck was on our side." John said. "Without Reg and Eileen, it would not have been possible; though I was determined to get you out before the operation."

"Operation? What are you talking about, John?" Mary asked, puzzled. John suddenly realized she knew nothing about what her

238

fate would have been had she stayed, and as gently as he could, he told her about Lowry's plan for her.

"Oh my God! What sort of creature is he?" Mary burst out crying and John put his arms around her to comfort her. "How could a person be so cruel, John? He's a doctor; he's meant to heal people, not destroy them!"

"I know, love," John said softly. "But you're safe now and that's all that matters. And we're together; how lucky are we?"

"You're right, John. I must concentrate on the good things and move forward," Mary said thoughtfully. "Still, that wretched place haunts me. I think of my baby boy everyday and I will never rest until I find him. I hope Lowry gets what he deserves one day!"

"And that day is now, Mary," John said cheerfully. "Lowry is being raked over the coals for his actions and I believe he will be suspended shortly."

"What's the point? He will only be free to spread his venom elsewhere," Mary looked sad, thinking of the damage such a person could inflict.

"Eileen's report has thrown the place into a spin and all the doctors are scrambling to check their past actions with the people who were in their care. Cases are being scrutinized and those who have no reason to be in the asylum are being discharged," John said reassuringly. "Care givers are on their best behavior and unsuitable staff are being fired right, left and centre. It's wonderful; the board of trustees is really shaking up the place."

"She's marvelous! I've read the news stories and as far as I am concerned, Eileen is the bravest woman ever!" said Mary; so proud of her friend. "Yes she is amazing! Eileen has achieved in a few weeks what no one could achieve in years. We owe her so much," replied John.

The Journey

"Does Reg know you're here?" Mary asked, and John nodded. "Says he's glad I'm here. Wants us to come down to the private dining room for dinner tonight; has something he wants to say to us." Mary shook her head worriedly and John said, "Don't worry, Mary; everything will be alright. I'm with you now; whatever happens, we'll be together and we will find your little boy."

Kelly came up to fetch John and Mary for dinner and Mary was so proud to introduce John to her friend. Kelly laughed and said, "It's nice finally meeting you in person; Mary has told me so much about you; I feel I know you already!"

"Ah, don't exaggerate, Kelly!" Mary blushed. "So, I may have mentioned John once or twice."

"Make that a million and you'll be closer to the amount of times I've heard you mentioned his name," Kelly teased. "Come on, let's go down. Reg has a surprise for you, Mary." Mary smiled, "And what's that, then?" Kelly just said, "It wouldn't be a surprise if I told you," and laughed as she skipped happily down the stairs. Mary entered the dining room and she was shocked at what she saw. Reg and Jill were there and so were Michael and Sheila. Mary broke down and wept tears of joy and heartbreak. All the years she had been parted from her family were lost to her. They had all lived separate lives, not knowing what had become of each other, each wondering where in the world the others were and whether they were well and happy. And now they were here and their love for each other came flooding in; filling every little space of emptiness and doubt.

"Thank you for this, Reg," Mary said when she could speak. She hugged her brother and sister tightly and watched them in wonder as they spoke. Michael and Sheila were beyond happy; their beloved Mary was back and they felt almost as if their mother was with them.

"I just thought you should meet before you leave," Reg answered and seeing the confusion on Mary's face, he added, "I think it's time for you to go to Dublin; It's not safe for you here anymore."

"How so?" asked John anxiously; Mary's safety was his prime objective and if she was in danger, he had to do something about it.

"As you know, the newspapers have been having a field day with Eileen's account of conditions at the asylum. People love these sorts of human interest stories and reporters are busy trying to find Mary," Reg explained to the solemn group. "There's one reporter in particular that's been snooping around lately; asking too many questions about Mary, he is. Knows about your escape from the asylum. Now that you are with John, I feel you must go where you will be safe."

"Oh, no!" Sheila gasped and Michael looked pale. Had they found each other only to part again?

"It won't be long, I'm sure," Reg tried to reassure the youngsters. "I am very hopeful that Seamus will return soon to sign your release papers Mary. When that happens, you'll all be together again." He could not bear to see the young ones suffer; he loved them so much,; as did Jill, and they comforted them with promises of visits and phone calls to keep them all in close touch, until Mary was free.

"When are we to cross the Lough?" John inquired. "I was hoping to see my parents before we leave; they live in Kilbarra and I want them to meet the love of my life and Mary wants to visit her mother's grave. I thought we may be able to do this before we leave."

"It's a risk for Mary to be about," Reg looked at their crestfallen faces and added, "Well if you take good care not to be noticed, then go but be very careful. The boat will be waiting for you tomorrow night, at nine o'clock, so you must be back by then."

241

The Journey

"Tomorrow night!" the siblings gasped. "Why so soon?"

"It's not soon enough," Reg insisted. "It just takes a second of carelessness to ruin everything that we have worked for. Do we want to risk our future happiness?" Everyone murmured, "No," and began talking all at once. There was so much to say and do and so little time.

John and Mary caught an early bus to the outskirts of Kilbarra, the next morning. How familiar the journey was and how little had changed. Mary wore her scarf on her head and her collar up, to shield her face; she needn't have worried as there was no one about who remembered her and everyone was busy rushing around, getting on with their own lives. Still; she was a striking young woman and her beauty stood out in a crowd; they were careful and went straight to John's parents' house.

The Magowan home was a nice semi, in a quiet lane, not far off the main road, where the bus stopped. The look of delight was obvious on his parents' faces, when they opened the door to find their son on their doorstep. After hugs and introductions they settled down in the living room with mugs of hot tea and a plateful of Mrs. Magowan's homemade scones and biscuits.

"Your amazing biscuits played a key role in my escape," Mary laughed. "Please share your recipes with me, Mrs. Magowan."

"For sure I will, lass," the good natured woman responded. "But only if you call us Aiden and Ciara."

"It will be my pleasure, Ciara," Mary looked at John's loving mother and thought it was no wonder John turned out to be such a lovely human being. Their home was filled with pictures of the family and it was fresh and bright. Most of their possessions had a history and Aiden and Ciara were more than happy to share their wonderful stories, and Mary could feel the warmth of these two loving people and found herself laughing at their tales. She was surprised at how young John's parents looked and when she mentioned this to John he told her they were both just forty-two.

"Started out young, we both did," Aiden said. "Worked as nurses, both of us; still do. There's plenty of life left in us yet; hope to see many more grandchildren and even great-grands before we go!"

"Speaking of going...," John told his mother and father about their plans. They were supportive and said, "Well you both just be careful and God be with you. Keep in touch as we want to know how you're getting along."

"We will," John said positively. "We intend to come back to Kilbarra as soon as we can. This is home; Mary and I want to be married here and bring up our children here."

"That's a fine plan, then," Ciara said joking. "Will be good to live close by so that I can go over my recipes with you Mary and see your biscuits turn out like mine!"

"Your uncle Reece is a lawyer, John," Aiden said. "He has his own law firm. Why don't you get in touch with him to help in the search for Mary's son?"

"That's an excellent idea, Dad," John replied. "I was a regular visitor at their home when I was working at the asylum; the family was always so welcoming."

They had decided not to invite John's siblings over, which was a pity since they lived just a few houses away on the same street. Though John longed to see his brothers and sister, it was important to keep the visit quiet. Mary enjoyed her visit very much, and what she felt and observed convinced her that John would make a wonderful husband and father. It was late evening when they left the Magowan house, and even then it was hard for John and Mary to drag themselves away.

John and Mary walked along winding country roads to get to the cemetery to visit Annie's grave. The sea mist was rolling in with its familiar salty taste and smell, and the dampness clung to the grass and tombstones and nurtured the moss that grew unashamedly wherever there was a space to accommodate its invasive growth.

It was a somber moment. The last time Mary saw her mother she was alive and well and now she lay lifeless in the ground; it was hard for Mary to make that connection.

"Oh, Ma," Mary wept bitterly and her face was covered with the flood of tears that had been waiting for this moment. Her tears gave testament to the love and deep friendship that existed between Mary and her mother, and even in death this would not change. "I wish I was with you when you needed me. I wish you were there when I needed you! I'm sorry that I couldn't be with you during your final days; I'm so sorry...so sorry! But I promise you this, Ma... I will find my son, your grandson...I will re-unite Michael, Linda, Sheila and Seamus as a family and, this I will achieve with the man I love that is standing beside me. He's a good man, Ma and I love him so dearly." Mary turned and looked at John, with tears still streaming down her face and she could see that his eyes had misted up at hearing the words pour out of her.

Mary turned back for one last look at the grave of her mother. "Ma, I love you with all my heart and I always will; goodbye until we meet again," her sobs were wrenched from her heart and John allowed her this moment to connect with the reality of her mother's passing. When he led her away, Mary was limp with grief and stumbled over the uneven stones that were scattered among the grass like intruders. She glanced over at the spot where Gerald had molested her all those years ago and could feel the stones against her bare back. As they crossed over into the church to light a candle and say a prayer, a priest came up to them and introduced himself.

"I'm father Creagh; this is my parish," he said smiling. "You folks must be new to this area or I would have met you before."

The Journey

"It's you who is new here, father," John said. "We were both born, and grew up in Kilbarra. Been away awhile, but we intend to return soon, for good. What happened to Father Kennedy?"

"Right you are," The priest said smiling. "I suppose I am new to this parish; been here almost a year now; came to replace Father Kennedy when he had a stroke. He's now in a nursing home," Father Creagh said. "Poor man lost all his faculties and can't speak, but he knows what's going on. Very sad it is to see him lying there so helpless; may God have mercy on him."

"I noticed you were visiting Annie Harper's grave," Father Creagh said. "Her husband is buried in the cemetery, but in a different grave; perhaps you would like to pay your respects to him while you're here?" He noticed Mary's face blanch and quoted from the Bible, "In him we have redemption through his blood, the forgiveness of sins, in accordance with the riches of God's grace."Mary and John made a quick stop at Paddy's grave and said a prayer for his soul. Memories come rushing back and she found that for once they did not overwhelm her. Though Mary was far from forgiving her father, she had shed that feeling of intimidation and as she left the church with John beside her, she felt calm.

On the walk back into Kilbarra, they held hands and hardly spoke. They had a journey to make tonight and that played on both of their minds. Leaving the security of the hotel for the unknown was scary for Mary, but John reassured her.

"Don't worry, love," he said. "Reg has made the arrangements so I'm sure everything will be alright. Once we get to Dublin, Reg said his friend Willie Maginn will meet us on the other side of the Lough. He's the manager of a hotel in Dublin and Willie has agreed to give you a job and accommodation for both of us. I'm sure I can find a job at a local hospital; nurses are always needed."

"Especially ones as good as you!" Mary said, smiling at his attempts to put her at ease. "I'm not worried, John. It's just that so much is going on and at times it's hard for me to deal with it. I do feel bad about leaving Michael and Sheila so soon, but I know we'll be back shortly."

"The thought of being free and safe is too good to be true," John said excitedly. "Just imagine Mary, by this time tomorrow all our worries will be over!"

At the Royal Hotel, they gathered for a quick meal before Reg drove Mary and John to the Lough; where the little rowing boat would take them across to the South and to freedom. Kelly was there, to see John and Mary off and she had brought Grace O'Brian along to meet Mary, having sworn her to secrecy. The three of them had been such good friends in the past and it was a joy to be together again, in spite of the circumstances. Grace told Mary that the new baby had put a damper on their going to America and now that her Billy had enlisted in the army, their plans would be on hold for a while longer; but they still intended to go. As Grace cuddled her young son; Mary thought, "My boy is about Charlie's age; I wonder where he is and what he is doing at this moment." She felt a sharp pain stab her breast and longed to hold her son once again.

Michael and Sheila kept holding on to their big sister; even though they were older now and secure under Reg and Jill's care and Mary could see how much they loved each other. She then thought of her little boy who must be near four years now, and prayed he was loved. "I'm going to find him even if it's the last thing I do," she promised herself; with John beside her she felt as if she could move mountains. Putting on a brave face she wished her siblings goodbye and once again she moved out of their lives. Kelly and Grace hugged their friend and promised to get together sometime soon.

Jill held Mary and whispered, "Don't worry about the children; we'll take good care of them and they will be fine." Mary held her tightly and replied softly, "I know Jill, and I'm so grateful to you and Reg for everything you've done for us."

"I'll be back soon," Reg promised the children."And when I return we can go to the pictures, if you like, what do you say?" he teased them and tickled them till they smiled through their tears.

"Be relieved when you get across the Lough," Reg told them on the drive from the Royal. "That reporter chap was sniffing around again today; asking the staff all kinds of questions about you Mary. I had to tell him to leave the premises. I also heard there's a warrant for your arrest at the Kilbarra police station, Mary. I do hope Seamus gets back real soon and deals with your release."

"Everything will be alright, Reg," Mary said. "Once we get to the South, we can begin our lives as free human beings. That's something. John and I can plan our future for a change, instead of hiding like fugitives. You and Jill have taken such a good care of the kids; I can never thank you enough for that! It's a huge weight off my mind to know they are with you. Thank you, my dearest friend!" She leaned across and kissed Reg's cheek, and he brushed her off, "Aw, stop all that nonsense. Brought me such pleasure, those two have. Can't imagine life without them. We'll visit whenever we can; Dublin isn't all that far away and Michael and Sheila will be bothering me to take them over to see you. Now just take care of yourselves."

"Well that's that then. All that remains is for me to find my son and then there's a wedding to plan," Mary said and John enquired, "Is that to be the order of it, then?"

"Yes, love. I want us to have our whole family with us when we stand at the altar," she replied. "It means a lot to me, it does. You don't mind, do you?"

"If that's what makes you happy, my darling, that's the way it will be," John looked lovingly at Mary, the woman he had adored since he first saw her all those years ago. He could hardly believe they were together; this was more than enough for him; anything else would be a bonus. As they arrived at the Lough, someone on the shore flashed a torch at the vehicle and Reg dipped his lights in reply. John was alert and said, "Let's just deal with the present. The boat is waiting for us!"

"Hurry, let's go," Reg told the couple and they grabbed their things and hurried towards the boat. The boatman seemed nervous and in a rush to leave and Reg understood his apprehension. The coastguard and the police were patrolling these waters regularly for smugglers and spies; it was war time and they had to be vigilant for unwanted aliens sneaking into the country. Mary stepped into the boat and John was handing the boatman their suitcases, when there was a flash of lights and the sound of whistles; and four policemen came running towards them.

"Stop, or we'll shoot!" one of the constables threatened, and Reg's worst fears were now realised. The boatman tried to make a run for it but he was quickly apprehended. Mary hugged herself in the boat that was dragged ashore by two of the police officers.

"And what may you folks be doing on this lovely night?" a policeman asked sarcastically. He shone a light on Mary's face and shouted, "Well now, if it isn't the Harper girl. If that don't beat all!" He yanked her out of the boat roughly by the collar of her coat and dragged the terrified girl onto the shore.

"Leave her alone!" John shouted and tried desperately to hold onto Mary. "Stop! Take your hands off her!" Two constables pulled him off while Mary's screams pierced the stillness of the night. "Let me go! Please let me go!"

"Not a chance, girl," one copper said excitedly. "It's back to the asylum you're going! We have a warrant for your arrest"

"No! No! No!" Mary shouted as she kicked and struggled to get away from her captors. "Please let me go!" Reg and John stood by helplessly, listening to Mary's cries as Reg and John were handcuffed. One of the constables shouted, "Get over here Sarge; look what we've found!" The sergeant came rushing over and Reg exclaimed, "Arthur! Arthur Brice!"

"Mr. Calhoun! Mary Harper!" Brice said, surprised at the night's catch. "What are you doing here?" To his men, he said, "Calm down, lads! There seems to be a bit of a mistake here. Uncuff these people at once!"

"But, but Sarge," Wilson stammered in protested. "Mary Harper is a wanted criminal. There's a warrant for her arrest at the station; saw it myself today."

"Criminal my backside!" Brice shouted at Wilson.

"And what's the charge against this wanted criminal, then?" Brice barked his question at the man who mumbled, "Don't quite know, Sarge."

"I know Mary Harper well; she's as sane as you or I, she is. The lass ran away from the asylum," Brice yelled at his team. "Wouldn't you do the same if you were in her place? Free them this instant, I tell you and that's an order!"

"Sergeant Brice, this woman has escaped from the Lunatic Asylum and it is our duty as police officers, to return her," Logan replied defiantly.

"'Tis an illegal crossing these folks are trying to make, Sarge!" McFee protested.

"To be sure, you know all about illegal crossings, McFee!" Brice yelled back. "And you, Logan? Doing a few smuggling runs yourself lately, have you? The whole bloody lot of you are the ones that should be behind bars. You think I don't know what my boys get up to when they are off duty? Sure, before I joined the force, I might have done a little bit of smuggling myself. What's a fella to do to put a wee bite of bread on the table? Have some compassion men; these folks are not criminals; let them go and save your energy for the real criminals!"

"Please let us go," Mary begged, sobbing. "I just want to find my son and live in peace."

"Give the lass a break, lads," Brice coaxed his sullen team. "She's had a hard time, that's all. Don't add to her misery." Grumbling, men turned slowly and walked towards their van that was hidden behind a mound. Brice shouted against their retreating backs, "Listen, McFee; and the rest of you eejits; if you ever mention a word about this night to anyone, I will see to it personally that the only job you will ever get will be working for the rest of your lives as Herring Gutters. Is that clear? And don't you forget; if you ever think about double crossing me; my uncle is the Police Superintendent and your careers in the police force would come to an abrupt end!"

"Thank you so much, Sergeant Brice," Mary cried, shaking with fright. Her teeth were chattering and she looked as if she was about to faint.

"Off you go, Mary," Brice replied. "Your mother was a fine woman, she was. She would've done anything for her family and it's her I'm thinking about when I see you in trouble. And you, Mr. Calhoun; why didn't you come to me in the first place; I could have handled this without a problem?"

"I didn't think things would go wrong, and I didn't want to involve others more than necessary," Reg said. "Thank you so much for stepping in and helping."

"What nonsense is that, sir? It's because of your generous annual donation to our station that the police widows and orphans are taken care of. That counts for something in my book, for sure. Shudder to think of what may have happened if I wasn't on duty tonight," Brice said thoughtfully. "I usually prefer day duties myself; getting on a bit; I like to be home before dark. Next time you have a problem Reg, please come to me and save us all a lot of bother."

"This is John Magowan," Mary introduced her fella to Brice. "He helped me to get out of the asylum, and we plan to marry as soon as I find my son."

"Well, nice to meet you, John," Brice said as the two men shook hands. "You mind you take care of the little lady."

"I will, sir," John replied. "Mighty grateful for your help tonight, that's for sure!"

"Not at all, lad," Brice was embarrassed by the gratitude. "All in a day's work, it is. Helping good people like you, is what we do; not create more problems for them. Now you'd best be on your way; and remember, any problem and Brice is your man!"

"You tell Willie Maginn to call me as soon as you arrive in Dublin," Reg told John and Mary. "I need to know you are both safe, so don't forget."

"I will make sure you get that call," John promised. "Thank you for everything, Mr. Calhoun."

John and Mary got into the boat and the relieved boatman, who still shook with fear over his near arrest, was quick to row out into the Lough. John grabbed the other oar and began to row as well.

"We'll make better time if we both row the boat," he said and the boatman didn't argue; he was glad of any help he could get. Reg and Brice watched as the small boat disappeared into the mist that was covering the Lough. No words were spoken as Reg and Brice shook hands and returned to their vehicles. Reg got into his car and headed back to the Royal, where he knew his family would be waiting to hear that Mary and John had left safely. Inwardly, he shuddered at how close they had come to disaster and thanked his lucky stars Brice had been there. If not for him, Mary would have been arrested and taken back to the asylum and that would have

251

finished her for sure. It was a horrible thought and he wouldn't relax until he heard that Mary and John had arrived safely in Dublin.

With a heavy heart, Reg entered the hotel. He was tired and wished he could be home in bed, but the incident had exhausted him. It had been a long day; a very long and difficult day to be sure and now he had to face his family with a confidence he didn't feel. But it was important that the children were comforted and the thought of their expectant little faces gave him the strength to be brave for them.

"Oh, Mr. Calhoun," Diana at the reception counter called out as he passed. "There is a gentleman here who says he has an appointment with you." Reg turned to look at the man and did not recognise him.

"There must be some mistake, Diana," Reg said offhandedly. "I certainly have no appointments tonight, and I have no idea who this gentleman is." Reg turned to leave when the man said, "You asked me to come from Boston and here I am, Mr. Calhoun. I'm Seamus Harper; I've come about my sister Mary."

The Journey

CHAPTER 16 - RELEASE PAPERS

The Seamus Harper who stood before Reg was certainly not the seventeen-year-old lad he spoke to on the day Seamus and Linda left for America. The glasses he now wore added a touch of maturity and his fine clothes and confidence belied his roots. Heavily built and ruggedly handsome, this was a man who had returned and Reg stared at him with his mouth open.

"How ironic life is," he thought. Had Seamus arrived a few hours earlier, there would have been no need for that fiasco at the Lough. Mary would have been able to stay and meet her dear brother instead of being in the middle of the Lough right now; taking a huge risk to get to Dublin and safety. He shook hands with the young man and said, "I have never been so relieved to see anyone in all my life! Welcome, Seamus!" If Seamus was surprised at Reg's warm greeting, he just smiled and said, "Thank you, Mr. Calhoun. It sure feels good to be back in Ireland. May I see my sister, please?"

"Ah, you've missed Mary by minutes!" Reg said and when Seamus looked surprised, Reg put his arm around his shoulders and guided him to his office where Michael and Sheila were waiting with the others, for news of Mary. "Come, Seamus, we have much to talk about."

All eyes were riveted on the men as they entered the office. They stared at Seamus and it was seconds before the siblings gasped and screamed out their brother's name and flew into his arms. When everyone had calmed down, Reg said, "Mary and John have left and should be in Dublin in about two hours." He left out the details of the trouble that had ensued on the shore before the couple finally started on their trip across the Lough; he thought it was

254

pointless to add to the anxiety that Mary's siblings were under. Instead, he told Seamus what had transpired and the man had many questions for Reg.

"I'm sorry I wasn't able to come sooner," Seamus apologised. "I was a bit worried considering the way I left and I had to secure my business in the States before I got here. Worked too hard to let things go; in case I was arrested; I wanted to make sure that things were sorted out for Linda and the girls and the little one that is on the way."

"Better late than never, Seamus," Reg said happily. "There are no charges against you; I have checked this thoroughly. Now, first thing tomorrow, we must go to the asylum and you must sign Mary's release order. I think it may be a good idea to take Sergeant Brice and my lawyer David Agnew with us." There was such joy in the room in spite of Mary not being there. The fact that everything would be sorted out after all these long years of loss and misery heightened the jubilation and when the phone rang, the shrill buzz brought the room down to earth. Reg stared at the phone for a second: almost hesitant to pick it up. Willie's voice came across loud and clear, "John and Mary are safe, Reg!"

"Thanks Willie! Are they with you?" Reg asked and Willie replied, "Yes they are; we're sitting in my office in the hotel."

"Please put Mary on," Reg asked. "I'd like to have a word."

"Reg! We made it!" Mary gushed excitedly. "Thank you so much. I'm free!"

"Well, love, you have to return to Kilbarra tomorrow," Reg told the confused girl who just managed to say, "What? Why? What's going on? Is everything okay? Michael and Sheila...?"

"Everything's fine, Mary," he laughed. "I have someone here who wants to have a word with you."

The Journey

"Hello, Mary," Seamus said and Mary recognized the deep voice instantly. Her throat constricted and she could barely whisper, "Seamus!" over and over again. Incoherent words were exchanged and though they didn't make any sense, the brother and sister understood each other perfectly. When Reg finally got the phone back, he asked to talk to John and explained the situation to him.

"Come back tomorrow and this time take the train," Reg laughed. There was so much jubilation in the room; Reg could hardly hear himself think. "Seamus," said Reg, "We need to go to the asylum first thing tomorrow morning so that you can sign Mary's release papers. When Mary gets here we can have her checked by a doctor and have her sanity certified. Then she will really be free."

"You both have grown so much," Seamus said looking at his young siblings, and Sheila replied, "Well it's been such a long time since we last saw you! We had to grow up!" Michael smiled, "When Mary gets here we will all be together for the first time in over four years; isn't that wonderful?" Seamus replied simply, "Beyond words, Mikey; beyond words!"

"I notice you walk with a slight limp, Seamus," Reg said. "What happened?"

"I had an accident about six months after I arrived in Boston; hit by a drunken driver, smashed my leg in three places. Lucky to be alive I am," Seamus explained. "I was laid up for months and it really set me back, it did."

"The good thing is that you're alive, Seamus," Sheila burst out and threw her arms around her brother's neck. "I couldn't bear it if I lost you."

"Well the good Lord saved me for you then," Seamus hugged the girl tightly. "But I can't outrun you in a race like I used to."

"Aw, we'll let you win every time, won't we Michael?" she promised lovingly and Michael nodded. Seamus chuckled, "All right then!"

There was so much Seamus needed to know but he would wait for Mary to bring him up to date regarding everything that had happened in his absence. It felt so good to be back and he wished Linda and his two daughters were here to complete the family.

"It's late and we have to make an early start tomorrow," Reg said but no one was quite ready to go to bed just yet, so Jill asked one of the staff to bring some hot cocoa and said firmly, "Fifteen minutes then, and then it's to bed!"

"You're staying with us, Seamus," Reg said. "We live just a couple of miles away." When Seamus protested, "I can't impose...," Reg said, "Nonsense; you're family now!" He made a couple of quick phone calls to Brice and Agnew and asked them to accompany Seamus and him to the asylum the next morning, and they both said they were free and were happy to oblige.

As John and Mary boarded the train back to Kilbarra; the four men were in Reg's car on their way to the asylum. Reg tried to answer the questions Seamus asked and he told him briefly how Mary ended up at the asylum.

"How could my father do such a thing to Mary; to his own child?" Seamus puzzled over the question. "My poor Ma; I didn't want to leave but she insisted I go. I should have stayed; I wish I was with her to help her through her trials. I wonder what she had to put up with before she died? I just can't believe she's gone." Reg did not want to enlighten him and glossed over the details; there was enough to deal with without rehashing the trauma of the past. Mary would fill her brother in, for sure; it's best they handle the situation as they see fit.

"Ah, she was a fine woman was Anne Harper," Brice couldn't help remarking. "A jewel if ever there was one; much too good for the likes of Paddy Harper if you don't mind me saying so." His mind went back to the first time he saw Anne; the image of the sixteen-year-old girl, the fresh faced, slender lass stuck in his mind and that was the Annie he would always see until his dying day. The others remained silent; lost in their own thoughts and perspectives.

When they arrived at the asylum, Reg told the gateman they had an appointment with the medical superintendent and the surly man looked them over and checked their claim on his intercom. "Yep, he's waiting for you folks. Relatives of Mary Harper, you are; the lunatic that managed to escape? Now you take your fancy car and drive to the admin block; that's the one with the large brown wooden door," he pointed them in the direction and waved the car through the massive wrought iron gates. Seamus wanted to stop the car and punch the man in his face but Reg calmed him down by saying, "No point in tangling with that bloody imbecile, lad! We have more important things to do!" Hearing Reg curse snapped Seamus out of his rage; he was right; they had to get on with things, and signing Mary's release papers and putting this place out of their lives was a priority.

Dr. Browne had replaced Dr. Lowry as medical superintendent and the man was clearly intimidated by the presence of Mary Harper's team and stood up when Reg said, "I'm Reginald Calhoun, a friend of the Harper family," and firmly shook the doctor's hand. "This is Sergeant Arthur Brice of the Kilbarra constabulary; Mr. David Agnew our legal representative, and Mr. Seamus Harper, brother of Miss. Mary Harper."

Mary's escape and Eileen's revelations were bringing about long overdue changes at the asylum; the management board was urgently implementing radical changes, and a modern psychiatric hospital was being born. Mary's escape was still the most talked about topic by inmates and staff. People kept popping their heads into the office on one pretext or another, hoping for news of her. Following on from Mary's escape and the knock-on effect, over one hundred sane inmates had been discharged and more cases were being investigated for release. The inmates imagined they could make a dash for freedom just like Mary did and challenged the staff when they tried to enforce discipline with threats of writing to the newspapers. One had to laugh at the absurdity of it all even though the situation was an extremely serious one.

"I would like my sister Mary Harper released into my custody," Seamus said and Agnew quickly threw in some legal points to support his request.

"Yes, Mr. Harper; that is what we are willing to do," Dr. Browne replied, eager to get the job over and done with. Newsmen were after their blood and each day new stories appeared to damn the asylum staff and stir up the public outcry. Agnew and Seamus went over Mary's file and the brother exclaimed, "My poor sister was admitted against her will on a charge of 'moral insanity'! What in God's name does that mean?"

"Um...it was a question of loose morals; you see...a young pregnant female without a husband...," Browne tried to explain but Seamus was having none of it and shouted, "It's you and those like you who are the crazy ones; it's you who are immoral; you should be locked up behind prison bars to keep the public safe from you monsters!" Brice put his hand on the young man's shoulder to restrain him, "Many of the staff will have to answer to the law, lad. We have our own ways of handling offenders so don't waste your breath. We'll get them all in the end, not to worry."

"This was all before my time, gentlemen," Dr. Browne explained, trying to distance himself as a villain. He pushed some papers across his desk. "Please sign the release order, if you please, Mr. Harper."

"Yes, I do please!" Seamus spat the words out, scowling at the doctor. "There's nothing that would please me so much as signing your dirty, stinking forms!" Agnew pulled the papers towards him and read through them with his legal eyes. He asked Seamus to put his signature to the forms and the doctor tried to defend himself by saying, "It was the father who brought the girl here...," and that comment sent Seamus into another fit of rage.

"Just you shut your dirty mouth, you bully; you torturer of helpless women; you low-life maggot!" he fumed. "I don't want to hear another word from you, or I'll put my fist down your throat!"

"I am being threatened, sir?" the doctor said angrily. "I do not have to take this kind of behavior from the likes of you! If you can't control yourself, I will have you removed!"

"Have me removed, will you? Are you sure you don't want to lock me up in this hell hole on some trumped up charge?" Seamus roared. Reg grabbed the young man's arm that was begging for an excuse to strike out, "Calm down, Seamus! We have a job to do so let's be done and get out of here!" The doctor checked the forms and Agnew slipped copies of the forms into a large brown paper envelope and put it into his briefcase. Brice walked Seamus to the door and said, "We're done here; I think we can go now." Agnew lingered on; he had something on his mind that the others had forgotten in their annoyance and anxiety.

"What happened to the child, Dr. Browne?" He asked calmly and the doctor repeated. "Child? What child?"

"Mary Harper's baby boy, who was delivered in this institution? This is clearly stated on her file," he flipped open Mary's file and read slowly; "A healthy male child was delivered to Mary Harper. See, they even have the date and weight of the baby. I'm talking about the baby, that is mentioned in this file, that was taken away from his mother at birth!"

"Umm...," the doctor began and Agnew cut him off abruptly.

"Umm is not an answer, Dr. Browne. Where is he? What did the staff in this asylum do with Mary's baby son?" The lawyer asked

260

deliberately and everyone froze where they were, waiting for the man's answer.

"The asylum does not deal with babies on the premises; the moment a child is born; the baby is taken to the children's home, in Dublin, that is run by the nuns," the doctor replied. "Mary Harper's baby would have been sent to the Sacred Heart Children's Home like all the other babies born to women inmates at the asylum. You can go and check there, if you like." Agnew responded coldly.

"We intend to do just that, sir. I'm taking Miss. Harper's file with me; you will have no further use for it, I believe," Agnew said deliberately; not waiting for permission he put the file with the forms in his leather briefcase.

"I must say this is highly irregular," the doctor retorted and Brice asked sharply, "You saying you want to make a case of it, then, doctor?" Browne kept quiet; it was obvious he did not, and what use would they have for Mary's file now?

"Good day to you, Dr. Browne. Let's go, gentlemen." Grunted Agnew. As they drove out of the asylum, Seamus shook his head and said, "My poor Mary; imagine, four years in this place! What the hell was that useless, so called father of ours playing at? I should have stayed and been here with my family!"

"Don't fret lad," Brice patted his back. "You did the best you could at the time; don't give yourself a hard time, for something you couldn't help. What's done is done and regrets won't give you another shot at doing things over. The big job is to find the wee boy and return him to his mother's arms; that's what has to be done now."

"Let's head to Dublin now and pay a visit to the children's home," Reg suggested. "I'm not sure if they'll entertain us without an appointment but it's worth a try."

The Journey

The Sacred Heart Children's Home was a pleasant red brick building lined with tall leafy trees and paved grounds in front, where children were playing. They all seemed very young; from toddlers to about four years of age and as they ran around the playground, the sounds of their infant voices and laughter filled the air. Nuns strolled about monitoring their charges; it was almost an idyllic scene and Brice remarked, "They look well fed and well dressed. A right bunch of happy nippers, they are. Maybe this place isn't so bad after all."

"It's not about the place, Sergeant," Seamus replied. "It's about taking newborn babies from their mothers, against their wishes, never to see their child again. For Christ's sakes man; it's inhuman!"

Agnew rang the doorbell and a kindly looking nun opened the door and looked at the men curiously.

"We've come to inquire about the whereabouts of a baby who was delivered at the county down asylum and then sent here for adoption. Could we come in and have a word, please?" Agnew asked politely.

"I'm afraid we are very busy here; you would have to make an appointment and state your business so that we can be prepared to answer your questions," the nun tried to excuse herself.

"We've come a long way, Sister," Reg said. "Perhaps you can see your way to accommodate us; we only need a few minutes of your time. Please..."

"I'm listening, gentlemen," she answered firmly, refusing to open the door any further. "Ask your questions."

Agnew was the first to compose himself and asked, "My client is Miss Mary Harper. She gave birth to a baby boy on June 21, 1937 at the county down Asylum. We have been told that the new born infant was brought here. What we want to know is what happened to the child who was illegally separated from his mother?"

"Let me be very clear here, gentlemen," the nun replied. "The mothers all signed away the rights to their babies; either they did this or their guardians signed on their behalf. As patients at the asylum, these women were unfit to raise their children and the asylum does not have facilities for infants and children; which is why they are brought here. These babies are given up for adoption to couples who can give them a secure loving home. That's what probably happened to your client's baby. Now, if you'll excuse me, I have work to do minding the children we have here. Please make an appointment next time you want any information."

"And if we make an appointment, would you be able to tell us who the adoptive parents are?" Agnew asked.

"Certainly not! Those records are confidential. We cannot disclose the details of adoptive parents and adopted children," the sister retorted. "We have to safeguard their interests." Seamus shouted, "And what about the interests of the birth mother, sister?" She replied, "You should have asked that question before the woman in question became an unwed mother! What we do is clean up the mess made by these wanton creatures." With that, she slammed the door in the men's faces. As they turned to leave, Brice said sarcastically, "Full of kindness, she was!" Agnew commented, "We'll have to take the legal route; these adoption cases are extremely complex and the law is not on the birth mother's side; finding Mary's baby may be next to impossible, so don't get your hopes up."

"They all look so sweet and innocent; makes me think of my girls," Seamus said looking at the children as they walked down the drive. "Do you think one of them could be Mary's boy?"

"Perhaps; don't know," Agnew replied and shrugged. "What I do know is that I need a drink and a bite to eat. Let's stop somewhere decent and refresh ourselves; it's an hour and a half's drive back to Kilbarra." Seamus and Reg nodded and Brice said, "Good idea; let's do that!"

Sitting in McGinty's bar, just outside Dublin, sipping their pints, the men discussed the day's events. Seamus kept going through Mary's file and kept shaking his head as he read her reports, saying, "My poor Mary."

"It must have been terrible for Mary, finding herself locked up in a place like that," Brice added, and Seamus replied, "How could my father have done this to her; my poor sister? It says here, 'Inmate: Mary Harper; Age: 18 years; Address: 16 Cliffside Road, Kilbarra; Date of Admission: November 30, 1936; Condition: Healthy, 3 months pregnant, agitated. Remarks: Gave birth to a son, on June 21, 1937. Baby immediately removed to the Sacred Heart Children's Home in Dublin; Harper shows excessive violence towards doctors and nurses, attacking staff when they do not give her information about her baby, who she cries for persistently. Her eyes are constantly roaming to and fro, looking for something. She hardly sleeps at night and eats very little.' My poor Mary; how frightened and desperate she must have been!"

"Your father did what a lot of families do when dealing with such a situation, Seamus. The social disapproval of women who become pregnant outside marriage is intense and the unwed mother is seen to have shamed both themselves and their families." Agnew tried to explain. "Keeping the pregnancy secret and having the baby adopted is a priority with the families of many of these women, who are usually quite young, frightened and in desperate need of their family's approval."

"It still doesn't explain committing your own daughter and leaving her to rot, without telling a soul where she was," Seamus said bitterly. "She could have come to Boston; I would have taken care of her."

"You had just left Seamus; no one knew where you were at that time. Anyway, Mary told me it was very sudden. Paddy took her to the Kilbarra Hospital, supposedly for a check-up and she was driven from there to the Asylum and admitted." Reg said. "I myself tried to locate her but had no luck. To think I even visited the asylum once and they told me they had no such person."

"It's criminal, it is," Seamus raged. "And 'moral insanity'? What sort of illness is that? Do they make this stuff up? And then they take her baby away and give him up for adoption. Mary has a son and I have a nephew somewhere out there, and we don't have the right to know where he is? Is that justice?"

"I see why the pressure on women to have their babies adopted is intense. An unwed mother is usually shunned by family and friends. Adoption can give these children a chance of a better life. It means they do not grow up being looked on as inferior or seen by society as bastards because their birth had been 'illegitimate' as the law cruelly describes it," Agnew tried to bring up the practical aspect of a cruel system, but Seamus was having none of it, and fumed, "My sister was raped! It wasn't her fault! Some people don't have choices, but Mary had a family and people who cared for her. She was forced into the situation; treated like a prisoner and tortured mercilessly. As for the people who took her child; how could they be so heartless?"

"'Tis fate, that's what it is," Brice said sadly. "There was no one for her at that point in time and she was just sucked into the system and got lost in its labyrinth. As for the people who adopt these babies; they are just ordinary folks who long for children they can't have themselves."

"The adoptive parents are, in general, blameless in these events," Agnew said. "They believe, or are told, that mothers are pleased their babies are going to a good home. In some cases, they are told the baby has been abandoned, which is not true. Sometimes, they are told the baby's parents are married but can't afford to raise their child."

"Just a few meaningless words to sum up a life," Seamus said bitterly, slamming Mary's file shut. The food tasted like ashes in his mouth. "I will never forgive myself for not being there for her and Ma."

"Now, what are the chances of recovering the child, David?" Reg asked, trying to change the subject that was torturing Seamus. "This is where we must concentrate our energies. I failed Mary once, but I'll not do it again; her boy must be found otherwise she will never be truly happy again." Seamus said, "I'll not rest till my sister gets her boy back for good."

"If there's anything I can do, let me know," Brice said, mopping up the gravy on his plate with a piece of crusty bread. "I'm a very resourceful chap, you know." Reg chuckled, "That you are, Arthur; that you are."

"I must tell you that these cases are very hard to deal with and the law favours the adoptive parents," Agnew explained. "Documents are not allowed to be accessed and it takes time and money to follow up the lengthy and difficult process. You must realize that even then, results are not guaranteed."

"Are you saying that searching for Mary's boy is a waste of time and my sister will not get her son back?" Seamus asked pointedly.

"That's not exactly what I mean. It's a long process and you have to remain calm and keep going because you are going to come up against a lot of brick walls. You can try your best and you may get lucky, but I'm advising you to err on the side of caution," Agnew drew a bleak picture. "Don't expect a positive outcome; I have never seen one instance where a child has been returned to its birthmother and I've seen too many of these cases end in heartache for all concerned."

266

The Journey

"You just send off the official letters to those concerned, David," Reg said firmly. "We'll take our chances! Now let's be off; Mary and John must have arrived in Kilbarra by now and I'm sure Seamus can't wait to see his sister! Let's go!"

CHAPTER 17 - FAMILY REUNION

It is hard to describe such joy as was between Mary and Seamus when they met. They laughed and cried and talked and held on to each other and then laughed and wept some more. They knew it would take time to tell each other what had transpired during their separation; some things they would never know, but it didn't matter to them at the moment.

They knew they were lucky to find each other again and this was what they were going to build their future upon; the togetherness of family. Mary was examined by two well known psychiatrists and certified perfectly sane. Now she was cleared; the stigma was lifted and she was finally free.

The days that followed were filled with jubilation as the siblings reveled in each other's company. Mary could see how they were disrupting the lives of Jill and Reg; though the couple never gave any sign of this, but Mary knew it was high time to get on with their own lives.

"Nonsense!" Reg said when Mary and John broached the subject. "You stay on at the Royal as long as you like: at least until you decide what you want to do."

"You are an angel Reg, but we can't go on taking advantage of your hospitality," Mary insisted and Reg saw the old spark return to her eyes. "We can't stay here forever."

"You know, I wouldn't mind if you did!" Reg laughed. "Have you made any plans?"

"Well first we have to decide where we want to live," Mary said. "Kilbarra is my home and John's too and we both want to settle here. That's as far as our plans go for now."

"The money Michael brought with him should put you on your feet," said Reg, "and you know you have a job here whenever you want."

"I have a bit put aside," uttered John. "Didn't have expenses at the asylum and managed to save most of my salary. I think a home is the first thing we need to decide on."

"Let's look round Kilbarra this weekend and see what the situation is," Seamus suggested, and Mary replied, "Yes. Let's do that and let's visit the cottage! We can all have a picnic on the beach!" It was the first time Mary didn't feel apprehensive when talking about the old places and John was happy for her. Together, they would overcome the terrible memories and soon have their own family to love and cherish.

Michael and Sheila were delighted when they heard of the plans for the coming weekend and Reg marveled at the resilience of human beings. They had all suffered such trauma at Kilbarra and yet they had seemed to bounce back in spite of all they had endured and longed to go back to what they considered home. They had found the strength to deal with adversity and overcome great loss and tragedy and their love for each other was so strong that as long as they were together, they would survive anything that came their way.

"Would Michael and Sheila opt to leave Reg and Jill go back to their family?" the question plagued Reg's mind and he knew Jill wondered the same thing; yet they dared not voice their fears. Their doubts grew as they watched the young siblings prepare for their family weekend; still the youngster's delight was so contagious that their foster parents could not help but be happy for them.

269

That's what one does when you love someone; you set them free,"
Reg seemed to be telling Jill when he put his arm around her as
they waved the children goodbye. Jill's troubled, sad eyes were not
convinced and she wanted to hold on; just a bit more. Seamus had
hired a car and they would drive around the village and explore the
countryside. John's parents told them that they were welcome to
stay a night or two with them. The mood was jubilant on the drive
through Kilbarra and Mary said, "Calm down you lot! Ma always
said that too much joy ends in tears!"

"This is worth it, don't you think?" Michael asked, grinning
broadly, and everyone shouted, "Yes," and laughed even louder.

"Why are there so many American soldiers about?" Seamus asked
and John replied, "The Americans have now entered the war and
they have two bases on the edge of Kilbarra."

"So much has changed," Seamus observed. "New houses, roads,
people and traffic. Kilbarra's become a busy place; look there's a
new picture house and a row of shops! Wonder who's spending, as
there's still a lot of poverty about." He noticed children running
about the streets in ragged clothes and bare feet and his heart broke
for them. John told Seamus, "There are some new factories opened
up, that are providing jobs and making lives easier, and they have
really boosted the economy of the place. Sadly, many people are
still living in the past and find it difficult to change with the tines;
they are the ones that need help and it's up to the more fortunate to
reach out."

"Yes, it's something I'd like to do," Seamus said; the wheels of his
mind were already in motion and Mary said, "There's nothing I'd
like to do more than help children in distress."

As they passed the Church, Seamus said "Let's go in, visit Ma's
grave and attend Mass?" And they all happily agreed. When
Seamus had parked the car, they were all greeted at the church
door by Father Creagh who welcomed them, before leading the

270

group to a front pew. The church hadn't changed much but it felt less intimidating and the kindly open nature of the new priest made it feel inviting. As well the numerous activities on the bulletin board showed the level of the new priest's interest and commitment to his parish and parishioners.

In his opening remarks, Father Creagh said, "I would like to welcome the Harper family back to Kilbarra and hope that they will make this church their own, once again. The same goes for you, John Magowan; welcome back all of you." The church was suddenly abuzz with curious murmurs as people tried to identify who these Harpers were and from where they came. They looked so fine that no one could recognize them other than to guess at their identity: Must be Yanks who have returned to the old country. Surely these Harpers were not connected to Paddy and Annie Harper?

Kilbarra was going through a period of transition with new people settling in the village and the beach was a huge attraction, as was the low cost of land. The locals saw these newcomers as city folk, with money; looking to invest in Kilbarra and if it meant that there would be jobs for the villagers, so be it. Enough of their men had gone off to distant parts in search of work and so many had enlisted, that it seemed this was a community of old folks, women and children. A munitions factory had opened up and with the arrival of a new fish processing company, there were no shortage of jobs for the female population and thanks to these new avenues of employment, women became independent of their missing and drunken spouses; and their children didn't have to go to bed hungry.

When the service was over; the family stood with Father Creagh greeting old acquaintances and being introduced to new faces; it's strange how even the toffs were anxious to shake their hands and find out who they were.

271

"I'd rather not visit Ma's grave right now, Mary," Seamus said and Mary replied, "I understand; another time, then." It was an emotional moment and the young man needed to do this alone.

"Those blue eyes; I'd know them anywhere; brought each one of you into the world I did!" exclaimed Muriel Burns, the local midwife.

"Oh, Mrs. Burns! How lovely to see you! How are you?" Mary replied and hugged the lady.

"Ah, look at the lot of you; so fine you are! How proud dear Annie must be looking down on her children. Look at you Sheila; what a beauty you are and you Michael, a real heart breaker you've turned out to be. This has to be Seamus; I can hardly believe my eyes! What a treat to see you all again!" She began to sniff into her handkerchief and Father Creagh patted her on the shoulder and said, "Now, now, Mrs. Burns, 'tis a happy occasion to be welcoming these folks home."

"For sure, Father," Mrs. Burns said. "That's why I'm crying; tears of joy I'm shedding!" Her remark drew laughter and Mrs. Burns had to giggle through her tears. As they walked to their car Mrs. Burns said, "I was with your dear mother at the end..." Mary's open palm stopped her, "I want to hear all of it but not just now, Mrs. Burns. We have a lot to do; we have to find a house to rent and rebuild the cottage...so much to do..."

"I'm sorry, Mary. That was so thoughtless of me love," Mrs. Burns apologised; she could see how the mere mention of Annie's last moments devastated Mary. "Me and my big mouth; never seem to know when to keep my trap shut!"

"Would you like a lift Mrs. Burns? We're going your way," Seamus said and the woman accepted the offer happily. "You still in the same place then, Mrs. Burns?"

The Journey

"Well, actually, I've moved in next door with my sister since her old man passed away. All our kids are grown up and gone and there was no point in rattling around alone in my cottage; keep each other company, Millie and I do. Thinking of selling the place I am; just haven't got down to it yet. Afraid of being tricked by these con artists who are all over the place now-a-days; don't want to be duped out of my property, that's for sure."

Seamus looked at Mary. The property bordered their land; Mary and John could live in Mrs Burns' place while they rebuilt their own cottage; how unbelievably perfect was this opportunity?

"Would you consider letting us buy your property, Mrs. Burns?" Mary asked and Muriel replied, "Jesus that would be great. Are you sure you can afford it?" Mary nodded smiling and Mrs. Burns said, "It's a deal then!" John drove back into Kilbarra to collect the five hundred pounds that Michael had left with Reg; by the evening, the matter was settled and the Harpers had extended their property empire by another whole acre. There was a scramble to get the cottage in order and Millie and Muriel were a great help; lending fresh linen, kitchenware, and whatever else that was needed.

The place was in fair shape and with electricity and running water; sure it was more like a palace than a cottage. Soon the fires were lit and everyone pitched in to prepare the evening meal. It seemed such a luxury to buy bread, butter and milk; such things would have been provided at home when Annie ran her house. John had brought along his precious radio and music blared throughout the house and the youngsters tried out the latest dance steps they had seen in the films. His mother sent over a roasted ham and they added the contents of their picnic hamper to the feast. After dinner, John left to spend the night at his parent's house and the Harper family were alone together for the first time in four years.

The Journey

Looking out at the remains of their burnt out cottage, Mary and Seamus seemed lost in thought.

"I wonder what really took place, Mary," Seamus said softly. "I can't even bring myself to go over there. How are we ever going to live in that place?" Michael and Sheila ran out and jumped on the bikes that Reg had gotten for them; they peddled round and round the ruins of the cottage, laughing as they raced each other. The older siblings watched and smiled. Mary said, "How brave they are." Seamus nodded and replied, "Yes, they have more guts than I have. I should have been here for you Mary; I should have been here for you all; I'm so sorry!"

Mary embraced him: "Stop it this instant, Seamus Harper!" Mary scolded. "Things just happened. It wasn't your fault and it wasn't my fault; you had problems of your own to deal with and you did the right thing. It's over; that's what we have to remember; it's over!" She stood back and reached out for her brother's hand and together they walked to the old cottage. The youngsters got off their bikes, and holding hands the four of them entered the remains of what was once their home.

"I feel Ma's presence so strongly; do you think she's with us?" Michael asked and Mary replied, "She's always with us, Michael and let none of us ever forget that. Let's make her so proud of us all." Sheila piped up, "Don't worry, Ma will look down on us from Heaven and see that we don't want for nothing."

"That's for sure darling. Ma loved us so much," Seamus said. "She would be so happy to see us here all together. She will look out for us, I know she will."

Sheila started to speak; "The night before Gerald Fegan came to steal Da's money; Ma came to me in a dream and she told me to dig up the tin with the money from under the oak tree. I got up...it was still quite dark outside...light had just begun to creep over the cliffs. Da was awake; he left the cottage carrying a spade...he saw me and told me to stay inside until he came back, but I knew that he was up to something. I looked out of the window and saw him burying a large box under the tree and rolling the big boulder back on top of it."

The family's eyes flew to the boulder that lay under the oak tree. Sheila said, "Isn't that the money you took, Michael?" Michael shouted, "No!" and dashed to the new cottage looking for a shovel. Together Seamus and Michael rolled away the heavy rock.

"How the hell did Da have the strength to do this alone?" Seamus asked and Michael replied, "He called on Satan's help; that's how he did it!" Digging frantically, they reached a depth of three feet without any trace of the buried box. Panting and frustrated, Michael asked Sheila, "Are you sure you saw what you saw?"

"Are you sure you weren't dreaming, Sheila love?" Seamus asked ready to give up.

"Ma came to me in my dream; what I saw Da do was real!" Sheila insisted. Michael said, "Let's try another foot or so just to be sure." As he hit the soil with his spade they heard the dull clanking sound of metal against metal; they knew this was real. Seamus grabbed the spade and dug around the box that was now in plain view; he reached in and pulled the metal handle, and out it came. It was dark now and the only light was from the full moon and the open windows of the new cottage. The lighthouse was shut down due to the war and looked like a blind sentinel still standing guard over its territory.

"Let's fill this hole up," Seamus said; the four siblings pushed the earth back to where it belonged and rolled the boulder back into place. They were covered in dirt but they didn't care. Mary shook the box, trying to assess how much money, if any, was in it. Laughing, they dashed to the new cottage and tried to pry open the lock on the box.

"I thought Michael found the money that day," Sheila shook her head, confused.

"No, I didn't, Sheila," Michael assured his sister. "I didn't know about this box. What I took is what Da kept around the house; what Ma kept stored in jars and planted in the vegetable patch."

The lock broke open with a loud snap and the siblings were speechless at how much money the box contained. The all began to count the notes and when they were finished they could hardly say the sum total.

"Nine thousand, three hundred pounds!" Michael shouted. "That's a king's ransom! We're rich!"

"Enough money here to buy John and Mary one of them grand big houses and even one for Seamus and Linda," Sheila beamed. Mary laughed, "And one for you too, Sheila!"

"Ma is watching over us after all," Seamus said with tears in his eye. Mary put her arms around him and said, "She'd want you to be happy, Seamus. You know how much she loved you."

"You're right Mary," Seamus answered. "We're together and we have our health; thank God!"

"We'll share the money and property between us and that should leave us well off for the rest of our days; if we are careful," Mary said and everyone nodded in agreement. The youngsters were ecstatic and Mary cautioned them, "We can't mention this to anyone; and I mean anyone; do you understand?" Sheila and Michael replied, "Yes Mary; we won't breathe a word! It's our secret."

"It's money Da earned illegally from his smuggling," Seamus explained. "If we turn it in, there would be too many questions; I was once involved in the trade; I'm ashamed to say. Got caught up in trying to make money the easy way, though it wasn't really easy and the risks were great; not proud of myself I must say. Had to

276

leave you all because of the racket, as I thought the police were onto me and I run away like a coward."

"Don't say that, Seamus," Mary begged. "Ma wanted you to go and she was so relieved when you left; she never wanted any harm to come to her children."

"Yes, Seamus. Ma would talk about you while we worked. She would say she prayed you were well and happy," Sheila said, putting her arm around her big brother's shoulders. Seamus muttered, "I feel guilty every time I look at you all. I'm so ashamed of myself; how can you ever forgive me for leaving you?"

"Please stop, Seamus!" Michael pleaded. "There's nothing to forgive. We can't return this money so let's put it to good use; that's what Ma would have wanted. Please, let's be happy; there's been too much sadness in this family, so let's put it behind us and move on."

"How are we going to explain away all this money," Mary asked and all eyes were on Seamus for an answer.

"We can say I brought it with me from America," Seamus replied, "Let's just not spend it all at once. I have done well for myself in Boston."

"That well, Seamus?" Michael asked and Seamus smiled, "Yes, Mikey; I've done very well indeed!"

"Well, I know exactly what I'm going to do with my share; I'm going to build a cottage with all the mod cons; hot and cold running water and indoor plumbing included!" Mary said joyfully.

"Jill will lend you some of her magazines on beautiful homes," Sheila suggested. "They are full of great ideas!"

"I have the best idea of all; we should have the old cottage levelled to the ground!" Seamus said bitterly as if its removal would take away the memory of the bad times it represented.

The Journey

"No, don't do that," Mary protested. "Ma loved her home and I want to remember her there. Does anyone mind if I take the land with the old cottage, then?" Every one replied, "No!" and Mary clapped her hands with delight.

"I'm going to use all the old material and add to it; it's going to be the most beautiful cottage ever!" Mary was beside herself with joy and the others joined in her happiness. "I'm going to call it 'Cois Dara'. Cois means coast and Dara means oak tree. What do you think of that?"

"Brilliant! Ma would approve, for sure!" Seamus answered for the rest. They talked late into the night; it was like the old times without the threat of any calamity. Half a dozen times, Mary reminded it was late and they had to get up early for their picnic on the beach, before they returned to Kilbarra; still they continued until exhaustion overtook them and they passed out on the mattresses they had laid out on the floor.

John's loud knocking woke the Harpers up and a sleepy dishevelled Mary opened the door to a smiling John.

I thought as much!" John hugged Mary laughing. "You lot didn't get to sleep, did you? Bet you kept everyone awake with your chattering, Mary!"

"Yes, she did!" Seamus made a dash to get ready, shouting, "Last one dressed has to make breakfast!" Sheila and Michael dashed after him and Mary just groaned and held on to John for support. John put the tin of his mother's fresh baked biscuits on the kitchen table and watched Mary fill the kettle, get out plates and spoons and set them with the sugar, milk and cereal in the middle of the table. John listened to the sizzle of eggs and bacon frying, as golden toast was lifted away from the fire. The radio was on and Mary sang along with Vera Lynn.

"How happy my Mary is!" John though; his heart bursting with the love it held for her. He vowed, "This is how I'm going to keep her always." John and Mary had only swallowed their first mouthful of tea before the siblings returned; fresh and hungry. Mary went to get ready, leaving John to cope with her rowdy brothers as they battled over the last piece of toast.

It was beautiful outside; one of the last days of summer that made you yearn for its return. Mary noticed a line of cars parked near the lighthouse and wondered what was going on: she found out soon enough. The tide was out and the beach was exposed, covered in smooth golden sand. In the old days they would have been the only ones on the beach; now there were others, coming from near and far, invading 'their precious beach'. Children ran up and down the shore, yelling exuberantly and chasing each other; sometimes they stopped to catch their breath or pick up shells that were washed up by the tide. Sheila and Michael were off and running while Seamus decided to go for a walk alone. John and Mary sat on the large blanket Ciara had sent.

"You're thinking of him, aren't you love?" John asked, snapping her out of her reverie.

"I think of him always, John," Mary said. "He's always there, wherever I am; whether I'm happy or sad."

"We will find him, love," John assured her and kissed her lovingly. "I know that your happiness can never be complete without him and I won't rest until he is once again in your arms."

"I am happy, darling," Mary replied. "I never imagined that being this happy was even possible- ever, and I am grateful for every moment and feel like the luckiest person alive. God: thank you for bringing this man into my life. John I love you so much."

John looked into her large blue eyes. "Mary you are becoming more beautiful by the day?" Mary laughed and John whispered, "That smile just melts my heart."

Just then they saw Seamus in the distance coming back toward them. "Seamus looks a bit distracted," John said. "Is something the matter?"

"Just thoughtful," Mary replied. "He's had so much to think about in such a short space of time. He blames himself for not being here through the difficulties; he has a lot to deal with and no doubt it will take time."

"Seamus stood before John and Mary and announced, "I've made up my mind; I'm leaving Boston and returning to Kilbarra with Linda and the girls. This is our home; I've been away too long and I will never be truly happy unless my sisters and brother are part of my life."

"You need to think about this carefully, Seamus. Discuss it with Linda; you could make a good life for yourselves in Boston," Mary advised. "We'll visit and you'll visit; at least we know where we are. Don't make emotional decisions; think about this very carefully."

"I've thought about it," Seamus replied. "And I know Linda will be so happy here; she's a simple lass and I know how much she misses her family and friends. Whenever we talk of home, we always mean Kilbarra."

"I don't mean to interfere, but you do realize that once the war is over, this village will empty out once again," John said. "Making a living may not be all that easy then."

"You're family, John; always feel free to speak your mind; your opinion is appreciated," Seamus answered. "You're right; no doubt about it but I think I can manage if I manufacture here and organise outlets in the States for my products. I can provide jobs for the locals and keep production costs down. The war has created huge demands and I think I can take advantage of this climate of change."

The Journey

A family walking by stopped to ask if they knew of any tearooms close by.

"I think there's one tea room near the station," John informed them. "But there are quite a few pubs about if you're interested."

"It's more a family place we are looking for. It's a shame there's nothing available near the beach. The kids are tired and hungry and there is nowhere to take them for a meal?" Another family walked by and were drawn in by the conversation.

"Tearooms haven't caught on here," the husband agreed. "Seems to be a popular beach and tearooms here would be a good business to set up, and would certainly attract plenty of customers. My kids need the use of toilets and they want something to eat, but we have no choice except to drive into Kilbarra! It's such a pity."

"It's lovely out here and we would spend many a weekend if the proper facilities were available," the wife said, as she tried to round up the kids who were in no mood to leave.

"Sorry to bother you folks," the passers-by left with a friendly wave. Mary jumped up. "That's what we're going to do, John! Tearooms and maybe a couple of rooms to let! What do you think? Please say yes!"

"Hey, steady on. I'm not made of money," John the realist interjected to bring Mary down to earth. "These things cost a lot of money."

"Mary has a bit of money and I can give her the rest; if you both decide this is what you want to do," Seamus said quickly. He hated keeping things from John but he found it hard to trust outsiders. Perhaps one day he would tell him the whole story. For now he had to return and wind up his business in Boston and then return to Kilbarra with Linda and the two girls, and the sooner the better.

"What do you think, John?" Mary's big blue eyes stared at John looking for an answer. It was hard to refuse her anything, but he

281

did want to be the man of his house and provide for his family. "Let me just say, I think it's a good idea. But let's talk it through and work out the details; see what's involved," John said sensibly, but Mary kept on badgering him to say yes.

"Can you see what you're going to be dealing with, John," Seamus teased. "No one would blame you if you headed to Boston with me."

"I couldn't live without John!" Mary exclaimed, and went silent as the two men laughed. John looked into Mary's eyes and said; "Yes, love; if we can manage it; it's a 'yes'!" Mary was in his arms, kissing him joyfully, and Seamus was laughing, "You've only yourself to blame if you spoil her so outrageously. You could have made her wait at least fifteen minutes for a 'yes'!"

"I can't deny her anything, Seamus," John said, holding Mary tight. "I just love her so much!"

John saw Michael and Sheila splashing in the waves; so he jumped up and stripped down to his swimming trunks and shouted, I'm going to join them for a swim. You coming, Mary?"

"You carry on, love," Mary replied. "I'll just stay here and talk to Seamus." No doubt there was a lot for Seamus and Mary to discuss, so John sprinted down the beach to catch up with the youngsters who started wrestling with him in the water the minute they got hold of him. Mary and Seamus laughed at the antics and Seamus said, "He's a good lad, Mary. Take care of him." Mary nodded, "I am truly blessed. Ma's here; I know she has a hand in our new found happiness and that she will help me find my son; she will always be watching over us and I know it's her wish that we all move back to Kilbarra."

"I've been meaning to ask, Mary; what's to become of Michael and Sheila?" Seamus brought up a question that Mary didn't know how to address. "I've been wondering the same thing, Seamus. I don't know what to do. Reg and Jill were there for them when they had no one else. They brought them back to life, and they love them so much; they would be shattered if they were to part."

"Let's leave the decision up to the kids then," Seamus suggested and Mary agreed, because she just couldn't make the call. They peeled off their clothes under which they wore their bathing suits and joined the others for a swim. Back on the beach, they demolished the contents of their picnic basket and stretched out on their towels looking up at the sky.

"What a perfect day this has been," Sheila said and Michael agreed, "It is; wish Reg and Jill were here." Mary looked at Seamus and knew it was time to pop the question.

"I've been wondering," Mary said cautiously to Michael and Sheila. "Do you want to move in with us at the cottage or stay on with Reg and Jill? Please tell us what you prefer and don't feel you're under any pressure in making your decision. It's up to you both; whatever's best for you is okay with us." Michael and Sheila sat up and looked at their older siblings nervously.

"We've already thought about this and more or less made a decision," Michael said and Sheila nodded. "We love you both very much and Reg and Jill have also become our family and we love them very much too. Would it be okay if we stay with them; at least until we finish school?"

"Of course, darlings," Mary said feigning a cheerfulness she didn't really feel. She so wanted her family to be together. Seamus must have sensed what she was feeling, or else he felt the same. "It's not as if we're apart, is it?" he said. "We can visit all the time. Just be happy."

"All our friends are in Kilbarra village and we get on so well with them," Sheila said, and Michael agreed, "I never thought I would enjoy studying so much. I want to go to college; we both do and perhaps become teachers. Maybe we can teach here, in the school in Kilbarra one day." They looked at Mary and Seamus, their big blue eyes begging for approval.

"Who are these smart kids? What happened to our Michael and Sheila?" Mary teased and Seamus said, "I think they just grew up, Mary."

"It's time we were getting back," Mary said, relieved that things had turned out well. They would visit; often; after all Reg and Jill lived just five miles away from the cottage. "Let's clean up and get ready to go over to John's parents' home for tea; they're such amazing people and you're going to love them."

"If they're anything like their son, I think I love them already," Sheila said and Michael put his arm around John and unsuccessfully tried to grip him in a head lock, after which they compared their muscles as they walked back to the cottage. Sheila walked between Seamus and Mary, arms linked, enjoying the nearness of her older siblings, laughing at her younger brother as he tried to get the better of John.

"Are you both really okay with our decision?" Sheila asked as they neared the cottage. "I don't want to make you unhappy."

"We are both fine with what you want," Seamus answered. "It's a good decision. Staying in school is the best thing ever and I'm glad you both have been able to realise that. Reg and Jill have looked after you both so well. We're truly happy for you."

"I think this is one of the best days of my life," Sheila said and quickly added, "After finding you both again! I can't wait to see Linda and my nieces; what a happy day that'll be!"

The Harpers arrived at John's parents' home to find the whole Magowan clan waiting for them. John's sister and brothers, along with their spouses and children were there to greet them and they all wanted to meet the girl who had stolen their brother's heart. The news that they were returning to Kilbarra permanently, delighted John's family and they all had a wonderful evening; with John and Mary being pleased that everyone got along so well. Begging their leave and thanking the Magowan's for their hospitality, the Harpers drove back to the Royal hotel and John had decided to stay with his parents. John and Mary had agreed, to having separate accommodation and waiting until they were wed, before they shared the same home; this was proving to be a very difficult condition to stick to.

It was dark when they arrived at the hotel and the plan was to stay overnight and move out the next day. They couldn't wait to see Reg and Jill's faces when they told them the news about settling in Kilbarra and that Michael and Sheila wanted to stay with their foster parents. Diane asked them to go through to the office.

"We've got something to say to you both," Mary said excitedly, when she saw the couple waiting for them. Reg replied, "And we have some news for you too." Looking at their faces, Mary couldn't tell if the news was good or bad, and jumped in, "Let me tell you our news first, then!" In all of two minutes she blurted out what she had to say and looked at Reg expectantly, "Your turn now; what do you have to tell us?"

"Firstly, I must say thank you on behalf of Jill and myself; nothing could make us happier than having Michael and Sheila with us; I think you are well aware of that." Jill was sobbing and the children were hugging her and trying to console her. Sheila said, "I thought you'd be happy," and Jill replied, "I'm unbelievably happy!"

"What's your news, Reg?" Seamus asked curiously. "Don't keep us in suspense." When Reg hesitated, Mary looked up at him and began to feel the blood drain from her face and Reg spat it out, "It's good news, love!" He handed Mary an envelope; it was addressed to him and was from Agnew, Reg's lawyer. She took the envelope and instinctively knew without opening it, what it was about. Mary stood for a few seconds, staring at the envelope before it slipped out of her hands and she fell to the floor in a dead faint.

The Journey

CHAPTER 18 - THE REBIRTH

They read the letter again and again. The message was clear; in response to his enquiry about Mary's son, Agnew had received a letter from a Dublin convent stating that, "Miss. Mary Harper delivered a male infant at the County Down lunatic asylum, on June 21, 1937. Following the birth, the baby was taken to the Sacred Heart Children's Home where he was adopted on June 27, 1937 by Dr. and Mrs. Eric Byrne, in a private agreement and with the consent of Dr. Morgan of the Kilbarra General Hospital, Father Kennedy of Kilbarra Parish, and Mr. Patrick Harper of 16 Cliffside Road, Kilbarra; father of the birthmother and grandfather of the male infant. An undisclosed sum of money was paid to Mr. Patrick Harper for expenses incurred and all rights were signed over to the adoptive couple. The child James, as he is named by his adoptive parents, has benefitted greatly from the expert and loving care he has received. Unfortunately, the Dr. and Mrs. O'Byrne were involved in a motor car accident that resulted in the death of Mrs. Byrne, with Dr. Byrne sustaining injuries that have left him unable to take care of his son, James. As such, he wishes to have James returned to the Sacred Heart children's home and put up for adoption by suitable parents; that must be approved by him. James Byrne is now three years and two months old and is a healthy, active and intelligent child. He is presently being cared for by the Nuns at the Children's Home and the nuns there are in the process of selecting new parents for the child. Are we to understand that Miss. Mary Harper is interested in having the child returned to her custody?"

The Journey

"Is that even a question?" Mary sobbed. "Let's go and bring my boy back home, where he belongs! He has lost his adoptive parents and is in a children's home; yet he is just a baby and must be so frightened to be there among strangers; I have to go to him!" It was late and Reg said Agnew would be over first thing tomorrow morning to move the case forward.

"I must go to Dublin; I'm going to the Children's Home tomorrow; I want to see my son," Mary was beside herself with happiness and frustration; how she longed to see and hold her boy again. It was unbelievable how this good news had come out of the blue and it was a sign to her that this is how things were meant to be. She would be reunited with little James; it was a fine name and she decided not to change it.

"There is still a lot of red tape to unravel," Agnew warned and made an appointment with the concerned persons on the Board of child services in Dublin, to meet the following day. Mary insisted on going too as did Seamus, Reg and John. When Mary didn't show up at the new cottage the following morning as she was supposed to; John arrived at the Royal to find out what had happened. He couldn't believe it and neither could Mary, and they just hugged each other with joy; he was so happy for her and knew how much this meant. She had spent nearly four years in misery, begging for her child and now she had found him; or rather James had found her.

Seamus went out early that morning and bought a new car. He explained, "I figure we have a lot of places to go and we need a car! Everyone drives in America; Linda has her own car and it's time we had one too." Everyone agreed it was a good idea and Mary spoke up, "I must learn to drive!" and Seamus put his hands up in mock fear. They tested the new car out on the journey to Dublin and it handled beautifully. Mary wanted to go straight to the Children's Home but Agnew insisted the first step was to visit the office of child services where they had an appointment. It

288

turned out to be a preliminary inquiry into the case and questions were asked to which the answers were already stated over and over again. Agnew cautioned Mary to remain quiet and allow him to answer on her behalf.

"I'm James's mother," she protested to Reg during a break. "Why can't I speak for myself and my boy? Why are we wasting time rehashing things we already know? Why aren't I hearing permission to go and pick up my son now?"

"Don't fall apart and blow your chances, Mary," Seamus warned. "It's annoying, but let Agnew handle the legal aspects of this case; he knows what he's about." Reg nodded and put his arm around Mary's shoulders, "Please be patient, Mary," and she composed herself briefly for the sake of her child. When the meeting was adjourned after two long hours of going round in circles; Agnew was told that there were concerns for the welfare of the child; he would only be admitted to a stable two parent home and only if it met their stringent criteria. The despair began to bubble up in Mary and Seamus literally got up and took his sister out of the room where she broke down.

"Please don't let them see you like this, Mary," Seamus tried to calm Mary down. "They're not going to give me my son back, Seamus! He will be adopted by strangers and I'll never see him again!" Reg came out and said, "That's not true, Mary. They just want to verify the facts and ensure the welfare of the child." Agnew added, "Please remain calm, Miss. Harper. It's a difficult road we have ahead of us and we need to conserve our energy. If they see you fall apart at the first provocation, they will conclude you are an emotional, unstable person who finds it difficult to cope under stress. Please be calm."

"You sound like the doctors at the asylum, Mr. Agnew!" Mary lashed out. "They labeled me crazy when there was nothing wrong with me. Are you going to be the judge of my fitness as a mother to my own son?"

289

"Now, Mary, that's foolish talk; David is on your side; he is one of my oldest friends and I depend on his legal advice in all matters, and believe me; he's got me out of many a tight spot over the years," Reg said firmly. "I trust him implicitly and advise you to do the same, if you want a favourable outcome."John said, "Listen to Reg and David love; they mean to help you. Mr. Agnew knows the legal processes and has to work through them. Trust the people who love you, and have patience and you'll win in the end." She calmed down but flared up again when she found out they had to go home without visiting the Children's Home.

"We couldn't get permission, Miss. Harper," Agnew explained. "At this stage they believe such a meeting would be detrimental to the young boy."

"My little boy is all alone!" Mary wept all the way back to Kilbarra and when they arrived; Seamus dropped Reg and Agnew off at the hotel. He picked up their belongings and headed back to the cottage with John and Mary. John remained with Mary and Seamus, and they discussed everything that happened at the meeting.

"I just can't calm down," Mary sobbed. "Let's go to church and say a few prayers; it can't do any harm." Seamus and John were at a point where they would have done anything to stop Mary being so upset and a visit to church would hopefully soothe all their nerves. When they entered the church at that late hour; they found that they were the only people there and after each of them lit some candles, they found a place to communicate with the Lord. It must have been an hour later when they got up to leave. They felt drained, empty and adrift and the solace they craved eluded them.

Father Creagh appeared through the main entrance and recognized the three and noticed how unhappy they seemed. Mary had cried so much her face was swollen and she could hardly speak. Seamus ached for his sister and missed his own family all the more. He thought of his little Annie and Mary and knew he would die of heartbreak if they were taken from him. John felt Mary's pain. When she was unhappy, he was unhappy; when she hurt, he hurt; it was as simple as that.

"Come with me. Let's have a cup of tea and talk," Father Creagh said and walked with the three a short distance to the priests' house. They sat mutely and the priest had to ask, "What seems to be the matter, then? Perhaps I can be of help?" Haltingly, they told him what had happened and he said cheerfully, "I see this as a miracle! You have been trying to find your child and he has found you! You should be rejoicing instead of lamenting your fate." They looked surprised and were forced to look at the situation in a different light as Father Creagh guided them out of their misplaced melancholy.

"You're right, Father," Seamus smiled. "We've been foolish; it's counting our blessings we should be doing instead of moping around."

"As I see it, you should be getting your home ready; there's a lot of work to be done," Father Creagh suggested. "I definitely think a wedding's in order since your son requires a mother and father; what do you think?" Mary looked at John and said, "The sooner the better!" The three were smiling and the priest said, "Isn't it wonderful how positive thoughts can transform a negative situation. Work with the positives and leave the rest in His hands!"

He pulled a register out of the drawer in his desk and opened it up.

"Now what date can I put you down for?" At first the young people had no idea what Father Creagh was asking and when it dawned on them they began to speak at once and weren't able to decide. Seamus wanted Linda and the girls to come over for the wedding; Mary said she would have to discuss the details with Reg and Jill and get Kelly to help her choose a wedding dress. John said he had to inform all his relatives who would be highly

291

offended if they weren't included. They realized what a muddle they were in when they noticed Father Creagh's amused face.

"I would say you have quite a bit of planning to do; organize yourselves and give me a date when you decide," the priest advised and walked the happy trio out to their car.

"Thank you, Father," John said shaking hands and Seamus repeated the same. The smile on Mary's face expressed her gratitude. Father Creagh waved them off and shouted, "Don't forget!"

"What did he mean?" Mary asked as they drove out of the church grounds. "Don't forget to set a date; don't forget to inform him; don't forget to organize ourselves; don't forget to work with the positives?"John replied, "I think he meant all of them! Mostly, let's not forget to count our blessings."

"I think that Father Creagh is wonderful; I really do," Mary said. "I'm so glad he's here instead of the wretched Father Kennedy!"

"No negatives, remember," John laughed. "But yes; I'm glad he's here; that's a positive!"

"Let's find the best restaurant in Kilbarra and have a slap up meal!" Seamus suggested. "All this positivity had made me hungry." They changed their minds and picked up some fish and chips and went back to the cottage. They unloaded their luggage and relaxed in front of the fire, each with a pencil and paper before them. They began to jot down things to do and people to invite to the wedding and when the lists began to run into pages they stopped and Mary said, "This is no easy job; I need help. Lots of it!"

"I'm going to have a telephone installed first thing tomorrow and speak to Linda," Seamus said excitedly. "I want her and my girls here for the wedding; let's see; one week to shop for wedding clothes, my girls love to dress up; it takes about five days to make the transatlantic crossing: let's give them a couple of weeks to get here. You can set a date any time after that!"

"What about you John?" Mary asked. "When will you be ready to marry me, then?"

"Right this minute if it was up to me, darling!" he said enthusiastically. "But can I get back to you after I have a word with my mother?" That got a lot of laughs and wry comments about a boy's dependence on his mother.

"Father Creagh was right; we have a lot to do," Mary said. "I'll have to sit with Reg and Jill tomorrow; Michael and Sheila are going to be delighted and I need Kelly to help me; there's so much to do! Today's Thursday; let's speak to everyone concerned and try and fix a date by Sunday; then we can inform Father Creagh before Mass, so he can announce the wedding banns."

"Three Sundays gone there," Seamus agreed. "Let's fix it for the eighteenth day from today. How's that?"

"That's the twenty-first; what do you think, John?" Mary asked and he said, "Perfect! Now drop me back home; Mum's going to keep me up all night, talking about the wedding and planning!" More laughter ensued and John was jokingly advised to snip those apron strings or else he would have two battling women on his hands. Mary laughed with the others and said, "I love the affection between Ciara and John and it must never change. She's a lovely person and we are all going to get along just fine!"

The days went by in a blur of feverish activity and Reg was impressed by Mary's positive attitude. She now looked forward to having James with her, as soon as was possible but there were no more tears and a new found strength guided her thoughts and actions. Work on the old cottage was well underway and when the front was finished, Mary had a beautifully painted sign hung from a wrought iron frame, beside the front door, proclaiming its name; Cois Dara. The new cottage was made ready for Linda and the children; it would be packed to the rafters with family and Millie and Muriel offered three rooms in their home to accommodate any overflow of guests. Mary had asked Eileen to be her bride's maid and she agreed; she could certainly stay next door during the festivities. Sheila was also to be a bride's maid; the list went on as the wedding plans grew each day. John looked worried; always the practical one, he said, "Let's keep something aside for after the wedding, Mary; seems like the spending is getting out of control."

Seamus heard this and took John aside; knowing the years of hardship and suffering Mary had endured, he wanted to indulge his sister; this gathering would bring the family together in celebration and tell the village that the Harper family was back. He explained to John that for them, this was more than a wedding; he would take care of the expenses so John needn't worry. When the fancy invitations arrived John knew they didn't come cheap but even he had to marvel at their beauty. When the guest list climbed to sixty people, John said, "That's a lot of guests, Mary; didn't think we knew so many people."

"Family makes up most of the list, John," Mary said brightly. "And yes, we have more friends than I imagined; I want everyone to share our happiness!" There was not a whole lot John could add to that except to say, "Where will we find a barn big enough for the ceilidh?"

"Yea, it's going to take a big barn to accommodate around a hundred people." laughed Mary. John paled. "Is that how many guests we have now, love? "Mary threw her arms around him and laughed, "No, darling; maybe ninety-nine, but definitely not a hundred!"

"I hope this makes you happy, love," John said pulling out a little square box and placing it on the table in front of her. They were having a late breakfast before Mass; Mary stopped chewing her mouthful of toast and was speechless. She looked at the box and did not move until John said, "Open it Mary; it's for you!" When

The Journey

Mary had taken the top off the small box, John lifted the ring out and slipped it onto her finger; for a while they watched the little diamond flashing its perfection. John understood Mary's silence like he understood everything about her; she was beyond words and the moment was too precious to clutter it up unnecessarily.

The day Linda and the girls arrived was another cause for celebration. Mary, Michael and Sheila, hugged and kissed their nieces until the little ones protested; and then they followed the toddlers around and cuddled them again. Sheila literally attached herself to the girls and they were never far from each other. Linda looked very well. Like Seamus, she had matured into a woman of the world and it suited her. She had adapted well to her new home and circumstances, and was clearly a good wife and mother. She presented Mary with a big cardboard box tied with a ribbon.

"What's this?" Mary asked. "You didn't have to get me a present, Linda; just having you here is enough." When Mary opened the package she saw white lace nestled within the folds of tissue paper.

"Do you remember the dress you bought me for my wedding, Mary?" Linda asked her sister-in-law. "I had never seen anything so beautiful; I certainly never owned anything so precious in all my life. I'll never forget the feeling of joy it gave me and to this day nothing compares with the happiness I felt walking down the aisle in that beautiful white lace dress. I found this dress for you; the moment I saw it on the mannequin in the bridal store I knew it was made for you; I hope you like it." Mary and Sheila gasped when the bride to be lifted the dress out of its wrappings and held it up.

"It's gorgeous!" Mary exclaimed and the girls said, "Try it on!" and helped her into the gown.

"This is it, Linda! It's the perfect dress!" Mary turned around and Linda said, "You look like an angel!" and Sheila cried out, "Sweet

Jesus! I don't believe my own sister is this beautiful! I wonder what Ma would say if she were here."

"She's here, Sheila," Mary replied. "And right now she says to tell you not to take the Lord's name in vain or you'll feel the back of her hand, big as you are!" They burst out laughing and Sheila laughed; "That sounds like her alright; I'm sorry, Ma!" There was still so much shopping to be done and the women enjoyed this part of the preparations.

"My guilty pleasure is shoes, Mary. I can't resist a pretty pair; they all look so tempting in the shop window," Linda confessed after one of their spending sprees.

Reg and Jill were saints, and if not for them the wedding arrangements would have stalled hopelessly. Jill had each job listed and ticked it off when it was done. The invitations were sent out and one of the local barns- that happened to be the largest barn in the county; was prepared and decorated for the greatest party that Kilbarra had ever seen. Reg's present to Mary and John was to have the Royal's chefs prepare all the food and he made sure that the alcohol would be flowing like a river. Both Seamus and Michael would give Mary away. The Jenkins had offered a carriage and their two best horses for the occasion, as their wedding present, to take the bride to church and transport the couple back to the ceilidh; and of course these were gratefully accepted. There were many meetings with Father Creagh; whenever something weighed heavily on Mary's mind she visited the priest and he never failed to put her at ease.

"The wedding plans are a bit over the top, Father," she told him one day. "It's hard times this village is going through what with so many of the men off to the war; I do feel terribly guilty and John is always trying to rein me in as far as the spending goes."

"I understand your dilemma, Mary, and I commend John for being the practical, down-to-earth young man he is. However, I think the village needs something to brighten their lives and bring everyone together. They're going to enjoy your wedding like they have never enjoyed anything before"

"Father," Mary said. "Once the wedding is over and we've settled in, John and I would like to take an active part in the activities of this community. With your guidance I think we can make a difference to the lives of some children."

"I do believe your family can play a vital role in Kilbarra. It's important that young people become active in uplifting this place. I'm here for any advice you may need and the doors of this church and my humble home are always open."

"I can never thank you enough for what you've done for me, Father Creagh," Mary said gratefully and the priest laughed, "All part of my calling. Helping others is the greatest gift. By the way, I've been talking to the Fegans. They are alone and in a bad way; one son has been killed in the war and the other has taken to alcohol and they haven't seen him in years and don't even know where he is living. They lost their business some years ago after the death of Gerald; they just about get by now but worse than that, they are very bitter, miserable people."

Mary went cold at the mention of Gerald's name; there was no part of her that accepted the memory of this man.

"I am bitter and miserable too when I think of Gerald, Father. He ruined my life," Mary said. "The memory is so painful to me that I still shiver when I think of that terrible time."

"It wasn't right, Mary," the priest said softly. "No one is condoning what you had to go through. But He has a larger plan for each of us. Look at you today; you are alive and well and your whole life has certainly not been ruined; you found John and your family has come together stronger than ever and you have so much to live for. And then there's James; I have every confidence he will be with you soon."

The Journey

"You're right as usual, Father," Mary agreed; she did have a lot to be thankful for. She had avoided the mention of James since the meeting with the people in Dublin; even thinking of him was like a sharp knife stabbing her heart. The wedding would move her one step forward towards being reunited with her son and she needed to get over this first before she could move ahead in her mind. John was wonderful as usual and supported her throughout this trying process; he had told Mary he wanted to adopt James and Mary knew this would be the natural outcome for the three of them.

"Forgiveness is a great healer, Mary. It's time to forgive yourself," Father Creagh said. "Perhaps you can come along with me when I next visit the Fegans."

"They wouldn't want me anywhere near them; they blame my family for the death of their son. They hate me, Father; they think I encouraged Gerald's advances," Mary said unhappily. The priest said, "They don't hate you, Mary. They are your son's grandparents and James has an inherent right to know them. Don't deprive the three of them this experience; it may be the only pleasure the Fegans ever have. Try to put the past into perspective; I know it's not easy but I believe you have the strength to do this. I'm going over tomorrow morning and it would be a joyful surprise if you bring a wedding invitation for your aunt and uncle and come with me?"

Sitting with Father Creagh in the Fegan's little parlour; Mary realised he was right. The place was so bereft of human emotion she neither felt their love or hate. They had nothing of their family left; in their pain they had lost each other as well and there was no comfort to be found anywhere. Father Creagh carried the conversation and the rest of them mumbled a few words out of politeness; Mary noticed that there was no energy left over for hostility or antagonism. There was just nothing there and she recalled the bleak days of loneliness in the asylum when she felt

298

completely alone and that life was no longer worth living. Before she left, Mary leaned over and kissed her aunt on the cheek; the woman did not respond but neither did she push her away. On the drive back, Father Creagh said, "I'm proud of you Mary. These things take time but you are on the right track, for sure."

"Those people are my James's grandparents," Mary replied firmly. "I'm doing this for my boy."

"Whatever your reason, you did the right thing," he insisted and Mary couldn't argue with that.

Strangely, the days became calmer as the wedding day drew nearer. Perhaps it was because all the tasks had been completed and now all that was left to do was wait. Eileen arrived and it was great to see her again. Only John, Eileen and Mary could understand the events of that night, in the asylum, when they risked everything for friendship; that would be the unbreakable bond holding them together for the rest of their lives. They were able to discuss and dissect the events of the escape for the first time and Mary found out how much was at risk during those nerve wracking days and thanked God for John and Eileen.

"You've become a force to be reckoned with, Eileen," John teased. "Who would have thought that sweet, polite lady was such a champion of the people; your hard hitting reports appear regularly in the newspapers and baddies shiver at the mention of your name."

"I learned there's no point in keeping quiet and hoping problems will automatically disappear. You can't depend on human decency to right wrongs because most of the time this quality doesn't exist. If you don't speak out, who's going to hear you?" Eileen said softly; with her old friends she was her gentle self again.

Two days before the wedding, Mary had just got ready for the day and sat at the table looking out of the front cottage window, enjoying a cup of tea with Seamus. "Do you think we'll have such

299

lovely weather on the day of my wedding?" Asked Mary. "Not a chance; it'll rain cats and dogs for sure!" Laughed Seamus.

"You know something, Seamus?" she answered. "I won't even care just so long as John and I are husband and wife. I'm too content to be bothered by anything!" Frying up her family's breakfast, with each of them clamouring for something different, Linda good-naturedly tried to oblige. She smiled, listening to the conversation between Seamus and Mary; Seamus had never been so happy, and returning to Kilbarra was the best decision they had ever made. She too enjoyed having her family close by and the children loved having so many relatives around. She couldn't wait to get their affairs sorted out in Boston and return to Kilbarra for good.

"What's the plan for today?" Linda asked. "I haven't really planned anything;" replied Mary. "I'll just stay home and relax and John will probably come over later... oh, there he is now. What are Reg and Jill doing here and Michael and Sheila are with them; don't they have school today?" Seamus looked at the unexpected visitors getting out of the car, and just then Agnew pulled up, in his car, with Father Creagh and Eileen. "What on earth's going on?" Mary got up and walked to the open front door.

"Top of the morning to you, Mary! Isn't it a fine day today?" Father Creagh said joyfully and walked towards her while the others just stood around. "I have someone with me who hasn't had his wedding invitation yet; do you have one to spare, Mary?" Agnew opened the car door and John helped a little boy out of the car. The beautiful little boy with golden curls and big blue eyes smiled shyly. Mary knew who it was without being told and she instinctively dropped to her knees and held out her arms, and James ran straight into them.

There were lots of tears shed but none of them were by Mary; she just held on to her son, breathing in the delicious scent of him. She touched him, examined him and kissed him; listening to the words he spoke and telling him how much she loved him. The others stayed on and talked excitedly; apparently it had been a dramatic event. Mary heard brief snatches of conversations; Father Creagh had spoken to the parish priest in Dublin and they had gone to visit Dr. Byrne and the man was shocked and ashamed of the circumstances that deprived a mother of her child. Prior to them adopting James, his wife and he were told the mother had died and the child had no living relatives.

"Have we been punished for what we did, Father?" the ailing man asked. "I took my happiness at the expense of another. I have lost my wife and James; now pain torments me and I know my days are numbered."

"You had no idea of the truth; James needed loving care while his mother was unable to provide this to him. The Lord will bless you for your big heart and only He knows the purpose of the path he has chosen for you," Father Creagh tried to comfort the man. Dr. Byrne insisted, "James must be returned to his mother so I can be at peace. Please ask her to forgive me and tell her that her boy was greatly loved by Edna and I. Do give her these photographs of the boy so that she can see her baby's growth; I know it won't make up for lost time but these photographs are hers."

Father Creagh used his influence with the Dublin convent to release the child into Seamus and Linda's care until he was returned to his natural mother and Agnew had applied every legal tenet in the book to plead the case. Reg and Jill worked tirelessly for this, while Chief Superintendent Griffin and Sergeant Brice applied all the pressure at their disposal. Everyone agreed that it was when Eileen walked into the Children's Home and demanded to see James that things really began to happen. Eileen threatened to expose every last person in the system who tried to keep this mother and child apart, especially since his adoptive father insisted that James be returned to his birthmother. No one dared to stop her when she picked up the child and walked out with him.

The Journey

"This is kidnapping," Sister Julia said without conviction and Eileen shouted, "So, sue me!"

It seemed the whole village of Kilbarra was out to cheer for John and Mary. As the flower decked carriage, with two of the finest horses, you could ever set eyes on, took the bride to the church, strangers shouted, "Good luck, Mary!" Mrs. Murphy's music filled the church as John turned to see his beautiful bride walk towards him on her proud brother's arm: He couldn't put his feelings into words and his eyes glistened with tears of joy. Mary had never looked more radiant and beautiful. Family and friends packed the pews and familiar faces smiled back at her including John's parents, Reg and Jill, Kelly and Ralph, Grace and Billy; with the rest of the gang from the Royal Hotel. Even Sergeant Brice was there with Chief Superintendent Griffin and their spouses. Mary saw James, dressed in a little velvet suit, sitting in the front row on Ginger Fegan's lap. Bertie Fegan told James to wave to his mother and as he lifted his little hand, the most loving smile imaginable, spread across his face and his big blue eyes sparkled with such radiance; and a luminous feeling of peace washed over the bride.

There was pin drop silence when Father Creagh began to speak; his loud clear words reached the hearts of everyone present.

"And the Lord said, "Don't be afraid, for I am with you. Don't be discouraged, for I am your God. I will strengthen you and help you. Don't be afraid. I am here to help you. Be strong and of good courage, do not fear or be in dread of them, for it is the Lord your God who goes with you; I will not fail you or forsake you..." There wasn't a dry eye in the house when Father Creagh asked, the all-important question and the couple answered, "I do."

The bells rang out loudly, informing Kilbarra that Mary Harper and John Magowan were now man and wife. When the couple emerged from the church, Mary led the family to Annie's grave just as she had promised.

The Journey

"Here we are, Ma. Your children and grand-children are together again, all well and happy. Here's Seamus and Linda with little Annie and Mary and another baby due soon. Look at Michael and Sheila; how proud you must be looking down on them, they are with dear Reg and Jill who are taking care of them for you. And this is my darling husband, John. He is my sweetheart, the kindest man I've known and he loves me so much; just as I love him. And this is my son James who has returned to his family. The love and happiness that you installed in our hearts; has been ignited again and we stand here surrounded by family and friends. We love and miss you, Ma and we will never forget you! Rest in peace, mother." And as Mary bent over to place her flowers on her mother's grave, a tear dropped from her eye onto the white rose at the centre of her wedding bouquet; and for what seemed like an eternity, Mary could see her mother's smiling face looking up at her.

ABOUT THE AUTHOR

Jimmy Smyth comes from a mental health, nursing and social work background. He is the author of several children's books and a a number of non-fiction books.

Having since retired from the NHS in the UK, Jimmy is now a counsellor, life coach and mindfulness teacher with a number of charities and private clients and is one of the partners in the Health & Wellbeing Company, based in Northern Ireland.

The idea for The Journey came to him in 1980, when he was looking through old notes, in the basement of the psychiatric hospital where he worked. The hospital had opened its doors as a lunatic asylum in 1869.

To this day he wonders whether he heard the voice of a young girl incarcerated in the cold, dark, lifeless building. Steeped in history, the basement held the deepest secrets of the patients who battled their own minds and the brutality of the system they were imprisoned in.

Or maybe his imagination just run away with itself?

Regardless, the quest to tell Mary's story began and the idea to bring her to life in this novel was planted. Throughout the years Jimmy believes the quiet, sweet voice of the girl who spoke to him

The Journey

that first day continued to remind him of his goal.

As well as this novel, Jimmy is in the process of finishing a non-fiction book about the history of women and mental illness.

Meanwhile, what has become of the voice of the woman in his head desperate to tell her story? She's still there and isn't planning on leaving anytime soon.

The Journey

The Journey

The Journey

The Journey

The Journey